ETERNAL DAMNATION

A NOVEL OF THE AMAGARIANS

STACY REID

ETERNAL DAMNATION is a work of fiction. While reference might be made to actual historical events or existing locations, the names, characters, places, and incidents are either the product of the author's imagination or are used fictitiously, and any resemblance to actual persons, living or dead, business establishments, events, or locales is entirely coincidental.

All rights reserved. No part of this book may be reproduced in any form by any electronic or mechanical means—except in the case of brief quotations embodied in critical articles or reviews—without written permission.

ETERNAL DAMNATION

First Edition September 2018

Edited by AuthorsDesigns

Cover design and formatted by AuthorsDesigns

Copyright © 2018 by Stacy Reid

PROLOGUE

The planet Serange
The Golden Age
The Kingdom of Dxyriah—Castle Ashmir

"How peaceful our city seems when only a few months ago the cries of our people echoed with pain and despair," a soft, feminine voice murmured.

Rah Blevinstoke, the most formidable Baron of Princess Shilah Symonrah's remaining supporters, felt arrested at the sound of his former lover's sensual tones. He missed everything about Megladine and coming to meet her now was highly perilous. But hearing her voice made him think the risk was worth it, though, if he could convince her to aid his cause would be the true reward.

He considered the facade of peace and prosperity that blanketed their kingdom. He moved a few paces forward on the stone ledge jutting from the caves beneath their castle, which was built on the highest mountain of their nation. He peered down to the thousands of glass, steel, crystal, and crystalline sky-towering buildings below. A hovercraft flew by, the *Dxyrian* blue and purple symbol of peace prominently emblazoned on the side of the sleek silver aircraft. A deliberate move by their new ruler, Crown Prince Quan, a hopeful reminder to the people that he governed with peace, fairness, and love. They should scrub from their memories that only three months ago, bodies had dropped from the castle in the sky, and blood had stained the mountains and the steel-plated streets as he had overthrown the Symonrah bloodline's rule, slaughtering dozens.

"I will not forgive the pain Prince Quan has caused," Rah murmured. A piercing agony lived and breathed inside his chest, one he feared would never abate. "And I do not accept him as our prince." Without glancing at the woman by his side, he held out a robe stained with blood. "This belongs to our Princess Shilah who is the rightful ruler of *Dxyriah*. I want you to see if you can read her."

Megladine inhaled sharply and glanced around furtively, her left hand dropping to the high-power beam anchored at her hips. A dangerous weapon only a few were certified to carry, and which had the power to melt his insides from a single blast. A hollow ache formed inside his chest that she would even dare to rest her hand on its grip.

"You've been searching for Princess Shilah? Rah, that is treasonous!" she hissed, and unaccountably the fear in her tone soothed the jagged pain tearing at his insides. Her concern for his wellbeing meant she still cared, that he might convince her to render aid.

He shifted closer to her, subtly inhaling her scent of ripe peaches and the woman herself. He glanced at her and for a moment could not remove his eyes as the sight of her lush figure clad in a yellow sari woke memories of passion in his mind. Her fair skin reminding him of its softness, her rich midnight black hair like silk between his fingers, her lips full and moist on his. Their eyes met, and her light blue orbs radiated with awareness.

"We shouldn't, we mustn't…we can't." Her fear was evident, and he hated it. Another testament to the veneer of peace in which their kingdom was shrouded.

Although they were ensconced within the caves underneath the castle, spies lurked in every corner, and it was not the right time to be found conspiring. Several layers of rocks formed the caves, and solidified crystals, and ice covered the floor. They should hear if anyone approached.

Their kingdom was in turmoil, the ruling family had been brutally executed, and the reign of the realm had been wrested from Princess Shilah before she'd even ascended to the throne. The sun dipped, slipping lower and lower in the sky before disappearing behind the mountains and the Black Sea. The steel and glass city below slowly glowed with light as the respective Prime Sentient Intelligence (PSI)-1.5, which powered and governed each household, illuminated them. Their capital was still unsure of the new order, for nary a hover zipped through the air, most of their denizens staying at home. Everything had changed when the crown prince had allowed greed to fester in his heart and rule his actions.

"My family has served the Symonrah family for over two thousand years," Rah said, choosing his words carefully. "Seventy other Barons and myself pledged our lives, powers, and beams to Princess Shilah. The threat of death will not stop me from serving her. Our princess cares for her people and serves their needs and not her desires. The K'tair house has been loyal for years. The loyalty that's borne from love and not fear or hatred. I cannot credit that you would so easily forget your vows of allegiance, love, and respect. Now, will you help, Megladine K'tair?"

She seemed to consider his request for several moments before a troubled sigh slipped from her lips. "You believe her to be alive, along with Princess Kala?"

The last sighting of Princess Shilah with her younger sister Princess Kala had been near the border leading into the Kingdom of O'andor. The reports said Princess Shilah had held a dying Princess Kala clutched in her arms, and when the ruler of O'andor, Crown Prince Tarik tried to take her, Princess Shilah had ripped into his mind and almost taken his life. The prince had teleported to his kingdom's medical unit to save himself. No one had seen her since. "I hope it," he said softly, not speaking aloud how desperately he had been hoping and praying to all the gods his princesses lived.

Megladine faced him, touching his arms lightly. "Rah, if she is alive we *must* report it."

"We will not. And if you betray my confidence, I will end your life." And it was one of the most painful things he had ever vowed, for he loved Megladine with every emotion in his heart.

The slight figure before him trembled, and he could feel her pain. He was sorry for it, but it could not be helped. His loyalty must always be first with the Symonrah family. He had been searching for their princesses now for three moons, and desperation turned him to his former lover, the one person he had vowed to stay away from during these turbulent times.

He glanced away from the tears pooling in her eyes toward the vast beauty of the Black Sea. Megladine was a foreseer, a rare designation for a Serangite, each of the three kingdoms of their realm possessing less than one hundred seers combined. Megladine was one of the most powerful foreseers of Dxyriah, and he had not wanted to involve her in his search, but his Princess had vanished from the face of

Serange. She could be anywhere in the Omniverse. Or dead. "A report placed her near the portal leading to the world of Amagarie. I questioned the gatekeeper of that portal, and he did not see her. There is a possibility she had removed his memory. The one thing I am certain of is that she is not on our world. Or I would have found her."

He shifted and peered into the hardened beauty of Megladine's eyes, the scar that ran down her cheek, marring the face that had once been perfection. As a foreseer, her designation was that of an Omega—the second ring of power. She was not even close to being an Imperial, the most exceptional level of skill that could ever be attained with their abilities, yet he did not doubt her capability in reaching through the Omniverse to locate their princesses. She had foreseen the despair that came to *Dxyriah*, albeit the warning came too late.

"Will you help me, my Megladine?"

Her lips wobbled on a small smile, then his lover took the robe, her eyes fluttering closed. She swayed, and he clasped her waist anchoring her. The feel of her soft skin beneath his fingers was torture. He could not marry Megladine as he dreamed of doing. Princess Shilah had sensed his deep love for Megladine, who as an Impure was not permitted to marry or even allowed a liaison, and the princess had not reported them. They had been secret lovers for over ten years, and it was only since the rebellion that he had stopped going to her bed. For if they were discovered the punishment would be severe for both. What he asked of her now was just as dangerous but restoring his princess to her throne was not only his duty, it would put their world back upright, and he could be with his love once again.

Megladine gasped. "She lives!"

Relief blasted through him. "Where?" he demanded.

"I cannot see." Her brows furrowed in fierce concentration. "She gathers an army."

"An *army*? Where exactly is she?"

"It is not as clear as how I would hope," she said her voice throbbing with power. "She seeks to wipe out the hands that betrayed her and to reclaim her throne. I see our princess cloaked in shadows and darkness."

"Death?" he asked sharply.

Megladine's breathing fractured. "I cannot see it, but the shadows are sentient."

Impossible.

"Lies whisper and blind my vision. I sense destruction and pain, Rah. That is what our princess returns with," she expelled with a shaky breath. "She and Princess Kala are the last pure royals of the Symonrah line. Our princess must know that to return is to end her bloodline's reign. I too yearn for her, but I fear she is on the wrong path. Vengeance is not the way to reclaim Dxyriah."

He stepped away from her. "She is our rightful ruler, Megladine!"

"The darkness I foresee eclipses that which our kingdom currently faces. Our people have had enough death," she said softly.

"What are you saying?" he demanded, ice congealing in his heart.

"You know," she breathed, looking away from his stare.

"I don't *know*." And he prayed she was not suggesting...

She faced him and touched his arms lightly. "Our princess cannot be allowed to return. We must foil her arrival to protect our people from more devastation."

"You could be wrong," he rebutted her, unable to bear the idea of adding to the suffering of his princess now. He loved her more than anything in his life. He was the anvil to her hammer, and from birth, he had known his sole purpose was to serve her, *always*. For now, their princess lived, and it was knowledge they needed to keep close as it proved difficult to determine who her followers now were.

"We cannot fail her," his lover whispered. "She would want us to protect Dxyriah, even from herself."

1

Amagarie
102 years After the second Great War
Mevia—Kingdom of Sounds
The Emperor's palace.

Princess Shilah Symonrah, heir to the throne of Dxyriah, had one thought as she hurried down the long-winding hallway to meet with Emperor Jadon Khan, the sovereign ruler of the house of Zhang, and the emperor of Mevia. *I'm in deep shit.* That had been the response of the stocky bald human priest, Father Bramwell, with whom she had spoken to at length about her predicament last evening. He had explained his meaning, and while she had been horrified at his vulgarity, she entirely agreed. She was in the deepest of shits with no foreseeable way out, but she would not give up. The lives of her people, the life of her dear sister, Kala, depended on every move Shilah would make tonight.

Something had changed and whatever that was had nervous energy coursing through her veins. The emperor had summoned her for an audience, and the insolent way the guards had addressed her had been too familiar as if her status as a royal guest had been revoked. That did not bode well. How she resented the wings of fright beating so frantically against her breastbone.

She opened her mind, careful not to spill her aura and reached for her younger sister whom she'd vowed to protect at all cost. *"Kala are you well?"*

A gentle flutter stirred inside her mind, and she reached for the thread, opening her psychic eyes wider to sense her sister's aura. It was white.

Relief darted through her. Kala seemed well.

"I am bored. Father Bramwell entertains me with a game of chess and amusing stories of Earth. Quite fascinating how primitive they are with their technologies. He was positively riveted when I explained our household is organized and operated by PSI-2.1 our advanced sentient Intelligence, and that we have sentient robotic servants."

Shilah smiled, so grateful for the comforting presence of the human priest. *Be vigilant. Something has changed in the palace. I can feel the tension on the air.*

Her sister's aura flickered, to tinge yellow with her burst of alarm.

"The castle walls are rife with rumors of a beast being pulled from a Darkan and sent to Nuria, the kingdom of Eternal fire. Did you have anything to do with it?"

Shilah flinched. Guilt burned through her like acid. It hurt something deep inside of her to admit to her sister the blade the emperor held over their heads, and the vile things she had done because of it. *"We will speak at dinner."*

She closed her thoughts to her sister and reflected on the impossible thing she had done the previous evening. She had pulled two of the malevolent chakras buried inside captured Darkans into a corporeal form.

The young men had raged with pain when being invaded by her power, thrashed futilely in the chains that constrained them. The manacles, forged from the pure *valnetium* iron found in the hardened core of Amagarie, were unbreakable and the Darkans' terrible agony had battered at her psychic shields. It had drained all her energy to hold the two beasts to the physical realm, while a witch had cast spells of immense power to control them.

She had succumbed to a deep sleep to regain her strength, and in the comfort of her bed, she had dreamed of their residual pain. Shilah wished the young Darkans had been strong enough to escape the dungeons like their predecessor, but the emperor had learned from his mistakes. The empire had captured a female Darkan before and made the mistake of only binding her with five shackles of *valnetium* iron. When Shilah had started to exorcise the beast from her, the rage and strength she'd displayed had been breath-taking. Tormented by pain, she'd burst forth with madness, and had almost destroyed all of those that held her in the upper level of the dungeon before escaping. It was still a mystery how she had done so, for the cells were reputed to be impenetrable. The empire hunted her to no avail. Shilah hoped daily that the Darkan female had made her way to safety or back to her own people.

Shilah despised the Mevian emperor with all her heart. Of the seven kingdoms of Amagarie, the Darkage—the realm of beasts, shadows, and darkness—was the most feared though they had only a small fraction of the number of citizens within the other kingdoms.

Darkans were the only people who possessed something extra in addition to their unique ability to control a mystical element. The rabid rumors throughout the empire whispered that at a point in their history the king of the Darkage, in a bid for power tried to make a deal with the king of the

Demon realm, a mystical world far beyond the Jupiter ring, and the result had been horrifying.

Chakras from the demon realm had spilled into their lands burying themselves in Darkans and cloaking their domain in perpetual darkness. The chakras they housed were brutal and evil, giving them access to powers so destructive they were feared and reviled, and the emperor wanted to rule that evil to build an army. Shilah hated that she had aided his cause, even if she did so unwillingly under the threat of death or worse, enslavement to the emperor's depraved desires, and the death of her beloved sister, Kala.

Their affiliation had started as a bargain of mutual benefit, where she would use her powers at his request for a special interrogation with a few condemned prisoners, and he would grant her several thousand warriors from his unmatched army to return to Serange. She had done all he asked, but the Emperor had been delaying delivering on his oath. Instead, his demands for her to use her powers to serve him grew in large leaps, and he gave or promised nothing in return. It killed something inside of her to know she had been the one to approach him and placed her life in his hands, and that she had foolishly held onto some hope that he would fulfill his side of their bargain.

The Princess of Dxyriah *will become my personal slave...I will enjoy her tongue on me.*

That was just one of the sickening thoughts she had gleaned from his mind a few weeks previously. It made Shilah doubt if she were successful at controlling the vile powers in Darkans he would ever let her go. He coveted her for her telepathic powers, so he wanted to break her, and... he desired her body.

Acrid fluid rushed to the back of her throat. She took a few steadying breaths, then forced down the bile as she neared a massive door constructed from iron overlaid with pure gold. A sizeable ornate emerald gem glowed in its center, and twenty guards stood militant, dressed in bronze armor, their features covered with vizors, their feet braced apart, and their hands gripping the hilts of their swords.

She slowed her steps and lifted her chin. "The emperor has requested an audience."

Two of the guards whistled softly, and the emerald gem clicked several times, and then the door opened. Shilah entered, her slippers loud on the jade green marble floor as she traversed the impressive length of the chamber. The door closed behind her. She ignored the magnificent room with its exquisite golden tapestries illustrating the history of the Empire. They always took her breath away and invited unbounded admiration. She concentrated on the lone figure sitting in the most prominent position. His aura commanded her full attention. She could sense there were others in the throne room, but she did not divert her regard from the man on the high throne. Emperor Jadon Khan sat upon his throne, peering down on those he deemed lesser. White-blond hair hung down his back, and his eyes, the color of gold stared down at her. "How kind of you to join us, Princess Shilah."

The terrible power in his voice cramped and knotted her stomach, but she presented a serene mien and dropped into an elegant curtsy. "Emperor Khan, how may I be of service?"

I'll have you on your knees soon my sweet Serangite.

He deliberately spilled his thoughts, hoping she would hear them. She wanted to drop the pretense and let loose her power and kill him. Shilah would probably succeed, but such an action would be foolhardy. Death for her and her sister would be instantaneous for she could not defeat the massive army of his empire. Keeping her countenance tranquil, she met his gaze. "Are we to complete our bargain, Emperor Khan? I admit I am eager to depart for my realm. Each day I am away my people suffer." She had done everything he had demanded, and he should now be assisting with her demands.

His lips curved in a cold smile. "I have extended your stay in the empire for another year, Princess. Your sister's too, of course."

Shock stole her voice for precious seconds. His meaning was unequivocal. "I must decline," she said firmly. "My people await my return, and I fear I cannot extend my stay any longer in Mevia. Your generous hospitality will be remembered, and your aid to Dxyriah. You swore an oath to grant me fifty thousand warriors to return with by the end of this moon cycle for my aid, which I have rendered for the last several weeks in good faith."

Despite the chill of warning kissing over her skin, she would bargain fiercely for the liberation of her kingdom. She needed warriors, loyal to her, who would travel with her to Serange and help her take back her throne and aid her in avenging the senseless slaughter of her brother and his wife, and dozens of people loyal to the Symonrah line.

Familiar grief and hate welled in her heart, and she buried the emotions for they had no place at this moment.

"It is my will you remain another year," he pronounced flatly, with all expectation of being obeyed. He grasped a golden goblet studded with emeralds from the raised dais to his left and drank. The hovering servant hurried over and refilled it with wine, which he emptied once more before saying with a smile, "And you will do so."

Fury and despair filled her. "I have fulfilled the terms of my bargain with *honor*, Emperor Khan, I expect the same in return," she said with all her inbred arrogance. It would not do to appear weak though her stomach cramped. The enemy surrounded her on all sides, this castle sat in the center of the entire Mevian empire. In this room, she was near two of the deadliest individuals of the entire kingdom. For she could also sense the aura of Lord Shenzhen somewhere behind her. So, if the emperor decided to take her head, she would lose both her kingdom and her life.

Those cruel lips curved into another smile, and his eyes glinted with depraved anticipation, but also held a queer admiration. Instead of addressing her, the emperor shifted his regard to Lord Shenzhen, the ruthless grand general of his army, who was entirely without compassion and was Khan's most loyal supporter. As if she was a fly to be discarded as if his promises were made from ashes. As if there were no consequences for them in this despicable turn of events.

"The honor and judgment of the empire must not be called into question," she said with practiced diplomacy. "I urge you to fulfill our bargain tonight, as agreed."

The emperor considered her as if she were an interesting bug that invited study and vivisection. Lifting her chin, she held his penetrating regard, refusing to flinch from those cold and cruel eyes.

An enraged snarl caught in her throat. She had been deceived. Her sister's protection and aid to their kingdom had been promised, and she had foolishly believed. Now she would remain a prisoner of the empire. No longer would she delude herself into thinking she was a guest of the realm. She had the freedom to traverse the kingdom but always with several guards. And not just any guards. They were from the grand general's elite force, the most brutal warriors of Mevia. Now their purpose was evident, they were for her imprisonment, not for her protection.

She waited silently with foolish hope beating inside her for the emperor of Mevia to make his ruling. A ruling from one she perceived as the most dangerous man in the seven realms of Amagarie. Beauty should not sit so well on evil.

Nor should an evil rule be viewed as legendary across Amagarie. He'd been the only ruler of the empire of Mevia for three thousand years—no other leader in Serange or Amagarie had ever ruled uncontested for so many years. He'd held his throne against war and sedition. The tales of his rule had been why she'd approached him, not realizing that she dealt with a monster until it was too late.

"What have you to report, General Shenzhen?" The emperor drawled, finally taking his eyes from hers to look at a point beyond her shoulder.

He dismissed her once again and it stung. She reached out with her power, not surprised to see that his barriers remained fortified. The taint of a spell sparkled with a gray aura. She tapped gently, testing its strength and the complexity of its construct. It would take immense energy to break through his psychic barriers. Not that she could launch an attack with so many guards present and no viable plan of escape. But it did not hurt to assess his shields to understand the potential fight that loomed inevitably if he did not fulfill his bargain.

The grand general stepped past her and made his way closer to the throne and lowered himself to one knee and bent his dark head. Surprisingly, his ordinarily impeccable hair held in a queue behind his nape was loose and flowed over his shoulders. His black and red armor had blood specks in several places, and there was a slight discoloration on the lower part of his sharply chiseled left cheekbone.

"It is done, my sovereign ruler. The attack on the capital city of Nuria was successful."

Shilah cringed from the grand general's subservient tone. His voice poured forth treachery, yet the beauty of its pitch enticed her.

"You have proven invaluable to me, Princess Shilah."

Sweet venom dripped from the emperor's tongue. "*That* is a most coveted position to hold in my court. Value it."

A hum of satisfaction vibrated on the air, and the import of their words slammed into her stomach like a high beam laser. With every honeyed word from the emperor, the promise of freedom slipped away like ashes in the wind. She held tightly onto her self-restraint, it would never do for a princess to flinch and betray fear.

"She has failed, my sovereign ruler," Grand General Shenzhen replied with a frown, lifting his head to stare at her. His black eyes holding contempt. "The princess is not fit to be in the service of the sovereign ruler of the house of Zhang."

His obsequiousness sickened her. He was such a paradox —abjectly servile to the beautiful Emperor, yet deadly and powerful in his own right.

Shilah exhaled slightly, relieved when the emperor responded in a moderate tone. Sounds were weapons for Mevians. Their voices were not naturally beautiful. They merely had the ability to manipulate the variance of sound whenever they chose to turn their voices into a lethal instrument.

"Come now, General Shenzhen, the princess has proved her worth. She was able to pull forth each demon beast from its master into a corporeal form. That is extremely impressive."

Nothing moved inside of her at the smile that curved his lips. It was self-satisfied, covetous, and downright terrifying.

"But we do not yet have the king of Nuria, my imperial emperor. The attacks failed in its main purpose."

The emperor tapped his chin lazily. "We do not have the king, but we have something better."

Shilah tried not to be startled at the presence that simply appeared in the emperor's room. A Darkan and he had the witch, Amirah, clutched in his grasp. Shilah's stomach knotted, and she forced her mind to remain calm as the Darkan threw the witch that she'd worked with on the ground. She was a bloody mess.

A hard shaft of fear slammed into Shilah, and she cringed as the Darkan shifted his gaze to her, sensing her rising dread, for his kind fed on negative energy.

The grand general slowly rose from his kneeled position. "What is better than the Nurian king, my emperor?"

Fierce satisfaction emanated from the emperor. "A Dracan beast."

General Shenzhen faltered into complete stillness, an arrested expression on his cold face. "An impossibility, none has been recorded for more than a millennium, my emperor."

The emperor slashed his beautiful eyes to look at the witch who huddled on the ground.

"Report, my sweet Amirah."

The witch's aura wavered and flickered a deep violet, indicating the depth of her pain. The witch held her ribs and swiped at the blood that bubbled from her lips. "I incanted my emperor, for the Darkans and their beasts to attack the Nurian King at the Games of *Fyre*. I controlled the Darkan's demon beast with all my abilities and fulfilled my end of the bargain. I ordered it to capture the king, and the beasts tried but failed. The king of Nuria is a fierce and powerful warrior, and he drew forth the spirit of the *Phoenyx* buried inside him to defend against the demon beast. I tried using spells on him, but the king had a witch, High Duke Acheron, who incanted to counter-attack my spells."

She paused as she labored for breath, and then continued, "The Darkan and his summoned beast were defeated before the king was incapacitated for his retrieval."

"By a female warrior who has the tattoo of a Dracan?"

The witch trembled, yet she maintained eye contact with

the emperor. "She killed one of the beasts and its master. The king of Nuria killed the other."

Amirah flinched as General Shenzhen withdrew his sword from its sheath.

"The Princess and the witch have failed in the carrying out of their task, my imperial emperor. I ask your leave to take their heads."

The room spun quickly about Shilah, and abysmal fear wafted through her. She gathered her power and scanned the general's aura pattern, seeking a weakness and found none. She could not die here. The liberation of her people rested on her shoulders alone.

The emperor stood, his flowing silver robe studded with gems swirling around his ankles "Hold your sword, General Shenzhen. They have executed their tasks beautifully. They have proven that a Darkan can be controlled. They have proven that the chakras buried in the dark ones can be pulled onto this plane and controlled completely by us. We have found a most brilliant weapon in the war to come. And these weapons are the Princess Shilah and the witch Amirah."

The general hesitated, distaste flashing across his face. "My emperor?"

"The task I set before them was to breach the wall that separated man from beast, bringing the beast to the forefront. The princess executed that task exceptionally, and with the help of the witch's incantations, they were able to steer the demon into attacking the Games of Fyre, and the kingdom of Nuria."

"Their task was to *capture* the Nurian king, my emperor, and they failed."

The Emperor smiled, and it was so beautiful it forced Shilah to look away.

"The task was to show they could command a Darkan to draw forth his beast power and to direct that Darkan. Think of the possibilities, general, for our army. To have such a power in our control will be glorious indeed. And they discovered something that will position us beautifully. The woman who fought to protect the king of Nuria houses a most fearsome and legendary beast—*A Dracan*. I want her in my dungeon before the next moon night."

"And the king?" the General asked, canting his head to the side.

"We will use the Dracan to take the king." The laughter that pulsed from him wavered with his might.

Shilah's chest tightened as power lashed at her, biting at her skin. She breathed through it. "Sovereign Emperor of Mevia, I have fulfilled my bargain. I respectfully demand we complete our oaths." Her heart thumped in her chest, and she took some comfort from the fact that only the Darkan who looked on silently felt her dread.

Cold eyes settled on her. "The agreement my, sweet princess, was your aid in interpreting the book of Oracle to decipher a way to make the *Phoenyx's* power mine. Have you discovered the way?"

She hesitated. Had they not been over this? "Its power cannot be harnessed, emperor. It is pure rage. For the *Phoenyx* to be pulled forth from King Ajali, all would be incinerated. Its heat rivals the suns of the Omniverse," she rasped hoarsely.

Some indecipherable emotion flared in his eyes, and her stomach tightened.

"Then you have not fulfilled your bargain."

No! "The witch and I have scoured the book of the Oracle, the tombs, and scrolls. We presented our findings. The *Phoenyx cannot* be pulled from the King of Nuria."

"But it can be harnessed, hmmm?"

After a deep pause, she continued, "I doubt that I have the strength or control to call forth such a power, even with the witch's incantations. And doing so would be suicidal, for all present would be incinerated and the entire planet would be at risk of destruction."

He purred in pleasure as if planetary destruction would suit him well. "Are you confirming that you are useless to the execution of my plans, princess?"

Asked so blandly without a hint of power thrilling his voice, Shilah knew she faced death. "No." She could squeeze no more out of the tight clasp on her throat.

"You will soon be able to practice on the Darkan who houses the Dracan. If it takes you years, you will control this beast as you did the others."

Years. A petrifying knowledge slammed through her. The emperor had no intention of *ever* releasing her, a lifetime's imprisonment. She was a new prize for his army. How foolish she had been to place herself and her sister in his power. Shilah had been at once arrogant and naive.

He threw a thick book, and it landed at her feet. She picked up the massive tome. She skipped the first page and balked from the depiction drawn there. Even though a picture, it reeked of vicious evilness. She swallowed as she realized she held a tome that cataloged the Darkans' beasts, their strengths...and weaknesses? How had this come to be in the emperor's clutches?

"Learn about all that a Dracan offers, for I will have control of it."

She executed a shallow curtsy and then walked away from his throne. She ignored the garbled whimper from the witch, hating that she was unable to offer aid. Shilah had not been abused for her supposed failure because she was the only Imperial Serangite in the kingdom of Mevia. Witches peppered Amagarie after ripping portals into the Omniverse to abandon their realm eons ago. The Emperor could kill Amirah and have another witch in his service in a few hours.

To acquire another Serangite? That might take him another hundred years. Still, she reached out to her, brushing against her mental shields. The witch allowed her in, and before Shilah could speak, the witch said, *"I thank you for thinking of me Princess Shilah. But it does not make sense for both of us to die. If you try to render me any aid, the Emperor will make you suffer for it."*

Shilah faltered, her throat tightening at Amirah's pain and despair. *"I will bargain for your release—"*

"No! I appreciate your kindness but I have a plan and you interfering will only make my life more difficult. The Emperor will believe you care about me, and I will simply become another tool to control you!"

Swallowing back the denial, Shilah ensured she did not glance in the witch's direction as she rapidly walked from the chamber, quickly planning how to proceed. What to do? She had explained to the emperor the dangers of harnessing the power of the *Phoenyx* and binding it inside of himself. He was willing to risk war with Nuria to attain his obsession. There were many whispers in the castle of his plans to capture the Nurian King, but she had been disbelieving until they had been whisked to the outer walls of his palace to direct the beasts she and the witch had pulled from the Darkans to attack Adara, the Capital city of the Nurian Kingdom.

To capture the king of such a nation was undoubtedly an immense folly, but the confidence of the emperor shook her. He was either incredibly powerful, more so than she comprehended, or absolutely mad. The rustic beauty of the empire did nothing to soothe Shilah's frazzled nerves as she lightly ran up the thickly carpeted stairs that led to her guest quarters, passing several armored warriors who stood with rigid awareness along the large hallway.

Every passageway of the castle, the courtyards and baileys were manned by armored warriors leaving little room to escape the empire without a fight. The weapons she'd traveled with would hardly aid her, for Amagarie and the Empire of Mevia was nothing like her world with towering castles built from glass and topaz and refined steel. How she wished she had fled with Arrow, her PSI-2.1 friend who knew all the languages of the Omniverse and was possibly stronger than all the warriors she hurried pass. Arrow was skilled in many fighting styles and programmed to understand warfare and clever stratagems. How she missed him.

With a heavy sigh, she pushed open the door to her chamber and entered, closing the door gently when she wanted to slam it. Her current adobe was quite large, regal in its elegance, with several rooms and antechambers allocated for her sole use, including her own bath chamber, yet she knew her apartment for what it was. Her prison.

She made her way through the sitting room, eased open the door to her bedchamber and walked with grim purpose to her desk with its many parchments and inkwell. At least it was a comfortable prison with many luxuries provided. She came to a stunned halt seeing the man stooped rifling through the contents of the secret compartment in her desk. The one she'd believed she had cleverly installed.

Wariness rolled down her spine in a chilly wave.

"Who are you and what are you doing in my chambers?" she demanded.

He rose with animalistic grace and faced her. Her breath caught, he was power, strength, and so incredibly male, and too handsome. He was gorgeous, his face almost savage in its planes and angles. His frame was lithe yet muscled. Midnight hair was held back from his face at his nape, and his eyes were the most beautiful shade of amber, the color of rich, dark honey with bright flecks of gold.

Scanning his lean, lithe length, and striking features, she

registered his unfamiliarity. She fought back her rising temper. "I will not ask again, Sir," she snapped.

Her body hummed in shocking awareness and something wicked pulsed through her at his slow perusal. That look was almost physical. A caress. "I have told the grand general time, and time again I do not require a consort."

At his silence, she grew uncomfortable. "Speak," she commanded.

"I am not here for your pleasure."

She realized that seconds after she made her rash statement. He was not dressed like a consort in revealing silken clothing like the others that had been presented to her. He seemed…predatory? He stirred, a slight ripple of muscle warning of his strength. The power in him was so apparent it clung like a second skin. Shilah assessed him but sensed no aura.

Impossible. She was an imperial—the most powerful in her genesis of telepathy.

That absence of aura, the lack of sense of his true power, gave her the first inkling of fear. She gently flared out her telepathy, fluttering softly against his mind, and the shield that she encountered stunned her. She studied it with her psychic eye, reading its intricate pattern. It was a shield constructed from sheer willpower, and her mind was unable to see beyond its walls. Her heart thumped. "Are you here to kill me?"

"First a consort and now a killer," he said with such lazy amusement Shilah was almost disarmed. *Almost*. She slipped her hand inside the folds of her sari and gripped the hilt of her dagger. Her fighting skills were below par for most Amagarians, but she would not be taken without a fight.

The smile that curved his lips indicated that he'd seen her subtle move. If he attacked, even with the force of his shield, she would try and penetrate his barriers, seeking any weakness. She could attempt to trap him into a false memory or implant the suggestion to leave her unharmed or order him to stop breathing.

"Your injury is not my desire, Princess Shilah Symonrah of Dxyriah."

How deliberate he was with his knowledge. "I am sure that you do not expect me to be assured by such words coming from a stranger in my personal rooms. The emperor did not send you. Who are you?"

"I seek something that you have," he said with a deceptive shrug.

It occurred to her he desired to seem harmless, the notion ridiculous. Her instincts screamed he was a killer.

"You deliberately let me find you here. What is it I possess that you seek?"

His golden gaze moved over her predatorily curious. "Information."

"Why would I aid a man who has forced his way into my chambers and intrudes on my privacy?"

The soft hiss of a blade clearing its sheath sounded like a drum in the chamber. He looked distinctly—menacing. Shilah flared out her psychic eye, preparing for an attack even as she trembled. She gasped in raw shock when he gently clasped her from behind, his soft touch belying the cold press of steel against her throat. She swallowed. She had not seen him move at all. Not even the slightest indication of it. How was it possible for him to be so much faster than her eyes had been able to track?

"You will aid me, princess. I do not desire to hurt you, but if I must? I most assuredly will."

Fear slashed through her. "The emperor will have your head if you bring me harm," she said with false calm. She punched hard against his mind, trying to break past his mental barriers and met an impenetrable shield wall of will. She had never encountered such resistance. *Who was he?*

The soft laughter at her ear rasped against her skin like the sweetest caress. Undeniable awareness filled her, and she resented it, the feeling was unwelcomed from someone who threatened her life.

"The dungeons of Mevia, Princess. Tell me all you know about them."

2

Lachlan Ravenswood, an Archduke of the Darkage, inhaled the unique fragrance of the slight female clasped in his arms. The princess felt sublime resting against him. When Lachlan had spied her earlier, he had faltered, arrested by her stunning beauty. He'd stepped in her shadows, traveling with her for hours, learning and plotting. He'd discovered two things about her. She appealed to him despite being so petite, and the emperor of Mevia was her enemy despite the façade she presented. It was impossible for him to sense negative emotions as his fellow Darkans did, for he'd denied the existence of the malevolent chakra housed inside his body. Even without a demon beast's essence guiding him, he sensed that she feared the emperor, and, having spent several hours observing her carefully, he could identify the resentment and hatred which had burned in her eyes. It was that spit of fire amidst the fear that stroked his interest, but most compellingly she was a Serangite. Her mind was able to store a vast amount of information, dissect it and unravel its patterns. And also she was a telepath.

Would she aid him? That remained to be seen. The role

she played in the empire remained unclear. Earlier she'd had a meeting with the Emperor and his General, but Lachlan had not spied on it, sensing at least three other Darkans in the shadows of the throne room. An icy rage had filled him, for they were not in Mevia at their king's order. Hence they were traitors to his realm.

He would try to persuade the Serangite to help him explore the dungeons and would even use his blades if necessary, although he would prefer to use seduction as his tool. Lachlan tensed, analyzing his thoughts. It had been years since he'd bedded a woman or even had the desire to do so. The petite princess attracted him, but it was moot as his mission to uncover the dungeon of Mevia's stronghold was his main objective, and he could afford no distraction.

She inhaled, unintentionally pressing her softness into his hardened frame. The top of her head met his chest. She barely cleared five feet and was curvaceous though her loosely flowing sari hid most from his gaze. Her face, however, was shaped like the finest porcelain. Delicate chin, small nose, gently rounded cheeks, beautiful lips, and eyes hardened like diamonds appeared as if a star itself had been fractured in their depths. He ignored the flare of arousal that tightened his gut and pressed the blade closer to her beating pulse. Her soft gasp rasped over him, stroking the arousal that seemed to pulse inside of him.

He didn't trust his unfamiliar, extraordinary reaction to her. He should have ignored her presence, but he was racing against time. His kingdom had formed a recent alliance with Princess Saieke of the winds and mountains, and he was now honor bound to free Princess Saieke from the emotional pain that beset her because of her Queens Blades' imprisonment. They had been taken by warriors of Mevia who had hunted the princess only a few weeks past. They had been her guards for years , and she'd grown to regard them as family, ignoring the distinction of rank. Since their capture by the empire, she had been trying to rescue them. Lachlan owed her mate, Drac El Kyn, and he had called in his favor. Honor and friendship insisted Lachlan responded. Saieke's Blades' lives now rested in his hands, and he would complete his rescue mission successfully.

Lachlan had been in Mevia for precisely six days, but only in the palace for the last twelve hours. He had traveled through the kingdom in the dark, seeking those who had been rumored to construct the dungeons or anyone who had any knowledge of how to gain entrance. After endless searching and spying in the shadow space, it seemed as if the cells were a mystery to everyone in the empire. Yet he knew they existed.

The famed torture chamber of Mevia created fear even in Darkans. And for the civilians of Mevia who seemed to live in abject deference to the emperor and his warriors, talk of the dungeons were taboo. Infiltrating the palace required more caution because the emperor had Darkan traitors working with him who scanned the shadows for intruders. But Lachlan had absolute control in wielding his *shenkiri* of shadows and had been careful to stay a step ahead of those of his kind in the shadow space.

The Princess Shilah was a weak link to the empire and weakness should always be exploited. She was ironically a powerful weak link, one that held the key to what he sought. *Possibly.* He pressed the blade closer to her neck letting its cold caress her skin, and its threat imprint in her mind. She posed no danger to him with her telepathy. It wasn't that she was not dangerous. Far from it. She might be more fragile than other Amagarians, lacking their speed, strength, and their rapid healing capabilities, but Serangites made up for it with their mental prowess. But his shield, built through agonizing pain and loss, was impenetrable. He dipped his head and whispered in her ear. "The dungeons of Mevia, Princess. All that you know."

The trip of her pulse vibrated against the fine steel of his knife. "The dungeons?"

"I believe that is what I said. You were recently there." In what capacity he had yet to discover.

"I know nothing of the dungeons," she snapped.

"You visited last eve."

Every line in her body went taut. "You've been spying on me?"

He smiled at the outrage in her tone. "It is incidental that you captured my attention." He had been analyzing the underground area where he suspected the entrance to the dungeon was located. It was a smooth wall of nothingness. There was no evident opening, yet those walls had parted, and the princess had spilled forth with a witch and several guards. Lachlan had tried to shadow step into that space and had found himself paralyzed for several minutes. "I grow impatient, Princess."

With brutal deliberateness, designed to shock more than harm, he pressed the blade under her skin. Blood pooled and ran down her neck. Despite the danger to her, she slammed her head back, thumping his chest. She grasped his wrists, tapping her fingers across his pulse. Then he felt the soft flutters across his mind. He smiled. She was such a tiny creature. It was then he realized she was trying to fight back. How had she survived this long in the Empire? He was barely restraining her, and she could not escape his clasp.

Heat punched through him, and invisible hands yanked the blade down from her throat in a quick, powerful move, and that same force slammed him back with stunning might. Lachlan dug his heels into the floor, cracking the tiles beneath his feet as he resisted the blast of her ability, grounding himself to a halt.

She had telekinesis skills. *Impressive*. Most Serangites controlled only one of the four geneses—telepathy, telekinesis, teleportation, and foresight. Unless the information gathered by his dark king on the other realms were incomplete. He filed it away and studied her.

The princess had a jeweled dagger held up in an attack stance, a strange blue light emanating from the blade. Her silver-white hair fell loose over one shoulder, exposing the slim line of her throat and the softness of her jaw. Lachlan hadn't the heart to demonstrate how feeble she was against his power should he chose to unleash it. And as a woman who had the ear of the Emperor, he wanted no suspicion roused that an unknown Darkan was in their midst. He relaxed his stance, and with a deft flick of his wrist, sheathed his weapon. He tried to sound reassuring. Tried to appear non-threatening. "I do not wish a fight with you. I only seek information."

Her eyes narrowed. "I have no information to help you, stranger. My senses were masked by enchantment. No one can enter those dungeons without the Grand General Shenzhen or the Emperor's approval."

That was valuable knowledge. "A witch's spell?"

"Is there any other kind?" she asked softly, her muscles telegraphing her intent to attack.

"Do not be foolish. I have no wish to hurt you." The truth of it resounded in him. He was not a man who shied away from his brutality. Lachlan was a warrior and had always done difficult things for those he loved. Yet he couldn't imagine hurting her. She seemed too defenseless, and it was never in him to prey on those weaker than himself.

He considered her for an exceedingly long time, assessing every shift of her eyes, and the play of her muscles. Because he chose to bury his demon beast, he could not rely on the dark flavor of negative emotions to tell him when a prey lied, feared, or raged. Lachlan had made it a part of his abilities to assess his opponents, searching for those tell-tale signs to reveal deception. The princess, though frightened, radiated with innocent truth. "How long have you been in the Empire?"

A quick frown chased her features. "Almost three months."

"And in that time how often have you been to the dungeons?"

She glared at him before answering reluctantly, "About five, and only the upper floors."

"And each time you made it out, alive."

She flinched, and his curiosity stirred. What had been her purpose? To read the thoughts of others while they were questioned and tortured? "Do you know the witch who cast the spell that enchanted the dungeon?"

"I do not."

Another truth. "Why do you visit the dungeons?"

Her breathing fractured slightly, and the pulse at her throat fluttered, yet her eyes held steadily on his. "I read the thoughts of selected prisoners for the Emperor."

Ah…a lie. "Did you lie to me just now princess?"

Her lips curved slightly. "I owe you no truths or loyalty, stranger."

"I could take it from you, should I wish it," Lachlan murmured, his intrigue multiplying.

Her chin lifted, and her hand tightened on her weapon, and those strange but beautiful eyes dared him to try. For some reason, her defiance made him want to smile. "You will keep this encounter between us, Princess."

She arched an elegant brow. "The emperor will not be kind when he hears of your presence in his kingdom."

"Precisely. Now if I believed you would reveal that I am

here, I would be forced to silence you. Instead, we could be friends."

A scowl settled on her face. "Is that so?" she demanded caustically, using her free hand to touch the spot where he'd nicked her skin.

"The enemy of my enemy?" he asked smoothly, sinking into that empty hollow place that would allow him to snap her neck without remorse. "Do I have reason to believe you will inform the emperor of my presence?"

He watched her carefully for signs of deception.

"I cannot reveal you if I am ignorant of your identity," she said hoarsely, gripping the edge of her blade, appearing more frightened than manipulative.

"Then we have an understanding." He dipped into the slightest bow, then moved toward the windows. Lachlan shoved them open and stepped through.

With a gasp she hurried over, her eyes wide with disbelief as she peered down into the courtyard more than fifty stories below them. She glanced up, her eyes frantically searching the darkness for him. He was right there, at one with the shadows and darkness.

"Who are you?" she whispered, no doubt thinking he had left.

The soft question seemed to brush directly against his cock, startling him. He didn't have time for a liaison and hadn't had time for almost two hundred years. How odd this slip of female could even for a moment rouse his senses. Pushing her from his thoughts, he roiled with the darkness into the Emperor's throne room, the place where he'd observed a few guards dragging the witch who had spilled from the enchanted dungeons with the princess. Hopefully, it was her who had crafted the spell, and if not, with persuasion, she would direct him to the right witch or try unraveling the spell herself.

After determining that none of his kind lingered in the darkness, he stepped into the throne room's shadow space. The emperor paced the floor, his robe flowing about his legs, his eyes flat and cunning. The witch kneeled on the jade tiles, blood in a round pool at her feet. Her raven black hair was a tangled mess, and cobalt blue eyes burned with hatred and anguish. Three guards surrounded her, their swords held about her head, waiting on their emperor's command.

"Lord Zhang, I ask for mercy," she said softly, the despair in her tone clutching at Lachlan.

"Mercy? I gave you one task. Control the Darkan beast that had been summoned to a corporeal form. And you failed. I believe another witch with greater power will be better employed."

A dark primal, instinctive part of Lachlan's soul stilled. They had somehow managed to pull the chakra from one of his people onto this plane? The beasts that resided in all Darkans were pure mystical energy with their own cunning and intelligence. Only the most powerful of their kind were able to tap into that abyss of unrelenting strength and summon the beast inside to a corporeal form. And only the Darkan host could control that beast. How was it possible that the witch could call it forth and then control it?

The very suggestion shook his soul and an emotion that felt perilously close to fear slithered through him. The concept of anyone possessing the power to harness the will of their people was terrifying and had far-reaching consequences.

"I am with child," the witch continued, resting her hands against her stomach in a protective gesture.

It was then he saw the gentle swell below her flowing caftan.

"Oh?" The Emperor said, a look of cunning settling over his features. "And why should that be of any import to me?

Unless, who might be the father?"

She lifted her head and met the Emperor's curious gaze. "Another witch from my coven."

Lachlan sensed that she lied, and he stepped into her shadow assessing her.

The emperor held her stare. "There is a rumor you allowed a Darkan between your thighs. One whom you met at the Inn in Taryllion. And now you are with child."

She whitened, and Lachlan tensed. She had survived the wastelands? Taryllion was violent and lawless—thousands of miles of land which separated the borders of the seven kingdoms of Amagarie. It possessed flat lands that seemed to stretch endlessly before mountains rose behind them, dark and intimidating. Many did not know of its underground city built deep inside the caverns of the wastelands, made up of exiles from the seven kingdoms, thieves, and assassins. Ironically, it had an Inn, where all factions could dine and drink, and even bed down for the night without fear of losing their lives. That savage and lawless place operated with a code—anyone within the Inn's wall was safe.

And she had met a Darkan there.

The hands that pushed her dark hair from her forehead trembled. "A Darkan can only impregnate a mate, and I'm no one's mate," she said, grooves of strain bracketing her mouth.

"Ah...but you did allow one to ride between your thighs, my sweet Amirah."

She remained silent. The emperor flicked his wrists, and the guards sheathed their swords.

"I believe I have further use for you, my witch. You will be kept here until the child is born. If it is the child of a Darkan it will stay here...and you will be allowed to leave."

A ragged moan of pain and denial slipped from her. She struggled to her feet, and Lachlan wanted to howl at the damage. Those with power should never abuse those weaker than themselves. And they had toyed with her. Cutting into her skin with their blades. She bled from a multitude of cuts. If she had been fated to die, a clean death would have done the job.

She dipped into a clumsy bow and then departed. He followed her, cloaking himself in absolute darkness. Three guards also followed at a discreet distance. She made her way several floors down, before turning left along a long lonely corridor. The witch stopped at an iron door and waited. One of the guards inserted a key, the door swung open, and she entered.

It was a small airless room, the lone window high almost to the ceiling. Stark, cold, grey concrete constructed her prison. A lone narrow cot was pushed against a corner, and the room was void of a fireplace. She hobbled over to a small table, took up a pouch, opened it and collected a pungent smelling herb. She slowly mixed the herb into some liquid she had in a chalice, muttered under her breath, and drank it in a long swallow. Before his eyes, a few of the smaller cuts stopped bleeding, but she still appeared pained. A chill blanketed the room, and she grabbed the thin quilt and wrapped it around her shaking shoulders, lowering herself onto the edge of the cot.

Harsh, broken sobs spilled from her. She did not tarry in her sorrow, squaring her shoulders and resting hands on her stomach. "I'll not fail you," she promised softly. "How stupid of me to run from your father when I sensed his might. He is a power to be reckoned with my darling, and he can help protect us from the coven, *and* the emperor. I am so petrified to reach out to him. His kind are monsters."

The small mound of her stomach rippled, and a choked laugh escaped her. "But not you, my sweet, you are no monster," she murmured. "Half of me is within you too."

A dark curiosity bloomed, taking root too rapidly for him to crush. Lachlan stepped from the shadows.

She paled alarmingly, came to her feet slowly, facing him, breathing roughly. Her power rode the air, and the walls of the room contracted and settled. "Who are you?"

"I am an Archduke of the Darkage."

Raw fear chased her features. Her eyes flared wide before she inhaled deeply. "*Lies*. I sense no demon within you. But you stepped from the shadows. How is this possible?"

He ignored that demand. "What work do you perform for the emperor?"

Her eyes flashed. "I am here under duress. I do not willingly do anything for him."

A truth. "How did you pull the chakra from within the Darkan?"

The pulse at her throat fluttered madly, and she whispered too low for him to decipher. Her power swarmed over his skin like insects. Lachlan remained still, drawing the shadows in the room to coalesce around her. They twisted at her feet like snakes and her breathing fractured.

"If you try to cast a spell, I will not hesitate to rip your tongue from your head. And if you lie to me, I shall peel the flesh from your body," he said without any give or mercy in his heart. "Speak."

She lifted her chin defiantly, but he caught a glimpse of fear quickly masked. "I do not have the power alone to pull the beast from its master. The Serangite used her telepathy along with my most powerful spells to summon it. He was young and unbonded, and we called out his beast from him at the emperor's order." Her voice cracked before she firmed her lips.

Disbelief scythed through him. "The Serangite used her telepathy, and the beast simply came forth?"

The witch watched him warily. "Along with my spell. The

demon beast wanted to be free and did not put up much resistance to stay within its host."

His voice was a low growl when he responded, "Take me to the Darkan."

Her eyes were a striking blue, almost black and she held his gaze unflinching. *Brave*. No other would face death with such composure.

"He is dead."

Violence tore through him, and vengeance bled into his veins.

"Not by my hands," she said hoarsely. "We summoned his beast and then used our powers—"

"Who is the Serangite?" His gut told him it was her, but he still needed confirmation.

"Princess Shilah."

Regret slammed into his chest. A pity. She would not live to see the dawn for the crimes committed against his people. Only the oldest and most powerful Darkans could summon their *Cerja*—the distinct image of their beast covering their body—to a corporeal form, but this Serangite was able to do so in fledging Darkans. Even if he was of a mind to forgive it, she and the witch were weapons of Mevia. They could not be allowed a place on the war board. The empire was already too powerful.

Something inside Lachlan violently resisted the idea of hurting her. He frowned, not understanding that anomaly. He had lived centuries in a stark, lonely existence, but with honor, never breaking his code or betraying his oath. He had never been the kind of man to shy away from his duty and removing any weapon that could ultimately enslave his people was a duty to his king and realm. He was also not the kind to kill without reason and had even been taunted by his fellow enforcers that he had the morals and scruples of a human. They'd even dubbed him the peacekeeper of the

Darkage, for he understood mercy and compassion. A thing most of his people did not do well with, but he did not mind, for he preferred to be merciful when necessary than live with the unchecked brutality of his demon.

"Who killed him?"

"We directed the Darkan and his beast to attack Nuria and capture King Ajali. He failed. There was a woman there, another Darkan, whispers refer to her as Tehdra El Kyn."

With clipped tones, the witch told him of the fight witnessed, and Lachlan realized with a sense of shock that Tehdra El Kyn, sister to his good friend Drac had bonded with her demon beast. For her to have revealed herself in Nuria, someone precious to her would have been threatened. Her mission had been one of pivotal secrecy to uncover who in the Kingdom of Eternal fire plotted to murder their shadow king—Gidon Al Shra, and to prevent any assassination attempts on the Nurian King by Darkans.

It was imperative Lachlan returned to the Darkage. A meeting needed to be convened with the war council. The Emperor's action could not be allowed to stand. "Are there more Darkans being experimented on?"

She swallowed. "There are three captives in the dungeon."

"Do you know how to access the dungeon?"

"I do not. It is enchanted."

He considered her unable to detect if she spoke the truth. "In what manner?"

"I do not know. It is rumored a coven of witches designed the spell for the emperor. After they bestowed on him the words and the talisman, he had them slaughtered."

Such a ruthless move sounded like the emperor. Lachlan withdrew his dagger.

The witch's eyes widened with shock. "You are going to kill me."

"You are a weapon of Mevia, one used to kidnap and

torture my people for the power housed inside them. As an enforcer for my king, I judge you guilty. You are a weapon that cannot be allowed existence."

She jerked, paling even further. "If you kill me, Emperor Khan will replace me by dawn. What will you do then, eliminate all witches from Amagarie?"

"I felt your power witch as you tried to read my chakra. Only a few have your strength. I believe you will not be so readily replaced."

"I am a white witch, and there are more powerful witches than I am. The Emperor has a few red witches in his army," she said, desperation throbbing in her voice.

At his lack of response, her eyes glistened with enraged tears, and she demanded, "Will you kill the princess too? Or is it only witches who are expendable?"

"She will die." The words were cold and implacable.

The witch backed away, going as far as to hop onto her bed, the thin mattress sinking below her weight. She shrugged the quilt from her shoulders, tensing to defend her life. She waited, her breath sawing from her throat, and Lachlan considered imprisonment for the sake of the babe she carried.

"By the laws of the Darkage, you cannot bring me harm. I am with child and...and...." She took a deep, steady breath. "My child belongs to the realm of demons and shadows."

For a timeless moment, Lachlan could not breathe. "Who is your mate?"

She flushed. "I have no mate," she said firmly. "But the father of my child *is* a Darkan."

"And who is this Darkan?"

Fear and doubt clouded her gaze before she lowered her lids. It amused him to see a blush climbing her cheeks. "I met him at the Inn. I do not know his name. It was only…it was only the one night."

No Darkan would bed his mate and then allow her from his sight.

"You know nothing of him?"

"No." And her blush became redder.

He arched a brow. "Then I can only surmise you lie, witch."

Her eyes flashed. "They called him Hunter, and he wore an amulet with the king's sigil."

Lachlan's muscles locked. She carried the child of Ramiel Hunter, the leader of the small band of warlords of the Darkage. A man who was solitary and wished for no ties as he executed one of the most hated tasks of being the judge and executioner for the *Senji*s—those who had lost their sanity to their demons and fallen under its bloodthirsty control.

It was possible Ramiel had known the witch was with child and walked away. It was rumored a Darkan could sense the moment of conception. And Ramiel was one of the most merciless of their kind, called an abomination by those with little tolerance because he housed two demon beasts. It was possible he had walked away because she would become his weakness, and the enemy would know it and move to secure her at all cost. And the damn hunter had more enemies than a sea with sand. And if the witch were his mate, and she was taken, killed, then he could become the very thing that he hunted. An outcome his enemies would rejoice in. If the emperor knew the powerful bargaining chip he held, he would try to bend the hunter to his will.

They stared at each other, and the fear in her eyes left a vile taste in Lachlan's mouth. He lowered his eyes to her stomach, for the first time wishing he had access to his beast. Then he would be able to touch her stomach and feel if the child had a demon beast. Power would have bowed to power and darkness to darkness.

"I will take you from here, and no harm will come by my

hands." Lachlan could not allow the emperor to have her, even if it meant abandoning his mission to rescue the Princess's Queen's blades.

Hope burned brightly in her eyes. "Will you swear on your king's life you will take me to safety?"

"I do." He did not add that he would be taking her to the Darkage and to Ramiel, that would likely start a fight, and she would end up hurt.

She closed her eyes briefly, relief evident in every line of her body. "When do we leave?"

"After."

She frowned. "After what?" Then she sucked in another sharp breath. "You go to kill *her*, the Serangite." Disapproval throbbed in her tone.

Lachlan stared at the witch. "Can the emperor procure another Serangite for his army?"

"No," the witch whispered shakily, cleverly sensing the direction of his arguments.

"Then she is integral to him?"

Another slight hesitation, then a reluctant, "Yes."

"If the Serangite disappears from the palace will the emperor command his army to scour Amagarie for her? Leaving death and destruction in his path?"

The witch closed her eyes and then snapped them open. Such sorrow for a woman she perhaps hardly knew. "Princess Shilah is powerful. I…I believe her to be an imperial."

An imperial, the most potent level there could be to a Serangite's power. "Then tell me, witch, if I cannot allow the emperor to control her, and if I take her from here, he will send his army after her…what is left?"

"She needs to be removed from the board," the witch whispered, her blue eyes dark with sorrow. "I do not believe she willingly serves him. The princess is but a pawn in the emperor's game and must not suffer for it."

"She'll not see death coming."

There it was again, that peculiar feeling of loss, a sense of wrongness at the mere idea of taking the princess's life. He deliberately filled his mind with a lifeless image of her. Even without the chakra of his beast, he was capable of immeasurable cruelties, especially when it came to protecting the vision of his king to lift their people from the political and economic slump they resided in as a kingdom.

Gidon had created the seven orders of law for the Darkage and had a bold plan to lift their realm from the blackened stain over them. Their society had been a less barbaric one because of him, and trade within their walls had flourished, and their kingdom had grown. Yet there were those of their kind who preferred the anarchy and plotted to overthrow him. And Lachlan along with Drac and Talon, two of his closest friends, had vowed their friend and King would not fall while they lived.

The princess threatened that, so he would remove her.

However, something unrecognizable to Lachlan, somewhere unfamiliar inside burned with denial at the thought of her death. He brushed it aside. Personal feelings must never come before duty to his realm and king, and he hardly understood what he felt for the Serangite. He did not know her. Perhaps it was merely lust, and that was no reason to hesitate.

The witch held out her hands tentatively. "I am Amirah Ky'San."

He did not take her hand, not liking her sudden ease. She was too trusting. Clearly, she thought he would not harm her now since she carried a Darkan child. And she was right. He lowered his gaze once more to her gently rounded stomach, an odd arrow of yearning piercing him. For years he had been endlessly alone. A choice he had never felt regret for until now. Strange. He did not hunger for love or for a mate so why did he feel this odd twisting through his heart?

She took a deep breath for control, then let it escape slowly. "When do we leave, tonight?"

"It depends."

"On what?"

"The Emperor." And with that cryptic statement, he allowed the shadows to swallow him. Before he stepped into the abyss, he spoke, "If there is anything you need to take with you, have it on your person at all times. When I come for you, I will come with the shadows, and we will disappear from the empire."

She pressed a hand to her chest. "There are other Darkans in the shadows," she warned. "And they work for the emperor."

"Be ready."

Then he *shiktred*—using the shadows to travel—through the palace, covering hundreds of rooms within seconds, searching if any of his kind lingered within the palace walls. He sensed no other, and he relaxed slightly. His cold and calculating mind worked, as he assessed how he would find what he sought. It was rumored the emperor only took his most treasured prisoners to the dungeon. Those he did not deem valuable were sent to work in the crystal mines of Mevia or executed in the arenas in close quarter hand to hand gladiator *taijui* battles.

Lachlan would leave this place with the witch, but he must first complete the task to which he had committed. Princess Saieke, the mate of Drac El Kyn, waited with hope that her loyal Queen's blades would be found alive and rescued. Time was currently against Lachlan, for the place he needed to be most now was by his king's side.

All evidence pointed of an imminent attack against his

king to remove him from his throne. When that attack arrived, it would be brutal and all-consuming, for the betrayers would need to succeed on the first wave. In that wave, they would need to kill him and all the enforcers and captains that were loyal to the dark king for their coup to be successful. And he now had a good idea how they planned to succeed.

It was imperative Lachlan left this kingdom by the next day and returned to the Darkage. The very idea of Gidon being assassinated while Lachlan was not there knotted his gut into bands of rage. The Darkage could not lose another king so soon after the assassination of King Rajleigh, Gidon's father.

The only way in which to find the dungeons was to become a captive. The Princess Shilah would be required to deceive the emperor. Her death was not imminent. How curious more relief filled him at that thought. He assured himself he needed the Serangite to testify before the emperor, and he would have to lower his barrier enough for her to read the thoughts he would project.

The emperor must be enticed to imprison him with the rest of his treasures. Lachlan faltered at the thought of even allowing his beast any freedom. It had been a little over four hundred years since he had used any of its vile chakra. His people fed their beasts from the dark negative energy others gave off, and he had suppressed the savagery of his beast by erecting a shield inside, separating their chakras, and never allowing it any freedom.

The notion of parting the veil once more to peek at the beast that lived within him, when a demon beast had slaughtered his family, had rage burning through his veins. It hardly mattered that the slaughter happened at the hands of a Darkan driven mad with power of his beast. Because that Darkan had been his father, and Lachlan had inherited that same beast and the shame of his father turning into a *Senjis*, becoming a ravaging monster who had killed indiscriminately. That same malevolence lived within him, and he had drawn upon its powers until he had seen the corruption caused from using its chakra. He'd seen it first-hand in the broken bodies of his mother and her lover.

Brushing aside the haunting memory, Lachlan moved in the shadows, plotting. He would lower his barrier enough so the Serangite could read the intentions he wanted to communicate to the emperor and afterward, he would kill her.

No. The denial snapped through him, and he stopped in the shadow space. *Why?* There was something about her he couldn't quite grasp, something important, elusive, something that brushed against the sharp edges of his mind but refused to be caught. He shadow-stepped into her palatial chambers. She methodically packed a bag with clothes, daggers, and rolls of papers.

Why do I hesitate at the thought of ending your life?

Unexpectedly she whirled around, a hand pressing over her heart. She lifted her chin, displaying the soft skin of her neck, the pulse beating heavily at her throat. Lustrous silver-white hair rippled to her mid-back, and the beauty of her delicate face arrested his attention. Her eyes stared where he stood, and he smiled, wondering at her power. Somehow, she sensed a ripple in the shadows. Her eyes which had the brilliant diamond cast of a fractured star seemed to glow, and he felt the brush of her powers. He glided closer, drawn to the rare beauty of her eyes. He stared into them, and Lachlan felt like he was falling forward into an endless abyss somewhere beautiful and unfathomable.

Her hand went to her throat. She looked so young and defenselesss, he wanted to drag her into the protection of his arms. And Lachlan doubted then that he would be able to snap her neck. He stared at her, disbelief twisting through his soul. *What madness was this?* She was a weapon able to draw the demon from inside his kind and turn it against the people of Amagarie, a weapon the emperor could use to enslave his people, triggering the third great war of Amagarie, for their dark king would retaliate, and his heart was merciless. Their kind was almost impossible to defeat in battle, and she had armed the emperor with their powers. There should be no hesitation in his heart to remove her.

He didn't like feeling uncertain; it was foreign to his nature. Her tongue darted to lick her bottom lip, a nervous gesture, yet fierce arousal burned through him, rocking Lachlan back on his heels. His reaction confounded him, for it was not the monster in him urging him to lay claim. That need was all him. The princess was a sudden inexplicable force of chaos in his well-ordered and emotionless existence. He burned, he hungered, and he wanted to lift her in his arms, split her wide, sinking his cock deep, and ride her until they were limp with completion and her voice hoarse from screaming his name. In the dark cage of his mind, his shield rippled and contracted, and a soft yet taunting laugh echoed.

Lachlan's entire soul froze, and with infinite care, he slowly moved away from her, melting into the gray shadow space of the wall. He searched inside, unable to detect any chakra that was not purely his. He tunneled his mind deep inside of himself, to his center where he only saw light in his mind and the blue glow of chakra, his life force, running through his veins. And beyond that light, deep shadows wavered into an impenetrable wall of absolute darkness. He assessed the wall, and there were no cracks. Had it been in his imagination that he had heard his demon?

He prowled over to her, dipped his head close to her neck and inhaled deeply. She smelled like the rain. He could not explain why he was checking to see if her scent drove him to distraction and lust as others of their kind had described the sensations they endured upon finding their mates. Lachlan knew it to be impossible without the beast in him, but still, he had to check. And there was nothing but the sweet woman scent of her, the one that begged him to seduce, and take her. With a soft curse, he moved away. What would he have done, he wondered, if he'd had a visceral reaction to her scent?

There was no explanation for his enthrallment. She wasn't in his mind, that he was confident of. The witch had cast no enchantment, and that led him to the realization it was simply the woman before him.

The anomaly of it tempted him then to step from the shadows, clasp her slender throat and snap her neck. He should not allow any opportunity for her to become a distraction or worse a weakness. Something dark and dangerous stirred deep inside of him, and unable to understand the needs rousing through his soul, Lachlan watched, and waited.

3

𝒰nable to shake the feeling that something lingered in the dark, Shilah closed the small bag she had carefully packed. Several times she had probed her room with her telepathy, and no thoughts had rushed to her. She could sense no aura, yet her skin prickled with unfathomable awareness. Careful to not appear unduly alarmed, she moved around the palatial room, scanning the large four poster bed, and the gold inlay chaise lounge. Of course, no one was hidden, but she truly couldn't shake the feeling someone or something more was within the chamber. It was at times like these she wished this world operated like hers where each household had a personal PSI system, for the sentient intelligence would not allow any stranger into her domain as it was the first line of defense.

The memory of the sleek, golden-eyed man taunted her, and she glanced around the chambers once more. Perhaps she was naturally anxious about the path she would traverse. Shilah would need to flee the empire of Mevia, *tonight*, with her sister. Where they would go, she had no notion, for they were without allies in Mevia. They would have to flee to another kingdom or perhaps the realm of Amagarie itself. The seven kingdoms were on the edge of war, and she could see now that she had chosen the wrong realm to escape to and seek aid from. Perhaps Earth, or Titan—the world of cyborg warriors beyond the Jupiter ring would have been a more prudent choice. It was foolish now to look back with regret, and she must plot a new path for her and Kala. They needed allies, and Shilah had no idea where to get them.

"Shilah!"

Her sister's scream of fear slammed into her mind with such force her knees buckled. Catching herself, she rushed toward her door, flung it open, and headed toward the opposite end of the corridor. Fury and rage pushed Shilah to run along the mile-long hallway tiled with jade green marble at full speed. *"Kala, I'm coming."*

The steady silent screams of her sister battered her mind. The emperor had assigned them to opposite chambers at the end of the hallway, and always, at least two guards manned the halls. Shilah and Kala communicated telepathically as much as possible, careful not to spill their powers in the air. The emperor had several witches in his service, and she had come to respect their cunning and strength, even as she hated them for their loyalty to such a vile man.

A wail of pain tore through her, and Shilah stumbled, her knees slamming into the ground. Pain radiated through her, but she pushed through it, launching to her feet, and hurrying faster to her sister's chamber. How she wished she had been able to flash as the Amagarians did, but their ability to move at such speeds was born from their enormous chakra strength and control. A gift no Serangite possessed.

"Shilah!"

Blood rushed through her veins, adrenaline surged through her system, and she pumped her legs faster. *"Kala, what is it? Control your fear and tell me. Are you under attack?"*

"A decision has been made." The echo of her sister's voice throbbed with distorted power, and Shilah ran faster. Kala was a foreseer, and her visions were never wrong. Shilah neared the door, and the two guards drew their swords from behind their backs. Thank kings they hadn't thought to use sound waves to stop her progress.

Without thinking she blasted past their weak mental barriers and commanded them to sleep. They dropped, the thud of their bodies echoing in the hallway. She blasted the door open with her mind, and rushed in. Her sister was kneeling in the center of her bed, sobbing, her mass of red hair tangled around her face, her green eyes wide with fear and uncertainty. Mentally closing the door behind her, Shilah pressed her hands against it and pushed with the full force of her aura creating a kinetic barrier in the room. Then she rushed over to her sister.

"What is it, Kala?"

"Our future has changed."

Shilah's mouth dried. "I know. The emperor has no intention of letting me...us go. He wants me to stay for another year, but I fear he lies. Our powers are too much of a prize."

Kala's eyes snapped open, and the fear and pain in her gaze drove the air from Shilah's lungs. She gripped her sister's hand as a dark blue aura flickered around her. The vision had taken hold of her, and her body trembled.

"No, Shilah...*everything* has changed. I can no longer see you ruling or married to the crown prince."

Shilah stepped back, her heart pounding in fear. "Has our realm found out that I have a second genesis?" She had been anticipating that discovery for forty-four years.

"No, it is not that. Despite your fears, I've seen us...you in *Dxyriah*, sitting on the throne, the Crown Prince of Novar by your side." Tears pooled in her sister's eyes and spilled over.

Shilah had never believed in that future and had known

there would come a time it would evolve. She was an impure, a Serangite with two geneses, and such a joining in her world was forbidden. Since she discovered the Alpha telekinetic gene had manifested in her years ago, she had burned all the hopes she'd had in her heart for a family of her own. Impures were not allowed to breed, to taint the purity of the race, a law she believed in with her entire heart.

"I've always known it was impossible for me to marry Prince Novar, Kala. Our Senate may not know I am impure, but *we* know it, and I could not deceive them so and consent to be his wife!"

Her sister sobbed. "Yes, but what I've seen Shilah…I cannot comprehend it."

"Tell me," she urged hoarsely.

"Heavy is the burden for the one who wears the crown of darkness," Kala said, her voice dark and gravelly with power. "It will come for you—a creature of blood and rage. I see upon your head a crown of snakes and thorns, I see an army of beasts, and at your feet our kingdoms in ruins, the street flowing blood."

For one terrible, timeless moment, her resolve wavered. She snatched her hands from her sister and the connection severed. Kala pressed a hand over her mouth.

"Our future has changed."

"Someone made a decision, and it was not us." That could be the only thing to account for the change in her sister's vision for the first time in thirty-five years. The first time Kala told Shilah she saw her on the throne, they had wept their rage and pain. For their older brother had a wife and children, and for Shilah to sit on the throne so young, it meant they would perish before them. They had warned her brother, and he had taken precautions, but their enemies had slipped under their guard, and their kingdom had fallen. Shilah had promised vengeance, but the vision had remained the same—she would rule as the Crown Princess. She had silently pledged not to marry the Crown Prince of Novar, and the vision had stayed unchanged. Even after she had entrusted her plans with the emperor of Mevia to take back her kingdom, and the vision had not wavered.

Shilah stood and started to pace back and forth. "What if I stay with Emperor Khan for another year?"

Kala took a deep breath, and Shilah held out her hands. The scream that tore from her sister was wild and frightened. Kala released her hand as if she had been burned and dashed behind the silken screen to empty her stomach. Kala came out, and Shilah stared at her.

"What is happening?" Shilah whispered, hating how afraid she felt.

"If we stay...." Kala shook her head as if unable to voice her vision. "I would rather die here and now than have you stay. I see nothing but agony and broken bones and spirit. Staying as the emperor commands is not an option. You will pray for death, and I do not see the mercy of it."

Shilah's knees went weak, and she lowered herself onto the sofa by the fire. "But what did your first vision mean?"

"I cannot see it in full. Shilah, I am afraid."

So am I. "Someone made a decision that has altered my future. That someone has to be important to me for the ripple to be so far-reaching." *I see upon your head a crown of snakes and thorns.* What could that mean?

"Perhaps," her sister said, drinking deeply from a chalice of wine, no doubt to remove the taste after emptying her stomach.

Shilah stood and paced. "What if there is no delay and we leave tonight, right this moment? We do not try and plan, simply act with impulse and courage. What then?"

Kala paled, and Shilah understood. "It's all right. You do not have to touch me again."

The use of their powers was often mentally and physically draining. More so for her sister who had not yet come into the full range of her abilities. With each touch and decision made, Kala was able to peek into someone's future. Her current ring of power was that of an Alpha—the beginning grade of her skills out of the three levels for her geneses of foreseer. If she had been an Imperial, Kala would have been able to see the pathway and who made the decision to affect their futures, and the different probabilities surrounding the future based on all possible actions. As it were, only a few Serangites ever attained imperial powers from the existing geneses of telepathy, telekinesis, teleportation, and foresight. Most of the imperial bloodlines were contained within the royal families of the three kingdoms of Serange. "We must leave at once," she said. "It is simply too dangerous to remain any longer in the Empire."

"How will we escape?"

A thought struck Shilah. "Were you safe and alive in the new visions?"

Kala's head shook frantically. "I could not see."

"But before when I married the Prince Novar you were there, yes?" She had heard the vision several times, but she wanted to ensure that part had not changed since the rebellion in Dxyriah.

Her lips trembled on a smile. "I walked you down the aisle of the grand cathedral."

Shilah's stomach knotted, hating not getting a sense of her sister's fate. "It is foolhardy for us to try and decipher your vision. We can no longer trust the honor of the emperor, and we must act. The emperor will not dream that we would try and escape. We must do so, tonight."

"And the guards?"

"We must kill them."

Her sister flinched. Kala had never been able to take

another's life, and while Shilah had been forced to defend them since the rule of their kingdom had been brutally taken, the aura that clung to her after taking a life was vicious and would see her weakened for days. Three times she had been forced to use her powers to kill, and the very memory made her heart tremble. "I will command as many of them as possible to look the other way." But not everyone had the same mental barriers and readily accepted the planted memories or suggestions that would distort their realities and thoughts.

"There are thousands of warriors in the palace. Perhaps we should not return to Serange," her sister said fretfully.

"Do you doubt my powers?" Shilah asked.

She had ascended to an Imperial in her telepathic powers in the battle to escape with her and Kala's life. When utilizing the full force of her power, she could ultimately control someone's perception and push thoughts, feelings, or hallucinatory visions into the mind of another person, causing pain, paralysis, or unconsciousness, altering or erasing memories, or completely taking over another person's mind and body. She had never battled with the full use of her abilities, but even while asleep, she could feel the deep well of her power at the calm center of her heart.

"We have no allies, Shilah. It will be us against the empire if we are discovered fleeing. Perhaps Dxyriah will flourish under Crown Prince Quan's rule and maybe—"

"It is our home," Shilah whispered fiercely. "Serange was divided into three kingdoms and treaties formed to prevent so much power being concentrated into one family. Prince Quan wants to change that. He will lay siege to the other kingdom until he unites them under his rule. It will not be peaceful. The slaughter must be stopped."

Kala closed her eyes briefly and then nodded. "It must."

"And we *must* avenge our family and friends. Torren,"

Shilah started softly with her brother's name. "Parisa, Michaela, Thorin—"

"Savannah, Raven, Matthias, and Nia," Kala ended softly. "I've not forgotten them. Not a day goes by I do not remember their lifeless bodies taken in the name of greed."

They stared at each other, the memories flowing from Shilah's thoughts to her sister's. The good ones of when they had been happy and life had been simpler.

"We will leave Mevia," Kala said bravely. "And I pity the fools who would try and stop us."

"Tonight."

Shilah hugged her sister. "*Get dressed and pack a small bag only with essentials.*"

Kala nodded, and Shilah walked away and slipped from her sister's chamber with stealth. The guards were still lying on the floor. She stooped and gently touched each of their foreheads, piercing their natural shields which were even more relaxed. *Nothing happened. You did not see my sister or me earlier or tonight should anyone ask*. She brushed against their memories of seeing her rushing forward and psychically snapped the thread, which appeared like a web of spider silk, removing it. *You will stand in a minute, then open your eyes, and rouse to full consciousness*.

Then she stood, and raced along the hallway to her chamber, her powers flared wide, preparing to manipulate the thoughts of anyone who should see her. Thankfully, the corridors were empty, and she slipped into her chamber with a sigh of relief.

She gathered her heavy mass of silver hair and wrapped it into a tight coronet around her head. Then she grabbed her bodysuit from the closet. It was dark blue, sleek, and would fit against her body like a second skin. In this, she would be able to fight and run without hindrance. The material was also hard and would resist most slashes and stabs. She whipped the sari from her body, stepping from the sheer material.

A sharp inhalation had her spinning around. Shilah realized with an unpleasant shock, of fear, that someone was in her chamber and she had not sensed them.

"Who's there?" she demanded, balancing on the soles of her feet, pushing her powers out trying to read their thought. There was nothing. Only a formless void.

Her gaze riveted on the dark spot near the top of her bed. Somehow, she knew that was where the person lingered, despite being unable to detect an aura.

No aura. "Is it you?"

She tried to appear unruffled, but anxiety seethed inside her, making the effort excruciating. She felt his eyes on every dip and hollow of her naked form. Shilah suppressed the instincts that urged her to clothe her body. That inattentiveness would be all that was needed for the watcher to pounce. She felt the caress of the watcher's gaze on her face, and when it traveled down to her breasts and stopped. A flush ran over her body, and she reflectively raised her hands to cover herself. The soft hiss that rode the air froze her hands —it echoed dark and forbidding— and she slowly lowered them to her side. She wanted nothing to hinder her as she braced for what would slink from the darkened corner of her chamber.

Shilah could feel the beat of her heart through her tongue. Inexplicably she knew it was the stranger from earlier. Why had he returned? "I know it is you. Please show yourself."

He stepped from where he lingered in the shadows. The light splashed across his savagely honed features. He prowled closer, and she forced herself to not show any weakness by retreating. Not liking the hint of darkness that wavered around him, she mentally turned on the crystals bathing the room in a wash of bright light. She regretted it instantly. For he faltered, his eyes turning to molten gold as he stared at her. Her skin burned at the brush of his gaze.

"You are beautiful."

Her breath hitched at that reverent whisper.

She moistened her lips and dragged in air. "Why are you here?" It was safer to concentrate on that, instead of the insidious tension thrumming in the chamber. Shilah slowly reached for the sari she had discarded on the bed and held it in front of her covering as much of her nakedness as possible.

A golden gaze filled with banked heat collided with hers. "How old are you?"

She stared at him. He seemed bemused that he had asked the question. *How unusual.*

"Why is my age relevant?"

"Tell me." A flat command and a warning.

"Six years above two centuries," she said cautiously.

"You are a fledgling, you've hardly lived."

The heavy regret in his voice had tension stealing through her limbs. The entire encounter was charged with a dangerous tension she did not understand. She did not want to arouse his suspicion even though she doubted he worked for the emperor. However, no one must know she planned to flee tonight. For any chance of success, the element of surprise had to be on her side.

"Are you a Mevian?" she demanded carefully.

"No."

"Which kingdom are you from?"

A slow smile softened the hard edge to his mouth. "I cannot own to it."

Her anxiety deepened. "Why not?"

"I am a spy, and you are in bed with my enemy, in every way."

"I'm not the emperor's lover," she murmured, searching for his varied meanings.

"Are you not?"

"Why should it concern you if I am in his bed?" she asked, watching him as one would the most dangerous of animals.

The unspoken words were implicit in his penetrating stare. His face took on a cast of intense, aroused beauty, a touch of sensual cruelty about his mouth, *Oh!* He wanted her. That awareness drew a fierce, almost violent feeling from her, and a shock of heat darted between her legs, mortifying her. Breathing was nearly impossible as she waited for him to move, to say something.

An odd feeling of regret curled through her. Once she fled the empire, she would not see this man again. "At least tell me your name."

"Lachlan Ravenswood."

It suited him. Old world and elegant. "I want to be courteous and say it is a pleasure to be introduced, but I am anxious as to why you are here in my chamber without an invitation, again, Lachlan Ravenswood."

She got the sense he had been here a long time too. He glided closer to her. Power hummed beneath the surface of her skin as she tried to read his intentions. His lack of aura bothered her, but she sensed there was something inside of him, still and watchful and so full of danger.

A fingertip brushed against her chin. His touch was inexplicably soft, entirely at odds with the sensual harshness of his expression. Her breath left her lungs in an unexpected rush and wings seemed to flutter lightly against the inside of her belly.

"I demand to know why you are—"

He dipped his head, pressed his lips to hers, catching her world on fire.

4

Shilah stood transfixed for a timeless instant, then shock exploded through her. His arm curved around her shoulders and dragged her against the solid wall of his chest. Lachlan Ravenswood's kiss tasted like midnight, dark, deep, dangerous, and bone-deep satisfying. She gasped, and he stroked his tongue deep inside. She gripped his shoulders with the intention of pushing him away, and instead pressed her fingers into the muscles of his shoulders. Shilah trembled at the pleasure that arrowed through her with such exquisite delight. It startled her for she had never felt like this before, not from a mere kiss. He dragged the response from her with the raw force of his embrace, and she answered his desire kissing him back. Their tongues tangled, and she was at once helpless against the sweeping sensations working through her body and invigorated by the intense need humming through her. She got achingly wet. So fast she was mortified. Shilah could feel her flesh preparing for him, aching for his possession. Something deep within her belly quickened, sending sharp darts of longing through her.

I am kissing the enemy. For somehow, she knew this man was not an ally.

She pulled her lips from his, breathing raggedly. "I am the Princess of Dxyriah, I cannot—"

He kissed her. Again. Over and over.

The intensity of feelings he evoked had nothing to do with logic or reasoning and that brief protestation burned away under the tide of passion. Swirls of want and need denied too long came rushing to the surface. A muffled moan of surprise sounded against his mouth as she felt the cool silken sheets beneath her back.

When had he moved them? Her thighs were nudged apart and his heavy weight cradled between her legs. Tremors started in her stomach, delightful pleasure built, and she clutched at his shoulder, purring her approval. Even through his shirt, she could feel that he was pure muscle and sinew and strength. One of his palms cupped her breast, his fingers tweaking at her nipples, stabbing pleasure to the heart of her. She felt overwhelmed and tried to drag her thoughts from the hot pull of bliss. *This* should not be happening, not now.

Pushing at his chest, she tried to put some distance between them. His cock was thick and hard, pressing into the juncture of her thighs. He was large, at least twice the size of her previous lover. He gripped her hips and dragged her down so he could roll his hips against her, and Shilah arched into him, shivering as his aroused cock ground against her clitoris through his trousers. The shock of feeling him right there had her dragging her lips from his. She stared at him, suddenly and inexplicably petrified.

"Are you a witch?" she murmured, unable to accept any other explanation for her loss of self.

His ragged breathing puffed against her lips. "No," he said, taking her mouth once again in a too dominant kiss.

The dark, rich taste of him enveloped her senses. Then two fingers were thrust deep inside her sex. She grunted against his mouth, her muscles straining to accept the invasion. She hadn't taken a lover in years, as much as a half century.

"Your pussy is the tightest I've ever felt." His voice was a rumble of carnal threat and promise and awe. As if he were amazed by her as if he too couldn't help the desire arcing between them.

Then his fingers moved. Each stroke into her snug sex was a shock of agonizing pleasure. Shilah tore her mouth from his, her lips parted, but there was no breath left to scream. His eyes held hers as he split her legs even wider and moved his fingers deeper. His golden gaze on her was unrelenting, and she knew then he would take her. It was madness.

She moaned, terrified of the feelings coursing through her body and the sudden terrible need that welled up the depth of her soul. She had never had a casual lover, a night of burning passion, and the only consort she had ever lain with had been selected after months of careful consideration, and he had treated her like spun glass. Yet she was here, profoundly vulnerable and in lust with a stranger. Shilah distantly felt the force of his hunger, the painful ache in his cock, and the indefinable throb in his soul to claim her.

"This is madness," he snarled, echoing her denials as if he too struggled to understand the needs driving him.

An aching, terrifying awareness of how much she wanted him inside her shot through her. Shilah had never felt like this about a man in all her years alive. She was hungry for every kiss, every touch, desperate for release. The shivering sensation low in her stomach felt as if she were falling, and a sense of unalterable consequences beat against her thoughts.

A decision has been made.

She shouldn't have allowed his touch. Then his thumb glided with roughness over her clitoris, once, twice, three times while his fingers slid with slow depth into her wet sex, driving her toward bliss with the biting pleasure-pain of each fiery caress. And not once did he release her eyes from his. He looked powerful, intimidating, his face harshly sensual, and aroused. Heat burned between them. Perspiration trickled over her neck, between her breasts. Shilah's heart raced, beating a harsh, driving rhythm against her breast. She bucked in his arms, her head twisting against the sheets as her body tightened. "Oh, Please!"

He kissed her, his tongue stroking into her mouth in a wet dance, a perfect mimicry of his wicked fingers. She lost her breath, control of her body, and her mind as ecstasy tore her apart. She wailed into his mouth as deep shudders of pleasure claimed her. Her mind reached for his and encountered a void. The bed lifted with them before slamming to the ground, and with a whimper, she worked to control the wash of her telekinetic power.

"Shilah, is everything well, I felt the walls tremble?"

The brush of her sister's voice had horror icing through her veins. Kala waited, and here she was cavorting with a stranger.

"Get off me," she breathed roughly, shocked, her body still shuddering in pleasure.

With languid grace, he rolled from her and stood. Shilah scrambled from the bed, watching him warily. He looked sinfully beautiful, arms, chest, and things roped with exquisite muscles. She hurried to the armoire, grabbed a silk robe, and held it before her. His lips curled in a sensually cruel slant, and she narrowed her eyes. "This was a mistake, and it will *never* happen again, stranger."

"I agree."

That she'd not expected. "You do?"

"Most assuredly, Princess Shilah. Fucking is not what I want from you. My reaction just now was an anomaly that will not be repeated."

His slight smile sent a shiver up her spine, then a dark wave of power slid against her senses. "What was that?"

He canted his head, considering her. "What is what?"

"I…felt an aura for the briefest moment…it was unusual, and it came from you."

He went wholly and utterly still. "In what manner?"

"It was darkness."

He flinched as if he had been burned.

She moved back a few more paces, not wanting to be close to him. "What is it?"

Something savage and unknown emanated from him. It scared Shilah, and she slowly backed away even further, cursing herself for her stupidity in relaxing her guard. "I must ask you to leave, stranger, I require privacy."

His mien was an implacable mask. "Regretfully I cannot accede to your wishes."

"Why?" She kept her voice even, flat. She couldn't lose control now.

The golden eyes which had glowed with hot desire iced over. He prowled a few steps closer. Shilah's heart pounded. Though he had no aura, his every move communicated cunning and ruthlessness. She was abruptly drenched in a chilling sweat. "I…. You are here to kill me."

Her soft words settled into the quiet of the chamber. He made no replied assurance, and her throat went tight.

A decision has been made.

The continued silence tugged on her instinct to flee. But to where? Her prison had been the safest place in the palace.

And somehow, she knew this man would not let her escape his intentions whatever they were. "Answer me."

"Yes." There was a gentle finality to his words.

Her breath caught in her throat and fear cramped her stomach. "Why? I have no enemies in Amagarie." *Or friends.* No one should want her death. The emperor had not sent him, she was far too valuable to his army. And then she knew *that* was the very reason she'd been marked for death. "I am *not* a part of the Emperor's army. I am trying to escape him. Tonight," she said hoarsely.

Curiosity flickered in that flat golden gaze. "Were you?"

"Yes. Look." She waved her hands toward the small bag on the bed. "Everything that I value is there, and I packed to flee tonight. If you just let me go, I will disappear from Mevia and never return."

He moved toward the left side of the bed, but instead of reaching for the bag he picked up the book the emperor had thrown at her feet earlier.

"What is this?"

And somehow, she sensed he knew the nature of the book. Her hands trembled. "It is the Darkage's lexicon. It holds in its pages the origins of their beasts and how they mated."

"Why do you have this?"

"The emperor ordered me to study from it, but I have no intention of doing so."

"How many people have you tortured for the emperor?"

She flinched, guilt and regret rising to choke her. "Please, I—" she took a deep breath. "While I invaded their minds and read their secrets I did not take their lives. Even when he ordered me to."

"And the Darkans you controlled at his command?"

"I am not certain what you have heard, but I was only able

to pull forth the beast from two Darkans, and I did *not* kill them."

Something haunting and merciless flashed in his gaze, and she stumbled even further away. "You do not have to kill me. I *hate* working with the emperor. He is a man without honor or conscience. I swear on my honor I was leaving the empire tonight. It is the emperor himself and his vile machinations I am running from. You could help me leave here. I am the Princess of Dxyriah, and my people await my return."

"And do you believe the emperor will allow such a promising weapon as yourself to simply leave?" There was no mercy in that dark, expressionless face as he demanded, "A woman powerful enough to pull the chakra that lives within Darkans to life and then control it? Are you so foolish to believe he will not send his elite team of *geikans* to hunt you?"

She'd heard whispered rumors of *geikans*, that they were assassins of the highest order in possession of the deadliest and most unique abilities. How naïve? She hadn't considered the emperor sending assassins for her. "You could give me the chance to flee. There is no guarantee if I am hunted I will be caught. My realm is undergoing a revolution, and I must return at all cost. My people need me. I cannot afford to be recaptured, I assure you."

He smiled. Barely. "And what do you believe the king of the dark will do to you when he discovers you are a weapon to use against his people? What do you think will happen when he learns you mercilessly invaded the minds of his kind, tormenting them, breaking them on the orders of the emperor?"

Dread iced through her veins.

"The death I offer you will be quick and painless. If you are taken to the Darkage to stand trial for the crimes committed against King Gidon Al Shra's people, you'll beg for mercy, and it will not come."

She believed him. The rumors she'd heard of the dark ones painted a picture of unremitting brutality and a nation that was feared by all in Amagarie because every citizen of the Darkage housed a demon beast that was beyond powerful when utilized. She'd thought it mad that the emperor would try and capture even one of their kind. How had she not thought about the implications of the king of the Darkans finding out? Had the emperor prepared for that? "It was never my intention to hurt anyone," she whispered.

She thought quickly of the other rumors that spoke of the Darkage as the kingdom that was in desperate need of wealth and trade advantages. "I will make atonement to the dark king when I am able to. I am wealthy. My kingdom is rich in minerals and technology that will benefit the Darkage, and I will offer them in recompense. I will also offer you and whichever kingdom you are from unmatched wealth. Just let me leave without a fight."

Shilah saw no softening in his mien, and she sensed he would not be deterred. In battle Shilah would typically read the mind of her opponent, anticipating everything they did before they acted. His shield prevented that, and she hated the uncertainty that burned in her.

How could she defeat him?

She never took her eyes or her mind from him, her body remaining still and ready, perfectly balanced. His lips curved slightly at her actions, and she narrowed her eyes hoping the fact he underestimated her fighting skills would give her the opportunity to escape. Her slight stature and delicate build always made others believe she was weak. While she did not possess the deadly art of hand combat, or the ability to move with such speed she appeared a blur, Shilah had the will of her forefathers, and the hope of her people on her shoulders.

She could not allow this man to defeat her. And she wished with her entire heart she was braver. The knowledge she may very well lose had a hollowness rising through her.

"Kala."

The need to connect with her sister was instinctive. Shilah's throat closed, not knowing how to say farewell. A hated wave of vulnerability washed through her.

"What is it, Shilah? I have packed, and I am awaiting you."

"I am dreadfully sorry to ask you this. Could...could you try and see my future?"

The silence was chilling. Her sister's fear came through their mental connection acrid with an aura of blackness.

"I...let me try." A sob fluttered in her mind, then an enraged scream of denial. *"I saw myself on the throne of Dxyriah, ruling in your stead."*

Relief pierced Shilah. Her sister would live. And their birthright would be reclaimed. *"I love you, Kala, more than you will ever know. We've planned for this. Use your powers. Try and see the possible outcome as you flee to safety, do not wait for me."* Then she closed the pathway unique only to them before she could hear the protests.

Shilah attacked. She covered the distance between them in a single leap, her knife fashioned from pure aura aimed at his throat, her mind opened, searching for a weakness in his shield. If she could read his mind, she would triumph, for then every move and intention would be telegraphed before he executed them. He evaded the knife, a blur of speed she barely tracked. She kicked her feet high, slamming her heels into his chest with her full strength. Again, she failed to deliver a blow. Using the force of her telekinesis she flung her knife toward his throat, in a flash of blue energy, and he vanished. She breathed harshly, staring in confusion. Too late, she spun around to meet his attack, and a forearm roped with muscle banded across her throat.

His grip on her was brutal in its absoluteness. "Be still."

Her eyes burned. She sank into the center of her power, flaring her aura, concentrating on his shields. Something in her, strong and proud, could not relent, could not submit to the raw force of the man who meant to take her life.

"Cease your attacks or I will break your neck."

She flinched at his hard, merciless voice. "Let's bargain," she said hoarsely, determined to slow the frantic beat of her heart and the fear that was trying to cripple her.

He bent his head, his warm breath by her temple sending a shiver of heat coiling in the pit of her stomach. Rage bit through her that she could have such a reaction to this man. It was unpardonable.

"You have no bargaining power."

She absolutely wished to stick her knife into the arrogant bastard. "You are seeking the dungeons. I will do everything possible to help you find it."

"Accepted."

His quick capitulation alarmed her. "In exchange for my life and freedom."

"No."

Incredulity surged through her. "You are not stupid enough to believe I would ever help you, knowing at the end of it you will kill me," she snarled.

"In exchange for your sister's life and liberty."

Shilah jerked, then faltered into complete stillness. At this moment fear was an ugly, living thing she couldn't shake. Her throat burned and with a harsh gasp she realized tears rolled down her cheeks in a hot trail. They dripped onto his forearm but neither of them moved, and they stood like that for precious seconds while silent tears of misery wetted them both. "I accept."

"You do not wish to die," he said softly, a vein of curiosity in his voice.

A choked sound escaped her. "You *know* of many people who wish to be murdered?" she demanded sarcastically.

His hand slipped from her. "Death is a consequence of war. Some accept it with grace."

She lurched away from him, spun around, and backed away until she came upon the wall. "You and I are not at war. My battle is not here in Amagarie. It awaits me in Serange."

The sounds of shuffling feet sounded in the distance. She flared her telepathy brushing against more than one hundred minds, reading a few. Her breath shuddered from her, and she wasn't sure if it was in relief or dread. "Warriors are headed our way. Grand General Shenzhen leads them."

No expression flickered in his eyes, as if the notion did not rattle him. "The grand general is one of the most feared men in the empire."

Still no reaction.

"You'll be arrested," she said.

"You sound hopeful."

If he was arrested, then he could not kill her, unless he was to act before they reached her. He shifted, and she flared her telekinetic powers, regretful she was only an Alpha in that geneses. She mentally lifted him and slammed him into the door with such force it splintered, and he stumbled into the hall. She couldn't help feeling he had allowed her attack.

Shilah grabbed the sari she'd discarded and hurriedly tugged the floating garment around her body, then belted it at the waist with a gold rope. Then she slipped on silk undergarments, wishing she had time to don more serviceable clothing. The sheer dress did not allow for the concealment of a weapon. She pushed her feet into jeweled shoes. Grabbing the bag, she'd packed earlier, she pushed it under the four-poster bed, as the Grand General and his warriors came into view.

Lachlan struggled to his feet, and she frowned for her

attack had not been all that powerful. He withdrew his weapon, and Grand General Shenzhen whistled, and soundwaves undulated in the air. Shilah barely had the time to throw up a barrier of pure aura to protect her from the sound waves that slammed through the corridor.

A crack sounded, Lachlan's left leg twisted in a savage break, yet he made no sound as he went down hard. He rolled into a crouch and held his weapon in a graceful fighting position, analyzing the warriors with impressive calm. Or perhaps he was just addled.

The General smiled, and Shilah's heart trembled. Drop the knife she wanted to shout, for Lord Shenzhen took pleasure in the pain of others. He clicked his tongue, and she groaned at the force of the waves that battered against her shields. The sound compressed the air around her, shattering her shield. Pain exploded in her head, and she tasted the raw tang of blood. The casual strength and the power of how the General wielded sound was terrifying.

The attack stopped within seconds, and she swallowed the gasp. Lachlan lay on the ground, blood running from his eardrums and nose. The shirt ripped away from his chest, revealing a torso roped with muscles.

"And who is this?" Shenzhen asked, sparing a cursory glance at the shattered door before his dark eyes settled on her.

"An assassin," she said softly, wondering why he did not fight back. *It's too easy.* "I…I believe he was here to kill me."

"How curious," Shenzhen said. "The emperor must be made aware. Come."

Then he turned around and sauntered away, expecting to be obeyed. Two warriors stooped and gathered Lachlan, gripping him by his underarms and dragged him away. Shilah stood frozen until the General murmured over his shoulder, "Your sister awaits us in the throne room, princess. Surely you would not leave her?"

Her composure almost cracked. She opened the pathways in her mind and searched for her sister's thread. *"Kala?"*

"A dozen warriors came for me just now. I am with the emperor."

And Shilah knew then even without the interference of Lachlan Ravenswood, they would not have made it from the empire tonight.

The emperor had already been several steps ahead.

5

A few minutes later, they entered the throne room of the Emperor. Shilah furiously thought about why the emperor had come for them. Clearly, he had anticipated her fleeing, but he couldn't have known she would have acted right away. Squaring her shoulders, and lifting her chin haughtily, she advanced into the room, conscious of the hungry, predatory gaze of the emperor. He stood before his throne of gold, Jasper, and rubies. He was deliberately projecting the thoughts of how he wanted her on her knees before him. She refused to give him the satisfaction of flinching or betraying in any way she knew his vile musings. His long flowing robes swirled around his feet, as energy rippled around him. Kala stood by his side, with her hands fisted, her lips flattened in hard, determined lines. Her hair had been braided, and Kala had gotten the opportunity to slip on her full body suit.

Lachlan was flung in front of the emperor, and his skull slammed onto the tiles with a resounding thud. Though she should hold no sympathy for a man who had seemed bent on taking her life, compassion stirred inside Shilah. General

Shenzhen lifted a fist, and majority of the warriors filed out of the room, leaving ten men who stood in front of the door guarding it from the inside.

"A man was reported to be seen entering your private rooms, Princess Shilah, I assume this is he?" The emperor asked, his gaze penetrating and direct.

A report from whom? "I believe he was sent to kill me."

"Oh?"

She faltered. Surely, he didn't believe she worked with this man. "I prepared for sleep when he intruded. Our battle had just started when the General somehow seemed to know I was in need. I can only assume you have guards watching my chamber for my safety. I thank you, Emperor Khan, for sending him to my aid. My kingdom will not forget your generosity."

His eyes seemed to glow with genuine amusement at her attempts of diplomacy. "I am surprised you were unable to kill one man." He peered down at Lachlan. "He does not seem to be much of a threat."

He did believe she worked with the man. Cold suspicion lingered in his tone.

"I do not know this man," she said icily. "He questioned me about the dungeons, and when I gave no satisfactory answer, he drew his blade with a promise to end my life because I've been working with you, Emperor. I attacked."

The emperor lowered himself onto his throne and considered her.

"Why do I feel as if I am under suspicion?" she demanded with a lift of her brow, ensuring she infused her voice with the chilling hauteur of her rank. "Respectfully, I am the Princess of Dxyriah, I do not answer to the empire."

The General stiffened, caressing the cold steel of his sword, apparently taking offense at her audacity.

The Emperor glanced down at Lachlan for several

moments before making her the sole center of his regard. His mien of casual interest had vanished. Suddenly he looked invincible, merciless. "I am curious, Princess Shilah, why did you not incapacitate the intruder with your telepathy? He is only one man."

"He has a shield, one I could not penetrate."

"A mental barrier that an Imperial telepath could not penetrate?"

A charged stillness blanketed the room. General Shenzhen peered at the man on the ground, a tension invading the general's shoulders. He drew his sword, walked over, and with casual brutality drove it through Lachlan's right shoulder and twisted. A harsh groan echoed from his throat, and his hand flashed up and gripped the blade. She forced herself to watch and not appear weak when the general pulled out the sword, slicing open the palm of the hand that had gripped it. Another hiss of pain sounded from the man on the ground, and the metallic scent of blood wafted on the air. The grand general repeated his vicious attack at Lachlan Ravenswood's left shoulder, and then in his left side. She looked away from the blood pooling on the jade tiled floor.

"I believe his barriers are weakened, Princess. I want to know how he infiltrated the castle."

"My emperor, I do not believe—"

The emperor barely inclined his head, and one of the warriors stationed by the door flashed faster than she'd been able to see and placed a blade against Kala's throat. His move so surprised her, Shilah's tongue felt thick with surprise. She stepped forward, and blood spurted from her sister's throat, freezing her.

"Please, don't!" she cried out, her heart a war drum behind her breastbone.

"I find I am of a mind to teach you the consequences of

disobeying an order of the Empire, Princess, and correcting the misguided belief that you do not answer to me."

Rage burned through Shilah. "If you harm her further, there is *nothing* you can do to induce me to work for you," she snapped with icy contempt.

The emperor's cold reptilian gaze settled on her face. "You've grown claws," he murmured. "I shall be forced to clip them."

He glanced at the warrior and the man plunged his dagger through her sister's heart.

Shilah screamed, dropping to her knees, gripping fistfuls of her hair. Energy poured out of her, raging and churning, as she slammed into the warrior's mind with the full force of her psychic power. *"Stop breathing."*

The warrior dropped, his body clattering onto the tile, and she pushed her power toward the emperor's mind, rage and pain ruling all thoughts and actions. The barrier she encountered was crafted from several spells and enchantments so she could not breach his mind.

The Emperor smiled. "Be calm, Princess." He stood and glided with menacing elegance toward Kala who clutched her chest, her face a grimace of pain and horror as the blood poured through her fingers. The emperor uncorked a glowing vial he had around his throat and tipped it to her lips. With a harsh gasp, her sister swallowed, and the wound on her neck and chest healed within seconds, and vitality flushed her skin pink.

Shilah stared back at him, breathing rapidly, the taste of fear lingering in her mouth.

"This is the elixir of life, stolen from Boreas—kingdom of winds and mountains. I am in possession of several jars. I believe I will find immense pleasure in killing your sweet sister, bringing her back before death claims her, and killing her again. I wonder how long before her mind breaks?"

His voice was low, beautiful, and all the deadlier for it.

Kala's aura flickered with the yellow hue of fear. Hatred burned through Shilah's heart with such an intensity she trembled. She lurched to her feet, and without reply, shifted her gaze to the man lying on the floor. She flared her powers, brushing against the walls of his mind, shocked to find his barriers had indeed been lowered. She moved closer, sinking to her knees beside him, and cradled his head onto her lap.

"I know that you are conscious."

She frowned when he made no answer. She closed her eyes and sent her mind into his, surprised at the control he had over his pain. Shilah studied the shield, seeing it as a massive wall in her mind. Its depth and breadth were unfathomable. It rose with no end in sight, yet beyond it, she sensed a hovering darkness. She probed, and an opening appeared in the middle of the wall, showing several silver threads of memories.

"What do you see?" Grand General Shenzhen demanded.

Fragments of thoughts that were impossible to follow. She knocked at another section of the wall, curious as to the complexity of its construct. The fact a small square part had opened, implied he allowed it down, and not the pain of the grand general's power and sword damaging his body. She peered down into his face, noting the lack of tension across his brows. She almost smiled. He had been the one to lower his shields with the intention of manipulating the outcome of this meeting. She read the thoughts he wanted to be projected.

"He's here to kill me," she murmured. "And he'll not rest until he has done so." That thread of knowledge was at the forefront of his thoughts, and it was not a deception. It was an unshaken resolve. After he completed the mission that took him to the empire, he would end her life.

"You arrogant bastard," she whispered to him, searching for

a response. He remained a blank canvas. His control of the shield wall was impressive.

Was it her imagination she felt mocking amusement?

"And where is he from?" The Emperor demanded. "His kingdom?"

She examined the few threads of memories. "I cannot see." The rest of the wall was tightly constructed except for that small opening. She considered the will it took to only lower a controlled piece of the barrier and what it said about Lachlan Ravenswood. He had purposefully allowed himself to be captured and placed himself in the hands of someone as vicious as the emperor of Mevia, so he could discover the whereabouts of the dungeons. He was cunning. And arrogant. And foolish.

"You should not have allowed me this crack," she whispered deep into his mind. *"I sense what you are doing. You are giving the emperor enough information to consign you to the dungeons, but you are holding back enough where he won't want to kill you. His paranoid heart won't be able to rest until he knows which kingdom sent you. And you've buried that knowledge behind your shield. He'll be forced to imprison and torture you for the information. You are playing a perilous game."*

He showed no reaction, but she knew he heard her. Shilah pressed the flat of her palm against his forehead.

"But you did not count on me, or you underestimated my resolve."

A slow tension invaded his muscles, and she felt the flicker of curiosity deep in his mind.

"I do not care about the emperor or even why you want to find the dungeons so badly. The only thing I care about is my sister and my people. You promised to kill me, but you see, for my sister to make it back to Serange alive and well, I must live. And I know that without a barrier you cannot defeat me in a battle and kill me."

She unleashed the unremitting strength of her power and crashed into the walls of his mind, battering his shields. Aura glowed around her in a blue pulse of fiery energy. It traveled through the opening he had allowed, crumbling it from the insides. No doubt he believed he had been safe, but she was an Imperial, and her power over the mind was absolute. His hand snapped up, gripped her shoulder, and flung her with shocking strength. She spun across the tiles and crashed into several decorative suits of armor, smashing them to the floor. Shilah pushed past the pain lancing through her body and glanced up, frowning at the smoky tendrils of chakra that rose beneath him as if he were on fire.

Connected with his mind, she felt the cold fire of Lachlan Ravenswood's torment and denial. *"No!"* his roar echoed through her. Uncertainty pierced her when through the large hole now present in the wall of his mind, a clawed foot stepped from it. Bricks rippled in their minds as the wall tried to rebuild itself, but a power that was not hers battered against it, shattering the stones.

There was a monster within him.

The knowledge bloomed, and she tried to pull back, lending her strength to Lachlan Ravenswood as he attempted to reinforce his barriers. But whatever lurked in the deep shadows of his mind reacted and threw itself against his barrier. The blackest of chakra exploded from within him, swirling around him like tendrils of black smoke.

A harsh rasp escaped her throat. She'd only seen chakra like that from the Darkans in the dungeons. But surely this couldn't be possible. The prickle of unease grew until her skin felt as if a thousand pins and needles stabbed into her. Power clung to him as if he were power manifested into a tangible entity. *What was he?*

"What is happening?" The grand general demanded, his

dark eyes narrowed to slits, his demeanor one of battle readiness.

Lachlan had also frozen into profound stillness, and she felt his determination to repair what she had damaged. He lifted from the ground and stood as if invisible hands had drawn him to his feet. His hair crackled around him as if alive, and he raised his head and inhaled. Then he smiled. The man before her was the darkest creature she'd ever seen —merciless, ruthless, and implacable.

It struck her that he was also beautiful and wild, but so damn terrifying her heart nearly ripped from her chest. Shilah could sense the mass and energy of him in the room, like a storm threatening to unleash lightning.

"Shilah, what did you do?"

"It wasn't me Kala, it wasn't me. His wounds are healed, and his leg is no longer broken. You will run at the first chance you get, and you will not look back."

Another claw pushed from behind the shield wall in his mind.

"I won't leave you." Her sister's voice echoed fierce and determined.

"You will obey! I think he is a Darkan and the power I sense feels ageless." She sent the thought to Kala, hoping she understood the severity of their situation.

The grand general and the emperor slowly moved toward the man standing so still in the center of the room, and she wanted to scream, *run you fools*, for they hadn't grasped the significance of the black chakra swirling around Lachlan yet. Or perhaps they did for the emperor spoke, his voice rich with pleasure.

"A Darkan, how wonderful."

"Not just any Darkan," she said hoarsely, sensing the unfathomable well of chakra strength buried beneath his mind. "He is not a fledging like the others."

"How old is he and what beast does it control?"

How could the emperor not perceive what stood before them? Of course, the fool would only see another Darkan to imprison and control for his army. She ignored the emperor and twisted her fingers into a symbol, centering the strength of her aura and telepathy to that single anchor inside, desperate to build back the mental shield of Lachlan Ravenswood, caging the terrible storm she felt at his center. The emperor had used her to manipulate the chakras of at least four Darkans, and she had never felt such a force, and the wall separating man and demon had not shattered yet.

A primal scream of rage and dominance blasted through her thoughts, the sheer savagery of it akin to the sensation of a thousand knives stabbing at the insides of her body. She dropped her hands limply to her sides as the shield wall in his mind crumbled. She had never known darkness had a taste. It coated her senses, as something appeared from the ashes of the shattered shield wall. The first wave of energy hit her so hard it drove her to her knees, and a cry of despair tore from her throat. Violence and bloodthirstiness—dark, malevolent.

What have I done? Tears swam in her eyes, blurred her vision. A wave of inconsolable grief and rage washed over her senses. And those came from the man within as oily darkness conquered all the light that had shone inside him. She had taken that peace from him.

Shilah cried out her regret. *"Forgive me, Lachlan Ravenswood."*

Dozens of warriors rushed to stand before their emperor who stared at Lachlan, glee, and cunning in his gaze.

"Control him!" he snapped at her.

"I cannot tame such a power," she said hoarsely, staggering to her feet, and slowly backing away from the man who still had not moved. "You cannot feel it, or sense it, but what is buried in that Darkan cannot come to life." It gutted her soul to even suggest it, but she said, "He will have to be killed, now!"

Another wave of energy crested from him and rolled through the room, and the tiles beneath his feet cracked. The monster in him raised its head, inhaled, and fed hungrily, desperate to fill the terrible clawing emptiness it had endured locked away in his mind. It drew from the negative emotions that filled every crevice and heart of those in the castle. It fed on her fear, her sister's pain, the wail of the widow in the courtyard who just learned of her husband's death. She could see the thread of dark energy in the form of dark green light racing from several directions to be inhaled through his nose and mouth.

"No!" Kala screamed, her eyes clutching her throat as she stared at Lachlan. Wild eyes swung to Shilah and back, and then her eyes swirled with foresight, her voice became broken and garbled with the rush of it. "Upon your head, I see a crown of snakes and thorns. Queen of darkness you shall become, and our people will know desolation. I see an army of beasts by your side, and our kingdom at your feet."

Fear acrid in its harshness pelted Shilah. Her sister's vision had evolved. What did it mean?

It was then Shilah saw the tattoo spreading over Lachlan's skin as if painted by an invisible force. It painted over him in violent swirls and curled around his body like a possessive lover, the black, red, and purple scales hugging his chest around his shoulder, and then over his back. His beast revealed itself in a full-bodied tattoo. A leviathan—the high lord of serpents.

Dread unlike any Shilah had ever known cramped her stomach and dark dots danced before her eyes. *Upon your head, I see a crown of snakes and thorns...*

The emperor's order to bind him was a distant drone.

She tried to pull her thoughts from Lachlan, and clawed hands reached out and touched her. She felt the phantoms caress against her face. Her psychic eyes snapped open and tried to see through the dust swirling around the collapsed wall. There was no *aura*, no flavor, just a flatness that made her completely aware of what hopelessness tasted and felt like.

Warriors rushed toward him, *valnetium* chains in their hands. The chains whistled as they wrapped around Lachlan until his entire body was chained. The emperor glided closer but faltered as Lachlan laughed—low, dark, mocking, and dangerous.

Her mouth dried.

The chains shattered and dropped to his feet. The display of power shook her. All Darkans in the dungeon were held with fewer chains and they hadn't been able to move.

"Take him," the Emperor snapped to the hovering warriors.

Shilah rushed to her sister's side, expanding her aura, and holding it in place to create a barrier around them. Sound waves rippled into the room, curving around her shield, and slammed into her body. Kala screamed as her ribs cracked from the pressure, and Shilah struggled to breathe through the pain battering her insides.

And then the pain was no more, for, with a blink, more than a dozen warriors littered the ground. *All dead*. She hadn't seen Lachlan move. Yet he stood amid the bodies, blood dripping from his claws. The door was flung open, and more than one hundred warriors rushed into the throne room.

Powerful soundwaves poured from the Mevian warriors. Vibrations ran through the air, sinking into every crevice and shadow, battering Lachlan. With casual speed and strength, he moved through the force trying to pin him, went behind the lead warrior, grabbed hold of the man's hair and, with one sharp move, snapped his neck.

Then he ravaged. Shadows danced in the room, blood-spattered and arched in several directions. Jumbled thoughts filled with rage and terror filled her senses as the warriors battled with a force they did not comprehend.

The grand general drew his swords, the aura around him glowing red. Then he screamed. The beauty and energy from his voice roiled the earth, shaking her with its purity. Shilah pushed her skills to their limit further, building the strength of her barriers to protect herself and her sister from their terrible strengths. The sound waves slammed into her force field, and with a grunt she braced against it, digging her heels and toes into the cracked tiles.

The attack from the grand general had broken several of Lachlan's bones, and right before their eyes, he healed, the blackest of chakras twisting around his body. Then the tattoo slid sinuously along his body as if alive. *No!* He was summoning whatever demon he possessed, and Shilah knew if he were allowed to so do, everyone in the palace would die. "He is summoning his beast!"

Lachlan's snarl trembled on the air and vibrated with menace. She took no satisfaction from the unease that rushed from the emperor. Acting on instincts, Shilah closed her eyes and pushed the sounds of the battle, the snarls, and the screams of the Mevians as they fell under his claws. The cruelty and the unadulterated blood-thirstiness crawled through her body like a nasty poison. The pain of enduring such terrible rage dragged a whimper from her. She trapped all the emotions inside of her and dug deep into the immeasurable well of her abilities, seeking his mental barriers. A violent, gnawing need to slaughter and devour tore through Lachlan's soul and beat at her shields. She could feel the urgency of his needs beating at him. The beast had been caged for years, and it hungered.

The monster in him sensed her presence. And it paused. It was that slight hesitation which allowed her to sink deep inside her to the absolute stillness and blast out her telepathy. She tried to rebuild the barrier, but the beast gave her no quarter. Serpentine eyes snapped open in her mind, and his darkness slid against her light.

The profound savagery of his demon beast's chakra took her breath. Every part of him seemed dark and shadowed, and Shilah fought back her rising dread.

The creature in him froze, then inhaled deeply.

Mine...

A possessive roar rose from man and beast she did not understand. *What was his?* She felt its vile chakra pressing against her natural shields as if he wanted to enter her mind, and terror filled Shilah's soul. She hadn't expected it to try and reverse the pathway she sent her telepathy on. Death brushed against her mind, creating a chill in her soul. The violent wave of bloodthirstiness made her heave and sweat broke out on her skin. The pathway widened, and his chakra churned around him.

The ground cracked beneath her feet, and the walls of the throne room expanded as a wild blast of energy swarmed the air. Then another insidious probe at her mind came from him. Shilah dropped on her ass as if she had been kicked, while the wave of violence swamped her, and a white-hot pain exploded through her head, the mass of rage and brutal intensity too much of a sensory overload to her psychic senses.

A scream ripped from her throat, and she grabbed her head. White spots danced in front of her eyes. Energy rushed through her as she tried to escape the raw, swirling force threatening to form a connection with her. Desperation burned through her. Why it wanted to connect with her, she did not know or care to discover, but every instinct screamed that if she allowed it in she would irrevocably lose all sense of herself.

Shilah flinched as pitiless eyes opened inside of her mind and malicious laughter echoed.

Too late.

Abandoning creating the shield wall, she built an intricate illusion, one of rampant destruction for the beast, and one of calm and serenity for the man. For she could sense the profound depth of Lachlan's pain that he was losing control of the force within him. Energy so strong and sure surged inside of her as she tried to build the illusion to entrap him. She only needed a few precious seconds.

"I need the witch," she screamed hoarsely, not daring to open her eyes to see if anyone obeyed.

The sounds of a battle raged on, the clash of swords, the awful drip, and scent of blood, and the screams. She closed her eyes even tighter, trying to drown out the cry of pain and terror. She ruthlessly built the images, feeding the construct to his mind, coaxing him to believe the memories she planted were real.

A wash of breeze caressed her face.

"Here is the witch," General Shenzhen snapped, strain evident in his tone.

Ignoring him, Shilah concentrated on the mental pathway of the witch. Amirah's thoughts crowded her mind, and Shilah absorbed the knowledge that this Darkan had been the witch's avenue of escape.

"I need a binding spell, one effective enough to suppress his powers."

A slight hesitation, then a whiff of magic burned along her senses as the witch responded, *"I will try. I need his blood."*

"It is on my arms."

No other words were exchanged as Shilah tried to trap beast and man into separate illusions. The witch's spell rippled in the air, and her chant rushed through the room, echoing with the whisper of several voices lifted in eerie unison. Shilah then dug deep, weaving the illusions of peace and love for the man, and one of violent slaughter for the beast. Her fingers trembled, and a wave of exhaustion hit her as she poured her energy into saving their lives.

The taint of bloodthirstiness vanished as if it had been sucked in the vacuum of space. With a gasp, she opened her eyes and swayed. The throne room was a shambled mess. Dozens of bodies littered the ground, and blood coated the floor. She stood on legs that trembled, unable to grasp that he'd wrecked such carnage in minutes. He too was tumbled on the ground, wrapped tightly in *valnetium* chains. The witch drew symbols atop his forehead and cheeks, muttering, words of echoing voices in the room, and the strangest white light on the tip of her fingers.

Amirah straightened and glanced around at the bloodbath, paling. "The spell is one which dampens the capability by restricting the flow of chakra in the body. It cannot hold him. In truth, it is your illusions, Princess Shilah which have entrapped him, but I cannot say for how long they will last."

"Take him to the dungeon," the Emperor snapped.

Shilah turned to face him, surprised to see a brutal scar had flayed open his cheek, and that the hem of his robe was soaked with blood. How could he for even a minute think the dungeon could hold the force they had just tangled with? She did not care how enchanted those domains were, it was improbable. "He needs to be taken away from the empire!"

Cold reptilian eyes settled on her. "Put this Darkan in isolation and the princess with him in the cage," he ordered without taking his gaze from her face.

At first, Shilah was certain she misconstrued his meaning.

Then the horror in her sister's eyes had his meaning scything through her heart. *No.* Pain exploded in the back of her head, and it was as she crumpled she realized the grand general had hit her with the edge of his sword. He lifted her, and she wavered in and out of consciousness. Interminable minutes passed, and then she was thrown onto a pallet on a stone floor.

"The sovereign emperor wishes that you learn how to control a powerful Darkan, Princess Shilah. Control this Darkan, and you will live. Fail to control it, and he will rip you to pieces and perhaps everyone else imprisoned. Including your sister," he said with icy satisfaction.

She pushed up and tried to stand, but her weakened legs saw her stumbling to the ground. Several guards were frantically chaining an unconscious Lachlan to the iron wall of the cage as if they were afraid he would awake soon.

She had roused something monstrous in him, and Shilah sensed with every fiber of her soul she would not be able to manipulate him. "I cannot direct the mass of power I felt in him," she said hoarsely.

"If it comes to that…it means you are useless to us princess. We need a Serangite that is powerful enough to control beasts such as this one."

The door to the cage closed with chilling finality, and Grand General Shenzhen sauntered away impervious to her screams.

6

The dungeons were a pit of despair. A lone great torch barely lit Shilah's prison, and the drip of water against rock pinged in the chilling silence. At least an hour had passed since the Grand General left her to face death. Trapped with so many prisoners, at times Shilah struggled to keep her shield in place. Exhaustion weighed on her shoulders like a boulder and the few whose thoughts she hadn't been able to keep out reeked of hopelessness. The dungeon of the high lords of Mevia created a desolateness that corrupted and withered the souls of its captives. It was whispered throughout the Empire that what was left after being confined in the dungeons was the husk of a person–blank, empty, devoid of hope, emotions, and the will to live or die. A few of the minds she touched were like that, and the pain of it all made her want to weep. Their pain swarmed through the air, the intensity of it choking her, filling her until the pressure was unbearable. And she and her sister had been confined to its cruel walls.

She saw no avenue for escape. They were buried thousands of miles underground the empire, and a bottomless pit still loomed below their cage. When she looked down, she could see nothing but unrelenting darkness, and the only sliver of light was the lone torch hooked high through the small bars of the cage. The cage they were in hung suspended, and it seemed like the only one in the abyss. Several times she had flared her powers and sensed no other aura nearby. It was a wonder the grand general left the torch. Mayhap he thought it more fitting she saw the death that would come for her instead of the oblivion of ignorance. *I would prefer not knowing.*

A gentle flutter whispered in her mind as Kala tapped at their connection. Shilah did not want to open it for she had no ability to block the emotions tearing through her. She wrapped her arms around her waist, desperate to stop the continual shivering. Another knock came, and she opened the door slightly.

A red-yellow aura flickered. Shilah took a steady breath and did the best to mask her emotions. Her sister needed her. *"Kala there is no need to fear. He still sleeps."*

"I…I cannot see you in any of my visions," her sister said in a weary tone.

"Stop trying, Kala. I love you."

"I'm so scared, Shilah. And I feel so foolish for I am not the one trapped with it."

"It is not foolish to be frightened. Our situation is uncertain, but I urge you to not worry about me. How are your ribs? Has the pain lessened?"

"I'm fine, Shilah. My suit took most of the damage. How can I not worry about you? You are my sister and my dearest friend."

The echoes of her sister's despair-filled sob battered at her mind.

"We've prepared for all eventualities. Stop your crying and conserve your strength. You must be brave," she pushed back gently, close to tears.

"It is unfair. I am the useless sister. It should be me who dies."

"Kala! I forbid you from thinking so foolishly. Our destiny is whatever the fates deem it. And I promise you, your powers will manifest. You are only ninety years of age."

"Our kingdom cannot wait for my abilities to manifest," Kala said with bitter regret. *"You are Dyxriah's hope and...and I've seen it in brief flashes atop your body, it's terrible fangs piercing your throat."*

The chains rattled.

Fear tightened Shilah's nerve endings and made her heart stutter. *"Kala I must go."* Shilah closed their link. She tried to draw on the memories of Lachlan's heated kisses that had promised the hottest of lovemaking, mixed with sweetness and erotic heat. Building the memories of pleasures, she could feed to his mind.

He stirred, and she scooted back against the wall.

His body was chained to the wall encased in serpentine metal. It wrapped around his neck, shoulders, arms, torso, hips, and legs supporting him upright against the gray iron walls of the cage.

Brutal, sharply hewed muscles delineated every inch of his body, and the play of those muscles across his chest and shoulder had a strange, darting heat piercing low in her stomach. Even with death looming, the dangerous beauty of the man before her couldn't be denied. He could only move his head, and it hung limply on his chest with strands of midnight black hair hiding his features. She could feel him rising from the layers of false memories she had buried him under, and she dreaded the instant he would fully awaken. The witch's symbols had melted away, and she sensed the burning rage fanning through him. Horrifying aura leaked from him, an unfathomable supremacy she knew she would be unable to control lurked within him.

Her body trembled violently, nearly shaking apart. How

he would kill her remained unclear. Would he use his teeth, claws, or bare hands? Being in the same cage was slow torture.

A scream strangled in her throat as the chains rattled with greater intensity. She stopped breathing when his muscles bunched, and the manacles shook with ease. What had lain dormant had been disturbed by her. She'd violated his mind and stirred a sleeping predator of the most merciless kind. And to think she had believed breaking his shield was her best chance for saving herself from him.

Would he remember their brief, passionate encounter? Would he recall the way he'd touched and caressed her skin, brought her to pleasure? And Shilah admitted even if he did, it would not sway him, for he had been resolute in his determination to kill her despite their sensual play. Duty was very important to this man. And sadly, she understood, for she was honor bound to do everything possible to save her sister and their people from Crown Prince Quan. His taunting promise to unite the three kingdoms of Serange and concentrate all the wealth and power within his ruling family must not come to fruition.

Her only hope was to keep Lachlan Ravenswood trapped in the illusions until she found a way to defeat or rein him in. The illusion he slumbered in was weak because she hadn't understood the viciousness that her mind had brushed against. The eyes that had opened and ensnared her had been pitiless, empty with cold cruelty. She had pushed peace, love, warmth, trying to trap him in a world that must seem anathema to him.

Could she defeat him? Order him to stop breathing? She hadn't trained on how to wield her Imperial abilities. She sensed the vast untapped strength inside herself and knew in theory how her abilities should work. So, she would try. *No, I must succeed.*

The emperor wanted her to control him, but perhaps she should attempt killing him. Except she didn't believe Lachlan Ravenswood wished to know the monster within him, and the man and the beast were not the same. *Remember he wanted to kill me.* And now he had more incentive to rip open her throat. The beast buried inside him was a creature of blood and rage, and Shilha doubted it would understand mercy if she begged for it.

Tears flowed in torrents down her face, and ugly broken sobs filled the cage and wracked her body. It was all too much, to avenge her family she hadn't even gotten a chance to mourn, to protect her sister the only family she had left, to save her people. It all sat on her shoulders like a mountain. Failure was not an option, and not even for a moment could she allow herself to think of what would happen to her sister if she did not succeed.

She pulled her scattered thoughts into order, pressed the tips of her fingers together and tried to center her aura. She would reinforce the illusions while seeking the mental threads that would possibly put him under her dominion. Or the ones she could snap to take his life.

The chains rattled again.

The harsh pounding of Shilah's heart drowned out her thoughts. She flinched as the thundering became like a drum in her ear, her eyes widened, and the hands that she clenched together to stop their trembling strained to stay clasped.

The chains shook more fiercely, and the hiss that filled the cavernous dungeons seemed to surround her. The scream trapped in her throat as the head that hung limply on his chest slowly rose and eyes that were no longer tawny gold captured her gaze.

∽

Darkness burned away at the images that held Lachlan's mind. They did not belong inside of him. The warmth felt unnatural, the loving wife that rubbed his shoulders while the children played was discordant with the feelings that pelted inside. The images in his mind slowly washed with blood, the laughing wife's eyes glazed with fear as bloodthirstiness and rage wiped away the false warmth that tried to hold him cocooned.

He felt different. His senses appeared to be stretching and sharpening. Lachlan tried to sift through the murky darkness that pervaded every cell in his body and soul. The smell of fear and despair wrapped around Lachlan's senses, intoxicating him with the pleasurable rush of dark energy. His lips curled back, a rumble brewing in his chest. The snarl that filled his mind was so cruel, and unlike him, he stilled.

Evil roiled through him as he tried to sift through his mind to locate his barriers. Memories did not rush in to aid him, there were only fragments—the feel of brutality punching through his mind, the malevolent potency of his beast rushing in and filling every crevice of his being, melding the two essences as one.

A hiss of rage burned from his lips as the need to kill burned hotter inside.

The monster inside gnashed its teeth and clawed for freedom. The need to taste pain and agony was dark and exciting. If not for the ironclad control that he had gained over the past four hundred years he would probably be rampaging now instead of sifting through the needs that pelted inside. His command of the unrelenting hunger to kill was tenuous as Lachlan realized that he could not locate the psychic wall.

Impossible.

The snarl of rage seemed to feed the darkness inside of him. The surge of violent emotions battered at him, consuming his willpower. His bones felt as if they were trying to break out of his skin, so every tendon and sinew stretched with the effort it took for him to rein in the monster.

Yes. He stilled once more as the hiss welled from deep inside of him. He knew his beast, his darkness, his bane for all of his existence. Yet this was different. These were *his* thoughts. It did not feel as if the thoughts of another brushed against his mind. That was how it had been before when he pulled on the chakra of the darkness buried inside. He had always been able to separate its essence from his, always able to leash the violence of his beast imprisoning it behind psychic shields. His creature had its own unique voice pushing and inciting him to further darkness, urging him to use its powers. The monster that he felt rushing through him now slowly shaping itself on his essence belonged to him.

The smell of fear acrid and pungent filled his nostrils, he looked toward its source at the opposite end. He hissed, inhaling, loving it, and feeding himself. The need to slaughter burned through his veins and Lachlan fought down the terrible hunger tearing at his gut and roaring through his body. His skin rippled, shifting and he looked down. The tattoo of his beast stretched painting his body. He was bonded?

Impossible. There had been no fight for dominance. Lachlan delved deep inside his mind, his essence, trying to separate his beast from himself and could not. That should have been impossible. He had a psychic wall embedded to separate the wash of evil from his essence, preventing the two chakras from melding as one permanently. Even bonded Darkans, the ones who had dominance over their beast, had a psychic wall with which they could leash their beast and the destructive power of its chakra behind whenever they choose. He had absolutely no psychic barrier. The essence was now entirely his. He distantly realized that his body was more muscular, his canines felt jagged and sharper, and claws curled from his fingers. He vaguely remembered the force that invaded his mind, the shattering of his walls and darkness rushing in filling his pores.

Madness howled inside. A cross between a hiss and a snarl echoed from him as more darkness spread through his being. The iciness of the night whistled as it rode the wind. Where was he? It was cold and dank, and he was chained. His muscles surged, and the chains dropped harmlessly to the floor. He should not have broken them so easily. He tried to reason around the rage riding him. Power pulsed through his body, the darkness, the malevolence.

Lachlan held himself still as he studied his surroundings, he was in the dungeon, and he was not alone. It was a beautifully constructed prison with complex locks to hold them confined inside the cage. The width and depth of the bars were at least ten inches thick and made from pure *valnetium* iron. The size of the enclosure itself about twelve by twelve feet. The cage was also suspended hundreds of thousands of feet in the air, with several lengths of chains stretching from their cage to the cavern rocks it was embedded in. The cage was suspended hundreds of miles from the ground, and as he looked down, he could see hundreds of other cages that hung suspended in a straight line one below the other.

He tried to think logically around the savage feelings that seemed as if they were slowly killing the humanity he'd let the human priest living in his castle convinced him he had. *You have a soul, and you are not eternally damned.*

A foolish lie he had allowed himself to believe. He could no longer hide behind that strange comfort the human priest's words had provided. There was no division between man and demon.

He felt like darkness itself—cold, cruel, and merciless.

Nothing felt wrong. Everything was right. And he would slaughter and conquer.

There was another in the cage with him. A woman. He could feel her presence at the other end of the cage, yet he did not glance at her. She'd held herself in a ball most likely trying to appear as small as possible and be as still as possible. She was insignificant. He felt a stirring in his mind, a flood of warmth. *"Lachlan Ravenswood."* The familiar voice soothed offering calm. It was compelling, hypnotic, so mesmerizing it was almost impossible to fight.

"Sleep. Find peace and sleep." Riding the voice was an arrow, he could feel it as her voice pierced through his body, seeking, and hunting for the threads connecting his thoughts, and chakra.

He recognized the Princess Shilah. "Do not use your mind games on me, woman," he said softly.

She gasped, and he stilled. His voice echoed with the distorted rasp of his demon the underlay ominous and sibilant.

"Lachlan..."

The whisper of her voice caressed right over him, stirring a multitude of feelings—unknown and unwanted emotions. Madness hazed his vision, and Lachlan fought with all the control he had wielded for the past four hundred years not to howl, rip, and decimate. For he would kill the female in the cage with him if he were to rampage. "Why are you here?"

He finally leveled his gaze on her fully, uncertain why he had avoided looking at her for so long. She huddled against the wall of the cage. She was very small-boned but perfectly proportioned. The princess glanced away, before meeting his gaze unflinchingly. She lifted her chin, squared her shoulders, and stared at him boldly, but he sensed and saw the falseness in the fine trembling of her lips.

It struck him she wanted to appear brave.

"The grand general threw me in with you."

She shuddered as the iciness of the night swept inside of the cave, and the winds whistled and howled in symphony to the rage that pulsed inside of him. He watched the deep movement of her throat as she swallowed, the quick dart of her tongue to moisten her lips that had gone dry from nervousness. She tried to hide it by returning his stare, but he tasted all of the negativity she tried to bury.

"He wanted you to control me as you did the others."

Her hands fisted at her side and she lifted her chin a notch. "Yes."

Unfamiliar emotions surged wildly through him. Of course, his kind was a weapon the emperor needed by his side to win the war he planned to unleash on Amagarie. Turning from her, he gripped the iron bars of the cage with such strength they groaned and bent. Sinking into the well of shadow spaces he tried to sense other Darkans in the dungeon. Darkness slid against darkness as the demon in him roared. At least three of his kind were bound below him, with dozens of other prisoners.

A hard smile curved his lips as the stink of fear wafted from underneath him and from deep inside cavernous dungeon from the many that were enslaved. Bloodthirstiness lunged as he fed on the dread and agony that floated from those in the dungeon. Strength rippled inside, and he ignored her gasp as the tattoo on his skin stretched and twisted as if alive.

Their gazes collided, and her eyes perfect like diamonds were wide with fear and uncertainty. Lachlan inhaled. Air rushed into his body and took a most unique and beautiful scent with it, one of wildness and fire, something hot and spicy, earthy, and fierce, utterly contrary to the defenseless way that she sat and stared at him. It floated to him through layers of darkness and malevolence and captivated his senses. For a single heartbeat, everything in him, mind, body, faltered into absolute stillness. An odd moment of recognition echoed through his soul.

Instinctive and primal, knowledge filled him. The princess was his *lekia*, his mate—the one woman he was meant to be with for eternity. The one woman capable of soothing the demon within and leashing the unchecked brutality he could unleash on the world. The memory of tasting her washed over him, and he swore her flavor lingered on his tongue—haunting, feminine, sweet, and sultry.

Primordial possessive darkness welled from the depths of his soul and took hold of him. *Mine*. His mate. His salvation. His torment. And his downfall. Hunger burned through him to capture that smell of rain and wildness and flowers and keep it with him always. Arousal surged hot and greedy through his veins and the need to push her to the floor, mount and claim her in the most primitive ways hammered through him. His cock hardened straining against his trousers as naked lust dominated his mind. The urge to sink his fangs into her throat lanced through him even as he recoiled from it. The thought of her in pain made him release a sibilant hiss, echoing inside the pit.

He gritted his teeth as a dark, brutal need filled him as he looked at her mouth, her throat, and the soft outline of her breast against the flowing green sari she wore. A raw scent of fear came from his mate. It sank deeper, and he found its taste repulsive. The darkness inside the dungeon would be overpowering for her, but for him it was nothing. He was naturally of the shadows and all that was dark and unholy.

Her scent lured, tethering the emotions of rage that swirled through his veins. He inhaled once more, and his breath hitched as the rage slowly dimmed.

Her scent calmed the rage and leashed the demon's insatiable need to slaughter.

He stared at her penetratingly. She looked small and vulnerable and very, very afraid. He hated the fragility that he saw. Any woman that would walk by his side would need to be as dark and ruthless. The princess had no hard edges, no merciless will. She was all womanly softness and sensuality. Lachlan felt restless and hungry to claim her. Inexplicable wants wracked him—to lick the hot wet center of her, and then mount her soft curvy body with his and ride her until the deep need burning through his body eased.

He inhaled deeply to control himself. *A mistake*. His thoughts grew murky, replaced by urgent want. The savageness of his lust and rage rode him with unrelenting force. Enough that he was thinking about drawing her underneath him, instead of figuring out the way outside of the dungeon.

Her skin drew him. The cravings beating through his black soul for her were none he'd ever felt before, and he was a slave to the desires rioting through his body. Lust, primeval and savage, tore through him as he stalked to her and spanned her throat with his hand dragging her up against his body. She was soft, softer than anything he'd ever touched.

Her hand flashed up and pressed against his chest. That heated, delicate sensation jolted through his body, set his heart pounding, and heated the blood in his veins.

Her breath caught in her throat, and she stilled within his arms.

"Unhand me, Lachlan Ravenswood."

How brave she tried to sound, but her eyelashes held the sparkle of tears, and her fear turned acrid. Lachlan had endured centuries without contact with others, and now he craved to feel her skin beneath the tips of his fingers and the glide of his tongue. For so long he'd kept all emotions and needs tucked away, lest he tempted the darkness in him to rise. And now with such little effort, this delicate yet exquisite creature captivated him.

He was *not* going to give in to the rush of heat, the need riding him harder than he had ever imagined possible. He didn't need. He didn't crave. Never had he allowed himself such sentiments, not after the slaughter of his family by his father. Except earlier with her, he'd had a sublime fleeting moment of stolen kisses and petting. But that was not enough to abate the emptiness yawning like a tremendous endless hole threatening to swallow him whole. What would it be like…to taste, to indulge, to take a woman after so long.

And not just any woman…*her*.

7

Her hair was seized in brutal hands arching her neck at a painful angle. Shilah flared out her powers brushing lightly against his mind and recoiled, slamming up her mental shield. Never had she encountered such malignancy and venom before and she had only scanned the surface of his *aura*. Everything about him was different. The sleek contours of his muscles now bunched, still supple but more intense. His beautiful tawny eyes now had the cast of a serpent's. The edges were golden, but the inner ring of his eyes, elliptical in shape had seven different colors. She had never seen eyes so beautiful and strange, and it seemed as if he had some sort of coating over them that had been absent before.

His hands tightened sinking claws deep and letting blood.

She could feel the rapid thud of her heart, pounding like a war drum. "Release me," she said and pushing the command to his mind with all her waning strength.

"Silence."

His voice throbbed with violent power, deep and absolutely petrifying. He would kill her, she saw it in his eyes, and even as an Imperial she was defenseless against him. Death at the hands of a Darkan would not be easy. They savored pain and agony, prolonging the death of their prey so they could feed on that dark negative energy. She was in for a long and painful death. She punched hard and deep with her telepathic powers, breathing raggedly through the pain of the violent emotions that were a part of him.

"Release me now!"

His hot breath washed across her face as he leaned in closer and she tightened her eyes more. Then he smelled her...again. His hands dropped from her throat as if the hottest fire had burned him. His head canted left as he stared at her, seemingly fascinated by her.

She stumbled, pressing against the iron wall. "I am sorry I shattered your barriers," she said her heart beating so painfully. "I did not *know*.... I...I did not know." Her throat burned to recall Lachlan's roar of pain and denial as the malevolence of his demon's chakra had burned through him.

"You freed me," he said, his voice a rumble of power and darkness and satisfaction.

She blinked at that unexpected admission, confusion bursting in her heart. "You are not angry." And instinctively she knew it was the darkness within him that was pleased.

Lachlan smiled, a barely-there movement of his lips, and for a timeless instant, she forgot to breathe. How could anyone seem so deadly but so sensual? Unfortunately, nothing about that small smile rendered him approachable, he reeked of brutality. He took up the entire space, the very air, with his power and remorseless energy.

Those soulless eyes settled on her face. "You taunt me to madness with your scent. You need to leave."

"Perhaps it escaped your notice, but I am trapped in a cage," she whispered furiously, not sure why she had lowered her voice or where she got the will to be snarky. But how she loathed the terror in her heart.

He leaned in again as if he could not help himself and inhaled her deep into his lungs as if he wanted to trap her scent. Though her mind was not connected with his, she could feel the monster in him stretch and roar. Something had irrevocably changed within him and how uncomfortable it was that he could not stop smelling her. Her heart leaped, stuttered, and then began to pound. Survival instincts shrieked at her to pull away, but she stood her ground. He appeared like a wild animal gathering itself for a strike. He tugged her body as close to his as possible, fitting his larger frame around hers almost protectively. She peered up at him in confusion. *What is happening?*

He smelled her again.

"Stop doing that," she snapped, hating that her voice trembled.

He ran the tip of a clawed finger down her cheek before lowering his hand. Her stomach did an alarming flip even as confusion bubbled inside her. Not that she wasn't grateful the Darkan was not ripping out her insides and feasting on her blood. The fact he stared at her as if enthralled as if awed by her was nerve-wracking. Shilah wetted her lips, and his eyes followed the movement.

He reached for her once again, and she tracked that clawed finger, bracing for his attack. He cupped her cheeks, and her eyes widened. Shilah's wits scattered in all directions. His touch was soft yet absolute in its possessiveness. Her head pounded, and her skin itched and felt too tight for her body. Energy leaped between them, fierce and passionate, dark, and mesmerizing. Shilah laughed, then sobered instantly sensing she was on the verge of hysteria. What was happening?

"Mine."

The words were like a solid blow to the center of her chest, and her resolve to be brave. Shilah stared at him in acute shock. Had she truly just heard him in her mind? It could not be. Darkans were not telepaths, and the thread he used was unfamiliar...strange and far too intimate.

"You are under my skin, and I've no idea how you've gotten there. I want to do things to you..."

That dark rumble in her mind, along a pathway she'd never accessed before shocked her into absolute stillness. The words themselves made no sense. Her heart was beating loudly, a hard, steady rhythm. "Did...did you say something?"

"You are mine."

A tremble worked its way through her body, and a fear burned through her.

"Do not fear me little one, my life, my crown, and everything I am is yours. To harm you is to destroy myself."

"You have a *crown*?" she croaked unable to process anything else.

I see upon your head a crown of snakes and thorns. She slapped her hands together, flaring her power and slamming up her barriers, blocking all possible telepathic pathways.

"Why have you denied me?" His voice was dark, thick, his fingers tightening in her hair. "Open up your mind to me."

"No!"

She glared at him, lifting her chin, anticipating his rage, preparing to fight to the death.

His finger slipped down her throat and trailed over the swell of her breast. "Your heart beats for me." His voice didn't just whisper in her ear, but poured over her skin, touching nerve endings.

"It jerks in fear."

"Why?"

Was he serious? "You are...you are a Darkan." He was feared and reviled by all Amagarians, surely, he knew of his kind's fearsome reputation. *"And from the evidence of your tattoo, you are fully bonded with a leviathan for a beast,"* she pushed at his mind, testing to see if the telepathic pathway remained open.

His head canted left as he considered her. "I am Lachlan Ravenswood, Archduke of the eastern quadrant of the Darkage, and I am your mate, and you are mine."

His words felt like a decree.

She was still fighting to breathe, to shake off the trembling and fear and uncertainty. "Are you going to kill me?" she asked, ignoring that mate nonsense, truly too afraid to assess why he seemed so possessive.

She squared her shoulders, determined to show courage and the will to fight. From what she had heard in the empire Darkans respected strength and cunning. And her beleaguered appearance certainly did not say that, but she had to try.

"Kill you?"

How surprised he sounded. As if he was not the most menacing thing she had ever encountered. "Yes, kill me."

"No, I would not harm a hair on your beautiful head, but I am going to take you."

"Take me where?" she asked, hoping he had a plan for escape from the dungeons that would include her. Then she would turn her thoughts to escaping Amagarie to her realm.

Immediately, raw, provocative, and shockingly carnal images blasted through her mind, as if she had not erected a shield. Heat flared through her as the image of her on her knees, her hips arched, sweat slicking her skin and wild cries coming from her mouth, his body blanketing hers from behind, and the thickest cock she'd ever seen thrusting in and out of her with savage grace, flowered in her mind.

He placed one palm against the bars above her head, effectively caging her in, his body language blatant, possessive, intimidating, yet appealing with its raw savagery. "There," he rumbled, lust flavoring the chakra that leaked from him. "I want to take you there."

Shilah laughed then slapped a hand over her mouth, glaring at him, desperate to ignore the deep ache the raw pictures had painted and the fear at the blatant possessiveness in his tone. "I am Princess Shilah Malie Symonrah, rightful ruler of Dxyriah, and my hand is promised in marriage to Crown Prince Novar. You will not be taking me anywhere that resembles *that*."

A burst of violence blossomed over her, through her. The glow of his aura—black ringed with a deep red formed a halo around him, yet he was not the mindless monster she'd heard whispers of. He smelled feral, wild, dangerous. How did he have such control of the beast within?

"*Another thinks to claim what is mine?*"

His voice was a rumble of ruthless malice. She made a small sound of protest, of fear, but firming her lips and electing to not offer a rebuttal to his outrageous claim. *I do not belong to you.*

A soft laugh echoed through her thoughts, and she froze. Had he heard her?

His hand skimmed over her breast and circled her throat. She felt the surge of darkness, of danger, then his voice spoke in her mind. "*You are mine.*" Cold, and absolute.

Power shifted inside her body, the tight coil slowly began to unfurl, to spread and grow. Then she slammed it into him, pushing him away from her. He flew back and thundered into the walls of the cage, rattling them. Then in a blink of an eye, he was once again before her. How did he do it?

"If you had asked, perhaps I would consider your suit for you are a fearsome warrior," she hissed, rebuilding her barriers. All ridiculous nonsense for never would she indulge the thought of courtship from a Darkan. She stabbed at his chest with a finger, amazed at the wall of hardness. "I do *not* belong to you simply because you said it. I belong to no man, and when I eventually do, it will be because *I* desire it. If you mean to...to kill me, get on with it." Her voice trembled on that last bit and she scowled.

"Any man who touches you will die."

Her chest became so tight she could barely breathe. His voice was an accusation she did not understand, a curse, a promise of dark retaliation.

"Your claim is outrageous. I do not accept."

With speed she could not track, his hands lifted her to him, pressed his erection tightly against her feminine mound. "What—"

Then his mouth fastened on hers and took possession. He was not breaking or rending her bones…he was kissing her? His need assaulted her senses, his energy a live entity that broke through her telepathic shield. His lust was acute and intense and threatened to consume her. She pulled her lips from his, breathing raggedly. "Lachlan, I—"

He stole the air from her lungs by pressing his lips to hers. The warmth of his body drove away the shivering she hadn't been able to stop since she'd shattered his barrier. Desperation drove her to open her psychic eye to read him and encounter a violent wave of molten lust and need for her. She absorbed the ferocity of the emotions, alarmed when she encountered the vermillion hue of desire and *tenderness*. She gasped, her distress allowing his tongue inside. These were not the seductive kisses she had received from him before; there was no gentle nibbling, teasing foray, sweet passion. The need of the man and beast were one, and they battered at her mind, replacing her fear with a torturous heat. He stole her breath, her reason, her fear, and replaced it all with a burning, all-consuming desire. He held her like that for a long while, kissing her, letting her feast on the petrifying sensations he was evoking.

Shilah moaned as he slanted his mouth over hers roughly. Darts of fire raced through her bloodstream with the hottest arousal, frightening because she had no business feeling such need for the Darkan holding her as if he would never let go.

She flinched and tried to draw back as sharp teeth sliced at her lips. The metallic taste of her blood filled her mouth. The snarl from his throat had her stilling as fear warred with lust inside of her. He swirled inside of her mouth, licking up the blood and sucking at her lips. The sting immediately stopped, and her mouth tingled. He had her pinned to the cage, and his erection felt hard and heavy against her stomach. His enormous strength was intimidating.

He found her throat, soft and vulnerable. Then a sharp pain lanced through her as he pierced her flesh with his fangs. Shock and arousal tore through her body in a whip of flames. His throat pulled, and the snarl of satisfaction washed through her. The pleasure so intense that she could feel her body gathering, chasing the violent storm stirring inside.

HUNGER SWEPT THROUGH LACHLAN, a gnawing, clawing need that he feared would never be assuaged. His throat worked, and the princess's life force rushed into his mouth. An exquisite, rare taste beyond anything he'd ever known burst through his fucking soul, trickling down his throat to seep into his veins, pouring through his body like the elixir of life.

Find the Princess of Boreas's Queen's guards, the witch, and take them with his mate from the dungeons. *That* should be his focus but need battered at him with such force. It felt as if the beast in him was trying to claw through his stomach.

The princess stirred such depths of feelings after such a barren existence, it terrified him, broke him apart, and then melded him with the darkness. A terrible craving that tore through him, relentless, insatiable, he knew at this moment this yearning would never end as long as she existed. Sane thoughts caught at the sharp edges of his mind but couldn't carve its way through the dark mire of need and lust and pulse-pounding desire.

She was his…and he would take her. She tasted like nothing he had ever had, and he never wanted to stop consuming her blood. Fire, hunger, need, obsession. All those and more she made him feel.

Her taste was rich, dark, and evocative. He drank her blood, let the liquid slide down his throat, savoring the taste of it, and fed provocative images to her mind of what he wanted to do with her, of what he would do. She whimpered, and a growl rumbled from him as lust and fear wafted from her to him. The stench of fear from the woman he would give his life for was repulsive.

"Do not fear me."

He pushed it along the mental pathway he could feel forming between them, their *lei*—the mental path unique to all mated Darkans. He could see the link in his mind and felt it anchoring their souls together, darkness and purity, a joining that should be impossible. Along the thread connecting their souls, bright, vivid lights of blue, gold, and silver danced over her thread, and hovering around it was a thread of oppressive darkness. It tried to seduce the light, but it fled from the malevolence. And he saw it as an omen for how their mating would be. She was not of his kind and would run from his mating until he would have no choice but to bend her to his ruthless will.

"I cannot help but fear you."

Her response was a soft whisper along their link.

"You threatened to harm a man who was promised to me before you met me."

He retracted his fangs and released her throat, allowing her blood to trickle along her neck. Her skin was pale, almost translucent, her eyes enormous in her delicate face. She was everything he was not. Soft. Pure. Beautiful. And he sensed she wanted some reassurance from him, one that would lessen her dread, and it was beyond him to offer it. He would never lie to her.

"I made no such threat. I promised to slaughter anyone who would dare."

Her eyes widened until they were enormous bottomless pools, stark horror staring at him.

He lowered his head and licked her skin, closing the wounds on her throat, before reclaiming her mouth. He brushed his lips gently, almost reverently over hers, hoping to communicate that she would always be safe with him. Then he deepened the kiss, and with a muffled moan she arched into him, kissing him back with a beguiling clash of innocence and carnality. She was like a living flame, burning him with her sweet wildness. His body clenched into a painful, hard, unrelenting ache. He smelled her arousal, hot and spicy, and wanted to sink to his knees and devour the wetness he knew he would find.

He showed her what he wanted to do, and she trembled in the cage of his arms, the hard points of her nipples stabbing into his chest.

And yet…her fear never abated.

"Do not fear me, even in eternity I shall belong to you."

Confusion now flavored her chakra, and he had no notion how to explain what she was to him and what she would forever be.

"I…I do not understand. We do not know each other. What are you saying?"

Instead of wasting time with words she would never understand, he spoke with his tongue, his hands as he used one of his hands to palm her breast and rolled her nipple between his fingers. Arousal rode her hard, and her thoughts spilled to him along their tentative link.

She wanted him to touch her, to explore every inch of her skin with his mouth, to lick along her wet pussy, and then slowly feed his cock into her. The gentleness she envisioned, craved as he pleasured her felt strange to him. He wanted to dominate, to slake the lust rising between them with raw strength and passion.

He released her swollen lips and bent his head to place a kiss against the soft, vulnerable line of her throat. Shilah's skin was warm satin beneath his stroking fingers. Her pulse fluttered too fast, and he heard the rush of blood, smelled its sweetness, and succumbed to his lure. His fangs once again burst forth, beyond his control, and he sliced them deep into her throat, bemused by the need to give her all the tenderness she imagined.

The need to lay the world at her feet was a gut-wrenching necessity, and Lachlan feared he would never be able to give her the snatches of the kind of lover and life he felt along their thread. Savagery and darkness were bred into his very soul, and he had found the only sliver of light that could possibly keep him from being eternally damned. And as sure as the kingmaker would bring war to his realm, he would lose his mate before he would get the chance to claim her, for he did not understand love, or kindness, or mercy.

He was a monster, the darkest kind.

8

"Please stop," Shilah whispered, almost collapsing when Lachlan complied immediately.

His tongue rasped against her neck. She trembled, wanting to wrench herself from his hand, yet she burned for him. She hated the awful duality of need and terror twisting through her veins. Lachlan's head lifted, and he peered down at her. His mouth was set in a cruel, unrelenting line, his lips were ruby red with her blood, and his expression was one of violent pleasure and primal satisfaction.

"You bit me," she said faintly, touching her neck, surprised at the smooth, unbroken skin. "You…you drank my blood. Darkans do not consume blood." That much she knew about the dark ones.

She met his eyes, and Shilah flinched from the feral lust and cold cruelty.

"Do not fear me."

She wondered if she had unwittingly trapped herself in an illusion. This was the second time he was issuing such an absurd command as if she would just obey it. "I…I need…"

she pushed trembling fingers through her hair, desperate for some time to think.

"Whatever you need I shall provide."

Shilah stared at him. Every touch of his mind to hers making the connection stronger, more impossible to deny or even resist. *"How do you always find a way through my shields?"*

"I can feel you, in me, a part of me."

"You can?"

"The scent of your arousal, the feel of your skin, the sound of your voice feels as if it is imprinting on every cell within my body. I can see a clear bright thread of light in my mind, and it is the only light in my dark abyss, and it leads to you."

She hated that something in her heart and soul recognized his words. Shilah closed her eyes. She could hardly reconcile with the tender somewhat poetic proclamations of this fearsome creature before her. A beast which so far had killed everything in its path but was now ravishing and touching her passionately, claiming her as his. *I'm merely hungry and exhausted.* "I am not sure what is happening," she said aloud, refusing to speak along their unique pathway.

"You are my mate."

And what did that mean? She hadn't read the Lexicon the emperor had provided, and the rumors in the empire on Darkans only spoke of their might and unchecked brutality. No one spoke of mates. Did he simply want to mate with her as in bed her? Or was it more? *"What do you mean whatever I need you shall provide? Anything?"*

"Yes." Immediate and implacable.

"So, you will not kill me?"

"I cannot harm you."

Relief crashed into her. She did not remind him of his earlier resolve to end her life. His promise wrapped around her, soothing the fear in a manner she had never imagined. "You truly cannot harm me?"

"All the enemy needs to break me is to hurt you."

Her lips parted, and she stared helplessly at him. Nothing inside her could imagine the fearsome man before her broken or humbled in any way. But if she was hurt… suddenly, the weight of her importance to him settled on her shoulders. She opened her psychic mind to his, gasping when she saw that silver thread with white diamond lights with a tinge of black surrounding it. It led from her to him. She reached out her fingers touching the air, tracing the connection only those with immense psychic powers could even discern. And somehow, she understood that this thread that led from her to him was the only reason he wasn't a ravaging beast. And what if this thread were to snap? What if her light should be snuffed away?

"My retribution would burn Amagarie."

Her soul trembled at the brutal, and unshakable promise.
"You've just met me!"
"It does not signify."
"I cannot mean so much to you in so little time."

The darkness was deeply entrenched in him somehow, she was his only redemption. She didn't want that responsibility, the fate of her realm already rested on her shoulders. His soul was too much. Yet a part of her wanted to hold onto the promise of being the most important thing in his universe. Hadn't she always dreamt of a grand love? A sweeping, thrilling romance that would live through the ages that would inspire the poets to write ballads to be sung throughout the galaxies?

His insanity was apparently contagious. *This is not the beginning of that,* she harshly reminded herself, choosing to blot from her memories the way he had made her burn with a simple kiss. He was a demon of darkness, and there was nothing pure in the mind that she touched. Inexplicably she believed the man before her would give her anything she desired and would move the earth beneath their feet to see it done. Surely her imagination must be overwrought.

"I will give you anything."

Disbelief hammered at her. Could he read her innermost thoughts? Or did her aura betray her deep yearning for the things she has yet to gain? She stared at him in deep puzzlement while her brain worked quickly and logically. *"I want to be free from this cage and away from the Empire with my sister Kala who is also a captive."*

"It shall be done."

Hope was a terrible thing, pushing its way into her heart and soul, letting her dream and hunger for things she had almost given up. Without thinking the goals she had for her realm of ruling with love and peace, and kindness floated through her thoughts. *If only...*

Cold violence settled on his face like a second skin, the beauty of it eerily mesmerizing.

"I will make you Queen of all you survey, and those who defied you will bow before your throne."

Her mouth dried. *I see upon your head a crown of snakes and thorns. Queen of darkness you shall become.* Lachlan Ravenswood was the harbinger of her sister's vision. Shilah's entire soul trembled, and she knew at that moment, she should never succumb to anything he could offer.

"I must warn you, the emperor will not take kindly to losing my sister and me." She swallowed. *"And I...I must return home to my people."*

He stiffened, the movement nearly imperceptible. And his eyes—those beautifully wild eyes stayed on her face for far too long. Shilah released the shakiest of breaths when he slowly swiveled around to the lock of the cage. It was insanity to rely on his promises when his eyes glowed with such possession and invitation to sin, but she needed to find a way out of the mess she had landed herself and her sister in.

The one great torch in her cage barely dispelled the dark, but he behaved as if the darkness wasn't a deterrent. Of course, Darkans lived in a kingdom which had no sunlight and where their citizens, controlled elements of shadows and darkness. They had enhanced eyesight, hearing and speed unparalleled to those of other Amagarians.

Her eyes tracked him as he silently padded around the cage, muscles rippling across the breadth of his shoulders. Shilah flinched away from the stirring that quickened inside her. *What is wrong with me?* Each time he had kissed her it had felt like he stole a part of her, but that was no reason to be ogling the dratted man. But he *was* really a fine specimen. His tattered shirt no longer remained on his body, he was only clothed in his trousers and bare feet. His muscles were mouth-watering, and despite the fear he generated, Shilah had to admit that he was stunning. The midnight black hair against the paleness of his skin. A paleness that was now covered with a tattoo that she found hard pressed to look at. It seemed alive, and at times it twisted with sinuous strength over his body.

"The enemy below us cannot be underestimated."

His voice rasped with an undertone of gravelly menace. As if something else spoke with him. His beast? She cleared her throat to unclog the emotions that tightened it. "What do you require of me?"

Shilah swore that the coldness did not come from the caves but from him. His aura contracted, and the subtle red bled to blackness. She flared her telepathy against his mind as gently as possible, and her teeth chattered violently from the cold.

"Do you know of the guards of the Princess of Boreas being held in this dungeon?"

She gritted her teeth as not to flinch from the distortion of his voice. It was terribly unsettling. "I've not heard any rumors, but if they are in the empire, this is where the Emperor would keep them."

"Prepare yourself." The sound of his voice, dark, chilled, rasped over her senses.

"For what may I inquire?"

Shilah flinched as with a stunning show of strength he gripped the bars of the cage, bending and breaking them apart. She stood rooted in shock as *valnetium* iron gave way under his hands. Chakra roiled around him eclipsing the soft glow of the aura that she could see. Blackness churned, and the faintest of hisses filled the air, echoing down into the dungeon. The sound did not come from him, it echoed around. She stepped back as his skin bulged and twisted, as images moved sinuously on his body. The slithery sound that echoed rose, the hissing grating with menace.

Shilah stepped back as the coldness that came from him reached out and caressed her. It was his *chakra,* and its touch was repulsive to her. She shivered as she stared at him with false calm. She knew he sensed her dread; she could not bury it deep enough from his darkness.

The sounds of slithering grew louder, more ominous and Shilah recoiled as she saw that the very bars of the cage were filled with a writhing mass of snakes. She closed her eyes tightly, inhaled deeply and opened once more. They were still there—a curling mass of slithery evil. The aura that roiled around them a deep vermillion tinged with hues of red, yellow, and blue.

Shilah tentatively walked forward to assess them. They were only reptiles—nothing more abnormal to them. Where did they come from? The hissing echoed around her, and it came from the thousands of snakes that seemed to be coming from the rocks attracted to their cage for some reason. She hesitated to venture to the entrance of the enclosure with the torch. The patterns that she felt in their minds made her hesitate. Touching the mind of non-sentients was usually easy, but this seemed different. She tried to ascertain their intent as she spied several reptiles with fangs dripping with venom amongst them.

Shilah paused in confusion, there was no doubt. The intention gleaned from them was to protect her. The bars that Lachlan had ripped apart were now filled with snakes of all sizes and shapes, some dripping venom, some coiled as if to attack at any moment and some observing her lazily. Her stomach clenched in hard knots as she stared at their eyes. She swore to the gods that she was looking at Lachlan's eyes.

He had drawn them to the cage. Shilah stoically ignored the sibilant hiss that echoed so eerily in the depth of the cave.

"Do not close your mind to me. I must know at all times if you are in danger."

"Yes."

Then he just disappeared with the shadows.

LACHLAN TASTED SHILAH'S FEAR, even though she tried to bury it deep. It was repugnant to him. She hadn't felt fear as he kissed her. Only lust and perhaps a bit of uncertainty. A part of her believed she could walk away from his claim, but he would not allow it.

How curious it was that her pull on his mind was so strong. For so long he had accepted the necessity of his solitariness and had liked his bleak existence. Now in a matter of minutes, he disbelieved how he had existed without her for so long. He felt some regret that she was not a Darkan. He did not understand softness or mercy, and he already sensed she had too much compassion. When he had pressed her into the cage wall, next to his strength, she felt fragile, delicate, like a precious glass that could be easily broken. The taste of her lingered until he thought he might go insane with craving. Darkan males were sexually aggressive, and everything in him hungered to drive her to her knees, mount her, claim her. He wanted to bury himself so deep inside her that she would never get him out. That was a dangerous need for he did not wish to break her.

That primitive possessiveness stirred once more and with a ruthless will he pushed all thoughts of his mate from his mind. The mission had to be completed, and only then could he allow himself to be distracted by her allure.

Her safety was now paramount, and he had to take her away from the dangers of the dungeons. He hung suspended from the bars of the cage. Trusting the serpents to protect her and call to him should his mate be threatened, he released the irons. Lachlan plummeted into a bottomless hole. It felt like he fell for an eternity, and the closer to got to the bottom the crueler he felt, the bloodletter in him stirring.

Fear lies below...

He became distantly aware that he spoke to himself or the darker need that rasped against every crevice of his being. He breathed a sigh of pleasure, one borne of darkness that licked at his insides. Something shifted inside the moment he launched himself from the cage, away from the princess. The rage that had pulsed slowly inside of him conflagrated into something more—something hotter, darker, more destructive. The tentative leash that he'd held the madness under dissipated as if it never were. Her scent and taste had been the anchor.

The thought slid into him and the darkness that hovered slunk through him with seductive intent. If it had powered through and tried to steal his will, his anchor to sanity, he might have resisted. The sweet lure to destruction was more than Lachlan could resist as it seemed to come from the depths of him. He embraced the shadows within himself, allowed, for the first time, the darkness to take him. It settled over and into him, fitting like a second skin. Without her mind brushing his, he had no heart or soul.

He landed, one of his knees slamming into the earth with such force, the ground below him cracked in several places. Strength rippled in his body, his skin twisted, and power, unlike anything Lachlan had ever felt raced through him as he fed voraciously from those imprisoned. Their agony and pain were the sweetest nectar. He lingered in the shadow space, moving with exceptional speed as he explored the twisting maze of underground caves. The emperor would return to check how the princess fared, and soon. She was too valuable to leave with a beast they had thought capable of killing her. Or perhaps the emperor was merely confident of her capabilities. Either way, they would return soon, and he wanted his mate away from the slaughter he would wreak. He faltered, canting his head to the side. He could not kill the emperor. War would visit the Darkage, and his king was currently opposed to such a beautiful and pleasurable concept.

A chuckle rumbled from his chest at the very idea of the blood and slaughter he could partake in. He would have to try and convince Gidon treaties and laws were not the way to deal with those who thought to take his throne. Or perhaps Lachlan would simply incite a war by taking the ruler of the empire into the darkness and killing him. The honor bred into his heart and bones savagely protested any action that would jeopardize his king and realm. The ravaging monster in him paused, assessed the known might of Gidon Al Shar, and accepted that he respected his king's darkness.

His purpose was absolute—protect his mate and his king.

Lachlan moved past dozens of guards who felt no ripple in the cavernous underground mazes. Within minutes he found the Queen's guards of Princess Saieke. They were buried deep inside the dungeon in one of the many cells. Three of the walls of their prison were the cave itself, and only the front was made with *valnetium* iron and several other metals. In the stretch of the maze that he stood more than one hundred cells ran in a straight line. The Queen's guards were in cell number thirteen.

Two men sat on pallets, and they were a pitiful reflection of the images Drac's mate had drawn for Lachlan. Yet there was no doubt it was them. He observed their captors who stood with militant readiness close by. Twenty Mevians for two Borean Queen's blades—starved, beaten, and bloody men.

Lachlan stepped from the shadows. "Kamu and Thyon of Boreas."

They scrambled to their feet and gripped the open bars of their cage, yet neither man spoke. They stared at him fearfully, and it occurred to him their rescue might not go as seamlessly as Princess Saieke anticipated. There was no doubt what he was, and his kind was reviled by all.

The sounds of several swords unsheathing behind him pulled a smile to his lips. Dark anticipation roiled through his gut. The concept of mercy which he had held onto for four centuries was now abhorrent, foolish, and weak. With his chakra and his beast's merging as one, he now saw more clearly, and the murky looking glass no longer stood before his morality and conscience. For so long he had dreaded the hideous stain of his demon across his soul. He'd believed in damnation and redemption and yearned for the secrets of the latter. No longer. It mattered not if he could be eternally damned, Lachlan embraced the savagery blooming inside, vowing never again to cage his darker side.

He *shiktered*, moving with the shadows, breaking bones, slicing throats, and severing limbs giving them no chance to scream. Within seconds, the tunnel echoed with a chilling silence. He did not linger, but swallowed the shadows into his being, embracing the darkness even more, searching for his people, taking down every guard he passed in the labyrinth of the dungeons.

At times he touched his mind to his mate along the unique pathway they'd formed. The snakes had one directive, keep her safe at all costs. And though he was confident he had absolute control of their will, there was a need inside him to reach out to her, to feel her, to taste her essence and hold it deep inside him.

He came to a section that was isolated and manned by six warriors who were clearly a cut above the rest. He could feel the ugliness inside of them, sensed their depravity, and knew they were responsible for the sorry state the three young Darkans were in. Four of the guards were seated around a crude table, playing some sort of game, and drinking wine. Two stood ready and alert their hands on the hilt of their swords.

Lachlan ignored them and moved into the cell caging his people. The female whimpered, her eyes widening with pitiful hope and shock when she spied him in the shadow space. He inhaled, unable to sense a beast within her, assessing her pain and the blood beneath her on the cold floor. Her skin was pale, her veins a blue spidery network all over her naked form. They had beaten her mercilessly, and from the dark bruises and red smears on her inner thighs, they had raped her.

He shifted his attention to the two males chained to the wall, large nails driven into their wrists, ankles, and stakes in their stomach. They were gaunt and bloodied from their torture, but their eyes smoldered with the need for vengeance. They were young and without the full powers of their beast, and all related given their similar russet colored hair. No tattoos had formed on their bodies, placing their age below one hundred years. But he could feel the simmering darkness inside of them, waiting to mature and burst free.

Lachlan's lips curled in distaste. The empire had preyed on Darkans who were not old enough to call upon their beast powers fully to fight their way free. Moving in the shadow space, he made his way closer.

"I will free you," he said, pinning them with his gaze. "Then you will kill the guards. If you are unable to do this, I will not take you with me."

The female whimpered, and he lowered his gaze to her. Knowledge gleamed in her gaze that he would not tolerate weakness and anything that would hinder him while he removed his mate from this vile place. She struggled to her feet, slipped several times in her attempts, before finally standing straight. The guards around the table paused their gaming to peer into the cage.

She met his eyes steadily, and in hers, he saw pain, rage, shame, and a hovering darkness that hinted she was close to one hundred years. Her monster would soon be birthed, and dark satisfaction filled him for he sensed she would not suppress it. No…weakness would not be for her.

"You, I will take with me," he said, mildly surprising himself.

Her dried, cracked lips parted on a sigh of relief, and a few tears trailed down her cheeks. "My family will be in your debt."

The guards launched to their feet, pushing back the table and chair with force.

"Who do you speak to?" one of them demanded, scanning the area she stared.

Lachlan moved, and with a mere blink from the guards,

the two Darkan males were freed. The female was too weak to use the shadow space to leave the cage, but the men did not hesitate to roil with the darkness into the maze hallways. They were weak and bloodied, and even without the use of their beast, the control of their element—darkness and shadows—as they fought the guards was impressive.

The female stepped to a fallen guard and painstakingly removed his armor and his clothes. Lachlan offered no help, watching her and assessing her strength. Nor would she require it at this moment. Her lips were flattened in hard, determined lines, and her shoulder shook with silent sobs as she tugged on a shirt that fell to her knees. She tipped her head upward and breathed deeply before shifting to him.

"I do not believe the dungeon can be escaped from."

The battle had ended, and her siblings did the same, clothing themselves, and looking to him for guidance.

"I am Lachlan Ravenswood, Archduke of the Darkage."

In their realm, men were given rank for their might and power, and at his pronouncement, the hovering despair which had still clung to their chakra vanished. They snapped to attention, slamming their closed fist across their chest in their sign of respect and deference to his power. Questions glowed in their eyes, but no lips parted, they merely waited for his commands.

"You will stay in the shadow space and watch and be vigilant unless ordered to fight. There are other Darkans here in the Empire working for the emperor." He pinned the men with his gaze. "Your sole job will be to ensure your sister leaves this place alive."

They nodded, their eyes lowering to his tattoos, then back up to his face.

"You do not have your demons yet, but when you encounter the enemy, you will show no mercy. My mate is within these walls, and my sole attention will be for her."

Then he went to each guard, four in total, who had been incapacitated but remained alive. He shook them conscious one by one, staring into their eyes. They cringed with terror and whimpered. He reveled in their fear and misery, then he ripped their still beating hearts from their chests.

9

The mass of snakes pulsed and slithered away with surprising speed. Shilah did not betray any alarm at the re-emergence of Lachlan, a fact that pleased her immensely. She doubted five minutes had passed since he left the cage, and her frantic pacing had not helped her shattered nerves. She had restrained from reaching out to Kala, not wanting to offer her false hope of rescue or that he would have indeed returned for her. Shilah held up the great torch, the flickering light dancing over the play of his muscles. Blood splattered his chest, face, and his mouth. The flame dipped as her hand convulsed.

Do not react. Do not react. It took every ounce of courage she possessed to step to his side. "Did you find the princess's guards?" She was impressed at how calm her voice sounded.

He did not speak. Instead, there was a press against her thoughts, and a shadow crossed her mind, dark and sinister. Shilah forced herself to hold still and to accept the soft probe against her mental shields. The shadows shifted and then she was clasped from behind. She dropped the torch, sucking in a harsh breath as the sensation of plummeting hundreds of miles down created the dizzying sense of vertigo. The rough scrabbling of claws scraping the cavern side seeking a foothold reached her ears. Their descent slowed, and the grinding sound of his claws burrowing into the rocks traveled down echoing into the cavernous darkness below. They came to a sudden stop that had Shilah gasping for breath in the darkness.

A burst of breeze caressed her face, and then a great torch was held out to her. She gripped it and looked around the labyrinth. There was no doubt they were underground, the tunnel they stood in wove like a maze in several directions. He rolled forward with animalistic grace into one of the darkened maze-like entrance. After a slight hesitation, she followed swallowing her trepidation at the gore that splattered the ground.

She did not want to know what had happened. Her determined steps slowed the further they walked into the tunnel. The light from the torch unveiled the specks of flesh, bones, and blood that lined the floor and smeared the wall. Her breathing sounded loud and shallow even to her own ears.

Had he done this?

She sensed he was close by, yet she could not see him. The great torch's range only went so far. Shilah heard clamoring ahead and quickened her pace. Even though seemingly alone she did not want to linger in the body-strewn tunnel. She rounded a bend and gagged fighting not to spew. A horrid smell permeated the air beyond the scent of fresh kill. Recovering from the smell she took note of her surroundings, her throat worked, but no sound came out. Shilah could only stare at the carnage. Bodies littered the ground, but she could not decipher limb from head. They were in pieces. Blood and bits of flesh painted the walls, ceiling of the tunnel in a macabre testimony of the brutality of their death. A soft whimper escaped her lips, and her stomach roiled in dread.

She spun around, held the torch up and stared at him. He was watching her in that cold, unflinching way of his. He could have offered them a clean death, why would he do this? She sucked in a harsh breath as a revelation flowered inside. He was a Darkan, his kind fed on the pain of others, and now she understood a little bit more as to why they were so feared by everyone else.

There was another dark brush against her mind. She hesitated briefly, before opening her mind to his along their unique connection.

"Tell me, mate, are these men the ones I seek?"

Shilah flinched. His voice throbbed with such awful power it was almost unbearable to connect with him mentally. She lifted the torch, assessing the cage where two men stood, watching them, their expressions flat and hard. They were warriors or had been. The clothes hung on their thin frames, and several wounds covered their bodies. Yet there was fierce and determined resolve stamped in their gaunt and weary faces. She scanned their minds carefully.

The monster has returned
Why is he back?
I must prepare if he attacks.
His speed is unfathomable.
Sweet mercy, who is she?
She is enchanting.
She is with the demon.
What is happening?
Are we being rescued?
Is this my death?

The voices of several more prisoners seeped in, flittering through her mind with stunning speed. Their fear and uncertainty grated at her and glancing around she quickly lit several of the torches mounted on the wall of the labyrinth. Perhaps a mistake, for the tunnel was now lit, and the gore was unmistakable. She identified the source of the smell, it was rotting flesh. In several cells lay the dead, mangled bodies of prisoners. The smell of death and decay was intense and overwhelming. The psychic echo of their pain lingered, and with a shuddering breath, she reinforced her barriers. "The prisoners are confused as to what is happening," she said aloud, so the nearby prisoners could hear, and perhaps she might have relieved some of their fear. "They are not sure if you are here to kill them or rescue them."

"Neither."

She glanced at the cruel edge to his mouth. *"Neither? I thought you had a rescue mission?"*

"Of the two guards, your sister, and the witch. No more."

Of course. "We seek Kamu and Thyon of Boreas, the realm of winds and mountains."

"Who is asking?" the man she already knew was Kamu demanded.

His eyes and voice were heavy with suspicion and hope as he clung to the bars of the cage.

She mounted the torch in a holder behind her and stepped closer to the cage. A hiss rode the air, and she froze, shooting Lachlan a quick glance. *"What is it?"*

His cold eyes slowly moved from her to the men who had backed up.

"I won't get too close," she whispered across his mind, uncertain as to why she felt so warm inside.

She shifted her attention to the men. "I'm Princess Shilah Symonrah of Serange, and this man is Archduke Lachlan Ravenswood of the Darkage."

That is no man, but a beast.

She closed her mind to their racing thoughts. "He was asked by Princess Saieke to rescue you."

The two men faltered into complete stillness, and then

hope blasted from them, their aura's contracting from yellow to pure white.

"Is this true?" the one called Kamu demanded gruffly, staring at Lachlan.

"Princess Saieke of Boreas is the mate of Drac El Kyn of the house Dragos. As her mate, he must see to her happiness always. The princess will be happy with your rescue."

The men glanced at each other, disbelief, and shock evident in their posture. Shilah flared her telepathy, gently brushing against their minds.

Our princess with a monster. I must find a way to free her from their clutches.

What was our princess thinking? A Darkan? How is our kingdom dealing with this?

"Is Princess Saieke a prisoner of the dark ones?" Kamu asked, a green hue of fear and anxiety pulsing through his aura.

Lachlan's flat gaze encompassed them. "Shall I inform her you preferred captivity?"

The men fell silent, sharing several glances with each other, clearly assessing if it wise to trust the Darkan.

"Kala, where are you?"

Her sister replied immediately. *"You are alive! Do not ever close our pathway to me again, Shilah. I've been mad with worry. Did he...did he hurt you?"*

"No, and I am free of the cage. I will tell you all once we find you."

"We?"

"He's helping me escape."

"Why?"

"I am his mate, and I think that makes me very important to him." The echoes of her sister's shock beat at her. *"I will speak with you soon, Kala. Prepare to flee. Can you sense the people around you?"*

"Yes. I can feel the aura of dozens above and below me."

"I will find you. Be ready." Then she pulled her mind from her sister, but careful to leave the pathway not so shielded.

"Kamu, Thyon…Lachlan Ravenswood has sworn an oath to see you both safely to the princess," Shilah murmured. "Now we must hurry, for time is of the most crucial essence." Possibly more than an hour had passed since the emperor left her with the Darkan alone, so surely his return was imminent.

The men nodded, and then jerked as Lachlan appeared behind them without breaking down the entrance of their cage. Shadows swallowed them, and then within the blink of an eye, they stood before her. The men looked too pale and gaunt.

"Do you have enough strength to flee?" she asked worriedly.

"We will crawl on our knees if we have to. How will we escape this place?" The one she identified as Thyon asked.

Shilah glanced at Lachlan, instinctively reaching for his thoughts, and assessing his plans. "We will search every crevice for the weakest spot," she said.

"And how will we find that?" Kamu muttered.

"It will be the place in the dungeons with the most guarded protection for the very fact it is the weak link. We will also need a witch. Several of the dungeon's entrances are protected by enchantments."

They nodded glancing at each other, lips firming in determination.

"My sister is on the third level of this dungeon," she said glancing toward the Darkan. "*I need her with me, please.*" Then she sent him all the impressions gathered from Kala, even though Shilah sensed he did not need them.

And then Lachlan simply vanished and reappeared with

her sister. Shilah stared at him helplessly. How was it possible to move with such speed?

Kamu and Thyon gaped, glancing at each other, communicating some message silently with their eyes. Instinct made Shilah read their thoughts, grimacing at their deep mistrust and fear of the being before them.

"Shilah!" Kala sobbed, rushing into her arms.

They hugged fiercely, and she peeked at him over her sister's shoulder. *"How did you find her so fast?"*

The hard edge of his mouth softened into a small semblance of a smile. *"You wish to know more about me, mate?"*

She frowned at the rich underlying pleasure in his tone. To say yes felt like a trap she did not understand, and the pressure to understand what being a mate meant loomed with more intensity. And that she did not have time to process now. Instead, she replied, *"Thank you, Lachlan Ravenswood."*

She pushed her sister from her and gave her a reassuring smile then made quick introductions. Shilah gleaned from Thyon's thought he was struck dumb by her sister's beauty for he hadn't spoken, just stared at her. And confoundingly her sister blushed.

"I will travel ahead and ensure the path is clear. I will be twenty paces ahead at all times," Lachlan said.

His voice was such a menacing rumble. Her sister paled, not looking in Lachlan's direction.

"I know it can be unnerving," Shilah said to her. *"But I believe him when he says he will not hurt me. And he already knows harm to you will devastate me."*

Her sister nodded slightly, and in that eerie way of his, Lachlan disappeared with the shadows, but Shilah could sense him ahead somewhere even if she could not see him. Everything felt so uncertain. They were not remotely safe, and while it had been relatively easy to escape the cages, escaping the depth of the enchanted dungeon would be a different matter.

Shilah moved forward, moving swiftly along the tunnel corridor, her sister and Kamu and Thyon keeping pace. As they hurried through the tunnel, the prisoners in their cages stirred, and she could see the aura of hope surrounding each pitiful body as they sensed an escape was underway. Ignoring the sorrow and the regret beating through her heart, Shilah flared her senses wide seeking the enemies and hoping they were not running into a trap. It occurred to her that she wasn't as frightened as she should be, and she owned it to the presence of the Darkan. Her heart leaped at the awareness she trusted him with her safety.

A deep sorrow and agony pierced through the second level of her mental barriers, the emotions so sharp she stumbled, before faltering. Her sister almost ran into her back.

"What is it?" Kamu whispered, also grinding to a halt.

Without answering, Shilah turned around and went back up two cells. A young girl, a child really, clung to the bars of the cage, her grey eyes full of pain and fear, her lips sewn shut. Shilah brushed her mind against hers.

"Your name is Raven," Shilah said softly. "You are eighteen years of age. And you've been in this dungeon for six weeks."

The girl's eyes widened, and tears spilled down her cheek.

"Yes, I can hear your thoughts."

The girl's hand gripped the bars of her cage so tightly her knuckles turned white.

"Oh, please, please help me!"

Her cry of terror and desperation swarmed through Shilah's thoughts. She read the torture she'd had to endure, the pain and degradation at the hands of the guards. "Your entire family is in this dungeon. Your parents and your younger sister."

The girl nodded, her desperation creating an aura of dark yellow tinged with red.

"I do not know if they are alive, or where they are," Shilah murmured, reading her concerns.

The girl started to weep. The sound muffled and ugly but filled with such bleakness her throat hurt. She carefully opened the unique pathway that had been formed. *"Lachlan?"*

She jerked as he instantly appeared before her. Brilliant, glittering golden eyes with swirls of blue, green, and red ensnared hers. "We cannot leave them," she whispered, so everyone in their party could hear.

A sigh of relief escaped Kala, and it was then Shilah sensed how much it had pained her sister at the thought of leaving everyone else to suffer. The white light of hope slowly surrounded the girl's aura, and she gripped the cage harder, pressing her gaunt frame into the bars.

"Why?"

There was something immovable about him at this moment, something harsh and unrelenting, and she hesitated. Then she lifted her chin. "I can feel their suffering, and it is terrible. There are fifty-two prisoners in this tunnel alone, and with just a slight opening of my thought to theirs, their agony is unbearable. I cannot read any horrible crime from their sad thoughts, only that they have angered the empire."

"You want to show mercy to people you do not know?"

There was a silence, long and empty.

"You wish for me to show mercy?" This time he asked it softly against her mind. Yet she heard the vein of puzzlement. As if the very notion was anathema to him. Worse as if kindness was something foul.

"Have you no heart, Lachlan Ravenswood?"

There was a sudden dark, malevolent feeling in the air, heavy and oppressive. Kamu and Thyon shifted restlessly, and her sister shuffled closer to her. Lachlan did not remove his gaze from hers.

"I do…and it beats only for you."

Something hot and unknown tumbled inside her stomach. *"I see."*

"You will not be weak, mate."

"Mercy is not weakness," she said softly, sensing his disapproval, understanding on an instinctual level he would wish her to be as brutal as himself.

He remained silent.

"Am I asking too much?" she demanded softly.

Another cold silence. Desperate to understand, she reached for their mental pathway and read his unobstructed thoughts, going deeper into what he felt. She absorbed his fierce longing for her and the terrible, empty hunger he endured. Shilah was unable to banish the blush that crept over her entire body as she tried to see beyond the lust and the varied ways he thought of fucking her body.

She flared her powers and found his other threads. Even before the shattering of the barrier, Lachlan had never been swayed by emotions such as mercy or love or gentleness. He hadn't allowed himself to be ruled with emotions. His code was fairness. He'd assess a situation and made the judgment that was fair, and peace was held. He'd never waded in searching for a battle, enough would find him, and it always did. In the five hundred years of his life, he'd fought countless enemies from his realm, had ended many lives. Centuries of being a shadow assassin for his kingdom had honed him into a violent, brutal predator who only understood blood, death, and war. Now his mate asked him to be kind…merciful. She read that he truly did not understand the notion. Blood and death were stamped into his very bones.

There was an empty, hollow ache in Shilah's heart. How

could he have existed in such a life? How could she ask it of him if he did not understand?

"I must see to your happiness always. I will destroy worlds for you, and lay kingdoms at your feet," he said with merciless sincerity. "I need not understand the things you ask. Just know I will grant them."

Kala gasped, and Shilah could feel the shock from the guards they had rescued.

"I do not want anyone at my feet. I would only ask for mercy for those imprisoned. I would ask for their liberation."

"They are weak and broken many of them, and it will be difficult for them to fight, to run."

"But not impossible?"

"Most will not make it."

"But some will?"

"You are my main responsibility. While I was bound to rescue the Princess's blades and the witch, I will not risk your life for anyone. To try and escape the dungeons with at least four hundred more prisoners invites discovery and death."

Shilah nodded, her throat tight. *"Would...would we be able to come back for them?"*

"No."

And there was no hesitation in his heart at the thought of leaving so many behind to suffer. Their agony and forlorn hope battered at her shields. She walked along the lit tunnel, gazing into the many gaunt faces, and bloodied bodies. Some huddled into the far corners, whimpering, others stared vacantly at the walls, rocking themselves trapped in their silent misery, while others stood, gripping the bars of the cage a desperate hope shining through their aura. She flared her powers touching on the individual minds she felt. *"There are four hundred and thirty-seven souls in this dungeon. And I do not believe they are criminals, only enemies of the empire."*

"They are prisoners of war."

She nodded, knowing it was merely the way of the world and hating she could not help them. Whenever she had entered the dungeon on the emperor's order, it had been in the upper levels and had been shielded from the captives. She hadn't been able to feel their pain and despair so keenly. It would be impossible to try and escape with so many weak and helpless. The empire was so vast and powerful, and they were so few. "We should leave."

Then she turned and made her way back to the girl. It would have been easier to continue without coming back to inform her they could not offer any hope of rescue. "We cannot take you with us."

A whimper slipped from Shilah at the despair that swamped the girl's senses, and she stood there, trembling with her shields open, refusing to protect herself from the pain of the child. Shilah read her thoughts and flinched. Shoring her resolve, she allowed herself to feel every rape, every single torture, mental and physical that had been done to the young girl as if it had been done to her. Tears trickled down her cheeks, the heavy sorrow pressing in on her chest. She swamped the girl with thoughts of warmth and reassurance, a promise that she would be safe, and reunited with her family if they lived.

Kamu and Thyon stepped forward. "We are not at our peak strength, but we can fight. They will fight too. I am sure of it."

His words echoed empty, for they all knew the prisoners were too frail and broken to do much more than scrabble behind them as they fled. There was no strength to lend to any fight that could come their way. They were unequivocally a hindrance.

"I will be merciful and kill them," Lachlan said dispassionately.

"All of them?" Kala gasped rushing toward the cage and staring at the young girl. "You would murder them?"

The girl stared at him, and her thoughts blasted to Shilah.

"She would prefer it," she said. "She would prefer death to the ways she had suffered, and she is certain everyone else would too."

"As you wish."

He stepped into the shadows of the cage and gripped the head of the child. Kala spun around, unable to look at an act that should be one of mercy but was so terrible in its cruelty. The girl closed her eyes, seemingly accepting death, but Shilah read her fears of the unknown, the pain of never marrying or fulfilling all the hopes and dreams she had for her life.

"Stop! I do not wish it," she gasped, uncaring that her voice was rough with unshed tears. "If I cannot find a way to save four hundred people how can I save Dxyriah which has two million souls relying on me?"

"I do not like your distress, mate."

She swallowed back the tears, not wanting her compassion to be seen as weakness. Shilah did not want to analyze why, but it was important to her that he saw her strength.

He stepped back from the girl who had been seized with trembling. Her small frame convulsing and her fear beating at Shilah.

"All is well. You will not die today, I swear it."

"He is a Darkan." The girl's fear grew even stronger, the stink of it almost overwhelming to Shilah's sensitive senses. She sought the words to reassure her, knowing she had a history of revulsion for his kind to contend with.

"I'm his mate. And I...he would not ever do anything to hurt me I believe. And he knows I want to save you. So, you do not have to fear."

She felt him then, a dark hovering shadow in her mind

and knew he listened in on the conversation. How odd she did not mind him there. Taking a bracing breath, Shilah spoke aloud, "Lachlan Ravenswood, can you open everyone's cage?"

Her sister and the guard behind her froze.

"They do not face death?" Kala asked, glancing around as if she expected to be heard by someone else.

"No. I…I would prefer we attempted a rescue. I will connect with their minds and speak with them collectively and calm them. I know many might die, but dozens will also live."

Kamu stepped closer. "You are able to speak in their minds collectively? Are you that strong of a telepath?"

She lifted her chin. "I am an Imperial telepath," she said, uncaring of the arrogance in her tone. "I'll communicate their imminent rescue, and how imperative it is they move with stealth and follow all instructions. I will also implant the urgency of wanting to leave into their minds and their loyalty to each other as we flee."

Admiration and approval glowed in his eyes. She faced her mate. *No.* Lachlan Ravenswood. She needed to think of him by his name and not the abstract yet so possessive term she had yet to understand. "I believe it will be best if you stayed in the shadows at all times, Lachlan Ravenswood. The knowledge a Darkan is with us will be counterproductive to our fleeing."

His mouth didn't smile, but a hint of amusement crept into the dark abyss in his eyes.

"The four of us will stay in the shadows."

Her heart stuttered, and her eyes searched the shadows, flaring her senses, unable to detect any other aura. "You've rescued your people already?"

His head canted left in acknowledgment. Then shadows covered him, and he vanished, but she knew he lingered.

Shilah opened her telepathy, touching the thoughts of all four hundred and thirty-seven captive souls in the dungeon. "I am Princess Shilah, ruler of Dxyriah, kingdom of Serange," she said softly.

She felt them, each individual's shock, agitation, wariness, and curiosity as her voice touched their minds. There was little fear. And she sensed that almost all had given up hope and quietly waited to die.

"I'm here in the dungeons with you, also a prisoner of the empire. I am a telepath, and I speak to you all at the same time," she said, ensuring she projected into her sister, Kamu, and Thyon's minds as well. She'd found the Darkans' pathway and went only surface deep so they could hear her, but not that she was tainted by the malevolence of whatever beast they possessed. *"I am outside of my cage."*

As if a hive, each mind paused at that implication, taking it apart and testing it. Hope and despair in equal measure flooded her senses. Then questions and confusion came. She carefully sorted through their thoughts, picking up the most insistent worry they had.

"Yes. I am in the tunnel of the lower floors. If you wish it, you will be transported from your cages into the corridor, and we will all attempt a rescue. Most of you are weak and hurt, so we must help each other. Some of you might die, or all of us might die if we are discovered. The battle will be fierce if we are found, and the empire will not show mercy. If you wish to come with me on this escape mission, step from your cage when it opens. If you wish for the relief of death instead..."

She took a deep breath, hating to offer it, but already sensing there were those so broken they had no will to live. *"If you long for death instead, it will be rendered. I also offer another option. I am a telepath, and I have the power to remove the pain and the memories of your time here. If you so wish it, it shall be done."*

10

Shilah held her breath waiting for those who would accept death and those who would fight to live. She felt a wave of profound relief that battered her senses, and then the resolve of those who wanted to die. One hundred and eighteen souls wished to perish. A peculiar agony clawed through her as she arrowed in on their thoughts. She flinched at their silent screams, trying not to weep at the terrible cruelty done to them.

"I can wipe the memories away and replace them with good ones. This experience will not even be a shadow in your thoughts."

She offered this lifeline, wanting to weep at the torment they had endured. Beating and tortures so inhumane she could only brush against the surface of their memories. Reaching for Lachlan she showed him those who wanted to escape and connected to him on such a profound level, she saw as he used the shadows and transported each prisoner from their cage into the corridors of the tunnels. His speed as he wielded his natural element of darkness and shadow was a force to behold, and she found herself reluctantly impressed by his strength. They did not even have the presence of mind to be shocked by being out of their cages without their bars opening. A few minds struggled to understand, but she could already sense the renewed purpose filling their hearts from being out of their cells.

Trusting Lachlan to do his part of the job, Shilah turned her thoughts to those who did not desire rescue. *"Please,"* she attempted once more, speaking into their minds, searching for that part of their will that wished to survive. *"I can remove these terrible memories. They will not haunt you, or shape you, and I can replace them with good ones."*

It would take an enormous amount of energy to build new memories for so many people in the little time they had to escape, but she needed to try. Shilah bit her lips hard when no one took her offer. Instead, their resolve to die and escape the shame and degradation flooded her senses, and her throat closed.

She connected deeply into their minds, holding onto their thread of life, uncaring tears streamed down her face. Her lips parted, and yet the command for them to sleep eternally would not spill from her mind to theirs. A harsh breath escaped her, and Kala and Kamu pressed closer, an unexpected wall of silent support. Thyon she saw was carefully removing the stitches from Raven's mouth, murmuring soothingly each time she flinched and whimpered.

There was a stirring in her mind, and then Lachlan spoke, *"I will kill them for you."*

"No!"

"Then why do you hesitate? Time is of the essence."

In his voice and heart, she sensed no hesitation. Death was such a natural part of him, and she recoiled from the awareness. *"I...I am not a murderer."*

Suddenly he was there, a whisper of breath across her nape. Shilah did not scream when darkness coated her senses, and he took her into a world of murkiness, where everyone disappeared, and everything seemed as if they were in another dimension. With a gasp she stepped forward, reaching out to touch her sister who was glancing around frantically searching for her. And Shilah understood then she was in the shadow space, a world within their dimension that no one else could see or hear…unless they were a Darkan.

His arms clasped her hips firmly from behind. His strength was enormous, nearly crushing her bones. Instantly he relaxed his grip, rubbing the spot above her hips soothingly. Swallowing down her nerves, she twisted in the cage of his arms and faced him. The world he cocooned them in wasn't pitch black, but shades of silver and grayscale, and she knew he was the one to control how deep the shadows went. The shadows painted him in a silver shade as if moonbeams kissed his skin. He was so savagely beautiful, a blend of elegance and untamed beast. Something quickened inside her, and she wetted her lower lip, hating the sudden dryness. *"Why did you bring me here, Lachlan Ravenswood?"*

He used a single finger and lifted her chin. His touch was possessive, even intimate. Her eyes collided with his.

"Taking their lives would be an act of Mercy."

"I can take the memories of their torture," she desperately argued, hating the uncertainty that rioted through her at stealing their choices. They wanted to go to the beyond abyss, and she was thinking to deny them even that after countless months and years of cruelty.

"I am no better than the emperor, they have hungered for death and even that peace they were denied," she whispered to Lachlan, unable to understand why it was he she reached out to and not her sister. *"Thinking to take away their choice is despicable, but I have the power to save them…and just perhaps they could go on living."*

His unblinking eyes on her were those of a waiting

predator. There was no judgment or censure, and it occurred to her then how much a man like Lachlan would not be guided by what was deemed right or wrong. What did he act on? What was his guiding force? And how strangely curious she wanted to know more about the dark, mystifying creature before her.

The shadow space melted away, and Shilah slowly walked along the corridor, touching each of the minds who wished to die. Pushing away the discomfort she started to plant the first memory in a male captive. The mind pushed against her intrusion and a wail of anguish vibrated through her as the man realized she was taking his choice. She burrowed deep inside his mind, and a raw gasp escaped her. The threads connecting his thoughts and life forces were a twisted, tangled mess, pulsing with a dark red aura of agony. She could find no white thread of good memories to study and supplant with the dark ones, it was as if his soul was fractured, and nothing remained but the need to end his torment.

The dark memories crowded her thoughts, ugly and brutal, his pain rising inside to swamp her senses. She eagerly clasped onto a memory she found, of him walking with a small boy atop his shoulders, and a woman beside him, laughing lovingly up at him. Shilah took that memory and pushed it at the forefront of his thoughts, trying to use it to bury the terrible agony writhing inside them. His mind was too broken to accept her illusion.

Her heart squeezed, and sorrow made her bones ache. She murmured, "*Sleep.*" And with precision snapped his thread of life, taking him to the afterlife with a pleasant memory his last.

A fine trembling seized her frame after the same thing happened with at least six more prisoners. They truly had no will to live, and the work it would take to draw them from the abyss would be unrelenting. But she worked, trying to find at least one soul from the one hundred and eighteen who wished to die. In their thoughts, she could find no hope. There was only pain. Terrible, endless pain. And in her heart, a rage started to brew as she hated the empire could do this to anyone. After the fifty-seventh command to sleep eternally, her trembling increased and her resolve swayed.

Immediately, a hand touched the nape of her neck, drew her close, and her back was pressed against a wall of heated muscled hardness. The reassurance was only fleeting, for a second later he was gone. She sensed the intent in him, a relentless hunger to slaughter that grew until it became his entire world.

"Please no!" she cried out to him, but then it was too late.

She felt their threads snapping as he took their lives by slicing their throats with claws. He tried to close himself off from her, the need to protect her paramount in him, and she also felt his need to offer them a clean death. For her. Her mind frantically touched those who did not die instantly, and her breath caught at the relief she felt in those who lay bleeding out at the notion death had come for them. And somehow, that awareness allowed them to call upon the good memories they wanted to take with them to the afterlife.

Shilah slowly disconnected from their minds without offering the quick and painless absolution of eternal sleep. Seconds later she belatedly realized she was clasped in Lachlan's arms and in the shadow space. And in that shadow realm, she could feel at least three more people. Darkans. She hazily glanced over his shoulders to see her sister, Kamu, Thyon, and Raven running stealthily in the distance. As they ran through the endless corridors of the tunnels, more and more prisoners joined them, some keeping pace, others hobbling behind, determination burning the aura around them in a wash of bright blue.

Shilah shifted in his arms and peered up at Lachlan. "You can put me down now. I can keep up."

He ignored her, moving so seamlessly it was as if he skimmed the ground above which he ran. She narrowed her eyes. "Lachlan Ravenswood—"

"You will preserve your strength for the coming battle."

She tensed and peered down the endless corridors in which they ran. "Tell me of this battle?"

"In the corridor above, more than a thousand warriors are waiting for you. And more are filing in as we speak. They will attack in a wave with one goal in mind. To retrieve you, my princess."

My princess.

Flaring her senses, she tried to find the auras. "I sense no one."

His lips curved ever so slightly and the blood-thirst in his expression sent her heart into a hammer. "I can feel their anger and need to kill. The empire knows we are escaping. The weakest path of the dungeons is the cave wall ahead. I cannot feel an enchantment, but miles of compressed rocks are between us and freedom. And beyond those walls of rocks, a force will be waiting."

"How many?" she asked softly.

"Thousands. You are a prize they do not wish to lose."

She flinched and glanced back at the dozens of people trailing behind, their aura shining brighter with each step. Those who were stronger helped those who stumbled. Kamu had a young girl on his back, her legs hooked at his waist as he ran with her. They were in no state to battle a few, much less the thousand warriors ahead, and then to face the army waiting beyond. Her throat closed. Their escape would only be a temporary relief.

Their unique pathway opened. *"There is a witch, Amirah, can you connect to her telepathically?"*

She didn't question why he chose this method to communicate, instinctively responding, *"Yes. I can find her."* Shilah pressed the tip of her finger at the spot the witch had drawn the symbol. "*She touched you here, and I can still sense the echoes of her aura. I only need to follow it."*

"Tell her to work on a spell that could possibly dampen the enchantment around the dungeons. I tried using the shadows to escape and could not. Though I cannot sense the enchantment something is preventing me. Tell her to dampen anything that could counter darkness. Inform the witch my vow to take her from the empire stands, and she must prepare."

Shilah nodded, and delved into her mind, opening her psychic senses wide and pulsing with a blue halo. It was then she sensed the aura of the warriors waiting with such deadly intent. Pushing back the need to caution him to not run toward the danger, she centered her thoughts on finding the witch following the twisting white thread that glowed with powerful vitality until she located her.

She politely knocked on the witch's mental barrier, not knowing the full range of her powers and not wanting to start a fight. The echoes of the witch's hesitation vibrated down the thread, then the connection opened.

"This is Princess Shilah."

A profound surge of relief filled Shilha's mind.

"I thought he killed you."

"No."

"Did you actually control him?"

"No...I am his mate, and because of it, he cannot harm me. I am not sure how long his protective instincts will last for."

Shock and fear blasted at her before the witch controlled her emotions. *"It will last forever."*

Shilah's heart jerked with such force she felt light-headed. Pushing aside that worry for if they made it out alive, she asked for the spell and explained of their escape and the

Darkan's promise he would come for her was still intact. The witch agreed, and she pulled from her mind. Lachlan placed her on the ground and removed the shadow space from around her, yet he remained within its confines.

She turned to face everyone slowly coming to a halt, pushed out her power and connected them once again like a hive mind. *"There are hundreds of warriors just ahead. There will be a fierce battle to escape the Empire, but I believe we can make it."*

Shocked murmurings floated on the air, with cries of denial and anger. Some tried to run back toward their cages, fearing the retaliation of the Empire. The sounds of stomping feet, jangling armors rumbled through the tunnel as the warriors ahead started coming at them.

"Please step from the shadows Lachlan Ravenswood," Shilah said.

He complied, and a surge of fear filled those close enough to see. "We have a powerful ally who will help us win!" She did not believe it, but she needed them to feel anything but the rancid fear and horror filling her mind. He was just one man, and she already sensed his priority would be to get her to safety, not saving the quivering, battered souls before her.

"This man is Lachlan Ravenswood." She fed to their mind his image as she spoke. *"He is An Archduke of the Darkage and has sworn to help me as I help us escape."*

Their fears and horror amplified and swarmed their senses.

Shilah stumbled back from this, desperately connecting to the minds of everyone behind her.

"He will not hurt us."

She waded through their jumbled, panicked thoughts.

"Yes, he is a Darkan...but he is my Darkan." Her heart trembled when she felt the echoes of his amusement and pleasure at her absurd claim.

There was no calm in their minds, and the assault on her senses was becoming too much. Shards of glass seemed to be piercing her head with the effort to sort through their uncensored emotions. Yet Shilah could not give up, would not give up. How could she liberate millions from tyranny and save her people if she could not save these pitiful people before her? Grief welled up, enveloping her, driving away her logic and reason. *"There are three hundred and nineteen of you escaping with me. Not one of you will die,"* she promised, determination beating through her. *"I am Lachlan Ravenswood's mate, and he has vowed to lay the world at my feet... and he will start with this piece of the Empire."*

Kala cried out her denial. The air in the room thickened to a black malevolence and savage satisfaction burned along her senses. A flood of violence and depravity stormed into her as the blackest of chakra swirled around him. Palpable might and brutality emanated from Lachlan, and with a sinuous twist, the tattoo on his skin curled around his body.

Her sister flinched, her lips forming but no word emanating. Shilah faced him, a desperate fear in her urging her to take back the words, that there were unimaginable consequences to her plight to save these people but could not.

The warriors in the distance started running towards them, and she felt the people at her back braced for the brutal attack. She spared them no attention, centering her powers into the deep still well inside and pushing out the largest kinetic protective barrier around the people behind her. The blue glow of that aura rushed over their heads until it covered everyone in a barrier of cracking energy.

Lachlan tilted back his head and inhaled. Then a pulse of raw savagery and blood-thirst came from him as the tattoo of the Leviathan twisted off his skin and appeared before her. Shilah screamed at the wave of darkness and death that leaked from it.

Rage flooded Shilah, consuming her with the need to kill, to fill the terrible emptiness. She slapped a hand to her forehead, fighting to separate the demon's beast essence from hers. The link had to be severed. Her head was splintering, fragmenting as the pressure increased. An ugly, twisting darkness poured through Lachlan to her as the need to bloodlet lit in his veins creating an inferno, one that blazed inside creating an unrelenting need to kill.

Somehow, she created a shield along their entwined threads, and it was only then she could breathe. This…this was more than she could understand. And she had aligned herself to him at her peril. Her throat ached as the implication of the depth of trouble she stood in resounded.

That monster's head shifted. His pitiless eyes slid over her, making her flesh crawl, but with a sensual heat, revulsion and desire pulsed through her in equal measure. Lachlan's beast revealed itself, towering over her at least ten feet tall, the head was dragon-like with a massive maw with serried rows of pointed teeth. The body was pitch black, except for the massive ridges running from its head down to its tail. Those were made from the most beautiful scales of green, purple, yellow and red. It stood upon four legs, muscled with rope-like sinews, and ending in feet with curved talons that gleamed like polished silver scimitars. The beast's long pointed tail lashed in its eagerness to kill, its serpent eyes were pitiless in their barbarity, yet the creature was absolutely exquisite in its sheer savagery. Lachlan himself appeared as darkness. Chakra roiled around him like the blackest of smoke, and the wall of energy she felt rising inside him was unfathomable.

Heart pounding, tasting fear in her mouth, she braced, not sure what to expect.

"*Kill.*"

The command burned along their link to the monster,

and the beast screamed its triumph. Darkness descended, and Shilah could not see anything. Cries of fear and pain echoed through the tunnels, and the psychic overload had her doubling over. The terrible pressure in her head increased so that for a moment her head felt as if it might explode.

"What is happening?"

Her whispered entreaty was met with implacable silence from Lachlan. Only cries of terror and pain. Sound waves whistled through the narrow corridor and battered at the psychokinetic shield. Then as soon as the attack started, it ended, and the darkness relented.

Shilah stared. And then stared some more. She started to tremble violently.

Dozens of fallen warriors littered the floor. Hundreds of them and all by the hands of Lachlan Ravenswood and his beast. She glanced toward his direction and flinched. He was coated in blood, and thankfully the beast that had originated from the tattoo embracing his body was not in sight.

But she could feel the malevolence ahead.

The walls of the tunnel rumbled and shook with such force she cried out and leaned against one of its walls.

"What is happening?" she demanded.

"Come, mate, your power is needed."

Without her seeing him move, somehow, she reached for his arms and was by the beast. Its massive form was burrowing through the wall of the dungeon, breaking apart rocks and creating a tunnel leading through the earth. She was lowered to her feet.

Shilah's heartbeat thundered, and her blood roared in her ears as adrenaline pumped through her body. She was too close to the monster, the waves of malevolence pouring a sentient aura that rolled with sinuous intent toward her. *"What do you need me to do?"* she asked shakily, doing her best to not look directly at the monster which was staring at her unflinchingly.

"You will use your telekinesis and crumble the earth."

"I am an Alpha in that genesis, a mere fledgling. I cannot bring down a lone castle much less a mountainous rock!"

At his lack of response, she glanced up into cold eyes that seemed to judge and found her lacking. Its notion stung and gritting her teeth she moved over to the dungeon wall and pressed her hand against it. Shilah dipped into the well of her power and blasted at the rocks with her mind. There was a rumble as if the earth was alive and groaning its protest at her attempts. The ceiling above her shook and dirt drizzled onto her face.

Hundreds of stomping feet came from above, and she identified that more warriors were running along the maze-like corridors to stop them. The Leviathan battered at the gigantic rock, its enormous body and power digging through and creating a massive hole. The undertaking seemed impossible, for the beast would need to create a tunnel that spanned for miles to deposit them onto the surface. How could they do it in time, and before the general and his elite army reached them?

"You will do it or die in this dungeon, mate."

Shock stole her tongue for several seconds then she firmed her resolve. Now was not the time to hesitate and she should have known this without his brutal reminder. She took a breath, released it, and let herself find that place deep inside where there was only stillness. Digging into the well of her power, she pushed with all her might at the rock wall. An ominous groan vibrated through the walls, and the entire earth dipped and rolled. Shouts of alarm echoed from the captives waiting far behind them in the corridors.

Power ran through her body and with it, confidence. Shilah blasted kinetic energy at the earth, a piercing scream escaping her as something she'd never felt before rushed through her. The wash of power felt dark, unlike her, and she belatedly realized the monster had connected to her and poured his dark energy along their neural connection.

The boulder cracked. She felt the fissure as the earthquake erupted. The walls of the tunnel exploded, the ceiling crumbled, and ahead, the Leviathan was like a massive scaled snake roiling through the now loosened soil of the inner walls with unparalleled speed through the terrain toward freedom.

Screams of fear and pain echoed from behind her as the roof of the tunnel came down in a hail of rocks and dirt beating against the protective barrier she'd formed. Her barrier wavered under the onslaught, because she was unable to maintain it while pushing all her energy into the quake rocking and breaking the terrane ahead, and she could see cracks spreading along the thin shield she'd constructed.

The screams intensified, and their fear rose suffocatingly into the dark tunnels flooding her senses. And through it all, Lachlan Ravenswood stood and watched her, a silent predator, yet she felt the strength of his chakra pouring to her through their link.

Releasing the wall, she stumbled back, and he clasped her from behind. The trembling of the cavern stopped, and for a moment there was a hush, broken only by the gasping breaths of the those trapped beneath the rubble.

"I have to help them," she said hoarsely, pushing from him and running back toward the captives. "My sister…Kala!"

Lachlan whirled and dissolved in a rush of fleeing shadows, and before Shilah could process what was happening, she stood outside of the crumbled tunnels and in the cold refreshing air. Only seconds passed before her sister, and the Queen's Blades appeared beside her. Kala rushed into her arms, and they hugged fiercely before releasing each other.

They glanced around dazedly to the gaping hole in the side of what was now evidently a mountain.

"How is this possible?" Kamu murmured, staring as dozens of prisoners appeared in bursts from the shadows until all stood behind them. "I've heard of the powers of Darkans, of how they controlled the shadows and darkness, but I've never understood the depth of their might."

And the yellow-green hue of fear burned along his aura.

"And our princess has bound herself to one," Thyon said, a bitter curve to his lips.

"Be grateful you've escaped the dungeons. Does it matter if it was at the hand of a Darkan?" The reprimand in her tone was clear but, their eyes showed instinctive fear, and something crafty lingered. Shilah hoped they did not do anything foolish.

The captives appeared confused, stumbling with exhaustion and hunger, squinting their streaming eyes, and staring into the sky. The young girl Raven cried out and stumbled over to a woman and younger girl who clasped her into a fierce hug. They babbled and hugged each other, tears streaming down their faces. Another lady dropped to her knees and started to wail, and then she kissed the grass on the ground. Brushing against her mind, Shilah learned she'd been a captive for two years, and her crime had been to reject the advances of a General in the army for she had been married and loved her life partner.

Merciful gods. How cruel of the empire.

Lachlan appeared at her side, black swirls of chakra floating along his body. His beast had been called back to his body, for the tattoo was once again painted on his skin, except the beast was now positioned differently, and she swore the eyes shifted on his skin, following her. Then right before her eyes, red stripes burned his skin like fire, and though his lips did not move, a hiss of pain echoed along their link.

She stared at him, not understating. She could see his chakra flowing and twisting through his aura, the blue churning, as the black separated from it. Then his aura contracted into small balls with the darkest of energy, embedded at the center of the blue light.

"What is happening?" she asked faintly.

"The darkness cannot face the light."

Her breath sawed from her throat as she took in the changes wrought in his body. She realized the dark malevolence of the beast hid in the blue light of his natural aura. She glanced at the sun, wondering at the power it held over his kind, then she glanced back at him. He looked as dangerous and primal as she knew he was, but somehow less petrifying. His eyes had lost their serpentine cast and multi colors, only a heated tawny gold stared at her. The claws had retracted from his fingertips, and the wicked curve of his canines had receded. His body still rippled with power, but the tattoo had stopped shifting across his skin.

"Are you saying you've lost your powers?"

A small smile tipped his lips, and she blinked. He was even more impossibly beautiful.

His gaze was a piercing caress she couldn't evade. "Worried about me, princess?" His voice was smooth and sensual without the overlay of menace from his beast.

Her breath strangled at the amused taunt in his eyes, before his lids lowered. The man before her now seemed much more than a monster. He was still unapologetically brutal, but now there was a hint of something mysterious and seductive, and her entire body flushed and ached.

Shifting away from him she stared out at the waiting force, which numbered in the thousands. How could they survive such a force when he had no access to his demon's power? She glanced in the sky at the red hue, sensing the sun would soon sink, but by then it would be too late.

In the far distance, a flash of light so bright it hurt her eyes shot into the air. And with a sense of shock, she recognized the aura of the *Phoenyx*.

"So, this is the power of the *Phoenyx*," he said contemplatively while exuding acknowledgment and challenge along their link. "There is a battle in the Taryllion at the section between Mevia's and Nuria's borders."

"Yes, that power is from King Ajali's *Phoenyx*," she said softly. "And from the soundwaves trembling on the air, he fights Mevian warriors. I had wondered how the grand general wasn't here with this force to capture me. King Ajali and whatever he fights to defend is a greater force." And she suspected the female who housed the Dracan the Emperor coveted could be what the king fought for. It warmed something inside Shilah to know that he would battle for her similar to how she had done for him when the empire tried to capture him.

"The empire is confident these warriors before us can retrieve you. They did not count on me. I am of the shadows and darkness. I am a force they cannot comprehend."

She glanced up at him with a terrible fascination, unable to take her eyes off his expression of ruthless purpose.

He looked away from her. "There are two choices, mate."

She shifted her gaze to assess where he stared. Mist veiled the mountainous horizon and crept into the deep forest below them, and beyond the tree lines, thousands of warriors waited, their bronze armor shining under the sun. Her heart stuttered. "And those choices are?"

"I take you now into the shadows, and we leave for my Kingdom."

Her breath rushed from her lungs in a long gasp. "The realm of the shadow demons?" she asked, recalling every rumor she had heard whispered in the empire the three months she had been inside its walls.

"I will only take you, your sister, the Queen's guards, and the witch."

Shilah stiffened, understanding dawning. The captives would be on their own. "They'd gained no true liberation. Once we leave them here…they will be lambs waiting to be slaughtered or recaptured. They are weak and unable to fight. If they run, they will be hunted and found."

A thundering sound tore the false tranquility, and the warriors waiting on the horizon flashed toward them, their speed making them a blur. Her stomach knotted for they would reach them in only a few minutes and the slaughter would begin. The wind started to increase in strength, and dark clouds drifted overhead. The frantic murmurings subsided as the people behind her spied the wave of warriors flashing toward them. The despair that rose in the air almost choked her, but she sensed their determination to fight, even at the cost of their lives.

"Can you take them into the shadows and hide them from the empire?"

"How long can they hide in the shadows," he said flatly. "The emperor has a record of every prisoner in his dungeon. If they flee to the comfort of their home, they will only be retrieved."

She hadn't thought that far ahead, only the need to take them from that terrible place had burned in her veins. But had she just brought them to meet another death or imprisonment once again?

"Perhaps we could keep them in the shadow space until I come up with a plan." Her heart felt heavy with grief and failure, for she could see no foreseeable way to save these people.

"There are three Darkans in the shadows ahead. They are coming our way."

She wanted to scream her frustration to the sky. She took a breath, even though her lungs could barely drag in air. "I assume they are not with you."

"That is correct, mate." Yet he did not seem worried there would be a potential battle with his kind.

"What is the second choice Lachlan Ravenswood?" Inside she was still, coiled, waiting for some hope, bracing for the wave of attack from the approaching warriors, yet unaccountably confident he would allow no harm to her.

His lips curved, and primal anticipation throbbed in his tone as he said, "We kill."

11

The world around Shilah turned into chaos.

The captives hadn't been required to battle before, but now it was inevitable as dozens of warriors screamed out waves of terrible destruction. The sound waves were excruciating, an energy wave that blasted everything in its path, knocking her back, aching her eardrum. Shilah frantically erected her barrier of kinetic energy.

"Decide."

Lachlan's voice in her mind was a menacing rumble of power even without the darkness what had seemed stamped onto his soul. The soundwaves emitting had no impact on him, and he stood with his feet planted wide, the muscles on his back and shoulders twisting like a snake. He was leaving the choice to her, flee and protect themselves or try and help these people. *"We save them!"*

Before the swarm reached them, shadows snaked over the earth with shocking speed, grabbed the oncoming warriors by their neck and snapped, as if the shadows were sentient. Wicked clawed daggers appeared in Lachlan's hands, and he moved with the shadows straight at the incoming force. He was too brave, utterly mad, or totally confident in his brutal might. It was the latter she saw, as dozens of warriors converged on him, only to fall under the slashing blades and darting shadows. Whenever she saw him without the shadows, he was a thing of beauty, his body fluid and graceful, so fast he was a blur. Then he would disappear, and bodies would suck into the shadow to only appear seconds later, dead or dying.

She stood in a fighting stance, using the well of power in her mind to uproot trees from the ground, and massive stone boulders and throwing them at the oncoming force, slapping warriors away with brutal force. There was a fierce, burning need to survive and to protect the people behind her, and she let that dominate her will refusing to feel the terror over the hundreds of warriors pouring over the land like ants towards them.

The sun dipped, and it was as if a dark aura moved over the land. Shilah flinched, releasing the boulder she'd grabbed with her thoughts, spinning to find Lachlan. The tattoo twisted on his skin, and in a burst of raw, brutal power it leaped from his body and slammed onto the ground. The earth under the Leviathan's feet seemed to tremble, and the trees surrounding them shook. She could feel the need to kill and slaughter inside Lachlan, but instead of wading through the dozens of warriors rushing onto the open field, swords held high and spinning sound waves preceding them, he disappeared.

Shilah could spare no thoughts about why he went into the shadow space, she could only battle. Two warriors grabbed her, and spun with her, moving toward the wooded forests. They flashed so fast she could barely breathe, and she glanced behind her to see Kamu, Thyon, Kala and several others valiantly battling. Most of the warriors were concentrating on fighting the Leviathan which seemed to be rending them apart by the dozens.

Using the power of her mind, she grabbed the warriors' throats and squeezed. They released her and stumbled. She rolled onto the forest floor, and lurched to her feet, sinking into a fighting stance. Shilah did not free them from her merciless grasp, but unable to squeeze the life from them, she delved into their minds with the intent to command them to stop breathing. Then the part of her that could not casually end a life read one of the men's thoughts and saw that he had a wife and two children whom he loved. Acting on instincts, she delved deeper into his mind, and she peered at the memories of how he'd tormented the prisoners, even raping several women. How could a man so loving with his family be so vile?

The other warrior was more honorable, but did every bidding of his master, no matter how cruel the commands had been. With a gasp she withdrew from their minds, releasing her mental clasp on their throats.

The man to her left eagerly dragged air into his lungs, retaliating faster than expected. He dived into a roll, grabbing his swords, and flashing toward her at such speed he blurred, she could hardly keep track of.

She powered into his mind, ruthlessly ripping it from him. *"Fall onto your sword."*

And with brutal precision, he impaled himself through his heart.

The other warrior parted his lips to emit a sound wave, and a snake darted from the earth to wrap around his throat, cutting off the sound before it had even formed. The snake coiled itself around the man's body, effectively tying him so that it was impossible to move. The snake's head shifted, sinuous and menacing. It bared its fangs, and venom dripped from its pointed teeth. Then the snake's eyes collided with hers. Lachlan's eyes. Swirls of gold, and blue, and red.

It waited while the man groaned and whimpered. Stark sounds of garbled fear.

"Yes," she whispered, rejecting the mercy that was stirring in her heart.

It struck, its fangs embedding with brutal grace into the man's throat. The guard convulsed, foam bubbling from his mouth. She did not look away even when her soul cried out for her to glance away. She watched his death, felt his horror, and pain, and accepted that justice had been done.

Three small multicolored snakes about two feet in length slithered toward her. With a gasp she stumbled back when they launched toward her, sliding sinuously up her body. Two coiled on her arms and froze, and another wrapped around her hair like a twisted crown before they froze into marble effigies.

A sound alerted her, and she spun around to see six warriors powering her way, their swords drawn. Shilah attacked, mentally grabbing them, and throwing with strength into the trunk of trees, breaking bones, and shattering limbs. Another swarm came at her, and she did the same, wielding her powers, slipping into some of their minds and commanding them to sleep while using her telekinesis to break limbs and push them away from her.

A hand grabbed her from behind and spun her around, but before she could attack, the snake on her arm came to life and faster than she could track its tiny fangs pierced the man's throat and then the snake was back on her arm.

The warrior screamed, falling to the ground, and twitching, blood dripping from his eyes and nose. Shilah stared in disbelief at the serpent that was once again frozen in a decorative coil on her arm as if it was a piece of jewelry.

Lachlan had sent them, and she knew their command to protect her was absolute.

Spinning around, Shilah ran toward the battle, crying out at the dozens of prisoners falling beneath the brutal sound waves emitting at them.

Something dark and unknown spilled against her senses, and the Leviathan that was battling the horde disappeared. *No!* Shilah ran faster up the incline toward the battle, for without the monster to defend against, the empire's force turned toward the captives. There was a red haze of madness, a fire sweeping through her, a rage unlike any she'd ever felt. She hurtled herself onto the ground, sinking into the well of her power.

She forced air through her lungs as the pressure in her head increased until it felt as if a vice gripped her skull. Then it imploded, her powers surged, and she felt the life pulse of every Mevian on the battlefield except for those approaching in battle-ready formation about a few hundred meters away. The ones she felt numbered more than two thousand. It was impossible she should hold such power…so much power. With a thought, she could kill everyone, command them to bow at her feet.

She felt the echoes of approval from the beast and the dark invitation of the power he could grant her.

"Warriors of Mevia, heed me, you will defend the prisoners, kill any who advances on them."

The command blasted from her. Energy coursed through her and at its center was a malevolence not a natural part of her. Like the swarm of ants, they turned to the advancing troops and attacked in a wave of brutal fighting. The shrieks of horrors and pain swamped her as with efficient savagery they decimated each other. She sent her telekinetic power into the earth, imploding it beneath the fighting warriors. Dark energy washed over her as the psychic energy slammed into her. The violence struck her hard, taking her breath, pounding at her head. She gasped for breath, and then like a vacuum it sucked from her, all that darkness and negative energy. The trail of aura lifted from her skin and without looking she knew they went to Lachlan.

Limbs shaking and her heart jerking with shock and distress, she faced him. She doubted she could say another word without bursting into sobs. He stood there, a dark protective force. She longed to fling herself into the comfort of his arms and rest her head against his shoulder, crying her regret for the lives she'd taken. There were several scars on his chest and throat healing before her eyes, and his beast was once again on his skin. He had been in some battle, and it had been fierce.

"I fought three of my people in the shadows."

Her eyes widened, recalling he had said there had been Darkans in the shadows of the warriors.

A hard edge curved his lips. It was a smile. Shilah sucked in a harsh breath. *"You are pleased with me."*

"That I am, mate."

She shook her head, hating the burn of tears in her throat. *"I killed them."* And she was petrified to accept that hundreds of warriors lay on the forest floor dying, with a simple command from her. With great powers came great responsibility, and Shilah felt as if she had just abused hers. The knowledge that the empire was cruel and unjust did not soothe the sorrow rising in her heart. The men behind her had families of their own, people they loved.

He inhaled deeply. *"Some still suffer."*

And he fed on their fears and agony and took pride in the fact she had ended their lives. Shilah's stomach cramped at his unapologetic brutality.

"We are at war." His voice in her mind was a dark pulse of power. *"In a time of war, we kill, and we do not show mercy."*

"Mercy is for the weak," she replied, repeating his earlier lessons.

Yet her heart ached, and the fingers that pushed the tangled hair from her face trembled. Taking a deep breath, she lowered the firm hold she had on her psychic barriers and allowed the energy of those suffering to wash over her. The minds of those trapped under the mountain cried out their terror, those who lay dying, thought of their wives, and daughters, and sons. None thought of the war they were fighting for. *"I have to save them."*

He studied her face, his eyes lingering on each of her features. Searching for weakness perhaps, and silently condemning her for her compassion. A blink, and then he was inches from her. A clawed fingertip lightly brushed against her lower lip.

"Is this your wish?"

His touch so gentle she could barely feel it, yet electricity crackled in the air between them.

"Yes. Do you think me weak?"

She knew it did, and it affected her that he would think her a liability. Silly and outrageous for she did not want to be his mate. Yet it mattered, so much that her heart ached as she waited for his response.

"I think you are different from anyone I've ever known. Different is not weak."

His hands framed her face, thumbs brushing her frantic pulse. His expression was one of stark desire and unrelenting hunger. And in the midst of the battlefield, he kissed her. For a dazzling moment, the world seemed to go up in flames. She saw the monster in him, the utter darkness and rage, but instead of fleeing, Shilah embraced it.

"You hold what is left of my tattered soul in the palms of your hands."

With a whimper, she clung to him. She hadn't known her

body could be so alive. Lightning streaked from her breast to belly in a wicked caress. There was nothing else but his mouth claiming hers, whirling her into another world of agonizing pleasure she hadn't known existed. Her skin crawled with need, her mind was chaos as the darkness mixed with her light and seduced the hunger in her soul.

"You are my queen. I will give you all that you dream of—retribution...power."

She fought against the dark, seductive whisper of power sensing on a profound level what he offered. Shilah pulled her lips from his, and the darkness retreated to give her breathing room.

Then she burst into raw, ugly tears. She didn't question the why of it, but when he hoisted her into his arms, she did not pull away. Instead, she wrapped her legs around his waist, and buried her face into the crook of his neck and cried, distantly wondering why she hadn't run to Kala's arms.

She breathed raggedly, feeling a little shaky, on unfamiliar ground. He walked with her toward the fleeing captives as they moved deeper into the forest. Shilah peeked over his shoulders at the decimated warriors. It looked as if a massacre had taken place. As far as she could see, corpses and the nearly dead littered the ground, blood and entrails strewed around them, their weapons broken and useless. Carrion birds hovered, smelling the feast that lay below them. She stared at the destruction and unable to bear the revulsion of how they suffered, she connected to the minds of those still living.

"Help each other to safety. Tend the wounded. Do not pursue the prisoners."

Exhausted she disconnected from all the mental threads and rested against the warrior who carried her. They reached a clearing deep into the forest, and he lowered her to the ground. Several people were bent over a creek, greedily drinking water, while a few rested on the grass or trunks of the towering trees which seemed to rise to the sky itself. Her sister looked up from where she tended the wound of a man and gave her a weary smile. Shilah was shocked to see the witch, administering crushed herbs to the lips of the people they'd rescued. Shilah glanced up at Lachlan. *"You rescued her."*

"I traveled with the shadows for her."

She stepped from his side and made her way over to the small gathering. Songbirds fluttered above their heads, darting in and out of the tree canopy, calling sweetly and bringing a brief smile to few of their lips.

"We made it out, but we cannot rest here long," Shilah said, looking from one weary but hopeful face to another. "Only a few minutes at best. For now, the battle has been won, but to escape the empire fully, you will need to continue fleeing. I…I do not believe those from Mevia can return. Surely the empire will re-hunt you."

A few tired nods were given. A woman with wild blonde hair, blood and dirt-matting the thick strands together, and the greenest eyes Shilah had ever beheld stood. "I am forever in your debt Princess Shilah, and my house will repay." Those untrusting eyes turned to the man behind her. "And yours Lachlan Ravenswood. I am Ivory Markham, and I am a high duchess of the house of Ellesmere from the kingdom of Caelum. I only need to travel to the waters which I can feel only a mile away, and I will escape to my realm."

As Shilah understood it, Caelum—the kingdom of water was mostly under the vast oceans of Amagarie, with only a small portion of that kingdom above ground.

Ivory glanced at the people behind her. "Those of you who wish to escape Mevia are welcome to travel with me to my home. My holdings are vast, and there is ample space for everyone. I will try my best to offer protection to those who are weaker. Though the healing herbs from the witch helped,

I am not at full strength. My kingdom also possesses the elixir of life, and with a sip, you will be restored to full health and powers if you'd possessed any. I will open my home to you for as long as needed."

Several people stood and moved closer to the high duchess, their relief palpable. The witch stepped forward. "I will provide a cloaking spell for everyone. Returning to your family is dangerous. It is certain the empire's warriors will be watching. But the cloaking spell will hide you from them, even if they are before you. It will only last for seven days, but it will give you the opportunity to visit your family and assure them of your safety or even convince them to flee the empire with you to another kingdom."

Everyone surged toward the witch and the high duchess. Shilah almost wept at the profound hope shining through their auras. Amirah started her incantation, and the survivors' aura begun vanishing under the cloaking spell. A stir came through her mind.

"You did this," Kala said, pride evident in her tone. *"You saved them."*

Shilah glanced toward the tree her sister leaned on, and then made her way over. She gathered her into her arms and hugged her. "I love you, Kala. How brave you've been."

"I love you too. I saw you…kissing him."

Shilah stilled in the cage of her sister's arms.

"I could feel the desire you had for him through our link. I've never felt anything like it," Kala whispered. "How can you feel so much for a creature like him?"

She released her sister, and stared at her, unable to explain the madness and the hunger which had seized her. Kala's eyes were turbulent with fear and uncertainty.

"Do we travel to Caelum with everyone?"

A ripple of dark power came from Lachlan. Of course, with his enhanced senses he heard her sister. She glanced around to where he had been leaning with deceptive ease against a tree trunk. Somewhere between fearing death at his hand and escaping the dungeons, she had lost a part of herself to this monster of darkness, to this man, to this warrior, and Shilah doubted she would ever reclaim it.

The awareness was terrifying. Exhilarating.

As if he felt her stare, his eyes snapped open—dark swirling pits of possessive fury.

"No," she whispered, knowing he would hear. "We travel to the Darkage."

A cry tore from Kala, and before Shilah could explain, shadows and darkness coated her senses, and her breathing choked off as he moved with unparallel speed with her away from everyone. She buried her face in his neck, so she could breathe, and in the grey shadowed world, she could see the shadows taking her sister, the Queen's blades, and the witch with them.

12

The Darkage—the kingdom of darkness and shadows
Kerberos—Castle of the deep—main stronghold of
the king

The unrelenting darkness was overpowering to those Lachlan rescued. Their fear fed him, even as he moved with unparallel speed through the mountains of Mevia toward the wastelands separating the borders of the seven kingdoms. He used his shadows to create a great winged creature which the rescued people rode on. His mate clung to him, her face hidden against his throat, her heart pounding against her breastbone. A journey that would take other Amagarians days, Lachlan covered in several minutes as he headed to the Castle of the deep, the main stronghold of King Gidon. He spun with the shadows to the western keep, aware they would feel the brutal wash of his might as he drew close. He moved through closed doors as the shadows bent around them and deposited the Darkans to the healing chamber. Then with another blast of power and speed, he dropped the witch, the Queen's blades and his mate's sister in a room where his king paced. Lachlan did not wait, the need to care and protect his mate paramount. He took her with the shadows to the body of water underneath the mountains of the castle.

Lachlan's mate's body felt warm and soft and so giving against his. He lowered her into the heated pools deep underground his king's castle, basking in her sigh of pleasure. The caves were quite large and wide, with several caverns, and he took her to the deepest underground one where veins of silver and gold carpeted the floor of the pool creating a shimmering effect on the surface of the water. There were several other pockets of small water pools scattered about with layers of rocks around them. Large crystalline formations jutted from the walls and from the high ceilings and rose from the floor.

Her eyes darted around. "Where is my sister?"

"Your sister and the others are being taken care of. They are in the dining area with my king and company. Princess Saieke should now be reuniting with her Queen's blades, and your sister and the witch will be offered all hospitality."

"And your people?"

"I delivered them to the healer in King's palace."

He felt her unease rise then dissipate. He suddenly felt relief and humor over their *lei,* and the tension stole from her body. "You speak with your sister?"

"Yes. I never thought of Darkans as hospitable. It is a refreshing notion," she said as her gaze roamed around before settling on the walls of the caves which had several fierce depictions of man and beasts struggling for dominion. A massive sculpture of a three-headed monster was mounted above the steps. Below it, a mass of writhing snakes, their mouths open with swords jutting out from an eight-headed serpent, a black ridged back dragon spewing black flames, and a massive chimera—a fierce creature with the head and body of a Lyon, the wings of a dragon and the tail of a serpent.

"What is it?"

"The Cerberus is the sigil of our king, and the other beasts are those of his enforcers. The Leviathan with its army of snakes represent my house, this fierce winged creature is a Dracan and represent my friend and fellow enforcer Drac El Kyn's house, and the chimera, represent another friend and enforcer Talon Merinus's house."

"It's macabre but compellingly beautiful." Those shockingly beautiful eyes leveled on him. "You made a promise, Lachlan Ravenswood, of fulfilling whatever desire beats in my heart. I want warriors to return with me to my kingdom. They will return as soon as I've established order."

"It shall be done."

"I would not expect such aid to my realm without recompense. I will offer a fair trade for the warriors you'll gift me."

"I shall expect none. You are mine to protect."

He heard the stutter of her heart and scented the uncertainty that flavored the air.

The rigid tension which had held her while he flowed with the shadows to his kingdom now completely melted away. Her stomach gave an alarming rumble, and he stepped into the shadows moving with speed to the main kitchen of the castle and reappeared within a second with a plate of fruits and roasted meat.

"You can eat first mate or clean your body."

His princess glanced at the platter of food, then peered up at him. "I would prefer to remove the dirt and blood from my body."

She paused staring at him as if waiting for something he obviously should be aware of.

"What is it, mate?"

"Do you not intend to turn away?"

"I am already familiar with every curve of your body, mate, there is no need to be shy." Still sensing her hesitation, he projected the images of her naked before him in the emperor's room and how she appeared to him as he'd kissed and pleased her with his fingers.

A blush washed over her body, and she sank lower into the depth of the water and pulled the tattered sari from her body and threw it onto the stone floor. Then she sank deep, swimming like a water nymph to the bottom before resurfacing. A few minutes passed in silence as she lathered her face with a rose scented fragrance, before dipping deep into the heated pool once again. This time when she surfaced, she met his gaze.

"I get the sense that when you refer to me as your mate, you do not mean for a night of…bedding." Her voice was low, trembling, and his heart turned over in his chest.

Hunger clawed at him, creating an urgent, intense wave of lust. "I do not."

Carefully avoiding his eyes, she reached for the scented oil on the rocks and lathered her skin and hair. Her skin looked rose-petal soft and inviting. "Where are we? At your home?"

He lowered himself to his haunches, watching her. She studiously avoided his gaze and the frantic pulse at the base of her throat tripped even faster. Yet he felt no fear and satisfaction rushed through his veins. At last, she was beginning to understand what she meant to him. "We are at Castle Kerberos. Home of Gidon Al Shra, King, and *Ricarkri* of the Darkage."

"I see."

As an Archduke for the realm, and friend to his king, Lachlan had a standing invitation to castle Kerberos along with his own personal chambers. He could only imagine the uproar he had left behind, but his first duty was the care of his woman.

"Do you live here?"

"No."

Her lips smiled briefly, and it was the most beautiful thing he'd seen in a long time. It made him feel warm.

She huffed out a small irritated breath. "Are you always this succinct?"

"No."

She waited, and he just watched.

"Then where do you live?"

"I am an Archduke of the Darkage."

"What does that mean?"

He really liked her curiosity about him and his way of life. The pleasure that rippled inside his chest was unfamiliar but welcoming. "Our kingdom is divided into four provinces, and at each helm is an Archduke. I govern the east, Drac El Kyn sits on the seat of the North, and Talon Merinus at the south and Gidon Al Shar sits on the throne of the West, but he is also king of all. In my province, there are three million citizens. I must govern them by the laws of the Darkage and train the warriors of the east to be ready when they are called to arms to defend our kingdom."

"In my world, your title would be that of a prince. When I first crossed through my portal to Amagarie, I thought to approach King Gidon for the aid I seek. The rumors and history of the dark ones were offputting, they spoke of a kingdom that was awash in constant bloodletting and war. So, I went to the Mevian emperor. How odd that the first moment I feel a sense of safety since I left my world is at this place?"

"And what aid did you seek?"

She considered him for several seconds. "I wanted an army."

Something dark stirred inside him. "Why?"

There was a slight hesitation, then she said, "My brother, his wife, and children were slain."

Profound pain darted through her, and the taste of it was repulsive to him.

"We…my advisors, and I did not know who committed the foul deed. An investigation was launched, but we found no one. The ebb and flow of life continued, and a few months later, on the day of my coronation…" Her throat worked, and she visibly composed herself. "On that day, as the High Priestess of Dxyriah was about to place the crown on my head, my home was attacked. I barely escaped with my life. And the man who'd attacked my home and assassinated my family now sits on my throne."

"And you want vengeance?"

"I want justice."

"False morality serves as the only distinction between the two."

His princess glanced sideways at him and then quickly averted her eyes, her long lashes hiding her expression.

"Tell me more, my mate."

A flush worked its way up her neck and to her face. "I would like to discuss something else."

"I will indulge it."

Something fiery sparkled in her diamond eyes before amusement curved her lips. "You are arrogant Lachlan Ravenswood."

His princess shifted, gliding the oils over her face, throat, and down her body below the water. "Why am I your mate?" Her face was averted, the curtain of silver-white hair concealing her expression from him.

A pulse of anxiety came from her but no fear.

"Fate has decreed it so."

Her firm, elegant jaw tightened visibly. "But what does it mean?"

"By the laws of the Darkage, you are forever mine, by the primal call of the beast I am eternally enslaved, and if I should will it, so are you."

He felt it then, the slow spiral of terror before she subdued the emotion. She made no response, and he was content to watch her as she dipped into the well of the water washing away the battle of the day. Several minutes passed in silence, and he watched and waited.

She faced him then, her skin flushed pink, her wet hair clinging to her body with heart jerking loveliness. Water droplets beaded on her shoulders. A small rivulet coursed across her collarbone.

"How are you so certain I am your mate? Could…could there be another?"

How hopeful she sounded that such a possibility existed.

"There is a fire in my soul to have you by my side always. I want to know what makes you happy and provide it to you. I am a captive to the sensation and needs you rouse in me. My darkness is pleased by your light and your scent. With every beat of your heart, I want to sink my fangs in you and consume your essence and make it a part of me. Your scent is that of peace, of solace, of promise and belonging to something other than darkness. Only a mate has such a power over one such as me, and there can only be one."

She looked dazed, staring back at him, the scent of her pussy, heated and female, drew him, making his mouth water for her taste. His princess waded from the water and made her way up the stone steps and made her way over to him. He loved the way she moved, the sway of her hips, her purposeful yet sensual strides. She was so beautiful she took his breath away. Her high rounded breasts, gently dipping stomach, and flaring hips formed the most breath-taking body he'd ever seen. She drew a deep, shuddering breath as she halted before him. "You are a fierce and formidable warrior. Despite your savagery and even though I do not understand you…" She touched the tattoo on his chest, tracing the outline of a massive claw.

He closed his eyes and savored the exquisite feel of her touch.

She stared at him with a mixture of longing and apprehension. "I want you too, Lachlan Ravenswood. But I will belong to no man."

Her soft sensual notes slid inside of him, teasing and tempting him to devour her. He pushed the long fall of silken hair from her face and back over her shoulder, not wanting any of her body hidden from him. "Your eyes appear as if the stars are forever in their depths."

"You are trying to seduce me," she murmured huskily.

He touched her hair, rubbing the wet silky strands between his fingers. "I only spoke the truth."

"If I were to give in to the temptation beating in my blood I can sense I would lose myself to you. I do not have the power of foresight like my sister, Kala. But I sense it with every fiber of my being Lachlan Ravenswood. I cannot afford such an attachment, and I will be no man's slave. Not even for this hunger burning in my soul for you," she whispered. "I cannot stay in the Darkage. I must return to my world. I cannot fail my people."

Her eyes were pools of denial and pain, pleading for understanding. And that anguish hit him like a mighty blow.

"By the laws of your realm, must I accept your claim?"

Fury swept through him. Ugly. Dangerous. Ashes and darkness swirled at the edge of his thoughts. She sensed it, but she did not flinch from him, meeting his regard steadily. The idea of letting her go lanced pain somewhere in his tattered soul. He had never thought he would feel that for a woman. At the sight of her looking small and fragile and apprehensive, every protective instinct he had stirred. A fierce need to protect her welled up in him, even from the darkness prowling in him to dominate her, to bend her to his will. It was so strong it shook him. He dragged her close, pulled her into the shelter of his body, needing to be close to her.

He kissed her because he had to. Framing her face with his hands, he took possession of her mouth. He was without mercy as he slanted his lips over hers. A broken cry of need escaped her as she responded with wantonness. He savored the taste of her—hot, exotic, the promise of wet, fiery passion. His thoughts spilled to her through their link, of him splitting her wide, and her riding his tongue, soaking her pussy with anticipation before he claimed her. He wanted everything about her imprinted on his soul, so he would forever remember the taste and feel of her. His mind was merged deeply in hers, feeding off her pleasure, heightening it as she intensified his.

The scent of her arousal began to intoxicate him, to fill his senses with tormented desires that could not be slaked now. She pulled her lips from his and pressed her forehead against his chest. "You must stop kissing me."

He could easily smell her scent calling to him with her readiness. The smell of her arousal was like a dagger to his gut. So why the resistance? "Why?"

"I do not need to give a reason," she murmured and pushing away from him. *I cannot think when you touch me.*

He caught the edges of her thoughts before she pulled from their connection.

"I can smell your arousal. I can hear your heart beating for me."

She faltered into absolute stillness, her eyes widened. "You can smell me?" she croaked, her entire body flushing a becoming pink.

"Yes."

"You smell like fire and sweetness, and my mouth waters for a taste of you."

He pushed the image at her, of him before her on his knees, her pussy on his tongue as he lapped at her wet folds. His mate blushed even more. Before she could reply, he took her into the shadows and into his chambers on the fifth floor of the castle. They spilled into the room, and she glanced around dazedly.

"Your speed rivals those who have the skill of teleportation on my world. You are very impressive Lachlan Ravenswood. And this is a beautiful chamber."

She moved away from him, striving to appear unconcerned but he could see the fine trembling along her elegant spine. Nervousness flowed through their connection, and he sensed she was desperately fighting to deny the arousal thrumming through her body. She craved him, even if she did not understand why, and the awareness filled him with heady satisfaction. The scent of her wetness and spice had his cock hardening on a pleasurable pulse.

"I must meet with my king. I have delayed enough. When I took the witch in the shadows, I also collected the bags you had packed. They are on the bed."

She spun around to face him. "I thought…" Her eyes glowed with something dark and mysterious.

He could barely breathe with wanting, but how he wanted to take his mate could not be done in a few minutes or an hour. The night would be theirs when he claimed her. He moved with speed behind her and allowed his hands to settle at her hips, his fingers curling over her fragile bones lightly. "I will return soon."

Her lips parted, but he stepped into the shadow space and roiled with the darkness to enter the council room where he sensed Gidon, Drac, and Talon—the men Lachlan respected and considered his closest friends. He stepped from the shadows, and his king lifted his attention from the scrolls he'd been analyzing.

"You have joined us at last, Lachlan," Gidon said striding toward him. "It was not like you to drop visitors at our feet and disappear before we got the chance to—"

His king faltered, violence settling on his face like a second skin, the tattoos of his three-headed demon beast—the Cerberus—shifting on his forearms and under his raven black undershirt.

Without his mate's presence, without touching her mind, darkness blossomed through Lachlan as the anchor to his sanity melted away.

"You have bonded," Talon said, rising from the chair he'd been seated in with untamed grace. He moved closer, his piercing green eyes watchful and wary. "How did this happen, my friend? I know of your vows made in fire and ice that you would not allow your beast in your life."

Drac lowered his goblet carefully, and stood, canting his head to the side. "What happened?" He asked, his tone devoid of all emotions.

Lachlan could sense the stirring monster in his friend, but Lachlan did not shift his gaze away from his King. The immense pleasure of Lachlan's darkness sang through his veins, and he relished in it, the bloodletter in Lachlan surging to life on a violent wave.

Gidon stepped forward, the tattoo on his skin rippling to life, menace covering him like an entity.. They stood only a foot apart, and darkness slid against darkness. Lachlan slammed his closed fist across his chest in salute. But it was the demon beast within his king whom he saluted, for its well of power was unfathomable and crackling in the air with a blatant challenge.

"What are you?" Gidon asked, the question pulling Drac and Talon to his side, a wall of protective power.

Lachlan looked down at his body with a brief, humorless smile. Their flat, lethal gazes slid over him, noting the changes in his body, the claws of his hands, the tattoo of his monster, and the changes to his eyes.

"You have no shield," Talon said, eyes flaring in shock. Tiny embers smoldered in the depths of Talon's eyes as his beast stirred.

"I am what I am," Lachlan said, unable to prevent the dark rumble of menace in his voice.

His friends watched him, their expressions blanked, but he could feel the coiled readiness and the stirrings of their demons. He inhaled deeply, feeling a queer sense of belonging he'd never felt before.

"You are not a *Senji*," Gidon said, his silver eyes piercing and calculating.

"I am not lost to the monster." He was the monster.

"And your loyalty?" Drac demanded, his eyes cold and flat.

Lachlan slammed his fist once again across his chest. "To Remelius, then and now."

Black chakra burst from Gidon and settled on his body like a second skin, as the demon in him reacted to Lachlan's vow.

"And who is Remelius?" Talon snarled.

Gidon stepped forward and held out his forearm which Lachlan clasped.

"My demon," his king said, his voice a brutal throb of power and savagery as he and his beast accorded. "Hail, Orochi, high king of the serpents."

Something inside him contracted to hear his other name on the lips of his king. Talon sent Gidon a sharp assessing look as their king acknowledged the demon bonded within

Lachlan, for it hinted of power and knowledge they'd not known their king and friend possessed.

Lachlan glanced at Drac and said, "And to you Abaddon, hail." Speaking directly to the beast buried in Drac El Kyn. Immediately the tattoo on his skin—the fearsome winged Dracan shifted, its serpentine eyes opening, and darkness beheld darkness.

Talon had stepped back. "What are you?" his voice was more curious than wary, but Lachlan could sense the rising cruelty in Talon as he shifted the hold he had on his beast. "We do not know the name origins of demon names," Talon continued. "How do you know it?"

Another wave of power crested through Lachlan. "I am what I am." He met his King's eyes unflinchingly. "My loyalty is yours then and now, Remelius, and Gidon..." Memories washed through Lachlan of running through the snow of the high mountains of the Darkage, training together and honing their *taijui* skills, and the many nights they had dined together and spoken of the many ways in which they could lift their people to prosperity and peace. The darkness seeded through his bones and blood tried to bury the memories of how his friend had fought with him atop a mountain coated in black ice as Lachlan tried to find his sanity. But they roiled through his mind, anchoring him, and reminding him of the love and respect he had for his king. "And you Gidon will always have my friendship and loyalty."

That seemed to satisfy Gidon for he nodded, a smile curving his lips, his eyes forever filled with cunning glinting with an odd sort of satisfaction. And Talon's malice receded.

"Come, let's break bread, drink wine, and you tell me of the witch Amirah and the Serangite Kala you dumped on us. They were given a chamber each with servants to wait upon them. The Serangite watches us with fear and refuses to speak. The witch is with child, and I can sense the need in her to flee from us, and I can also feel the power in the child. Its origin is of darkness."

"I believe the father of her child is the hunter."

Gidon faltered, shadows crossing his face. "And she is unclaimed by him?"

"They may not be mated." While rare, it was possible for non-mated Darkans to breed with each other, and even others not of their kind. "They met at the Taryllion Inn, and somehow became lovers."

"Curious," Talon said. "The hunter is not known to allow anyone close."

For he was an abomination to some of their people, hated by his own kind for possessing two monsters within him, and a force only a few could reckon with. The hunter gave his loyalty to Gidon, uncaring to connect or blend with the society who had cast him aside as a fledgling, and it was for that reason he was the leader of the cadre of five whose sole job was to hunt and kill those Darkans taken over by their demons, the *Senjis*.

"It is interesting she got close enough for a bedding," Drac drawled, falling into step beside Gidon as they flowed from the chamber and out into the hallway.

"I will send word to him that she is here," Gidon said, sliding with the shadows, traveling to a high balcony overlooking his kingdom.

They followed, and Lachlan moved to stand beside his king, but not too close. A warning still hummed beneath his skin, and the darkness in him stretched, burning the memories away, inviting him to partake in murder and mayhem.

As if Gidon sensed the rising demon in Lachlan, his king shifted to face him, and merciless silver eyes ensnared Lachlan.

"Much has happened in the few weeks you've been gone. We've learned Emperor Khan is working tirelessly to prevent the Nurian King from consolidating any more power. The Emperor sees Nuria as a threat, and Darkans working with him attacked Nuria. In her fight to save the king, it was revealed Tehdra El Kyn is his mate. We have received a formal declaration from King Ajali claiming her as his consort only a few hours past." Unholy amusement glinted in Gidon's eyes. "He found it fit to point out in his missives that he considered all Darkans but Tehdra enemies of his realm and trading between our borders will remain closed."

King Ajali had been a powerful stumbling block in Gidon's vision of changing their kingdom's wealth and fostering trade with other realms to enhance the prosperity of the Darkage which had seen no economic growth in centuries. A stain of treachery followed their people, and they were reviled. Gidon planned to show the other realms they were more than their beasts and the merciless reputation that accompanied them. And a large part of his plan was contingent on presenting their people as rational beings who desired peace and wealth like the other kingdoms.

But the prejudice of the other kingdoms was so entrenched, they could not be told this, they had to be shown Darkans were people who loved and laughed with families too. And Gidon vowed to show them that side of his people.

Lachlan peered over the jungle like courtyard below. Great torches scattered about keeping the darkness at bay and washing the balcony where they stood in white light. The air seemed crisp and fresh, the night a cool blanket. A child's joyous, and unfettered laughter rode on the air, pulling a curious smile to Lachlan's lips. A young boy played with a *kruwak,* a carnivorous bird, whose claws rivaled Lachlan's own. What would it be like to see his mate's belly swollen with their child? Something inside his chest twisted, and unfamiliar sensations poured through him. They felt odd, as if they weakened him, for his heart raced in a manner not felt in centuries. "Are we certain King Ajali and Tehdra have mated?" Lachlan asked.

"Despite how strange it might seem to us, their mating is absolute," Drac drawled, leaning his hip against the balcony stone edge. "My princess and I were in Nuria ourselves only a few hours past, she said she felt the love the King had for Tehdra, and I witnessed King Ajali's reluctance to bring her any harm."

Lachlan considered him. "In our history, we've never seen Darkans finding their mates with others not of our kind."

"And now we've got two," Talon said, scrubbing a hand over his face. "Our elders are still researching the archives, trying to figure out what changes we can expect from the bonding in the non Darkans."

Three, Lachlan said silently, thinking of his woman in the heated cavern waters. How badly he'd wanted to join her. The need to slake his desire in her body was all-consuming, and it had taken every discipline and control he'd learned over the centuries to not take her in the caves. At times, her thoughts spilled over to him even when she tried to keep him out. She thought of him carnally, of him taking her with a tenderness that was foreign to the violence stamped in his bones. Yet she made him want to offer it to her, to strip her naked and worship her with his tongue.

He glanced down at the wickedly curved claws prodding from his nails. He would rip her to shreds touching her with hands like these. He had been indelibly altered. His beast wasn't a taunting voice in his head, a chakra that he had to be careful in how much power he allowed. He and his monster were one in the truest sense, their chakras now inseparable in a manner Lachlan knew no other in their history had ever experienced before.

He tilted his head to the sky, unfathomably at a loss what to do with his all too fragile mate. A large *gheelle*, with iridescent green wings, flew overhead, echoing a fierce cry through the valley as it hunted.

"I've learned much in the Empire. The Emperor had the lexicon of our beasts' origins and the various powers they manifested. Someone took it from our archives and handed it to him. For a brief time, I was locked in the dungeon, and three of our people were also there. They were young Darkans unable to fight against someone as ruthless and powerful as the emperor and his army. He has tortured our people without fear of reprisal. He is hiding his vile actions behind your vision of not starting your reign with slaughter and war."

"The Kingmaker has promised our kingdom my assassination is inevitable, and he has someone waiting to replace me. I will not anticipate the coming of the kingmaker. I will hunt him," Gidon murmured, savagery flowering through his chakra.

Lachlan lowered his eyes to Gidon. The Kingmaker was a legend within the seven kingdoms, his identity a mystery, with no recorded pictures of him in their vast archives, yet his existence was undisputed. Whenever he stirred, the terror and bloodshed that generally bathe kingdoms were unmatched. He was lauded in all Amagarie, and it was rumored that the revolution that had nearly decimated Caelum—the kingdom of water—centuries ago, was because the kingmaker had helped Farron Irsa become king.

"Is this possible?" Lachlan demanded.

"Our friend has not been idle while you've been on your mission," Drac said, the monster in him humming to life. "It is rumored the kingmaker has a secret, one he would burn all the realms to protect for if this secret were uncovered, it would be the key to bring him to heel."

He could feel the dark hunger stirred through Gidon at

the thrill of hunting something as dangerous as the kingmaker.

"What is it?"

Gidon's lips curved. "A daughter." His voice was a rumble of power and something shockingly carnal and predatory. "The rumor my *Tensuri* has uncovered is that the kingmaker has a daughter whom he values more than anything else. Her name is Sabine."

And if the King's *Tensuri* had unearthed it, the information was untainted, his team of six were the most merciless female warriors of their realm, their loyalty absolute, their life force bonded to him in eternal servitude. A choice they willingly entered, but whatever fate befell their king, they would also partake. Even now they were in the shadows, a protective force the enemy would have to reckon with if his Archdukes should fall in the bid to unearth him from his throne.

A burst of wind vibrated on the air, and Princess Saieke appeared on the high balcony. She rushed toward Lachlan and gripped his hands. Her eyes, the bluest he'd ever seen filled with tears, but her lips laughed, the sound enchanting with its happiness.

The menacing shadow in the corner smiled as he absorbed his woman's happiness. With her gentle femininity and iron-strong will, Princess Saieke was the perfect mate for the ruthless Drac El Kyn. "I cannot repay the service you have done me today Lachlan. My mind has finally eased that my Queen's Blades have been found alive. I've administered the healing elixir, and they are well. Kamu and Thyon will return to Boreas and their families soon, and it is because of you."

"It was my honor to liberate them for you, I trust you will now stop your moping."

Grinning she pulled him into a fierce hug, evidently

choosing not to comment on his altered appearance. Possibly a difficult thing for her to do. When he'd just met the princess one of the things he'd admired was her fierce inquisitive nature and kindness.

Something stirred in his mind. *"There is a woman in your arms, Lachlan Ravenswood."*

He stilled at the possessive bite in his mate's voice. Then he smiled, and his mate's rueful laughter brushed against their thread with intimate softness.

Princess Saieke sent him a curious frown before flashing with a burst of speed into the haven of her mate's arms. Drac cupped her cheeks and kissed her with unabashed hunger, uncaring of their audience. With a breathless laugh, she pulled away, curving more into his side, and faced them. "Princess Kala allowed me into her chamber. We spoke for a few minutes, and she is wonderful. I declare we shall be great friends. I believe she was relieved a non Darkan lived at the castle. She asked of her sister?" Saieke said with a pointed stare at Lachlan.

Everyone shifted their regards to him and waited.

Before he could proffer a reply, the walls of the castle shook as a piercing sound trumpeted over the hills from a great distance. In unison, it appeared as if all the winged creatures of the surrounding jungles took flight, reacting to the sonic waves booming across the sky in a shocking show of power, the message heralding the sound waves no one had anticipated. At least not for months, or possibly years to come.

Princess Saieke glanced at her mate, horror dawning on her face. "Is that what I think it is?" she murmured, swaying slightly.

Drac hugged her tighter, pulling her into the protective cage of his arms.

The sound came again, a trumpet blast that echoed in the

air for unending minutes, rolling over the seven kingdoms. It was the promise of slaughter and mayhem. A death knell for the weaker nations. A sound of retribution to those who had wronged its greatness.

The Empire of Mevia had declared war.

13

*E*yes the color of liquid mercury swirled with rage and power as Gidon overlooked the wild darkness of the land. "Something has pushed Emperor Khan to declare war before any nation anticipated. There has been no indication he would be moved to this. What has changed?"

"I must return to Boreas immediately," Princess Saieke said, pushing back her mass of red hair from her face with trembling hands. "The last Great War almost decimated my kingdom. They...*we* are not prepared for another war so soon."

Her whisper was dread-filled and echoed with fury.

"The kingdom of winds and mountains has an alliance with The Darkage, princess," Gidon said. "Your people will not suffer the same fate."

Denial and pain suffused her beautiful features. "But they *will* suffer. Thousands will suffer and die. The seven kingdoms have been at peace for years. Why is he doing this?"

"If anyone should have declared war it should have been King Ajali of Nuria for yesterday's attack on his kingdom.

What madness has taken hold of Emperor Khan?" Gidon growled, pacing like a caged beast.

"He has lost a key piece in his plot and machinations," Lachlan said with more calm than he felt, for fury churned in his gut at the threat to his mate.

Everyone stilled, and the floor of the high turret contracted at the wash of power swarmed the air.

"Speak," Gidon commanded.

As if she had been summoned by his king's will, the sweet flavor of earth and rain filled Lachlan's senses. He scented her, and she made no sound as she drew closer. Shilah stepped through the wide terraced window. Everyone on the high balcony stilled, and she hesitated in the face of so many Darkans staring at her.

She made a breath-taking picture in a dark green sari which bared her stomach and hung alluringly low on her rounded hips. Golden slippers encased delicate feet, and her mass of silver-white hair was piled atop her head. Wisps of hair escaped her topknot and framed her lovely features.

His snakes were curled around her upper arms like golden bracelets. She held his gaze, her eyes huge and heart-stoppingly vulnerable. There was a fear in her that he would never let her go, and she would be unable to escape and save her people. He was a dark shadow in her mind, and all negative thoughts rushed along their link, even though she tried to shut him out.

The sparkly depths of her eyes were reflecting so many emotions they took his breath and broke apart something unfathomable inside Lachlan. There was a primal, turbulent need in him to ravish his mate so thoroughly and so completely that she would never hunger to leave his side. He wanted her bound to him for all eternity

There have only been two laws identified which have any impact on a beast's behavior, and they both pertained to mating. The first law is that the demon mates for life. The second law not recorded anywhere and kept secret by all Darkans, a mate cannot be claimed without their consent. Everything in Lachlan could clamor to bind her to him forever, but if she did not accept his claim, he could not force her. Until she allowed the mating, he had no rights to cage her to his will, and even then, Lachlan knew she would fight any claiming that might override her sense of self. And he didn't want that. Her beauty was fragile, and she didn't have the physical prowess of Darkans or even Amagarians, but she had the heart of a warrior. Even if it was mystifyingly weakened by mercy and compassion.

The darkness in him stirred, and violence sang through his blood at the notion of losing her. There would be no light left within him, no reason to feel the warmth tumbling through his chest now, no reason to feel the desperate need to be different…to be gentle.

"And who is this?" Talon murmured, glancing from her to Lachlan.

He felt her mind search; it brushed at him like the wings of a delicate creature. *"I heard the sound of a gong. The walls of your chamber shook, and I felt along the thread that connected us that you were close, so I followed it…to here."*

Lachlan knew no one else saw the silver thread that connected their souls. He could reach out a finger and run along the bright silvery white thread with the darkness twisting sinuously over it. The thread led from his chest to hers, and it hummed, a vibration of peace and pleasure as she moved a bit closer to him.

His mate paused, shy a few feet from him, and glanced at his cadre of friends who did not disguise their unabashed curiosity.

"This is Princess Shilah. And it is for her the Empire has declared war."

Stillness blanketed everyone on the turret, and Lachlan dared not move.

"Why is she valuable to him?" his king demanded, the coldness emanating from him causing Lachlan's mate to shiver and pale.

"She is Princess Shilah of the house of Symonrah, rightful ruler of the kingdom of Dxyriah of Serange. She is an Imperial telepath with the power to demolish the psychic barrier between man and beast in Darkans. Not only is she able to shatter that barrier, but she is also half of the power needed to force the demon from its host into a corporeal form and place it under the control of the Empire of Mevia. Retrieving her will be the focus of the empire, and only death will come for those who think to hide her from the Empire's might."

His mate paled and stumbled back, bitter fear leaking from her. Pain and betrayal rode the wave, and she stared at him with widened eyes.

"What you claim is impossible," Talon snapped, scrubbing a hand over his face. "The kingmaker has promised a new leader for the Darkage, and that bastard is plotting with the empire to murder Gidon. And for what? So that he can torture our people for the power within us?"

"If the Emperor had Darkans in his army, whom he had absolute control of, his might would be unmatched," Drac said, his gaze hard and piercing on Princess Shilah, whose anxiety was like a living entity as she fed them with her fear. "I surmise my friend; the princess is the reason you and your demon has merged in a way I've never seen in our kingdom. She broke your vow and your mind at the order of the emperor."

Retribution throbbed in his friend's voice, and Shilah stepped back a few paces.

"Princess Shilah and the witch Amirah are the ones who

directed and pulled the demon beasts that attacked the Kingdom of Nuria from its host."

The shocked silence was profound.

"Why is she alive?" Drac asked with palpable menace.

Princess Saieke gasped, and Lachlan felt the promise of death leaking from Gidon. His king's eyes were those of a predator waiting, watching, promising retaliation. He had judged Shilah, found her guilty, and her death was imminent.

Lachlan held out his hand to her. Her mouth trembled as she hurried over to his side, and she placed her hand in his. He carefully gathered his mate in his arms, barely holding onto the rage beating through his soul. It was unexpected and even unsettling, this desire to be gentle with her. She stirred, and he glanced down. How pale she seemed. His princess was so small and delicate, so curved and soft. She was light to his darkness, compassion to his merciless nature. Yet so powerful in her own right.

He breathed in her fragrance, absorbing the feel of her petite, curvy body against him. Nothing had ever felt so right to Lachlan. Despite her light and purity tethering him, violence blossomed through him and his monster twisted across his skin, its eyes snapping open. "Anyone who tries to harm her will only know pain and suffering," he said, his voice hissing with feral undercurrents.

She tightened her fingers around his. He could hear her heart, the rhythm too loud.

"By the laws of the Darkage, I claim Shilah Symonrah as my mate," he said, his voice low, but the tone one of absolute authority and the darkest of promise. "My life, my honor, my fidelity, my rage and my all belongs to her for eternity. A threat to her is a declaration of war. And I will answer the call of the empire and anyone who wishes to harm her with a message of my own—death and suffering which has never been endured."

∼

WITH A SENSE of shock and fear, Shilah realized that Lachlan's loyalty was utterly hers and belonged to no one else. *"Lachlan."* Spoken along their unique pathway, his name came out so husky, her voice shaking. In that instant, she accepted Lachlan would kill his king if he were a threat to her. Her heart denied such a betrayal, yet her soul rejoiced. She could hear the steady rhythm of his heart, a reassuring beat. The warrior behind her was not frightened at the danger that suddenly rode the air at his brutal, unshakable promise. She stared at him, unable to prevent herself from moving closer to his heat. The king watched them, his silver eyes cold and cunning, entirely at odds with the small smile of amusement about his mouth. The hair on her arms stood up, and a frisson of fear slid down her spine.

A shadow shifted from the corner of the balcony, and a man stepped into the light, a ravishing red-haired female by his side. Shilah blinked, her eyes darting to the cruelly sensual lips of the man and the black mark on his pale cheek which looked like a claw, finally accepting that all Darkans were handsome and downright terrifying.

"But not as handsome as me."

Shilah glanced up at Lachlan, disbelief pounding through her. *"Are you making a jest...at this moment, Lachlan Ravenswood?"*

"He is Drac El Kyn. My friend. They are all my friends."

His voice moved in her mind—soft, tender even. So at odds with the harsh brutality of his handsome features. She could feel no amusement, the buzz of raw power about her slapped at her skin like a thousand knives. Their lives were in danger and from the very people he called friends. The malevolence in the air, shifted like a tide, pouring over her skin and sinking into the cervices of her soul.

She was unprepared for the feeling of his gentle fingers stroking her skin.

"If *anyone* thinks to harm her, my retribution will be etched in the history of the seven kingdoms," he said, his voice a terrible iciness with its complete lack of feeling.

Talon let out his breath in a long, slow hiss. "They will come for her," he murmured, observing him. "They will not stop until she is back at the Empire."

"Let them come. Examples must be made."

Shilah felt as if he'd wrapped her in a protective cloak of violence. A threat to her would be suppressed mercilessly. Shilah did not like the fear that lingered within her. She did not know him or understand his world and the brutal code he lived by. A deep terror stayed inside that if she allowed herself too close to this man, that chill of violence and rage would entwine around her soul, and that would be the sure way to unfold her sister's prophecy.

Queen of darkness you shall become.

Lachlan was there instantly, flooding her mind with warmth and reassurance, feelings that must be strange to him, but here he was providing them for her. Unable to help herself she peered up at him, sinking into the promise she saw in his eyes, wanting to desperately return it. The madness of it did not escape her, but she hungered to be what he wanted even if for a moment in time. His mate. Even though she did not understand its full implication.

Somehow it felt important, more important than any love she'd ever dreamed. But a connection she'd always desired. The only thing she was absolutely certain of was that it promised passion in his arms and a reprieve from the duty that sat upon her shoulders always tormenting her with doubts and fears of ever saving her people. A reprieve from the knowledge that as an Impure it was against the laws of her land to ever marry and have children. She envisioned a lifetime of loneliness. The weight of it would crush her if she gave into the feelings. The promised pleasure was something she hungered to taste, but the man currently present was so different from the one she'd had her brief encounter within Mevia.

His slow smile made her tremble, and her sigh of need and acceptance vibrated on the air as his mouth descended to take possession of hers. It was a brand. One that seared her insides with molten heat. It truly was frightening how she reacted to him.

Before she could fully respond, he lifted his head and faced his friends. "I present my *lekia*—my mate."

She waited for a heartbeat until her pulse settled, then stepped forward and dipped into a brief curtsy. "It is good to meet you all," she said meeting their gazes with an arrogant tilt of her head. She was the princess of Dxyriah and the mate of Lachlan Ravenswood, she would not cower.

The red-haired female was the only one to offer her a warm smile, and then they bowed, and Shilah was almost charmed by their elegant synchronicity. The king stepped forward, his measure of her chilling. A kiss of danger whispered across the back of her neck, a faint disturbing prickle as if talons and claws scraped against her skin. She lifted her chin. "King Gidon Al Shar, I am deeply regretful I allowed my desperation to obscure my honor. In doing so, I dishonored the sense of justice my parents instilled in me, and I hurt people who were under your protection. I offer you reparations."

"Recompense will be paid," the king said.

"And I shall pay it," Lachlan said.

"As her mate, it is your right," Gidon murmured, assessing her closely.

Shilah could not imagine what they could demand of Lachlan, but the need to protect him burned in her veins, dominating all else. "I am responsible for my actions, and I would be the worst sort of...of...mate to allow this man to suffer for my failures. I made a decision, it has consequences, and I will pay the debt demanded by your nation with honor."

A growl rumbled from Lachlan and amusement glinted in the king's eyes.

"I do not require flesh and blood Princess Shilah, merely a trading alliance with your kingdom. Serange is notorious for being stingy with their trading borders, and none of the seven kingdoms can trade within your walls or enter your portals. The gatekeepers are reputed to be merciless in defending your world."

She curtsied, shocked at his courteous and forgiving nature. "It would be my honor to broker talks of trade between our realms when I reclaim my kingdom."

Dark Amusement flowered in her mind from Lachlan. *"King Gidon is not forgiving, he is cunning and manipulative. Our mates are treasured more than our lives. He would not do anything to hurt you."*

The king nodded, admiration swirling in those silver orbs.

Lachlan's incredible heat flushed against her back and she leaned into him, uncaring if it made her seem weak.

"I take leave with my mate. I will call upon the Western Keep tomorrow," he drawled.

"Stay," Gidon commanded. "Drac and his mate, and Talon and his mate intend to stay for dinner. I invite you and Princess Shilah to do the same. The war council will need to convene, and your presence is needed."

Shilah smiled tentatively. "We would be honored—"

"We leave for the Eastern keep now," Lachlan said, his tone rough, sensual, and possessive.

"Why?" Talon asked with an arch of his brow. "My mate

has wanted to speak with you, and it has been weeks since we've all dined together."

She felt Lachlan stare at the top of her head and she glanced up at him. Lust blasted from him and raked against her senses, and her eyes widened. With a gasp, she snapped her gaze forward to his friends. A blush engulfed her body for she suspected they knew Lachlan's intention.

Her heart thundered, and with trembling hands, she pushed a tendril of her hair behind her ear. He planned to ravish her once he took her away. She was not ready, Shilah doubted she would ever be prepared to take a lover as brutal and uncompromising as the man behind her. Without warning, shadows swallowed her, and she was gathered into his arms. She wrapped her legs high around his waist, hooked them behind his back, gripped his shoulders, burying her face into the warmth of his neck as they moved with unparalleled speed.

"War has just been declared, Lachlan Ravenswood. Should you not be meeting with your king and rallying your warriors," she said desperately.

"Armies do not march on the first call to war, my mate. Kingdoms will begin assessing their strengths and weaknesses, securing their borders, and collecting intelligence about the enemies in preparation for the upcoming battles. Alliances will be formed, possible Allegiances— joint heirship of kingdoms by two rulers marrying, for the most powerful will win the war that is fated to tear the seven kingdoms apart.

"This is because I ran, I—"

"War has been trembling on the air long before you arrived on Amagarie. This call now by Mevia is a show of force by the empire to frighten those who harbor you for their might is great. Their population is almost three hundred million citizens, and they have an alliance with

Avindar—the kingdom of lightning, and that kingdom has over two hundred million. The Darkage in comparison only holds fourteen million people, Boreas one hundred fifty-two million, Aria one hundred and ten. The size of Caelum is currently unknown for their kingdom is under the vast oceans of Amagarie. As of such the empire army is greater than all the six kingdoms' combined forces."

Shock and sorrow tore through her. "I am so sorry," she whispered.

"You will not apologize again, mate. The Empire has no right to you, and I will protect you," the menace in his voice echoing once again with unfathomable power.

Sudden fear tore through her for him. "Once I leave the Empire will cease hunting me."

He made no reply, and with a sense of profound shock, she caught the edge of his thought that resolved he would never let her go.

She suppressed the need to reach out to her sister, not wanting to share her fear, when Kala had enough to shoulder. The visions haunted Kala, and drained her energy, for she constantly searched the future for another outcome. Shilah had reached for her earlier and had almost wept with relief to find her sister slept, resting peacefully for the first time in weeks. For that gift alone, Shilah would repay King Gidon in wealth from her kingdom.

Shilah buried her face in his neck and held onto him as he traveled with them for miles. Those minutes passed in silent anticipation, and with a peculiar vulnerability beating through her. He stirred in her mind, flooding her with warmth, and hunger, and the burning need to belong to him in every way. Just for a moment, a reprieve from the lonely existence she had consigned her heart and life to as she served her people.

Panicked, she could barely breathe, her lungs burning for

air. *"I feel scared."* The sense of tears was thick in her voice now, and she hated the anxiety searing through her. He felt so raw, so primal, so unstoppable.

He remained silent in the cage of her mind, but she could feel the fire of lust rising in him, sweeping along her senses in a wave of pure fire. His arms tightened around her, and the darkness and shadows danced, painting the blurred world with strange silver-grey auras as he moved with unchecked speed. He scattered soothing kisses to her jaw, along the edge of it, down her neck.

Then he said, "We will wait until you are sure of me, mate. Then I will take you…there."

Raw, provocative images of his cock bruising her lips as she sucked his thick length deep, of her riding him with wanton hunger, of him gorging on her blood while he took her from behind with primal force. It wasn't fear that filled her at his violent sensuality. It was a deep ache of want and complex needs. Her nipples became tight and tender, desperate for the stroke of his tongue over the tender tips, the sucking heat of his mouth as it would travel down, and the rasp of his teeth over her clitoris. But beyond the temptation of desire, there was another emotion pouring through her. A thing she'd never imagined feeling with a man like Lachlan Ravenswood.

His promise felt forged in iron. His arms felt safe.

And in that moment, she knew she could love this fierce creature with every emotion in her soul.

14

A few minutes later, they came to a stop, and the shadows retreated. Everything stilled—the surrounding forest holding its breath. There was a winding pathway leading to a castle perched on a hill in the distance. Dozens of torches lit the cobbled trail, and she moved forward onto the path, not questioning why he hadn't taken her directly to the castle. It wasn't that she was uncurious, but her throat felt too dry for speech, too many nerves thrummed in her veins for the coherent formation of words.

Shilah sauntered ahead, and the walkway gradually steepened. She could feel his eyes on her and every single step she took sent more heat rushing through her body. Though the great torches helped her see the cobbled path before her, it did not do much in illumining the surrounding land. Darkness hovered at the periphery of the light, and she tilted her head, fascinated the stars seemed to be much further up in the sky than seen from the other realms. It was as if a layer of darkness covered the beauty of the night sky, dimming the shimmering brilliance of the stars.

The incline grew sharper, and when she paused, he took

her in his arms and as if in the blink of an eye she was at the top of the pathway. The castle sat atop a mountain overlooking the rest of the Eastern quadrant. Trees rose to enormous heights with vines and flowers sprawled for miles. They moved past the front courtyard which too had dozens of great torches lit, illuminating great winged beasts, massive snakes with ridged backs, wolvyes, lyons all frozen in eternal fight or flight.

His castle was starkly graceful, with an air of chilling elegance pronounced in every sleek line, which seemed to rise to the heavens. The massive stone structure, with the most beautifully designed buttresses Shilah had ever seen, was awe-inspiring. Cascading vines dripped from the castle, twining around the statues that perched on its highest peak. Its dark beauty strangled her breath.

He had dozens of gargoyles, many caricatures of massive beasts perched on high turrets. Some stared somber, some snarling, and some with their heads thrown back howling to the heavens. Some Shilah couldn't decide what they were, some sort of Lyon with wings.

"How breath-taking, Lachlan Ravenswood."

With another blink, she was somewhere else similarly lit with torches. A cliff it seemed and below lay a valley, and beyond that valley, the sound of crashing waves hitting rocks reached her ears.

"Where are we?"

He moved to stand beside her and then replied, "A place I've visited when I seek peace."

Shilah stared at him, never imaging there was a moment in time a man such as he could have craved for peace. She shifted her attention to sounds coming from the valley—the rustling of creatures, the cries of birds, the rushing of water. She allowed that serenity to seep into her and soothe her own turbulent mind. There was a shift in the darkness, a shape emerging, and she blinked wondering if she imagined it. Then a hulking beast appeared, its tongue lolling from its head.

Shilah jumped and shrieked, stumbling back, dropping on her ass in the grass. Mortification crawled through her, and she hurriedly lurched to her feet.

A deep, yet soft chuckle brushed against her skin, she whirled around. *Oh!* It was inexplicably the most beautiful thing she'd ever seen—Lachlan Ravenswood with a smile on his face. While she still struggled to control the beating mess of her heart, the great brute bounded over to Lachlan only to skid to a halt, its lips curling back in a savage snarl, wicked canines dripping with saliva exposed, its ridgeback hackles raised.

What was it?

Lachlan rocked back on his heels. "Easy, Cronus, it is me. I am a bit different, but it is still me."

The growls became more savage and its muscles bunched as if it primed for an attack. A ferocious sound burst from Lachlan's chest and vibrated on the air with domineering menace. The creature paused, the muscles relaxed slowly, and then it bounded over to Lachlan and licked his face. He grabbed it around its neck with surprising affection, sliding his hand through the creature's thick hair. Ropes of muscle rippled beneath the creature's sleek fur. She felt his blast of pleasure through their link and sensed he had missed the beast.

Her heart tumbled inside her chest in the most alarming flip. Her entire body was flushed and alive, acutely aware of him. "You have a familiar?" she asked, tentatively moving closer. She'd read about them, at times wishing her world had animals that offered some comfort and ones with whom she could play. Some planets called them familiars and others called them pets, but she'd never seen one before.

"Is it like a dog?" She sent the impression of a large animal she'd seen in the mind of the human priest when he'd described the animal to her and Kala.

"You dare compare Cronus to something so small and feeble," he said, sounding genuinely affronted.

Shilah laughed, and he glanced at her, desire making his eyes even more golden, the swirls of color more vivid. She looked away briefly, burying the raw lust that burned through her veins. Taking a steady breath, she faced him again, to see him staring at her with that predatory way of his. Fighting not to fidget under his unswerving gaze, she took a few more steps closer.

"Would you like to touch him, mate?"

She snatched the hand she'd been slowly reaching out with and placed it behind her back. "No."

Lachlan's lips twitched again, and she marveled. "Do you know that you are smiling?"

His face was void of expression when he answered, "My lips are not unused to the action."

"Are you also jesting?"

With a barely-there smile, he lowered himself to the ground and lay back in the grass and tugged her down. She landed against the hardness of his chest with an *oomph*. Shilah lifted her face to the sky that shone with muted stars.

"Your kingdom is beautiful."

He faced her. *"You can see it?"*

"I can see the aura of all living things. I can see the small winged creature flying above your head. More like its shape and the red aura surrounding it. I can sense the age of the trees, and I can see the silvery green aura which streaks from the trunk and way up as if it would touch the sky."

Unable to explain the need, she slid her hand against his and entwined their fingers. His hand swallowed hers, and his claws pricked the skin below her knuckles, beading blood.

She swallowed when he lifted it to his mouth and licked the small dots of blood in one sensual glide.

Heat blossomed through her heart, traveled down and lodged between her thighs. She squeezed her legs together, fighting the sudden desire arrowing through her body.

This time when he lowered back their hands onto the grass, he was careful to ensure his claws did not pierce her skin.

"I too have a castle in the sky," she murmured with a smile. "My castle sits on the highest mountain of Dxyriah, and from my bedchamber, I can see every home in my kingdom as it sprawls for miles with majestic grace." She showed him the image of her city, and the sheer beauty of it when the sun hit the glass buildings, and they winked like yellow diamonds. "I never expected to see such graceful beauty in the Darkage. I pictured your kingdom to be filled with boiling lava pits an unsuspecting visitor could drop in at any time and be devoured, not to mention the bits where it is rumored Darkans feed people to their beasts."

"We do have those too."

She jerked her head up and laughed at the dark amusement in his eyes. Resting her head once again on his chest, she thought of why he had brought her here. He had evidently felt her turbulence and wanted to soothe her.

"Who are you Lachlan Ravenswood?" She could feel the monster in him lurking, his darkness twisting along the silver thread that connected them together. What was even of more significant concern was that her silver light seemed to like the darkness and the two essences were merging even more. She reached out to that invisible thread of energy and plucked at the strings. Its resonance vibrated throughout her entire body.

"I'm a Darkan."

The pale ones. The dark kinds. The demons. She recalled

every whispered fear she'd heard in the empire of his people. "Tell me what it means to be a Darkan." *Show me.* "Tell me of your kind, please."

"We Darkans are not born knowing our beasts. The first century of our lives is spent experiencing the joys of childhood freedom, the crushes of teen years' transitions, and the thrill of young adult discoveries. A great part of this time we spend training to hone our chakra and ability to control the shadows. But all the while we can feel the hovering power of our demon, but we do not understand its breadth and depth until we reach our one-hundredth year when it awakens. We then undergo a brutal battle to fight for control and build up a psychic barrier, so the darkness in us does not rule our action. The rest of our lives is spent either accepting the vile malevolence of our beast and honing it into our weapon or fighting to keep it at bay to retain our sanity. In the past, I would come here and repose on these grasses, watch the forest, and feel a sense of calm that was hard to attain."

His voice was a pulse of petrifying powers, the rumble of a violent storm that could destroy everything it touched, yet no fear surged in her heart. She felt safe with him. She turned her head on the grass, inhaling the oddly sweet scent. "I could feel the deep apprehension of your friends when they looked at you." She glanced over the rolling hills, the aura of each unique being, whether it be a plant, birds, or insects, creating the most beautiful effect as she saw the landscape through vivid colors of purple, green, white, and black. I can also see you are different from them. You feel darker Lachlan Ravenswood."

He tugged her closer to him, and with a sigh of contentment, she rested her head on his chest, listening to the soothing lull of his heartbeat.

"The beast inside all Darkans is made of pure chakra. That essence is very powerful and malevolent. We learn at an early age to manage the psychic barrier that we are born naturally with, to keep that chakra from corrupting us wholeheartedly."

Shilah's heart pounded. "You speak of the shield I shattered within you," she breathed, struggling to push from him, but he held her to him until she settled back.

"We feed our beasts which has its own cunning intelligence on the darkest of energies—rage, fear, and pain. The more it feeds, the stronger it becomes, and if we are not vigilant and strong enough, the beast can become dominant, and when it does….it kills and slaughters, then feeds and feeds. Some of us chose not to ever lower our psychic barriers so not to tempt ourselves with the power the monster inside us offer."

"You had done that. When I just met you, I could feel your barrier, and I was impressed by its intricate construct."

Lachlan was silent for several minutes, and Shilah remained still in the cage of his arms, listening to the roar of his heart.

"For years I lived in fear of the other entity rising inside me, that it might try to steal the control I'd honed over the years, and slaughter what's left of my family. Or worse, force me to betray my king. I am five hundred and thirty-nine years of age. I lowered my barrier once and used the powers of my beast to kill my father, and then I shut it away for over four hundred years."

Images bloomed in his mind and flowed to her more like memories. She could feel all he had endured the moment he saw his father ripping his mother's heart from her chest. The agony of her torture and the scent of her horrifying death had driven a young Lachlan to his knees, and he'd screamed his denial until he'd been hoarse. The pain had gone so deep in his heart there was no adequate way to express it, except through fury.

His father had appeared terrifying, eyes flame red with bloodlust, his skin covered with the blackest of chakra and red scales, with vicious fangs protruding from his mouth.

"He'd turned into a Senji*. Darkans who are no longer in control of the chakra inside, and it is the demon's essence who rules."*

The memories continued of Lachlan fighting his father, and almost being killed himself. Her heart was a beating aching mess, and Shilah distantly realized she wept as she sensed the hopeless despair he had felt as he fought his father —a man he loved, a man whom he'd believed to be honorable, a man he'd believe to worship his mother despite the fact they hadn't been mates. Lachlan's limbs had been broken, deep gouges in his side, blood pouring from his multitude of wounds as the demon toyed with him, savoring his pain, and still, he'd struggled to his feet, determined to fight, resolved to protect whoever was enclosed by the large oak door behind him. It seemed impossible that he could win such a battle with the powers so unequal. But he did not give up, even when he lay dying, his hand still scrabbled to hold onto the ankle of his father. It was at that point chakra exploded from him, and she saw the awful memory of the first time his beast took control from him. How hideous it had all been. His wounds had healed, and with terrible wrath he'd went for his father, and they battled.

Unable to bear the rage that had pelted from them, the assault against her senses too much, she pulled from his mind, gasping raggedly.

"Somehow I won," he murmured. "I defeated my father by taking his head from his body and his heart from his chest."

She read his thought that he believed it had been sheer luck and the fierce quickness of his retaliation which had not allowed his father the presence of mind to summon his beast to a solid form. If that had happened, everyone in their home would have perished. She could feel the echoes of his torment that he'd lived with ever since.

"The demon in me ruled, and my sister whom I'd fought so hard to protect, I turned on her."

Shilah trembled, praying he did not reveal he had taken her life. The connection between them leaped once more to life, against her will, and she struggled to separate herself from the mental link. Her mouth dried, and when she sat up this time he allowed her. Shilah pressed a hand to her chest, gasping as the memories powered through her.

With a slam of his fist, the door had splintered open, and a young girl, a child of no more than about ten years of age, sat in the center of the bed trembling and sobbing. The demon went for her, grabbing the child up in his clawed hands, inhaling her terror.

Her breath caught as unfathomable anguish gripped her by the throat.

But this agony was not her own, she absorbed the emotions Lachlan had felt being trapped in the demon and unable to stop himself. Another Darkan had swirled into the chamber in a burst of shadows, grabbed hold of Lachlan and took him atop a mountain of black ice. And there he'd roared and fought for days, battling the unceasing hunger of the demon's will to devour and kill. His friend, who was revealed to be Gidon, fought with him, doing everything in his power to keep Lachlan atop the mountain. They battled for days, weeks, until Lachlan who'd been so buried under the ravaging lust for blood, started to fight, to regain control, to rebuild his barriers and honed it into an impenetrable shield born from pain and loss.

The connection severed, and she slumped against his chest, gasping harshly.

"You contained it," she said wiping at the tears tracking down her cheeks. "You held that monstrous force behind a shield for centuries." A piercing ache filled her heart. "A barrier I callously took from you. Will you ever forgive me?"

"There is nothing to forgive. You freed me from the shackles of my limitations. The kingmaker has risen, and he has promised a new king for the Darkage. The Empire has declared war, and if the kingdoms respond the third Great war of Amagarie will unfold. I am better able to protect Gidon when the enemy comes for him. And they will come, with a force unlike any we've ever seen. For the enemies know his might, and they will have to be greater than Gidon to take him."

He touched her lips lightly. "I am better able to protect you."

"I do not understand, why aren't you fighting with the beast in you?"

"You obliterated the threads that held the barrier. There can never be a division again. This goes beyond a bonding."

For a moment she struggled to understand who the primal throb of satisfaction came from, the man or the monster. She searched the threads of his memories, moving through with light agility. "That has never happened before in your history," she breathed in shock. "Normally when the beast takes control, the thread of the barrier still exists even though the demon is in control. And when your people bond with their beasts, there is an alliance between man and demon, reliance on each other, a barrier away from the darkness when the host wishes it. But you are not that…."

Acting on instincts, she rolled on top of him, her knees pressing down on each side of his waist and peered down at him. His eyes now held a swirl of gold, blue, purple, green and black, still held the cast of the serpent, and his face while impossibly beautiful and sensual, held a cruel edge. "Your beast has manifested in you in a manner never seen before. That is why your friends were so apprehensive."

Her fingers stroked his hair and began to make small

circles over his temples. "Let me try and help you build back that thread. I am an imperial telepath. Maybe there is a way to reverse what I did."

"I am what I am."

A calm, brutal acceptance Shilah would never comprehend. She couldn't find air to drag into her lungs for precious seconds. "If what I am reading from your memories Lachlan Ravenswood is correct, in Darkans who are bonded, they have absolute control over their psychic wall and let the demon out and cage it at their will. You do not have that. *I* took that from you," she said fiercely, tears pricking from behind her eyes. "What peace will you ever have but to be eternally damned?"

"I have you, my mate." *My soul. My sanity. My everything.*

Her breath hitched in her throat as her mind caught the center of his thoughts. Another rough sound escaped. *"Your soul, Lachlan Ravenswood?"*

"My soul has been branded as unredeemable at my birth, but you are my light, my mate."

And at that moment Shilah knew, once he touched her, claimed her, made her part of him, she would be irrevocably lost. She started to tremble. "I *must* return to my realm, I cannot stay in the land of shadows and darkness." But how he made her crave to abandon the solitary life she would confine herself to once she returned to her world. *But I'll save thousands of lives*, she fiercely reminded herself.

"I agree."

"I did not expect you to so readily agree to me leaving the Darkage."

"The empire will not take lightly to losing you. Even without your Imperial powers, Serangites are coveted. There are traitors within our walls, working with the kingmaker who has aligned himself with Emperor Khan. They can strike at you anytime. It is best you return to Serange as soon as possible. I will come with you, my mate. And you will have your army to take back your crown."

"And what of King Gidon and the ones who wish to take his head?"

"I will return to the Darkage when he has need of me."

She smiled, relief lifting her heart. With him by her side, Prince Quan would have no choice but to abdicate. "And I would like you by my side Lachlan Ravenswood, thank you."

She desperately wanted to lean in and take his mouth with her but held back out of uncertainty. The deep attraction confused her. Her reason for being in Amagarie had nothing to do with taking a lover, only the freedom of her people. Yet there was an undeniable hunger in her body for this man, and she would deny it no longer. *"Kiss me, Lachlan Ravenswood."*

The ground beneath them roiled, and something unknown trembled on the air.

"No!" The force of her sister's scream roared through her mind and had Shilah scrambling from off him, lurching to her feet.

"A decision has been made."

Fear seized her throat as her sister's voice hissed with terrifying promise as she foresaw the future.

"Queen of darkness you shall become. I see upon your head a crown of snakes and thorns. Your mercy and love will be our kingdom's downfall."

Shilah gasped. "Mercy and love for Lachlan?" she demanded.

Kala continued without pause, *"At Lachlan Ravenswood's feet, blood will flow, and bodies will drop from the castle in the sky as he slaughters. If you pledge your love to him, our people will know true suffering, and it will be endless."*

There was a choked cry and then she said, *"Please Shilah, run!"*

15

Shilah ran away from him, sprinting down the hilly slope, uncaring of where she dashed, the flowing length of the sari twisting around her legs. Her side ached, and she did not stop until she stumbled. A lake stood in front of her, the hovering darkness overwhelming, the aura of the creatures in the depths of the water creating a bright shimmering surface atop the lake. Trees hung over the swollen banks of the lake, the purple aura of their gnarled roots covering the ground in snake-like patterns. The great torches in the distance were a small beacon, but she pulsed forth her kinetic energy, creating a silver-white glow around her. She tasted such awful fear in her mouth. *"Kala, what does it mean?"*

"Lachlan Ravenswood must never be allowed into Serange."

"He has promised to help me, providing the army we need to root Prince Quan from our kingdom."

"Another way must be found, Shilah!"

"You said my mercy and love will be our kingdom's downfall, do you speak of the feelings growing in my heart for him?"

There was a tense pause, and Kala said, *"I cannot see. Let us leave this place soon, sister. We must find another way."*

Shilah closed the connection with her sister, hating the sense of helpless rage that filled her. Taking back her throne was not worth the cost of the pain in her sister's vision. If she returned to Dxyriah with Lachlan and his promised army, her people's blood would stain the streets and the mountains. Why? How might her love and compassionate nature lead to such an awful outcome?

Suddenly he was there, the warmth of his body penetrating the chill that wrapped around her earlier. She sensed when he bent his head, felt the brush of his lips against her hair, the warmth of his breath on the nape of her neck. "If I ask you to promise you will never hurt my people, what would be your answer?" she asked hoarsely.

"Whatever you wish will be done."

She did not allow relief to fill her, instead asking, "And if they should hurt me in the fight to reclaim my kingdom? Will your promise stand?"

He needn't answer for a wave of violence and retribution flowered through her along their link. She closed her eyes and spun to face him. "You cannot return with me to Serange."

He caught her chin between his thumb and finger in a firm grip. "Why?"

Her gaze jumped to his. "My sister is a foreseer, and she has visions of you killing hundreds in my kingdom. And her visions have *always* come to fruition. Those are my people. I *love* them, and I must protect them even at the cost of my own desires."

His eyes watched her, but he made no reply.

"I cannot vow to stay and accept your claim. Do not demand it of me."

A low growl rumbled warningly through the night, and she tipped and pressed her finger against his lips. "I want you…more than I desire my next breath. I crave you with an intensity that petrifies me. I want to feel pleasure, I want to feel alive as only your touch has ever made me feel in all my two hundred and six years alive. I want to bask in something other than the doubts and fear I feel for my people and the path I am on. I want to *feel*. I want to burn. And I want you to give it to me, Lachlan Ravenswood for another has never awakened this hunger I feel."

The tension swirled and thickened around them.

Shilah brushed her mind against their telepathic thread. She found a hunger so deep, so wild, so urgent, it scared her, even as it called to somewhere deep inside. She couldn't rely on him to help her take back her throne. Somehow, she had to do this herself. *Queen of darkness you shall become*. If she submitted to his claim Shilah sensed with her entire being she would be changed. But she could make love with him without handing over her soul, and the destruction of her kingdom, couldn't she? She closed her eyes, blotting out the utterly foolish thought. This man would not take in part and be satisfied. He was a conqueror, and he would demand her irrevocable surrender—to the man, the monster, and everything he represented.

"I will give you one night," she said softly. "To hold me, to love me, and then I must leave. If you swear to let me go after…."

A burst of lust swept from him and covered her. He smoothed the pad of his thumb along the curve of her lower lip, ensuring his claws did not split her lips. He was going to kiss her, she could feel it, and how desperately she wanted his lips against her. Logic didn't seem to have a place in her heart at the moment. *"Say something, Lachlan Ravenswood."*

His head dipped, and he pressed his mouth against hers. And she wanted to weep at how gentle he was. They stilled, and her lips trembled against his. A very strange but sweet twisting ache stirred in her belly, and her heart quickened.

He traced the curves of her breasts, sliding down to explore her tiny waist before moving down to the swell of her hips. *"I like touching you, Shilah."*

The sting of his claws had her flinching. He withdrew his hand, a frown slashing his brows as he stared at the wicked claws jutting from his fingers. Shilah felt his fierce concentration along their link. Power surged, and right before her eyes, his claws retracted.

She pressed her hands to his chest, moving even closer to him. *"I like touching you too."* Their mental connection leaped, burned to life in a pulse of silver-blue aura. Though her eyes remained closed, her lips pressed to his, their bodies unmoving, and she could see the image of them standing by the lake, a strange aura surrounding them clear in her mind. The silver-blue glow around them, expanded, and the nearby flowers which had been covered in darkness now burst into bright colors.

Her fingers slid over his face, the angles, and planes, memorizing his features. If only she could have him for a brief while.

Queen of darkness you shall become.

Pushing aside that forbidding prophecy, she leaned deeper into his kiss, parting her lips to his slow licks and nibbling.

"My mate." This brush against her mind felt deeper, more intimate, and she opened her physic eye peeking at the thread through which they connected. An arrow of shock darted through her as a smoldering burn seared her belly and flared through her core with a dark heat that threatened to consume her. She ached. She got wet. And he inhaled.

"I want your pussy on my tongue mate. Let me lap you up."

A rip vibrated on the air as he rent the top of her sari

from her body. Hot lips trailed along her jaws, her neck, and along her exposed breasts. With a blink of the shadows, she was on her back, lying on the grass, his powerful body coming down over hers. The hungriest of eyes devoured her naked breast.

A gentle breeze washed over the hill, and Shilah smelled the rain, inhaled the scent of it, then felt the cold drops on her skin. A groan of thunder rumbled, the ominous sound a portent for her possible future. She slid her legs up his pants, loving the feel of his muscles, and over to his hips to lock them behind his back. To keep her ankles locked behind his back, her hips arched sharply upwards, flushing her wet, pulsing core directly against the hardened ridge of his cock.

He groaned. She sighed. And they kissed.

She looped her hands around his neck and held on. Shilah became lost entirely in the taste, the scent, and the feel of him. His skin stretched, the tattoo slid sinuously along his body and hers, and she did not flinch from it but coasted the tip of her finger over his back and up to his shoulders. Ropes of muscle rippled and twisted beneath her gentle glide, and she felt the dark predator in him rise, incinerating the leash that caged the storm in her arms.

Water dripped from his body onto hers and trailed between the valley of her breasts and down her belly to the junction between her legs. Shilah parted her lips, letting the drops wet her mouth, hoping it would cool the burning hunger erupting inside.

"I could consume you," he breathed against her lips.

Their kiss changed as his mouth slanted over hers with sensual, domineering mastery. He rolled with her, never breaking the fusion of their hungry kiss until she was seated on top of him. Cold brushed against her skin as he ripped the bottom part of her sari away, and strong hands palmed her ass and squeezed.

He pushed a hand between the tight fit of their bodies, trailing his fingers down to touch her wet center. He slid a finger inside her, a slow penetration that arrowed a thousand darts of fire to burn her from the inside.

The sky cracked, and icy rain lashed at her skin, but Shilah was too drunk on pleasure and the promise of more to come to care. Around them, the forest had become another world. The sound of the rain was a soft rhythm, the soft lash of it against her skin a pleasure of its own. He slid her up his torso, broke their kiss, and with another swirl of the darkness he was once again on top, and she was pressed into the earthy scent of wet grass, her legs split wide as he settled between her splayed thighs.

Shilah shook with fear and pleasure as he captured her nipples and pulled firmly. The sting of lust was deep, and so were the bites of pain as fangs scraped and pierced her nipple. He lifted his head at her cry and Shilah trembled at the lust that darkened his eyes and wafted from his *chakra*.

Arousal shivered through her as he ripped away the silk garment that protected her core. His knuckles brushed against her outer lips of her wet sex, and Shilah swallowed back the moan at the surge of desire his action caused.

"I want you so much I burn, but I do not want to hurt you. I am so much bigger than you are, so much more brutal."

His voice whispered in her mind. Caressing her insides, calming her fear, and allowing her to control the mass of energy churning through her veins. *"I only fear you will stop touching me."*

Another swirl of shadows and she was in a room. The fireplace burned brightly, and the room felt warm and inviting. It was a bedchamber, and right in the middle sat a large, canopied bed with green layers of heavy curtains around it.

Smooth silk glided against her skin as her back pressed

into the bed, and he was naked. His speed was incredible. *"I love how you move with me."*

She braced on her elbows, crawling backwards to the center of the bed, never removing her gaze from the man standing at the foot of the bed. Shilah was bemused by his sheer sensual beauty. Her gaze traveled up his body, admiring the ripples of muscle over his stomach, the power of his thighs. Her eyes centered on the thick erection straining from between his thighs, hanging low. Her lungs refused to draw air. He was thick and significantly larger than the one consort she'd had.

"Draw your knees up." The words were a soft, gentle whisper in her mind.

She glanced up at his face. He was beautiful and so gracefully savage.

"Open them wide…I want to see the pink folds of your pussy."

The voice was a throb of carnal intent, and Shilah whimpered, her body reacting with a tidal wave of pure fire. Yet she could not move, her limbs too weak with lust to obey. Suddenly he was on the bed, crouching on his knees before her. He looked so powerful and predatory, reminding her just how fragile and softer she was to him. His hands spread her thighs. He didn't speak, simply positioned her with his hands. She felt her sex bloom like a flower under his stare.

"A beautiful pussy," he said, his voice a deep, rich growl. A slow smile softened the hard edge to his mouth. "I will be fucking you all night, my mate."

It was a promise, a warning, and her body reacted to him, going soft and pliant, her sex wetter. She was so lost in him already. Shilah moistened her lips, wanting to answer, but no sound would come out. She took a breath and breathed him into her lungs—dark and earthy, like a storm itself.

He brushed a kiss over her mouth again. Her lips trembled in response. He savored her taste, her moans, then he consumed and ravished, taking her lips with shocking carnality. He seemed to feed at her mouth, kissing her again and again. Desire crawled through her body, and between her legs, she could feel the hot dampness spreading. Claws bursts from his fingers as he flicked them over her nipples eliciting a sensation that she was not sure if it created pleasure or pain.

His mouth trailed fire across her stomach to the silken triangle at the junction of her legs. Tiny bites, the scrape of his canines dragged along her inner thighs before his tongue stroked over her wet, aching pussy. Her hoarse scream strangled in her throat. The roughness of his tongue created the most delicious friction, causing shards of pleasure so sharp it was nearly painful. He licked her drenched sex, forcing a piercing pleasure through her swollen clit every time he caught it with his tongue in a rough glide.

Her clit swelled with aching hunger...and right there, he licked it, sucked it into his mouth and destroyed her.

"Lachlan," Shilah screamed, her hips arching off the bed, fisting her fingers in his hair as sensations tore through her body.

His claws retracted once more, and he slipped a finger inside her, then another finger joined the first then, burning her with bliss as his mouth suckled her clit, his tongue flicking, pressing, ravishing her. A ragged moan burst from her when he added a third finger, working into her, stretching her, and she shuddered under the shockwaves of pleasure.

The next moment she was lifted against the muscles of his stomach, braced wide with one leg on each side of his muscular hips. He reached between them, fisted his cock, and pressed it against her sex, and pushed. Her breath gasped from her at the burning sensation. Her abundant slickness barely eased his way, but he'd only slid quarter way inside of her before the tightness of her body stopped him. He was too wide for her. Lachlan gripped her ass with both hands, and she clasped onto his bulging arms, as he arched her up more, splaying her legs even wider. His powerful grip stung the soft flesh of her bottom, and she trembled.

She cupped his cheek, brushing a tender kiss over his lips. The beautiful colors of his eyes had darkened, the savage cheekbones flushed with aroused sensuality. He held her gaze as he pushed his cock inside her, the thick ridges rubbing along her sensitive core. Shilah found it increasingly hard to focus on anything but the stretching tightness between her thighs. Ecstasy mixed with the pain of the full, relentless penetration.

A sob caught in her throat. *"Lachlan."*

He snarled, his own instincts clearly fighting to take over and ram into her. With a growl, Lachlan dug his fingertips deep into her ass and shoved, sinking deep inside her sex. Shilah screamed, clinging to his shoulders, gasping through the shock of the pleasure-pain. The pressure felt unbearable, the muscles of her pussy fluttering and clenching over the piercing thickness, struggling to adjust to his cock.

Black chakra exploded from his skin, caressing over her body in a sensuous caress and down to her clit where it stroked over it like fingers. Sweet, mind-shattering ecstasy rushed through her, making her wetter and her muscles relaxing over Lachlan's girth. The chakra coiled around her, gently caressing her skin, kneading her breasts, and stimulating her nipples.

He leaned slightly back and looked at where they joined. She blushed furiously as he rimmed her entrance where she stretched around him so tightly. Pleasure streaked through her as nerve endings came alive from the scrape of his claws. She swallowed as he ran his fingers to her clitoris and pressed, creating a firestorm of lust to bolt through her. "Ughhhh!"

He pulled from her with excruciating slowness, the drag of the ridges of his cock in her tender sex, filled her with bliss, then he thrust to the hilt once more inside her. A wild cry tore from her throat at being filled so deliciously. His cock fucked inside her with a rhythm that had her gasping at the savagery of the biting pleasure.

With one hand curved around her back, the other holding her buttocks, he slammed her down onto his cock, over and over with bruising strength, his chakra back at her core working her clitoris, squeezing then caressing the sensitive nub filling her with sheer bliss. She fisted his hair in her hands and dragged his mouth against hers. Their tongues dueled in a provocative kiss and with every thrust into her wet, smacking sex, his control melted away.

The monster in him rose, their thread exploded in a bright silvery light with the hovering darkness consuming it more and more. The two merged, creating a dark silver aura, that burned with lust and blood-thirst. The protest that swelled against her lips only came in wild cries of bliss. Fear sneaked into her heart as with every lunge, every swivel of his lips, he shattered her barriers, breaking her control. Shilah whimpered as the heat became hotter and more destructive. White-hot pleasure snapped through her body, and Shilah screamed in release. Her body convulsed, and he gave her no respite, riding her through the waves of brutal pleasure.

She became wild, unstoppable in her passions. Her hips rose, her nails raked his sweat-slicked back, her teeth sank into his shoulders drawing blood as he thrust deeper and the pleasure became hotter. The need for another release was growing, tightening, burning inside her until she felt as though flames were consuming her alive. Shilah did not surrender. He wrenched it from her, and despair filled her because she felt as if he owned her. He owned each cry, each scream that petered out to gasping pleas and moans as his intensity grew.

His head lowered to the vulnerable crook of her neck, and he licked with erotic hunger the sensitive flesh over her frantically beating pulse, and struck, his fangs sliding deep.

Fire and ice. Pain and pleasure.

A growl of triumph and ecstasy burned along their link as he consumed her essence. Their minds merged, the thread connecting them wrapped around them like a heated dark silver chain, his pleasure became hers, and she sobbed with the sheer power of it. The walls of the room shook, the ground undulated.

His thrusts into her body were hard, penetrating, and deep as he took her with brutal carnality. Perspiration layered her flesh as the pleasure expanded inside her, a noise escaped her throat, a high keening sound of bliss. She was dimly aware of the hoarse cry forcing its way out her throat as she finally shuddered in orgasm. His roar reverberated in the room as a hot splash of seed released inside her.

She wilted onto his chest, relaxing into the haven of his embrace, her body still shivering through the aftermath of such untamed loving. They stayed like that, he kneeled onto the bed, their flesh still connected, her legs wrapped around his hips, her torso resting intimately against his.

Shadows coated her senses, and then she was in some sort of cavern. The cave was lit with several great torches, sending a soft glow dancing over the ceiling. Water gushed from a rock, steam rising from around the basin it pooled in. He flowed with her into the water, taking her over to the fall, then he withdrew from her body. She moaned in protest, her body aching. Then a sigh of pleasure as the heat of the water soothed the soreness of her muscles.

They remained silent, and she smiled when a shadow darted over the surface of the water, to lift a flagon and fill a chalice which he carried to her. She took the goblet and sipped, the zesty wine bursting with rich flavor and sweetness on her tongue.

The shadows deepened, creeping along the walls and floors of the cave, and then images formed as he entertained her with the dancing shadows. Shilah laughed, thinking how incredible it was that he shaped the shadows to look like people, as he showed her a story of a man and woman walking along a cliff, then dancing under the sky, then making love using shadows alone.

It wasn't odd to her that they did not speak. There was a level of comfort in the silence and a barely lit cave she'd not thought possible. The shadows brought fruits next, strange, and oddly colored but quite delectable.

Sheila ate and drank wine, and not once did they speak. With a replete sigh, she leaned into him sleepily, feeling secure in the arms that wrapped around her waist.

"Why do you drink my blood?"

"It is a need...a compulsion I cannot fight or deny. Does it repulse you, my mate?"

"No."

"Good."

A slow fire started to build in her belly, and she quivered, a soft moan slipping from her. Black chakra curled around her like smoke and then dipped below the surface of the water. Something grasped each of her legs beneath the water and opened them, then slid sinuously up her calf to her knee, a long, slow, very even stroke up to her exposed sex. His chakra glided over her flesh with sublime pressure, pressing in the tender wall of her pussy, and up to her clitoris. She panted, need making her slick with welcome. He was relentless in how he worked her clitoris, the power of his shadows and chakra moving the hood covering that tender bud, rubbing, and squeezing her nub, filling her with bliss. She tried to move out of the caress, the unrelenting stimulation, the aching sensation too much, too brutal, and there was no ease.

She leaned back against his chest with a whimper. One of his hands banded around her waist, slid up to over her belly, through the valley between her breasts, where he lingered, stroking her flesh, tugging her nipples, then up to span her throat. The strength in his touch was unmistakable. Everything about the dark creature behind her spoke to her most primal lustful instincts.

With a simple nudge, her neck arched, exposing her throat. His teeth scraped along her pulse, and the breath left her lungs in a rush. His fangs scraped her flesh, he took a small nip, sending streaks of fire through her veins, making her whimper and moan his name.

"I love feeling you under my hands," he murmured. "I love these sweet hot little noises you can't help but make as I break your pussy into my cock."

She writhed against him, but there was no ease in his sensual assault. She felt a fire swell and grow in her belly as the ache in her clitoris became overwhelming. It built, and her limbs trembled. He spun with her and eased her over the rock, his shadows holding her legs apart as he notched the head of his cock at the needy entrance of her sex.

He waited, and she arched inviting him to burn with her, mindless with the pleasure twisting through her body. His chakra rubbed her sensitive clitoris harder, faster, driving her beyond pleasure. She shattered, and it was then he slammed deep inside her, jerking her to the tip of her toes, her buttocks arching against his body. Whimpering at the unyielding pressure she tried to shift, but she was impaled so deep on his cock she could barely move. A weak moan whispered past her lips.

His growls of pleasure and dominance echoed in the cave, and dark, primitive lust flavored his chakra. With a burst of shadows, they were in the room, and he tumbled her down onto the bed. He grabbed her by the waist and flipped her over onto her hands and knees, his powerful body looming over her from behind making her feel small and far too vulnerable. She'd never been so aware of her delicate femininity.

He swept her wet hair aside and brushed a kiss along her neck. She turned her face, her cheek sliding against silk sheets. A glimpse of a stark, raw hunger that made her shiver in anticipation. His hand banded across her waist to keep her from moving, and then he shoved his thick girth deep into her in one stroke.

His primal groan of satisfaction echoed in the chamber and drowned out Shilah's wailing scream. Lachlan started to move in her, a relentless rhythm that had her thrashing and sobbing in ecstasy. His chakra worked her clitoris, rubbing circular motions into the sensitive bud. He drove her hard toward insanity, toward rapture, toward losing all sense of herself. She became a creature drunk on pleasure, craving him more and more, despite the thick, rough penetration as he ravaged her trembling pussy. Her body spasmed weakly as his chakra rubbed her aching nub firmer, forcing devastating pleasure into the already overly sensitized nerve endings, sending sharp shocks of sensation through her.

His teeth sank deep in the curve of her neck. The pain of the bite gave way to the erotic ecstasy, and a wild cry tore from her as white hot heat consumed her. Fire roared and spread through her body in an unending pulse of pleasure. Their minds merged, and Shilah became lost, swept away in the firestorm of his desire, absorbing all the monstrosity in his soul, all the darkness, and all the desires as he released with a rough satisfied groan.

He retracted his teeth from her throat, and licked her skin, closing the wounds.

He tilted her head up a little and bent his neck, capturing her lips in a soft kiss. His kiss was searing and possessive despite the gentle caress. Shilah shifted so she rested almost on top of his body. She curved herself around the hard outline of his chest and thighs, listening to the muted roar of his heartbeat still glowing in the pleasurable aftermath of the rapture.

Strong arms closed around her back, pulling her closer to his powerful torso. "Thank you for this gift beyond price. I will treasure it for all eternity."

She pressed her nose into his neck and inhaled deeply. *"Thank you for tonight,"* she murmured almost shyly against their link.

A brush of amusement, bloodlust, and tenderness caressed her through their thread.

"The night has just started, my mate."

HIS MATE'S silver-white hair was spread over his silken sheets, her eyes glazed and bright with the shy awakening of her sensuality, her slit pink and swollen from his excess, glistening with their combined release. She was the most beautiful thing he had ever seen. He had relinquished all concerns that she might get hurt by the brutal pounding as he'd claimed her. Lachlan had slightly lost control, but she had burned right along with him, accepting his rough carnality, surrendering to pleasure several times. She'd moaned his name, over and over, her hands fisting in his hair, holding him to her. Noting the paleness of her skin, and the dark bruises under her eyes, a fierce need to protect her surged through him. He'd taken too much of her blood.

Reaching up with a clawed finger, he sliced into his neck deep. *"Come and drink of me."*

The slightest hesitation wafted from her, then she slid along his body with sinuous grace and licked the blood from his neck. Eyes widened, and pleasure flowed along their link. *"This is delicious."*

"Suck harder. I took a lot from you, and you need to replenish."

Her throat worked on a long pull, and then she swallowed. She arched into him, her body soft and pliant. She moaned against his flesh, a breathy little sound that sent a lash of erotic heat rushing through his body. Each stroke of her tongue, tug of her lips, pounded lust through his veins. She pulled from him, pressing a finger to her blood red lips. *"How is it that your blood tastes so wonderful to me?"*

"We do not know the full of it, but when a Darkan mates with a non-Darkan, there is a craving for each other's blood, especially during the mating heat."

He tugged her silky soft curves tight against the hardness of his body. Her eyes widened at the feel of his erection, and shock and intrigue burned along their thread. "Again, Lachlan Ravenswood?"

He stroked his fingers down her cheek, infinitely gentle. "For the entire night, my *leika*. But not at this moment."

She stroked a hand over his chest, pleasure curving her lips at the simple act of touching him.

"Come, I shall feed you properly and take you to your sister. Then the rest of the night will belong to us once again."

The fractured stars that were her eyes seemed to brighten, and she moved away from him to her satchel holding her clothes. He watched her as she went into the bath chamber and took a quick bath and dressed. He felt fascinated by her energy, the quick, lithe way she walked, her shimmering sensuality. He felt the ebb of the connection between them, the sharing of mind and body, the dark flow of his blood rushing through her veins. He'd been half alive for four hundred years…and now every dark crevice of his being hungered for her light.

I am bewitched.

16

Shilah stirred sleepily, pushing back the curtain of her silver hair from her face. The overly large bedchamber was lit with dozens of great torches, and a steaming bath which had not been present earlier was now in the center of the room. The tattered remains of her sari littered the plush carpeted floor. Free of sensual distractions, she glanced about, admiring the raw elegance of the room.

Windows encased an entire wall of the palatial chamber, and fluorescent flowers crept along the glass on vines. Somehow, she could smell the unique flowers hovering in the darkness beyond, hear the cries of wild creatures, the gurgling of a stream, and the thunderous roar of a waterfall. It was as if the castle was in the center of a wild forest, and its king was Lachlan Ravenswood—a dark, merciless predator.

She slowly pushed herself up from off the bed, her legs trembled, but she forced herself to stand. The softness of the green carpet tickled her toes, and she took a tentative step and halted. Shilah winced at the ache between her legs. She moved slowly to the bath, faltered at the large glinted mirror before it, and gasped. She looked a fright with her damp hair pasted to her nape. There were red strawberry marks everywhere on her body—her throat, breasts, stomach, and thighs. Those were the places he had nibbled and licked, sometimes nipping with his fangs. Her lips were red and swollen, and she pressed trembling fingers to her mouth.

At some time during their sensual feast, Lachlan had speared his clawed tipped fingers into the silken weight of her hair, bunching the strands in his hands as he held her head in place, staring down at her as he fucked her mouth with slow, shallow strokes. Connected deep to his mind, she explored him, lashing him with tormented pleasure. Her entire body blushed red at the carnal memory. How thorough he had been in his debauchery and cruel sensuality. Sweat had run in rivulets down her skin as he had taken her for hours, riding her through multiple orgasms.

His features never softened to that of a gentle lover. There had been a time her thighs had trembled with the effort to remain open, and he had flipped her to her stomach and drew her to her knees, or atop him. He had been without mercy to her hoarse screams, the hands that twisted the sheets as he took her body to the utmost heights of terrifying pleasure. There had been times when the erotic bite of pain had overwhelmed the pleasure. Those were the times he'd stopped, and took her pussy in his mouth, licking and sucking on her center bringing her to orgasm over and over before mounting her again.

Their hours of loving had been wicked, hedonistic, and Shilah sensed on a deep level she would never experience such shattering bliss with another. "And I would do it all over again," she whispered to her shattered reflection.

She pressed a hand to the smooth curvatures of her stomach, knowing their mating would not result in a child. Yearning struck her heart, the desperate ache of it smarting her eyes. If only it were possible. She was up to date with an injection that prevented unplanned conception. There were at least ten more years before the nanotechnology would disintegrate through her bloodstream. Not that if conception occurred, she could have kept her child in her realm. As an Impure, she was already condemned to a solitary existence. Crown Princess or not, she would be punished to the full extent of the law if she knowingly created life with the knowledge she was a multi-genesis, threatening the safety of an entire planet.

Lachlan Ravenswood made her hunger for impossible things. Shilah had wanted to stay cocooned in the lust he'd stoked in her. The guilt of wanting to be free, never to return to her kingdom almost felled her. She had momentarily yearned to be unshackled from it all and drown herself in the heat, taste, and scent, and a life with him, filled with possibilities of happiness that could not be attained living in Dxyriah.

She felt a peculiar wrenching in the vicinity of her heart. She was perilously close to falling into this man, and that was a situation her kingdom could not afford. It was to only be one night, she reminded herself fiercely, hating the prick of tears behind her lids. *"Kala are you well?"* she asked knocking at the psychic door of her sister's mind.

"Yes."

Shilah frowned. *"You are distressed."*

"It cannot be avoided," the soft resigned whisper came in her voice.

"What cannot be avoided?"

"One of you.... Either you or Lachlan Ravenswood has decided on a path. Until that decision is altered, the only future I see is your death and the slaughter of our people. I've seen several possible futures, and they all ended the same."

Shilah stilled. *"You've unlocked another level of your powers?"*

"Yes. Three days ago."

Shock blasted through her. *Three days?* She had been ensconced in this chamber and in his bed for three days? *"Oh Kala, why didn't you call me?"*

"You were...busy."

Heat suffused Shilah's entire body, and her sister's soft laugh brushed against her senses.

"Each time I tried to reach out I was met with a haze of lust that I quickly drew away from. I was entertained by the court, and King Gidon is very charming for a monster. I've been made to feel very welcomed."

The precise cause for a transition had not yet been identified, but it had been linked to specific scenarios, such as traumatic emotional experiences, abnormally stressful events, and some developments had occurred with age. However, the sources of a transition still varied among different individuals. The past few weeks could most definitely be described as emotionally traumatic, and abnormally stressful. So, the change from an Alpha to an Omega couldn't have been easy for her sister. The power would have roiled through her, stretching Kala's mind and body as it sought to accommodate its depth and essence. *"Has your Omega symbol formed?"*

"Yes."

It was absolute then. Each ring of power manifested in a white translucent symbol on their right arm. It was only when an imperial level was attained their eyes changed and evolved. There was a part of Shilah that did not want to know the new outcomes of the foresight, but she girded her herself. *"Have you any idea of the decision that was made?"*

"I see a monster. It is pure darkness with a rage I've never seen or felt. This monster decimated our kingdom because you...you were killed. No one was spared."

Her heart beat with such brutal force she feared fainting. *"How did I die?"*

"I see you lying on a floor, your hair flowing around you, your suit soaked in blood, and your lifeless eyes staring at the wall."

Shilah made her way over to the bath, and lowered herself into the heated water, sighing as the warmth seeped into her muscles.

"I think as Lachlan's mate...I am very important to him, Kala. And the notion of it is scary. He hardly knows me. My death should mean nothing to him." The very idea that she could mean so much to another was petrifying.

"Only you had anchored it to the light, and with your death, its only purpose was slaughter."

"We will leave here together," Shilah whispered, blinking away the burn of tears. *"I've made a mess of everything. I shouldn't have run, Kala. I should have stayed in Dxyriah, gathered my supporters, and demanded the Senate convene. I stupidly ran, and it has been over three months since we've left our home. Once you saw me on the throne, ruling with Prince Novar. That vision changed the instant I met Lachlan Ravenswood. I think it is also constant because I am with him. Once we leave the Darkage and Amagarie itself, perhaps the precognition will evolve once again."*

Her sister remained silent, but she could feel her anxiety and doubts. And Shilah understood. It was almost impossible to alter the future a foreseer predicted. Though sometimes the visions were not interpreted in full, and the outcome could be far different than feared, the steps seen always came to pass.

"How has King Gidon been treating you?"

"With kindness."

Shilah paused in lathering the cleansing oil over her body. Was that fascination she'd detected in her sister's tone. *"Do you like the king?"*

"I find him...interesting."

"Be careful Kala, there is no one I trust in this kingdom." Except for Lachlan Ravenswood.

The hitch in her sister's voice indicated she'd caught the edges of Shilah's thought.

"You be careful, sister," Kala whispered and then closed their link.

Quickly bathing, Shilah emerged from the bath and used the soft cloth she'd been accustomed to using to dry the wetness from her skin. In her world, a pulse of heat would emit in their bath chamber, and her skin would be dried in a second. She moved over to the chaise longue near the windows and picked up one of the garments clearly intended for her petite frame. She slipped into the dark green kaftan, appreciating the soft feel of the cloth. It hugged her upper body like a lover, then flared from her hips to her ankles in flaring chiffon and silk. She slipped her feet into matching slippers and hurried to the mirror. Using her telekinesis, she arranged her hair in a single plaited braid.

A low growl in the room had her whirling around. Cronus seemed to peel from the wall itself and prowled toward her. Vicious canines lined his mouth, glistening white and sharp. She jerked wildly as the beast that was easily the same height as her approached. Shilah laughed when his massive ridgeback head carefully butted her shoulder. She swore she saw concern in the depth of its eerily blue eyes.

"Were you in here, all this time you great beast," she murmured, touching him tentatively. Shilah brushed her mind against his, unraveling the pathway that was constructed with less thread than peoples'. "I am well Cronus," she murmured, rubbing his head, and smiling when he purred.

The door opened, and Lachlan framed the doorway. She was immediately aware of him, every one of her senses springing to life. He was dressed in stark black with only a white shirt to lighten the overall impression of darkness. Every part of her body ached, hurting for his touch. She dropped her hand abruptly from Cronus' head and stood, confused at her reactions to Lachlan.

"Lachlan Ravenswood, hello," she said softly, a dangerous thrill bursting in her heart.

"Shilah Symonrah, hello." His enigmatic smile was fleeting, but she could feel every nuance of his stare as it skimmed across her features.

He walked over to her, gripped her chin, and lifted her face to his. His eyes searched her expression for the longest time. Then he leaned in and took her mouth with his in a long, slow, incredibly tender kiss. And in it, she felt the apology and sensed the fear he had been too rough with her throughout their time of loving.

"Are you well, Shilah?"

She peered up at him and almost against her will a smile softened her mouth. *"You did not hurt me."*

She felt the burn of relief along their link and wondered at it. He took her lower lip between his teeth and bit down gently, teasing her lips to part with soft nibbles and hot, urgent kisses. *"Are you certain?"*

"Yes." Her stomach grumbled alarmingly. She only recalled eating food once but consuming his blood at least three times.

"Were we really in here for three days?"

"Yes."

And through their link, she saw him as he held her sleeping form cradled against his chest for hours. Then when she roused he would take her repeatedly. Then the same rest and frenzied loving would repeat.

His eyes darkened as the memories flowed through them, lust flavored the air, and inexplicable heat speared down to the valley between her thighs. Shilah smiled, truly amazed she could feel the stirrings of sensual need so soon. *"I am dreadfully hungry."*

And with a burst of shadows, she appeared in a large dining hall, a table laden with savory meats, fruits, and wine. Dozens of great torches lit the room, and she appreciated that his castle was a beautiful and elegant one. Beautiful tapestries graced the stone walls, their color magnificent, and the cloth rich and vibrant, unlike anything she had ever seen. Her home was just as beautiful but different with every graceful line shaped in cold steel and crystal glass. It did not feel warm and comforting as this castle.

"Eat." A soft command in her mind—tender, intimate.

Shilah glanced around the empty hall, then back at him. "Are we to be joined by others?"

"No."

She lowered herself and ate her fill, painfully aware he watched every bite, every swallow, and hum of greedy pleasure she made as each unique flavor and spice burst on her tongue. "Will you not join me?"

"No."

Shilah barely prevented the need to roll her eyes. The realization of how little she knew him filled her with an odd sense of discomfort. She had spent the several nights in his bed, his body connected to hers, driving her to heights of pleasure and she did not know what he dreamt of, what he despaired. She only knew that over the centuries, the other kingdoms had failed to recognize Darkans as people, instead seeing them only as monsters, demons, or mindless beasts worthy of fear and disdain. In her opinion, it was the Empire they needed to fear.

Lachlan was a ruthless warrior who did not hesitate to kill when he deemed it necessary, and he was an incredible lover. But surely there was more to the man silently watching her on the chair.

When she'd had her fill, and cleaned her hands, Shilah stood and faced him.

He held out his hand to her. *"Come with me mate."*

"Where?"

"I want to show you your army."

A million birds took flight in her stomach, and insidious temptation slid through her veins. Shilah placed her hands in his, he took her in the Shadow space, and within a few seconds, she was in a large courtyard overlooking hundreds of training warriors in some sort of stone paved battle arena. No battle cries rung, or pants of exhaustion or even effort. Their silence was eerie as they flowed in a fighting style that seemed ageless and almost beautiful in the brutality of the moves it displayed.

She walked to the top of the steps watching the warriors below. The courtyard was lit with hundreds of great torches, and at the edge of the courtyard magnificent stone sculptures of massive monsters—wolves, lyons, dragons, snakes, chimeras, hydras—frozen in eternal combat surrounded the ring in which they trained. Beyond them, massive trees rose as if towering to the heavens, and through the tree lines, she spied rows upon rows of elegantly large stone dwellings with bricked roofs.

It took Shilah several seconds to realize her vision in the dark was perfect. Shock tore through her.

Heat stirred through her mind. *"What is it?"*

Her lungs felt a little as if they couldn't quite get enough air. *"I...I can see as if the land was under the sun. I can see for miles beyond the hills and the houses sprawled below, I can hear the flapping of a bird too far for me to hear, and I can feel the insects crawling through the earth. My senses have transformed."*

Her heart was a painful thud, and he seemed undisturbed by her revelation. With her enhanced eyes, the dark appeared to her like the blue-grey skies after the passage of a winter storm, like silver moonlight with bursts of vibrant color of life at its center.

She stepped to him and laced her fingers through his. *"I do not think this is a new development in my telepathic abilities. I can feel this energy in me...and it is very different from what I am used to. Do you know Lachlan Ravenswood what is happening?"*

He tilted his head, regarding her steadily. An image flowered in her mind, of her licking Lachlan's blood, of being pleasured on his cock over and over while she sucked his neck. The change had begun then she realized, and she had been too enraptured to be alarmed. And now it metamorphosed, a dark wave of energy pulsing through her, her eyes sharpening, as images more than several miles out appeared as if they were before her. Shilah felt the strength in her bones, heard the winged creatures zipping through the sky hundreds of miles away. *"Your blood has changed me."*

She almost laughed at the beautiful, cruel irony. How could she disguise from her people that she was different?

"Will there be a physical manifestation of the changes your blood has caused?"

"There is a possibility. You will become faster, possibly stronger. A tail and two horns on your forehead. There should be no other outwardly changes."

"What?!" She snapped her head around to look at his face where amusement glowed in his eyes. *"Now is not the time to jest, Lachlan Ravenswood."* But she couldn't help the smile that curved her lips.

"I do jest, but only partially, speed and physical strength are known to develop with cases like ours."

She was suddenly terrified by a thousand different feelings and sensations assaulting her. He tugged her closer, his scent filling her lungs and calming the wash of terror. He gripped her chin and lifted her gaze to his. His eyes, despite reflecting his beast, were so beautiful they made her heart clench. *"I feel scared, yet I am not sure why."* The emotions had risen, harsh and intense.

"You are my mate. All of me belongs to you, and I would never allow anything to harm you."

That outrageous, inexplicable desire filled her once more. She wanted to be his sanity. His pleasure. His mate. His everything. And that desire petrified her to her soul. "There is a part of me that hungers to be all that you desire," she murmured.

Primal pleasure flickered in the golden depth of his eyes. His thumb slid over the sensitive skin of her inner wrist. "What is an impure genesis?"

Shilah stiffened, feeling his dark stillness in her mind. He had been there like a shadow, and she hadn't felt it. Or was it that he was becoming such an intrinsic part of her, having him in her mind no longer felt like an intrusion. There was a sharp snap along their thread as if something had been realigned.

A curious stare assessed every nuance of her expression. "I heard the condemnation of yourself in your thoughts."

And he did not like it. The warmth that filled her was unfamiliar with how sweet and achy the sensations were, but she welcomed it instead of shying away. "In my world, I am considered an Impure. I am an impure-genesis because I possess both telepathic and telekinesis powers."

His eyes were filled with grim darkness. "The more powerful you are, the more celebrated you should be."

How much his uncompromising statement revealed about the man before her, and the world he had been bred to. "Not in my realm. A man's character is revealed by the level of his power. We believe absolute power corrupts and withers the soul, and such raw power must never be allowed to flourish in our lands again."

He pulled her into his arms, his chin atop her head, his

hand around her waist as they faced the unnervingly silent training warriors, who synchronously shifted with speed from one fighting stance to the next with brief pauses in between. Each fluid motion was precise and beautiful. She could see the power vibrate into the air as they adapted each stance, indicating the force of the blow to their invisible opponent.

She glided her fingertip over the roped muscles of the forearm wrapped around her midriff. "Serange had once been a mighty empire where the control of multiple geneses was lauded. From that regime emerged a leader who was a Na'Vita—a being that controlled all the geneses. He was a force no one could reckon with, a law onto himself with Imperial telepathy, teleportation, and Omega level telekinesis and foresight. The power of his mind was so vast, his hunger for knowledge and dominion grew in terrifying leaps, breeding in his heart a violent conquest of Serange and other realms."

A sharp gust of wind rolled over the mountains, twisting the dress of her caftan about her legs.

"A rebellion occurred, war was waged. Our world was wrapped in chaos, our people on the edge of starvation, and it had little development in the way of advanced technology and medical care. The unrest after the rebellion was so great, the cry for a division of the powers was a thundering roar that cracked the fabric of our society and reshaped it. The leaders decided that one person should never hold such power again. New orders and laws were formed, and Serange split into three Kingdoms—Dxyriah, Arcadia, and O'andor. Families and friends were divided as people with similar capabilities were designated to live in different areas, and laws were enacted to prohibit the geneses from cross-breeding. That was over two thousand years ago. It is extremely rare for anyone to have more than one genesis since those laws, Over the years any citizen to display more than one ability was branded impure and illegal."

Apprehension tightened low in her stomach. "Almost one in every generation. There is a birth that is wrong. And the absolute law of our planet is the bloodlines must remain pure. I am an Impure, and I've hidden the knowledge from my family and kingdom for years. It was my secret, and I despaired anyone ever uncovering it. But with the slaughter of my brother and his heirs, I am the oldest Symonrah and the next in line to rule."

"What are the consequences should you be uncovered?"

She remained motionless for several moments. "If the Senate knew I would have been taken to the medical unit and my ability to have children taken from me. I am also required to never have sex with another or marry," she whispered. "I either submit to the law or choose exile."

He stirred in her mind, absorbing the memories of how she had cried when she discovered her flaw, and how she had battled with her honor and duty to the law. She'd wanted a family of her own and had struggled to accept the solitary existence that stretched before her. If she'd procreated knowing of her multi-genesis inheritance, the punishment was death. For such actions threatened the peace and enrichment which thousands of Serangites had given their lives for during the rebellion. The purist ideology was so entrenched, the fear of history repeating itself, even with sterilization, no impure could ever take a life partner. Her wits and intelligence, beauty, wealth, and strength would not matter, only that she had the capability of tainting the bloodlines.

"You sacrifice much for your people."

A shuddering breath escaped her. "I agree with the law."

"I feel that you do."

Her throat went tight. "I have always known the day would come I would have to reveal my status. Kala would then ascend, but she is so young and untutored. I promised her to keep silent until she is better prepared to rule. If Kala would have her wish, I would never reveal myself. I have already committed treason by not self-reporting the minute I discovered my second genesis."

What she had done instead was sought a consort, in the hopes of indulging pleasure just once. Prince Novar had declared his love, and she had chosen him to be her consort. While the experience had been pleasant, Shilah hadn't repeated the encounter to the prince's distress. He had proposed marriage several times which she had always declined. It was one of the reasons she had never understood Kala's vision that she saw them married.

The monster in the cage of her mind became so still, the blood chilled in her veins. She turned in the cage of his arms and wrapped her hands around his neck. "I am sure you've had other lovers, Lachlan Ravenswood."

"I suppose with that logic I must spare this prince's life."

Though his lips curved with slight amusement, at the heart of it a dark violence had blossomed.

Shilah slapped his chest. "I declare you must."

"I saw your sister's vision in the thread of your memories of you marrying this prince."

The menace in his voice had her mouth drying. "I have no plans to deceive anyone from my world so. And that vision is no more," she said, a lump forming in her throat. "It has been replaced by death and darkness."

They stared at each other, and the violence quieted, and an emotion she could not identify in full throbbed along their link, it tasted of loss and pain before it quickly vanished.

"You have a visitor."

She twisted around to see the Princess Saieke strolling toward them, her waist-length hair rippling behind her like fire. *"Perhaps the princess visits you, Lachlan Ravenswood. From our brief meeting, I could tell she held immense affection for you."*

He grunted, and said, "From what I know of the princess' inquisitive nature, it is you she has come to visit, my mate."

"Then I shall greet her," Shilah said with a smile, pulling from his embrace, and walking down the steps leading to the vast, open grounds. She skirted past massive stone structures of carved beasts and did her best to ignore Lachlan's familiar, Cronus, who was poised atop a hill in the distance, but the dratted creature bounded toward her. Shilah braced herself as its massive body bounced into her, and she tumbled to the ground. She held her self still as it licked her face, baring its teeth.

Laughter rushed from her, and she reached her mind out to his. The patterns were primal, but she sensed the intelligence within it, and that it liked her, and this was its greeting. She stood, and only had to turn her head to stare into its eyes. How monstrous this creature was, but also beautiful. She rubbed her hand atop its head, and it butted her underneath her chin.

With a light laugh, she sauntered ahead, and he prowled at her side, a protecting and comforting presence. There was something ethereal about the beautiful red-haired princess. Shilah smiled at her in welcome, and the princess's sapphire blue eyes glittered with pleasure as she dipped into an elegant curtsey. Shilah returned the honor and walked with the princess along the cobbled pathway.

"Lachlan Ravenswood believes you are here to see me, Princess Saieke."

She smiled. "I am. I remembered how unsettling I felt the first time I came into this realm. I've been making friends with your sister. Kala is simply wonderful, and I also wanted to put your mind at ease if fear had lingered within your heart."

Shilah stared at her, assessing the princess's aura. How different it was to all those Shilah sensed around her. "I thank you for such considerations. You are not a Darkan, yet I can feel the imprint of their essence on your aura."

"I am the mate of Drac El Kyn." Rich pleasure, love, and satisfaction were stamped into her voice. "That is the essence you sense within me."

Curiosity stirred in Shilah. "You are not afraid of his claiming."

The princess smiled, the radiance of it dazzling, the love pouring from her aura blinding. "I am not. I love Drac with every emotion in my heart, and he treasures me with such depths there are days I still struggle to understand my importance to him."

Shilah glanced down at the threads leading from her to the man in the distance whom it seemed heard every word exchanged with the princess. He was now in the center of the training circle, a group of ten Darkans surrounding him. He moved with the assurance of a man confident in his skills and at ease with his brutality "Your mating is young?"

"I only met Drac three months ago when the Empire of Mevia hunted me to this realm. He saved me."

She moved away from him, walking closer to the forest, Cronus by her left and the princess to her right.

"I can feel your fear," the princess murmured.

Shilah snapped her eyes to Saieke. "You have telepathic skills?"

"No, of course not, but I am able to sense intense emotions through your life force. Your energy is different from other Amagarians, but I still sense it. Lachlan would never hurt you. He...he is different from the friend I've come to love, but he is still the same man. Honorable and Kind."

"I do not doubt it," she said, moving with lithe speed and

skill through the pattern of the princess's mind, finding a pathway to connect on.

The princess gasped, and her eyes widened. "I just heard your voice in my mind."

"Forgive the impertinence of the intrusion. It was ill-mannered of me, and I forgot the courtesy we exist with on my home planet. I assure you I am not reading your thoughts. I would not invade your privacy in such a manner. I only went deep enough to project my thoughts to you."

"I took no offense, I was merely startled. The only person I've ever communicated in such a manner with is my mate," the princess said, with a gracious smile.

A warm feeling unfurled in Shilah's chest, and she knew if she stayed she would be wonderful friends with the poised and effortlessly charming princess. A slight buzz vibrated through the princess's pathway, and Shilah laughed. *"You will not be able to speak on a thread directly to me. But if you think about it, I will hear what you want to communicate."*

They strolled in silence for a while, and Shilah was content to bask in the wild beauty of the land, her hands resting lazily atop Cronus's head. *"I can feel a well of mystical energy several hundred miles north of this castle. Are you familiar with it, Princess Saieke?"*

The princess faltered. "I am."

"Is it a gateway portal to the other dimensions?"

She felt the unease of the princess. "It is."

"Does it have a gatekeeper?"

Princess Saieke glanced back toward Lachlan and stared at him for several long moments before she faced Shilah. "It does not. At least not on our side. But the journey to the portal is perilous at best. That was where I traveled to, hoping to escape a blood oath marriage by running to Earth. The wastelands to cross are dangerous, Princess Shilah. I would not recommend attempting it."

Shilah would take Princess Saieke's warnings about the perils of the journey into account as she plotted the best way to get herself and Kala to the portal safely. She also needed to understand the mutations she was undergoing and talking to the only mated non-Darkan she knew was an excellent place to start. "Have you undergone any changes since mating?"

Princess Saieke looked at Shilah with a knowing smile on her face, "Yes, I have. I was startled at first to awake with enhanced hearing and perfect vision in the dark. But as time progressed I realized that the transformation was a complete physical enhancement. All my senses were heightened, my bones and muscles became harder and stronger. I could run faster, leap further, and hold my breath longer. And possibly best of all, my rate of healing increased at least a hundred folds, such that wounds which once were fatal would now heal before death could claim me."

Knowledge bloomed in Shilah's mind about how these new abilities could aid in her taking back her family's birthright from Prince Quan. "I have experienced clear vision in the dark and improved hearing. It is amazing to think how much more sublime something as simple as experiencing the forest has become from having these abilities."

Princess Saieke laughed. "That is just the cusp of it. However, I am not sure if you will experience the same changes I have given you are a Serangite and I am an Amagarian. None of this is documented, bonding with non-Darkans let alone non-Amagarians is all new to the Darkage, and this is all happening at such a perilous time."

They spoke for several more minutes about the bold plan of King Gidon to lift up his people and how the princess planned to help, before the Princess flashed away, moving with such graceful speed she was a blur. Shilah turned to the north, opening the full range of her psychic eyes, assessing the portal and the energy running through it. The portal led to five possible planets—Serange, Amagarie, Earth, Titan, and Ceres. Why the portals only opened to those planets in the Omniverse no one knew, but a biosphere of dimensional energy seemed to connect to these worlds from the gateways which had the appearance of a tree crystalized in blue-white energy with five branches leading to each of those worlds.

A lazy wind swept across the mountain and Shilah inhaled the crisp cold air. *"In my world, there are few trees. Everything is different there. Our buildings are not made from stone and brick likes yours."* She sent Lachlan images of elaborately curved buildings with their intricate towering spires, some cylindrical, others squared, others shaped like triangles, some curved in perfect arcs and full circles, all made from glass and gunmetal grey iron. While the cities of her world were not dotted with trees and animals, the landscape surrounding each building was exquisite, lust verdant grass. *"Our worlds are so wildly different but so very beautiful."*

A heavy sorrow beat at her, and she ached to return to her people. She needed to know they survived, and that they were not suffering under the cruel regime of Prince Quan.

"I would like to know more of your Kingdom, my mate."

"And I would love to tell you."

A dark wave of energy rolled toward her, and she glanced toward the man moving toward her with such unhurried, savage grace. His scent traveled on the air, and she inhaled deeply, wanting to trap it inside her forever. His flavor was dark and elusive, predatory, yet so male.

"I would also like to show you my realm. I will be by your side, and you will be safe."

It never occurred to her she would be anything less. *"I would be honored to see your world."*

"Kala...." She called along the pathway to her sister, her voice firm, her determination unwavering.

Her sister was there instantly. *"Yes?"*

Lachlan was suddenly there, taking her in his arms, his eyes hard, brilliant amber with flecks of blue-green, echoed a bleak, stark loneliness. For the first time she realized for four hundred years he'd endured terrible isolation. There had been no lovers. He had not allowed himself sentiments. His purpose had been cold, merciless duty to his realm and protecting others from the monster within him.

Her heart twisted, for she understood loneliness, even though she had only endured it for the last fifty years when she had discovered she was an Impure and would never have the life her parents had, the lover and family her brother had, or so many of their citizens. She would be like the exiled ones, like the foreseers who were banned from ever marrying and procreating. It had been a life she accepted, for she believed absolutely in the law that outlawed crossbreeds.

Her breath hitched, and their thread jerked with a painful resonance. The sob in her throat threatened to choke her as she swallowed it back down. She pressed her forehead to the muscles of his chest, closed her eyes, blotting out the impossible needs beating at her.

"Kala, we leave tonight."

17

The Western Darkage
Naiyma—the capital city of the Darkage.

"*The realm of shadows and darkness is beautiful.*"

The sweet, soft, whisper in his mind was a soothing balm to Lachlan's soul. His mate's face glowed with rich pleasure as she sampled wine from one of the merchant's stall. They had been walking through his kingdom, at times moving to the other cities with the shadows for the last five hours. Now they strolled through the capital city of the Darkage, which buzzed with laughter and chattering as men, women, and children enjoyed the outdoors before the heralding winter.

He peered down at the delicate woman curved into his side, her eyes devouring the buildings and people as if she wanted to imprint them on her memories. He'd taken her to the great stone temples high in the mountains to watch the energy lights in the shadowed sky, then to the waterfalls of the East and West, and an underground cave which crackled and glowed with blue energy.

"While in the Empire I felt a sense of fear, even when I was simply strolling through the streets. There was always an air of menace, a sense of waiting for something terrible to happen. War has been declared, and even days later your people appear quite unconcerned with anything but the current flow of their lives."

Lachlan allowed the history of his realm to flow along their link. The Darkage people had not been involved in the last Great War which had lasted for fifteen years, and which had claimed millions of lives. Their ruler at the time, Gidon's father, had watched it from a distance and had not involved their realm since they owed no kingdom any alliance or allegiance.

The pain of the war, the horror of it had ridden the air and had fed many of their people who used the powers of their beasts. It was only recently, they learned some Darkans had sold their skills as death dealers during that war, creating enemies the Darkage had not known about. And the betrayal would be even greater this time. Now their own people would work alongside the Empire in the battles to come. And if Gidon called them to war, the security found in the obscurity and segregation from other kingdoms, even in a world as harsh and uncompromising as theirs, would be shattered.

The only reason a sense of normalcy lingered was that the war had not yet arrived. The kingdoms would be busy organizing warriors and food stockpiles, sending spies to infiltrate realms to uncover their weaknesses, selecting generals and captains to lead the march to war. Yet the Darkage might never show such preparations, for his King was not a man to be ruled by fear and emotion. He was cunning, smart, brutal, and would answer the call when he was ready. In that time, Lachlan must prepare his armies of the Eastern keep, while rooting out the traitors.

His mate laughed as a small, multi-colored bird flew into

the palms of her hand. He could feel her resolve to leave, to rescue her people from the dangers she had left them in. With war declared, it was not in their best interest to leave his kingdom for hers, and Lachlan did not believe he had the willpower to let her go. Duty, sacrifice, death, and war were carved into his very bones, and he needed a woman who could understand him and learn to accept the darkness in him for it was forever entrenched in his soul. A Darkan female would have relished a mate such as himself and celebrated his monster and his strength.

His mate had the potential to fear him.

She smiled, and his name whispered achingly from her lips. Something hot and urgent tumbled over inside him, and he gathered her closer to his side. The heady scent of her unique flavor sent his own pulse pounding. She might not be a Darkan, but she was a fierce warrior with the same values he held about loyalty and duty. Even if she was too soft. In time, he would hone her skills until she became more ruthless, more prepared to deal with treachery and betrayal.

Lachlan halted them before a towering building made of brick and white stones. "This is our temple of Artefacts. There is also an underground tomb where all Kings and Queens are buried. Would you like to visit?"

She nodded eagerly, and he took her into the shadows, appearing on the third floor, an immense space that stretched for miles with hieroglyphics on the wall, illustrating their history. The story of the Darkan legends and birth, even though it was written in Darkanian. She traced her fingers over the symbols of their language.

"What does this say?"

"It tells the story of our first dark queen, Luna Al Venfir, believed to be a primordial goddess for she had held within her all the beasts of the Darkans. It is said she had ten mates, one for each beast within her."

Shilah gasped. "Ten lovers!"

"She gave birth to ten sons and five daughters, each born with only one distinct beast, and the first generations of our demon beasts were manifested."

"I heard whispers in the Empire that once a king of the Darkage tried to bargain with the king of demons for more power."

"That man, King Amun Al Venfir, was Luna's husband and first love." Tracing the symbols, he continued reading, warmth punching deep inside at her enraptured expression. "The Shadow King, Amun, was not satisfied with our piece of Amagarie. He felt the power unequaled. We had suns, we had no monsters, our people were happy, but there was a restless hunger in Amun that could not be sated. His wife, Luna, the other half of his soul was all that was sweet and beautiful, and she tried to show him their love was all they needed. He was undeterred. Amun's search took him to the stars, and he found the realm of demons. Using magic and the shadows he made his way there and encountered such darkness and power. He was seduced..."

At his silence, she sent him a scowl and slapped his arm. "Continue," she ordered, imperiously.

Lachlan laughed, the sound shocking him. "Evil seduced his heart."

"What evil?" she demanded, her eyes widening.

"The king of the Demons lived in a realm of exile. Some call it Hell, others called it Hades, some purgatory, others call it the Demonage. The king was intrigued by the appearance of this man in his world when he had been bound in chains for years and unable to leave. The king promised Amun power and might, he only had to get the spell to weaken the walls of hell. Amun got it, how we do not know. Witches perhaps? Amun was so desperate, he did not once think that the Demon King was filled with treachery. The spell was cast, the sun that shone over our kingdom exploded, and chakras of the demons tried to escape their world and into ours. Dozens of beasts, hundreds legends said poured into Amun driving him mad. He fled back to our kingdom, and Luna greeted a ravaging monster. She was a light that anchored him against slaughtering his people, and when they mated and shared blood, some of the chakras within him found its way into her."

His mate inhaled slowly, then softly expelled. "And she birthed a nation of beasts. What happened to her? Does the story say?"

He took her in his arms and shadow stepped with her to a tomb where a flawless black pearl was mounted above a beautifully carved sculpture, with surrounding images of twenty different stone beasts guarding it. "She went on to live for centuries before her death. She lies here."

Another hour passed as he enthralled his mate with stories of his kingdom, her interest unending. He showed her the first plates his kind had used, their oldest clothes and furniture, rare paintings and sculptures by their greatest artists in history.

When she'd seen her fill, he spun with her in the shadows, taking her out into the streets. "Are you ready to return to the castle?"

"No, your world is very mountainous and teems with such wildlife. And the people, look at them," she said wistfully, lifting her chin to two children darting away from their mother, only for her to grab them with shadows and throw them into the air. Their peals of laughter echoed in the air. "How normal everything seems. I wonder if Dxyriah currently feels peace or are they in turmoil."

"Have you not tried to connect with any of your people?"

She darted him a quick glance. "I have tried. The distance is too great, even for my powers. I have no notion of how my people fare. It hurts somewhere deep inside that every day I am away, they might be suffering under Prince Quan's rule."

"Tell me about your world, my mate, and how did you end up in Amagarie?"

She faltered for a few seconds, before resuming her walk. "Prince Quan, the man who assassinated my brother, has no right to the realm. The heirship of Dyxriah's throne can only be inherited, or another house can challenge my rule and demand a trial by combat. Prince Quan has no Symonrah blood. The legal way for someone not of our bloodline to rule would be to petition the Senate for a trial by combat, and only after he proved to the Senate, I am unfit to be a ruler by our laws. Prince Quan ignored those laws, and he slaughtered most of my family and friends when he took my kingdom. My sister had seen a vision of this, but my brother did not take adequate precautions," Shilah said, an aching regret heavy in her tone. "Kala could not predict the timeframe, and when he consulted with other foreseers, they did see such a future for him. Because she was just an Alpha, he doubted her ability, but I believed her."

He sensed the agony burning like a fiery ball of pain that buried itself in her heart. If there had been hatred, it was now muted. Only a sense to seek justice was entrenched in her thoughts.

"After the attack, it took me five days of hiding from the prince in the network of crystal caves underneath our kingdom before we escaped through the portals. The prince's powers lie in the telekinetic genesis, and he is an Imperial. Twice he almost killed me, even though I could read his thoughts and anticipate his attacks. Soldiers who should have been loyal to me worked with him, and I was so frightened I would lose Kala and my life I fled."

Shame and regret were thick in her voice, and he felt the echoes of her tears in his mind. The memories of the prince wielding the power of his mind to use a sword to cut down dozens in her court rushed to him. The horror as he'd snapped her uncle's neck with the force of his thoughts alone. Soldiers close to her had rushed into the temple to save her, but they hadn't gotten a chance to pull the high beam weapons from their hips. Another prince whose powers lay in teleportation, moved through their ranks, cutting down her supporters with shocking ease.

He gathered her in his arm and flowed with her to the *Moire*—their largest jungle which connected the quadrants. There he took her upon a steeply sloped hill overlooking the capital city in the far distance. Using his shadows, he lay her down on the forest floor and lowered himself beside her. There they stared out into the great abyss, the jungle of his realm, and the obscured stars in the heavens. He'd already assured her vengeance, and he would lay her kingdom at her feet if she so desired.

"My Imperial powers awakened during the attack, and I did not understand how to use my full abilities. We have scholars who train and teach us how to hone our geneses, and though I could feel the well of energy at my center, I could not call it forth. I learned more about the level of my abilities while in Amagarie. I should have stayed, and fought," she whispered. "Instead, I handed him the key to my kingdom by running."

"Your instinct to survive roared to life. This is not something to be ashamed of. Retreat is a battle strategy. Amassing more power to return and defeat an enemy is a sound plan."

"The army I wanted was to only be a show of might, to force the Senate to convene so I could challenge the acceptance of his atrocity. To force him to give up a rule he had no right to, and to demand a trial where he would stand judgment for his crimes."

"Tell me of your realm and their powers," he demanded, wanting to understand the force he had to decimate.

"Serange is quite small, even smaller than your eastern quadrant here. My kingdom, Dxyriah has a population of two million denizens, and the entire planet only holds seven million people."

"And they all have mental prowess?"

"It is bred into our genetics. However, most of our wealth and power is concentrated in the aristocracy through a system of selective marriages. There is a strict division of class, so the most powerful of the geneses are clustered in the upper echelons of society. Almost all the Princes and Princesses of Serange have Omega level powers. There are only a few Imperials, and most are scholars at our temples. All other citizens are Alpha level. In Dxyriah every citizen is registered on a psychic network, where we can ask permission to speak with each other telepathically through that neural network."

"Your people do not speak aloud?"

She laughed lightly. "Of course, we do. But the network is there, where anyone can reach out at any time. But there are protocols of communication, so privacy is not invaded, and rights trampled upon. Permission is asked and granted. Like all kingdoms, we have laws that govern our people. Laws that prevent us from ripping into each other's minds, invading citizens' privacy, or stealing information. Once you are a citizen of Dxyriah, you must register on the psychic network. That way, it is easier for the PPF—PsyNet Protectorate force, the law defenders of our kingdom, to detect when there is a breach in the network and know when a crime is being committed. We are a peaceful kingdom with little to no crime. This is the reason Prince Quan's attack had such success. Our generation and several before us had no concept of war."

"Your people knew you were attacked."

Her breath hitched. "Yes. My cry spilled throughout the network, and my Barons responded. I could feel their worry and the multitude of knocks that wanted access to my neural net. I had to close myself off from the assault and concentrate on saving my sister's life."

"Is the Prince Quan a part of this network?"

"He is not of my kingdom."

"What is he?"

"He is the crown prince of Arcadia. Their power lies in telekinesis."

"What does he gain from the attack of your kingdom?"

"I fled," she whispered closing her eyes. "I only know at that moment he desired the ending of my bloodline. And I fear he is seeking to end the segregation of the three kingdoms. He would have support for this, especially from those people who are Impures and those who crave more power."

"Is he now the ruler of your kingdom?"

"It should not be possible, but he was crowned before I escaped. When the Senate called for me, I remained silent."

The image of her crouched in a cave, bleeding from her mouth and nose rushed through his mind, as she worked frantically to save her dying sister. Shilah had screamed and pleaded with the gods to not take her sister, the last of her family. She had been impervious to the mental call of the Senate as they had blasted calls for her through the psychic network, and hover crafts had whizzed through the air searching for her.

Her terror had been a living entity which had consumed her, and her entire heart and emotions had been concentrated into one relentless goal—to save her sister's life. She had lifted Kala's body, stumbling under the weight several times before dogged determination and sheer willpower had her carrying her sister for miles to the portal.

Lachlan turned over her predicament, dissecting it from all angles. Fleeing to save her sister had been the best move, as far as he assessed, or she would be dead now. He understood duty to her realm and people, and if he caged her and did not allow her to return, a man who apparently had goals of taking back her kingdom to the time of anarchy and tyranny would have free rein.

"I will send fifty Darkan warriors with you, and they will be under your sole command."

"I am tempted, Lachlan Ravenswood, but I've seen that even with just a peek of a possible future, my sister's visions cannot be ignored. It is not only you, but any Darkans must never enter my kingdom."

Denial roared through him for he did not see in her mind and heart a plan to return to Amagarie after she reclaimed her throne. She envisioned a solitary life, standing beside her sister as they ruled their people with love and fair justice. He hadn't dreamed of a mate, but now that he'd found her, it was impossible to imagine enduring living without her warmth, the light that shone from her, her taste, and her scent.

"I will do what I should have done," she continued softly. "I will find my Barons, those loyal to me, and take back my kingdom with as little bloodshed as possible. I did not give my people or my supporters a chance to stand with me, and for me. I made fear rule my actions, and I acted without thought, running and hiding away, relying not on my strength and capabilities but on others. I've forgotten the teachings of my forefathers, and it shames me. I must reclaim honor for our house and do it without costing my people any more anguish. I am their crown princess, and though I was not trained for the role like many before me, I must show them I am more than capable of protecting them and ruling our kingdom."

He sensed the tears in her mind, and the terror in her

soul, for she could feel the harsh and ruthless resolve forming in him to never let her go, that he would not stay at a distance and do nothing as she stepped into danger. She lurched to her feet and stumbled a few paces away. Gentle slopes gave way to steep ridges, deep ravines cutting through the forest and she headed in that direction.

It struck him with the force of a hammer, it was for this reason she feared being with him so much. Reading her thoughts, feeling her pain, she believed with her entire heart that should he know that her people harmed her, he would slaughter them. And she was right.

He moved with the shadows to stand beside her. "I will trust in your skills and determination. I will not send Darkans to your world." At this time, he couldn't promise he would not come should she have need of him, and he ruthlessly kept the thought from spilling to her.

She whirled to face him. Pleasure lit in the fractured depth of her eyes, and she rushed over to him with such speed she was a blur. His blood was already changing her physiology, making her faster, her bones denser, her body less susceptible to bruises. His little mate did not perhaps realize how fast she moved, for she only flung herself into his arms, tipped on her toes, and pressed her mouth to his with the sweetest of heat. *"Thank you, Lachlan."*

Using the pad of his thumb, he traced a slow line from her collarbone to the tip of her breast. With a shaky laugh, she pulled away, her newly enhanced strength and speed taking her several steps from him.

Her eyes were luminous with arousal. "You are dangerous to my willpower." With a frown she glanced at the distance between them, and then her eyes widened, her shock burning along their link.

"I…what?"

"Your strength and speed now rival most Amagarians with superior chakra control."

"This is not possible," she breathed, pushing tendrils of her hair away from her enchanting face. "I know you said my speed would increase but I never imagined with such proportions." Then as if to test it herself, she flashed toward him and slammed into his body. "I am fast. Let us race!"

Then she took off deep into the forest, running with such speed she covered miles within a minute. *"This is incredible. I can feel that I am stronger."*

She glanced at his side where he easily kept pace. *"Will I ever get as fast as you?"*

"No."

Her joy and fascination pulled a smile to his lips. Her reaction was far different from Princess Saieke when she'd learned of the changes to her body from mating Drac. Even now the princess searched their tomes and great archives, trying to understand the full effects of the extraordinary changes. While Serangites' mental capacity was superior to several species, they had a similar physical construct to humans, and Lachlan's princess seemed of a mind to revel in the newfound freedom of moving with such speed and stamina.

They covered several hundred miles, before she faltered, panting. "I should be worried, shouldn't I?" Then she laughed, enchanting him. With a flash she was before him, pressing a soft kiss to his lips.

He absorbed her happiness into his being. He allowed himself the luxury of getting lost in the sensations of her taste, drunk on the heady scent of her. He wanted her so much he could barely breathe. She moved away with a burst of speed, and with a sensual, tempting smile, toed off her delicate slippers.

Her eyes glittered with wicked, playful promise, and his

heart warmed in a manner he'd never experienced before. The sweet, spicy scent of her arousal rode the air, and he smiled at her bewitching boldness.

"My senses are getting even stronger than earlier. I can hear the sound of water miles away, the scuttling of small animals and insects. I can hear—"

Shilah's pained scream pierced the air.

Lachlan swirled with the shadows, but his mate's body was already flung into the sky by a spiral of sands, with a speed that rivaled how he wielded the shadows. Roots burst through the vegetation, streaking through the air to wrap around her throat and tangle around her body, before slamming her against a massive tree in the forest. The hold was merciless, and she screamed as the pressure cracked her ribs. His mate's precious blood dripped onto the ground, and onto the branches which had been formed into the spears used to crucify her body to the tree. The thick, twisted root coiled and stabbed inside her chest with wicked precision.

He felt the impact like an arrow through his heart.

Blood spurted from his mate's chest, and her cry of agony echoed to his very bones. For a second, his sanity vanished. An enraged, primal sound tore from his throat as his heart and soul cracked.

18

The demon on Lachlan's skin hissed, the sound a dark promise of retribution.

"We want no war with you, Darkan. We're only here for Princess Shilah of Symonrah," the Arian said, the earth parting as he rose from it, and stood with his feet braced deep into the soil, as he tethered his connection to his element. "We were given permission by the true king to hunt in the Dark lands."

Lachlan showed no reaction that others already gave allegiance to the man who was supposed to take the place of Gidon after his assassination.

"Something is crawling toward my heart," his mate gasped, her fear and pain bitter, tugging at the darkness within him. *"I can see it, root like tentacles digging deep into my flesh."*

"He is an assassin from Aria— the kingdom of Earth and Sands. Arians with great chakra control command anything of the earth. The minerals and iron found within it, the rocks, the dirt, the sand. This display of power indicates an elder from their kingdom, those with immense strength is rumored to control anything that has its origin from the earth's crust, even the trees, and lava."

With calm deliberateness, Lachlan closed their telepathic link, not wanting to subject her to the remorseless violence surging through him.

"Don't close your mind to me," she cried, tears streaking down her cheeks, her voice rough with pain and fury.

His claws lengthened into long, razor-sharp talons, his senses sharpening, all the light disappearing from his soul as he became the monster. The darkness was far thicker and much uglier without her anchor. They had come for her, in his world, and he would not show mercy. "No," he growled, his voice a distorted wash of malevolent power reverberating through the forest.

"Please…I need to feel you in me."

Everything in him repulsed at the terror leaking from her. He'd failed his mate. Lachlan had underestimated the reach of the enemy, thinking her safe within the walls of the Darkage with him by her side. He'd allowed himself to be distracted by the heat of mating, and now his woman bled before his eyes, her fear an affront to his senses. And at the center of it, there was a weakness inside he'd never felt before, for she was hurt, in tears, with death only seconds away.

The earth rolled beneath his feet, and lightning split the ground as an assassin from Avindar— the kingdom of lightning, arrived in a whirl of crackling energy. His speed unfathomable as he came with the lightning before the thunder. A sonic boom echoed in the air pushing back Lachlan several feet and pulling a scream from Shilah.

He slipped in her mind, offering her the comfort of the connection. *"I won't leave you, my mate."*

She grasped eagerly at their thread. *"Lachlan…they are here to take me back to the empire, and this newcomer's psychic barrier is weak."*

The Avindite slapped a hand to his forehead, as Shilah's

power buzzed in the air. With almost unparalleled speed, a slice of bright light flashed from his hand toward her. Lachlan moved with the darkness, dipping into the well of his rage and full power to beat the speed of light, appearing in front of his mate as the bolt hit. Pain slammed into his chest, as it cut into his flesh and bone like the sharpest of knife.

His mate's cry of rage and terror echoed in his mind, along with her disbelief that he'd been hit. *"He is an elder from Avindar. His control of lightning is beyond anything we can comprehend. His speed as he moves within the storm and energy of the lightning can rival that of a Darkan."*

Lachlan sent the full power of his element into the force of nature that held his mate captive. The shadows darted and slashed, piercing the tree and splitting through the middle from the root up. Before the assassin who controlled the earthly elements could react, in a blur of speed and darkness, his claws sliced the branch that had lodged itself inside her chest.

His mate fell forward, and he caught her. He swallowed her with his shadows, trapping her in unrelenting darkness, removing her from the sight of the enemy. He built layers of his shadows around her like a wall. A shield that kept away the world. He pierced her chest with his shadows, and she screamed thrashing in his arms.

"I have to find the roots he left within you. Forgive the pain."

His shadows grabbed the root like tentacles and yanked them from her chest. His mate heaved, sweat slicked her skin, her mouth white with the awful pain. He slashed his wrist and placed it to her mouth, merging his mind with her and coaxing her to drink. She did, shuddering at his taste, at once appalled and aroused by the idea she consumed a part of him. He could feel the power of his blood working through her, checking the flow of her blood and knitting her from inside.

Then he pulled the stake from her chest. Another scream tore from her throat, pain shuddering through her body. The control of his shadows was so absolute it was as if they were sentient. They curved around her, creating a place for her to lie down, contorting to give the impression of comfort.

"Stay with me," she gasped. "Their well of power is more volatile than those who had waited for us in Mevia. We can leave with the shadows."

"They cannot get you here, my mate. It would take another Darkan hours to pierce through my shadow barriers unless he is a force like myself. And there is none."

"I am worried about you!" The cry was torn from her throat, from her soul, and the anguish in her voice tore at him, even as it soothed.

There was no time to offer soothing words, he stepped from the cocoon of the shadows, the bloodletter in him rising with swirling madness.

"Take me with you. I am already recovered. I can fight."

"No."

Her frustration burned through the link. *"I can sense the power the two men before you have,"* she said, a tremble in her voice. *"And dozens more are coming, I can feel the wave of energies drawing closer, and their thoughts are uncensored. They are bounty hunters, and the Avindite is a powerful tool for the empire. He assembled them. There is also a warlord, it was his spell which found me, and he is casting a cloaking spell over this area so we won't be getting any reinforcements."* A hitch of hesitation traveled along their thread. *"I will build a compulsion for them to turn away and give up hunting me. My call will be loud and insistent. Please Lachlan, I can turn them away."*

And for the first time since he woke to find his darkness entrenched with his soul, he paused and genuinely considered another option. For her. And only for her. For she meant everything to him.

But there was none.

She was so innocent, too damned naive despite everything she'd experienced.

It gutted something inside of him that he could not give this to her—mercy. He could feel the rage and the menace from those converging on them. He could allow them to leave, give his woman the latitude to plant suggestions in their minds, distort their memories of even finding her, but a message had to be sent to the empire, one stamped with a promise of his own.

The waves of his mate's telepathic energy rushed through the air, brushing along the minds of the advancing enemy. He peered into the well of darkness he had hidden her in. She sat on the shadow chair, her legs curled beneath her, her fingers twisted in a triangular symbol as she sank into the well of her powers. Her hair crackled, and the thin fractures in her eyes seemed to shatter into more pieces as her powers expanded.

Rage and bloodlust hammered in him with each beat of his heart, clawing and raking for supremacy, but the purity of his mate leashed it. Lachlan looked inside of his being where her light lingered, a bright glow in the darkness of his soul. Chakra pulsed through his body, curling around her silver thread in a protective hold, cloaking the mating link that connected them in unrelenting darkness, pushing her away from their mental link.

Then he coated himself in a savagery that filled him with exquisite pleasure as he moved with the shadows and the unrelenting power of the monster inside him, tearing out throats, and ripping hearts from their chests.

Blue lightning streaked through the darkness as the elder assassin from Avindar breached the shadows, a bolt of crackling energy poised at his fingertips as he crouched. Lightning forked in a spectacular display, streaks stretching through the shadows, ripping it apart. Lachlan twisted, diving left to avoid the pure energy slamming toward him.

In the flashes of light, he could see the assassin atop the lightning itself, his speed almost too great for Lachlan to track. He rolled out of the dive toward the assassin, moving with such force and speed it was as if time slowed. The dirt as it erupted from the ground seemed as if it stood still, the trees tumbling on the forest floor appeared as if they'd frozen in mid-fall. Lachlan twisted, spinning with the shadows, dodging the bolts of raw energy, and barreling toward the assassin, slamming his hand into his abdomen and ripping deep with his claws. The Avindite shifted avoiding a fatal blow.

A piercing shriek echoed in the forest as the lightning seemed as if it ripped the fabric of the atmosphere itself. The lightning ran across Lachlan's skin, slicing deep, eating through flesh to his very insides like fire. The power of it slammed him back several paces, and blood poured from his side down his leg in a hot torrent.

Once he touched the Avindite assassin he would be struck by lightning, an absolute defense. But would it work if the touch was a fatal one?

In a coordinated attack meant to find his mate, bolts after bolts of incendiary lightning struck the shadows, the ground rolling and cracking apart as the Arian assassin used his earthy element to rip apart the forest floor. Lachlan summoned his demon, and with a pulse of unremitting power, it launched from his skin and slammed into the earth. His Leviathan roared a battle cry that echoed for miles throughout the kingdom.

The assassins exchanged an uneasy glance, fear shimmering in their eyes. There was no doubt they hadn't anticipated a Darkan who had the power to summon his demon beast. Black scales rippled and covered Lachlan's body. The assassins' tried to track his beast. A fatal error. He stepped into the shadows then appeared behind the Arian assassin and plunged his claws towards his chest. A wall of crystallized minerals formed but not fast enough, for his heart was already ripped from his chest and dropped to the ground.

A gleam of light slashed from above and Lachlan jerked back avoiding the Avindite's attack. He flowed with Lachlan striking toward his midsection at lightning speed. Unable to dodge Lachlan blocked the attack, but as the Avindite's blow was parried another piercing sound ripped through the air lashing Lachlan with crackling lightning. It threw him several meters into the forest breaking all the trees, and boulders in his path until he crashed into the side of a cliff forming a vast crater.

A menacing roar rang across the forest as Orochi decimated the last of the Avindite's support. Only one remained, and though the warlord was cloaked his fear revealed his location. Lachlan would save him for last, for now, he would let the warlord believe he was safe behind his spell.

Orochi's sight levelled on the Avindite and he was aware, for he summoned the depths of his strength scorching the ground and destroying all life in a hundred-meter radius around himself. Lightning danced over his skin and crackled from his eyes. He appeared at the height of his power. The state Lachlan wanted him at, for the edge of fear from the warlord had now disappeared. No doubt confident in his leader's ability. In this form, the Avindite would be ruthlessly vanquished before his subordinate. An example of the difference in power between an elder Avindite and a bonded Darkan, the tale of might which needed to be spread.

Simultaneously Lachlan and Orochi shot off toward the Avindite, their speed leaving a path of destruction behind.

The Avindite was fast, his reaction instantaneous, lightning spilling from the sky with deadly intent toward both man and beast. The lightning struck, but Lachlan and Orochi were already ahead of it, the electricity on their heels charring the wreckage in their wake.

In an instant they were upon him, his lightning always a few feet behind, but his reaction once again was quick, for he blasted a wall of electricity toward them, adding a frontal assault to his trailing lightning. But where there is the light, there is always the dark. Both beast and man stepped into the shadows to re-emerge before the Avindite, Lachlan went low, and Orochi went high. Lachlan tore out a chunk of the Avindite's torso, ripping through several vital organs, while Orochi took his head.

There was no lightning defense, instant death rendered it null. The Avindite's body fell to the ground, and Orochi roared its triumph.

A wave of dismal failure rushed into Lachlan's nostrils. He stepped with speed toward it slashing with might into a force field which distorted to reveal the warlord. He was young, with markings on his face making him look skeletal. His hair was wild and midnight black falling to his waist. His body was covered with symbols, and he wore a shoulder guard of humanoid skulls. His eyes were lifeless but filled with ambition and a hunger for power.

The energy barrier cracked under Lachlan's strike, and the warlord smiled, incanted a phrase then stepped into a portal which closed behind him.

Lachlan inhaled seeking negative essence. There was none. With the enemy crushed, he stepped into the shadows and removed the barrier protecting his mate. Through the red haze of bloodlust still pounding through his veins, the softness of her fingertips on his chest barely registered. Her scent of rain filled his lungs, and a soft head butted his chin, like a feline vying for the attention of her mate. He arched her to him, raked his canines over her neck, his lips and tongue easing the sting as he made his way to her collarbone, then lower to the soft curve of her breast where he struck deep with his fangs.

A wild cry tore from her throat, but she held his head to her, and he felt no fear. His throat pulled, and he shuddered from the sheer pleasure of it. She tasted exotic, exquisite, her blood centering him as the violent storm within quieted. He pulled from her and swiped his tongue over the punctures, healing them. She eased back from him and their gaze collided. She looked mesmerized and terrified, unable to look away from him. He bathed his skin in shadows, hiding from her sight his clothes that were drenched in blood.

She slipped her mind into his, and her energy poured over him like molten lava, filling the cold, dark crevices of his soul. The white purity of her light burned away the darkness, and their mind merged deeper than they'd ever gone before. He felt her every breath. Her heartbeat and it was inside his own chest. Her fear felt like his own. Her relief that he lived swept through his body. And all the aching hunger, fears, and hope in her soul became his. She was crying, and he felt her pain as though it was his own. The immense pressure that sat on her shoulder became a boulder in his mind. The acrid fear that if she allowed him in her heart, she would lead her people to more damnation pummeled her. And the desire she had for him. His heart trembled. It was a living flame in her soul, a need so profound it shook her.

Knots of tension Lachlan hadn't known held him eased. And it was then he acknowledged there had been a fear inside him that she might not return the intensity of emotions that he felt.

Someone groaned as a body slid along the ground in a bid to escape. Lachlan's shadows caught and wrapped around the man's throat. The scent of the man's terror was the sweetest of perfume, its fragrance an addictive aroma, urging him to torment and torture so he could feed more.

"Please, Lachlan let him go." The soft touch of Shilah's hand on his chest did nothing to ease the primal violence churning inside him.

"He intended to cause your death."

Vulnerable pain and fear flashed across her expression. "I am alive, you saved me." She glanced at the bodies on the ground, and he felt the need rising within her to vomit. Stepping back, she heaved, looking everywhere but at the carnage.

And he could sense her desperation inside, and with a burst of clarity, he realized their mateship hinged on his mercy. There was a dark fear inside of the bloodletter within him. Then he recalled her sister's vision that he would harm their people. Lachlan knew an outcome like that was only possible if they hurt her, and anyone who caused her pain could not earn his forgiveness even if he had been inclined to the odd emotion.

He suspended the man in the air and tightened his shadow around the man's neck, compressing his windpipe strangling the air from his throat.

"Please. He has a wife and three daughters. His wife is ill, and their healers can do nothing. They have need of money to purchase the elixir from Boreas or Caelum. For citizens of his lower orders, the cost is equivalent to five years' wages. He is desperate, and that is the only reason he responded to the call of the bounty."

The pain in his mate's voice crawled through him, burning straight to his soul and searing him with white fire. He withdrew the shadow and dropped the man. He scrambled back, breathing erratically, eyes darting back and forth between Shilah and Lachlan.

"Go," she said softly. "Do not hunt me or you will only meet death."

Lachlan felt the buzz of her power as she planted the suggestion in the man's mind. Then she tugged the small dagger from her side and threw it at the man who caught it deftly. It was embedded with precious stones of rubies and jasper. The man stared with surprise, and his eyes flared with something akin to hope.

"This should pay for a vial of elixir and will feed your family for years. Go *now*."

The man nodded, lurched to his feet and ran away. Lachlan inhaled deep, marking the scent of the man, the predator in him knowing he would never allow a threat to his mate to go unpunished.

"Do not, Lachlan. I gave him my word he would live. I searched his memories he is not a murderer. He is a good man."

He truly believed only his mate could think a man who had resolved to take her life for money was good. She waited, staring at him with her beautiful eyes. She looked vulnerable, young, and all too fragile.

"As you wish it, he will not die by my hands."

Her relief at his mercy burned along their thread, and she hurtled herself in his arms.

Her voice filled his mind, the tones soft and so achingly familiar. *I need you.*

19

An indescribable warmth slowly infused her body. The forest was still, the raw scent of blood fading from her nostrils, and carnage no longer in sight. Shilah held onto him as she moved them into a clearing, her muscles relaxing now that they were safe. Despite the shattering brutality of the past few minutes, she could live there, in his arms, their bodies entwined, hearts beating in harmony forever. And that was why Shilah knew she had to leave him under the cloak of secrecy, tonight, through the portal Princess Saieke had planned to use to escape to earth. Even now she could feel its phantasmic energy, and with her enhanced strength and speed, it should only take her a few hours to reach the portal.

Her people needed her, as his King needed him. If she left, her entire soul would cry out to him, and he would follow. Even now, something gaping tore at her heart, and she had to ruthlessly build barriers along their link, so he was not aware of the riotous feelings beating inside her.

"You are distressed mate."

She closed her eyes, swallowing back the burn of tears,

and the aching regret and pain already hammering through her. "Lachlan."

A hand soaked with blood cupped her chin and lifted her face to his. How wild and feral he seemed, how dangerous and brutal, his chakra still pulsing with a remorseless fury, yet his touch was inexplicably gentle.

For a terrifying moment, she'd thought he had died. And the fear that had lived and breathed in her had all been for him. The sense of loss and sorrow had been great, for there was so much more she wanted to know about this man. A thousand birds took wings in her stomach, and Shilah crawled up his body and wrapped her legs around his waist. The look in his eyes stole her sanity. The combination of raw strength and tenderness shifted something down deep inside her. She pressed her hand over her heart, suddenly barely able to breathe. It was impossible not to fall more and more for him. "I crave the taste of you, and I burn for your body."

Every detail of Lachlan Ravenswood would be etched forever into her mind and heart. He'd stolen a piece of her that she hadn't known existed, and she would not fight to ever reclaim it back. Even with the Omniverse separating them, he would always have that part of her.

She did not have to verbalize her need, he understood perfectly. He kissed her, and his embrace thrilled her, sent her into another world of pure sensation where she lost herself. He delved his tongue in to taste every part of her. He tasted like violence, like the rain, like comfort, like lust and sin.

"I need you...in me. Love me, Lachlan."

She was only dimly aware of her clothes being torn from her. Their mouths stilled fused together, a waft of breeze over their body and then they were perched on a rock's ledge, a waterfall pounding their bodies, washing away the blood and violence.

Another waft of breeze, a swirl of shadows and she was lying on her back on the wet grass, that felt sublime against her sensitive skin. The waterfall pounded off the mountain in the distance, and thunder rumbled in the air. Hard, muscled, his larger body blanketed over hers, licking along her neck, down to her collar, and over her tight, aching nipples. She arched as he sucked the tip of her nipple with a strong pull of his mouth.

He didn't linger, moving lower, parting her legs wide. The touch of his tongue on her clitoris was such a shock of pleasure that she couldn't hold back her cry. Her world narrowed entirely on the pleasure crowding her senses. He raked his teeth over her straining nub, then licked it hard. He alternately savored and consumed. Her heels dug into the earth, hips lifting, a cry tearing from her as his tongue pressed inside. Hungry, desperate moans spilled from her, mingling with his low, gravelly murmurs of approval fluttering against her wet sex.

She moaned and bucked under the carnal lash of his tongue, but he was unrelenting. Her hands went to his hair, fingers fisting the thick locks. She shivered as he pressed her harder onto the grass. Drawing her beneath him, he parted her thighs with his own, pressed his cock at her damp and welcoming slit, and surged deep, burying himself in one smooth stroke.

White lightning streaked in her veins. *Lachlan!*

He started to ride her, and his name became a whimper, a cry, a plea, a gasp, a moan. He whispered something low and guttural. His body was hard and powerful, moving against hers. Her core ached, and she would be sore for hours to come, perhaps days, but all she could do was feel a desperate, agonizing need for more.

He rolled with her, until she lay atop of him, his pelvis surging up from below, never stopping his pounding rhythm which she rocked her hips to meet, arousal becoming molten in her veins. She held onto him, one hand clutched at his back, the other around his neck. Shilah panted, sweat glistening on her body as she rode him in a deep, sensual glide, her hips circling, sliding up and down, as she fucked him like he surely fucked her. He caressed the globes of her ass, the hollow in her back. He touched her gently, almost reverently.

Chakra exploded around her, caressing all over her body, slid sinuously around to her wet sex. It delved between her folds and rubbed. Her clit throbbed, ached, swelled painfully at the friction his chakra generated. Her head fell back, the curtain of her hair rippled over her back brushing his thighs, a hard shudder wracking her body.

Despite the cold air, her body sheened in sweat, pulsating, throbbing with a fever of need. She released his neck to touch his beautiful mouth. *"I could fall in love with you Lachlan Ravenswood."*

Then she lowered her mouth to his throat, to the irresistible rush of his blood calling to something dark and unknown inside her. She found the pulse beating on the side of his neck, stroking her tongue across his pulse once, twice, in a small caress then biting down.

His hoarse cry of pleasure filled her mind, even as the sweet taste of his blood rushed into her mouth. The taste was nothing like she'd ever had, for riding the taste of blood was energy that rushed through her veins, tugging at the powers buried inside her.

His savage features twisted into a grimace of sublime pleasure *"I am already there Shilah Symonrah of Serange. I am already there."*

Her heart cracked, yet a joy trembled through her soul. She released his neck and licked, distantly shocked that her bite wounds healed instantly and that the wounds were the punctures of retracting canines. Claws exploded from his hands and sank into the soft skin of her back. Another swirl of shadows and she was on her knees, her hips arched in the air. He pushed her to her stomach, moving behind her, hilting deep in one stroke. His head lowered, his teeth gripping the sensitive area between her shoulder and neck as she screamed out in pleasure-pain as his fangs struck deep. A primitive, throaty, growl echoed from him, demanding her surrender, her submission.

The sounds called to something deep inside her, something unknown, feminine, but powerful. Sensual but innocent. Calm but ravaging. His hips rolled, and he shafted into her wet sex with an untamed strength not present in their previous mating. She sensed the freedom in him, the unfettered lust, knowing she was less fragile because of his blood, her body more able to withstand the roughness of the mating demands burning through his soul.

Shilah whimpered. That bite of pain only heightened the sensations, as he gripped her hips and rocked her harder and deeper onto his cock, her pussy hurting on his thick girth, but such a good hurt. *"Lachlan, please!"*

Shilah did not know what she screamed for as she became lost, if it was more of his untamed loving or an ease from the intense wash of lust. She begged, arching, writhing beneath him as so many sensations seemed to converge on her at once. She could barely gasp for air the sensations were so brilliant. Her climax rushed over her like a tidal wave, tearing through her soul, stars exploding behind her eyes as her powers roiled through the mountains and down the valley. She took his mind under, his soul into hers, his pleasure becoming hers and hers becoming his, and with a hoarse growl, he released his seed deep inside her body.

She collapsed onto the forest floor, and he tucked her body close to his, and she inhaled, breathing in his scent, his warmth. His arms tightened around her, his heart racing as he took her into the safety and comfort of the shadows.

Exactly three hours after she had fallen asleep in Lachlan's arms, Shilah's lashes fluttered open. She shifted in the bed, seeking the protective warmth that had held her as she succumbed to sleep. She flared her senses, unable to feel him in the chamber. Their thread twanged, and she ran the tip of her finger over the silky, yet unbreakable bond.

"I am meeting with King Gidon, Drac, and Talon at the Western Quadrant. I shall be home within a few hours. There is a great library on the second floor. I believe you will find great pleasure there, mate."

Home. How oddly comforting those words were? And it wasn't Serange she thought of. But here, in his arms, at this castle. She pressed one hand to her midsection hard, desperate to stop the quaking flutters, fighting to stick to her decision. *"Until I see you again, Lachlan Ravenswood."*

The presence in her mind stilled, and she felt its predatory intent as he assessed her words, the sorrow in her voice. Tension wound Shilah tight, coiling her stomach tighter and tighter. Moving from the bed with her newfound speed, she hurriedly dressed in a black caftan that molded her petite frame. Her hair was quickly caught in a tight plait, and she slipped her feet into delicate slippers. They were not fashioned for fight or flight, but they were all she had access to. After a brief hesitation, she took up the golden armband that was fashioned from snakes. She could sense no energy within them, but they had come alive when she had been threatened. Taking a deep breath, she slipped them on, and then opened her psychic eyes.

"Kala."

Her sister answered instantly. *"I am ready."*

"I am coming for you now. We will need to move with stealth. Can you see if our escape will be hindered?"

"No vision comes to me. I am no longer at the King's castle, but I dine with Princess Saieke at her home in the Northern fort."

Shilah slipped deeper into her sister's mind, assessing the friendship and care she felt for the flamed hair princess, and looking at the picture of the Northern castle. *"Be ready, trust no one."*

Kala's fierce determination echoed, and Shilah slipped her mind from hers. She sank deep inside, closing off the mental pathway that led to Lachlan Ravenswood with a ruthless will. Then she flared her telepathy, sensing that his castle currently housed eighty-nine souls. Only ten of those were warriors, and she could detect them in the shadows, the brief touch of their aura, red and malevolent. Their goal was to protect her until Lachlan returned.

There was a stillness at her center, and she reached for it, drawing on white energy as she pushed her power before her. Using her telekinesis, she opened the door and exited the chamber with stealth then she hurried through the castle. She passed servants, and visitors but none saw her, for she built the illusion in their minds that she was not there. Shilah made her way to the highest tower on the highest landing of the castle. There she lifted her head to the shadowed sky and sent her mind hurtling through the air with sharp precision. She felt all the animals on the ground and all the creatures in the air. Something large rolled through the sky at a distance. Dipping into its mind she waded through its memories, assessing his strength and speed.

She called it to her, pushing the compulsion deep, one the massive creature could not resist. The winged creature zipped through the air, hurtling itself toward her with shocking speed. It landed on the large balcony, standing over six feet on four clawed legs, its feline body covered in grey feathers, its head birdlike with a beaked mouth.

She went deeper into its mind, building its loyalty to her, overriding his primeval nature, binding it to her command, feeding it the urgency to escape to the Northern Keep for Kala. It crouched in a bestial grace, and she hopped onto its back, the powerful muscles beneath her thighs twisting with sinuous power. It hurtled through the air, a wild cry echoing from its breast. She held on with all her strength, lowering her face against the wind, breathing easily. The journey felt as if it took forever, and her tension mounted with each dip and roll of the massive body beneath her.

Shilah flared her psychic ability, sensing the intent of all animals and Darkans far and wide. She caught the minds of several people below assessing if they sent any alert. Their minds were filled with peace, lust, love, and war. She felt the surprise of a warrior who thought he scented Lachlan but did not see him. Her heart lurched when that warrior glanced up, but the idea flitted away from his thoughts as he went back to seducing the laughing Darkan female by his side, carrying a basket of fruits.

Though the creature's speed was great, it took almost two hours of flight before it reached the courtyard of the Northern keep. It landed, and Shilah hopped from its back, grateful for her enhanced stamina. Her sister waited, and the Princess Saieke was by her side.

"Kala?"

"It would be impossible to disappear from beneath her nose," her sister said with wry amusement. *"Her curiosity cannot be deterred."*

The princess smiled and stepped forward, her eyes flicking to the beast. Shilah found it curious she was alone, but then she felt the auras of the warriors in the dark, and Shilah blinked, for more than twenty lingered, their aura cold and calculating, and she sensed they had one directive, protect the mate of Drac El Kyn at all cost.

"Does she know that we escape?"

There was a hitch in Kala's breathing. *"She only knows you come for me, but she is very quick and witty."*

If Princess Saieke had a similar bond with her mate like Shilah had with Lachlan was it possible she had told her mate of Shilah's visit?

Shilah stared at the princess, and in the depth of her sapphire eyes knowledge gleamed. Shilah dipped into her thoughts, some of the tension easing when she saw that the princess did not mean to betray their actions tonight.

"You will need to see for yourself that he is the other half to your soul."

The princess's uncensored thought burned through Shilah's mind, and she made no reply as Kala mounted the animal after her. Shilah ordered it toward the forest leading to the portal, commanding it to soar through the air with speedy stealth.

A ripple of awareness roiled through her. Her nerves stretched taut as Shilah sensed a dark, silent force behind her. She glanced over her shoulder expecting to see a winged creature following. There was none. Yet she knew with every fiber of her being Lachlan was close by. She could feel his rage swarming the air, the brutal resolve trembling through the sky. And she increased her pace, a sob tearing from her chest for she ran away in vain.

She glanced below, able to see the houses, the forest, and even the people on the ground. They flew over a vast lake the wind touching the surface of the silver so that ripples danced over the water. She glanced at the towering trees, some tall enough they brushed the underbelly of the animal. Leaves fluttered wildly as if something passed between them, and the taste of something dark and too primal coated her senses.

Behind her Kala stiffened, her hand tightening around Shilah's waist, a wave of energy pouring from her. *"It worsens. I see our city burning and blowing away like ashes in the wind. No one will be spared."*

Her sister spasmed, and Shilah gripped onto her as the vision held Kala in its ruthless grip. When it released her, she sobbed softly, her tears wetting Shilah. She wanted to open her mind and plead with him to let her go, but she was petrified to a depth she could not explain. It was then she acknowledged a deep part of her still feared the monster within him.

Tears burned behind her eyes and clamped down hard on her emotions. She couldn't afford feelings. The winged creature soared through the sky with dizzying speed, her mind directing it toward the pulse of raw energy deep into the open lands connecting the borders of the seven kingdoms. They escaped the tree line of the Darkage, moving from the pitch black of night to dawn. She could see the sun far off in the distance. But she felt no relief that she was no longer in the realm of shadow and demons.

Below her she saw no movement, she detected no aura, but a wave of dread filled her as the stark wasteland spread before her. It resembled death itself, with sharper jagged edges its main décor. Lifeless plants, twigs, and barks indicated a once thriving forest full of animals all erased by a force beyond their comprehension. The creature dipped in a rolling swoop, his enormous wingspan flaring wide as it glided low, and then landed. They hurriedly slid from its back. "Thank you," Shilah murmured, releasing it from her mind control, and it took to the sky once more.

"Hurry Shilah, I can feel the portal through the woods, just there."

She didn't have the heart to tell her sister she could feel Lachlan in the shadows. Shilah ran with her sister toward an opening in the barren forest of the wasteland. The trees were bare without leaves, and the earth cragged and without grass. They scrambled over several small boulders, climbing to what looked like the mouth of a cave.

A wave of dark energy made her stumble, and Kala cried out in fear.

"Keep going," Shilah said, turning around and searching for him. Opening her mind, their thread vibrated with a resonance she'd never felt before. She could not see him, but she felt him deep in her soul where it mattered. "You are a man I never imagined experiencing," she whispered. "I thank you for our time together, for I will cherish the memories forever, and I will crave you always. Your world is on the brink of anarchy, and your king needs you. Mine is on the edge of a revolution and I am needed. Please, Lachlan Ravenswood, let me go." Her knees weakened, her heart beating sluggishly within her breast. "You are the harbinger of death and destruction for my city…and I would have no choice but to declare us *enemies* if you do not relinquish your claim, Darkan." Her heart cracked, and she trembled violently.

A cold, menacing snarl rumbled in his chest. The ground shook, and the acrid flavor of betrayal coated her senses. A low, mocking laugh, cunning and cruel filled her mind. And at its center she felt the bloodletter reveling in the challenge, the need beating in him to force her submission. And he still did not step from the shadows, yet she could feel him *beneath* her skin.

Inside there was a terrible wrenching as if something was tearing her body apart. It was a pain as she'd never felt before, and she did not understand the depth and breadth of it. Their thread jerked, the pull from her chest burning with live agony, and she could not separate his feelings from the ones swirling through her veins.

The control on her fear was a thin gossamer thread, for if he took her with him into the darkness, she doubted she could fight him. Doubted she would want to fight, for everything in her would cry to submit, and he had the power to make her surrender should she try to resist his dominance. Then everything would be lost.

Warily she stepped toward the shimmering energy that would take her back to her realm. Shilah moved deep into the darkened cave, dipping low to avoid the sharp edges of the crystals hanging from its ceiling. She breathed through the sheer raw power emanating from the portal. The tree glowed pink and silver in the distance, and Kala stood at a sparkling branch waiting for her.

Her sister glanced back at her but made no sound, only touching the tip of the branch that would lead back to their realm. A bright light pulsed and her sister vanished. Shilah stepped forward, reaching the tip of her finger toward the branch.

A harsh sob tore from her, and with a sense of shock, she realized she cried.

Phantom kisses ghosted over her forehead, and down to her lips. She touched the tip of the branch, and she was sucked through a vacuum of whirling stars and blinding energy.

"Goodbye," she whispered, her throat tight and aching.

Then her world went dark.

20

His mate had left. And he had let her. Lachlan had not expected the terrible wrenching, dagger-like pain piercing through his soul where only darkness should reside. She had been a brief light that had filled him, and the echoing emptiness that had been his life for over four hundred years had abated. She'd stilled his mind. Made him sentient, made him feel.

His eyes were damp. Darkans didn't cry. They didn't feel sorrow. Their brutal souls were damned, so why did he feel as if a part of him had broken and would never be whole? Why did he feel this peculiar weakness in his heart, this tearing agony because their thread no longer hummed with a soothing resonance?

His heart stuttered, and he stretched, reached, unable to let go of her. There was only a void. The ravaging hunger to slaughter and drink the darkest of essence burned in his veins. And this part of him had made her flee, the most natural, instinctive part of him. The bloodletter, the monster, but she didn't flee in fear of it, she fled because of how protective it was of her. He knew if any harm befell her, he would repay her pain with blood.

If his mate were to die before him as her sister's vision implied, he would indeed annihilate her kingdom, that was just his way, and there was no changing that. And understanding her love of her people and loyalty to them, he respected her choice and loved her even more for it, so he would not follow her and endanger her world against her wishes. Their mating had been complete, they had exchanged blood, and their *lei* had formed so he could force her to stay. The monster wanted to, but he wanted her to love him and come to him of her own will. If that would ever happen, he did not know.

Turning away from the portal, his hands clasped behind his back, he prowled on foot over the vastness of the wastelands. He could feel the crouching creatures of Taryllion, their hackles stirring as they smelled the predator walking through their lands. He could feel the darkness rising, that hollow emptiness yawning like a tremendous endless hole threatening to swallow him whole. A poisonous rage flooded through his veins, a dark red stain that spread rapidly, encompassing all the light that had tethered his soul. The sheer intensity of his rage threatened to rip him to pieces, but he set his jaw and kept walking, his mind filling with cold purpose.

He was going hunting.

Hundreds of assassins across the seven kingdoms had answered the call for her recapture. It did not matter that she had left and might never return, they would all be made to understand the depth of their error. And all the pain and rage he felt now would have an outlet. Darkness roared, the bloodletter rose in him and he embraced it, for the monster was familiar, the beast was a comfort, and the absence of his mate was an unrelenting pain he only knew to assuage in blood and death.

~

S<small>ERANGE</small>
T<small>HE</small> K<small>INGDOM OF</small> D<small>XYRIAH</small>.

R<small>AW</small>, pounding energy tore Shilah apart as she spun with nauseating speed across the stars. The color in the nexus constantly changed, swirling with a deep purple through dark red then with blue and green. The humming at the center grew louder, and then the multi-colored whirling force spewed Shilah and Kala out with such power they slammed into the floor of the cave. Kala cried out her pain, but with Darkan blood coursing through Shilah's veins, she barely felt the jarring impact.

"Princess Shilah?" a familiar voice whispered, emotions roughing the tone.

Glancing up, she watched as the gatekeeper, Herron, used his telekinesis to weave back the barrier in place, shutting away the shimmering effect of the portal. He stared at her as if he'd conjured her, before scrubbing a hand over his face, and quickly bending his knee to the stone ground.

"Please stand, Herron," she said, unfamiliar emotions tearing through her.

He rose, his mahogany brown eyes shimmering with so many emotions. "I've long hoped you would return to us, Princess Shilah, Princess Kala. The statues have been raised for you both. I…we…I am delighted you are both here."

The honorary statues were only erected after a prince or princess has been declared dead. She carefully brushed against the psychic network of her people. Shilah wanted to weep at the aura surrounding the wall of their connection. It was a deep purple, which hinted at the unrelenting pain. They mourned her, and they mourned Kala. Shilah did not want to risk going deeper if traitors lingered within the network seeking the pathway to her and Kala.

"Do I have your loyalty, Herron?" Shilah asked softly, her gaze darting around the underground cave. They were deep within the mountain trails, leading to the network of the caves. Few knew of the location, but surely Prince Quan would set spies in the mountains and at the portal. She flared her telepathy and sensed no other aura for miles.

"Always, Princess Shilah," he hurriedly assured her.

And from his thoughts, she gleaned his honesty. Even though she had known of his love and fidelity to her family, she had to check. His family had pledged fealty to her house when her father had granted a group of Arcadians refuge from political unrest which had broken out in their kingdom. To please the purists in Dxyriah, all the refugees and their descendants who chose to remain within the territory had to be registered and were required to bear a mark on their foreheads. It had been Herron who had helped them escape to Amagarie after swearing an oath to not reveal where they had fled to. But much could have changed within the last few months.

"Rah Blevinstoke has been relentlessly searching for you, Princess Shilah. He bid me to direct you to his location should you resurface. I did not inform him of where you escaped with Princess Kala, but he seemed to be aware of it, and of your imminent return."

Her stomach tightened. Rah had no doubt used a foreseer to try and find her, and she sensed he'd used Megladine, his great love whom he could not marry for she too was impure. Rah had been a friend of her father, a mentor to her and she trusted him. Yet she hesitated, hating that sense of mistrust she had for her people which had taken root and flowered since the betrayal at her coronation. "And what directive were you given?"

"To safeguard the portal till your return. And the Baron showed me a map, but I did not understand it, nor can I remember it."

She walked over to him. "With your permission, Herron."

"Most certainly, my princess."

She delved deep into his mind, moving past his barriers sifting through his memories. She saw that the prince was persecuting Herron's people as traitors and all who remained were in hiding. She pushed past his pain and anger and finally came to the map as he'd seen it. Shilah studied it, locating the marked networks of a cave deep underground her castle which led toward the Senate and was perilously close to her home. Unease filled her that he would choose to meet so close to the enemy, for undoubtedly Prince Quan lived at castle Ashmir.

"Thank you, Herron," she said, stepping back.

"Princess Shilah, for days our new…Prince Quan has had a hovercraft patrol these parts of the mountains. Many whispered that you fled the realm and would return to your rightful place. I believe these whispers have also reached his ears."

"Thank you for the warning, I already suspected the prince might be vigilant. These caves are my home, and Prince Quan and his followers do not know them as I do. Please rest easy, Herron, I will be cautious."

Questions swirled in his gaze, but he bowed deferentially. Kala who had stood silently during their exchange walked over to him and enfolded him in a hug. She whispered in his ears softly, telling him of a future she saw, a wife that would bring him great happiness and children.

Herron closed his eyes, and hope burned his aura bright yellow.

Kala released him and hurried over. Drawing her sister close, Shilah made her way deep underground the cavern, skirting past large crystal stalactites, and going deeper. She'd missed her home and her people. But she missed Lachlan Ravenswood with such intensity it bordered on pain.

"I am still in disbelief we are home," Kala said, a smile on her lips but a vein of fear in her tone.

"I too am pleased, Kala."

"You mourn him," her sister said with a gasp of surprise.

Shilah paused. "Who?" Though she full well knew her sister spoke of Lachlan Ravenswood.

"You will deny it, but I see visions of you curled on your bed, screaming your tears and sorrow into your pillow. Oh, Shilah, I never realized you had such feelings for him!"

Kala's arms were suddenly around her, holding her tight as Shilah returned her embrace, wrapping her arms around her sister comfortingly.

"You made the right choice, and I promise you the pain of walking away from him will pass."

Relief pierced Shilah. "You've seen it?"

Kala stiffened but made no reply. Shilah brushed against her mind, absorbing the images of her staring listlessly above her kingdom as snow blanketed their streets and buildings. She released her sister, and stepped back, pasting a forced smile on her lips.

"So, in eight months' time with the arrival of winter, I will still be mourning him." The pain of it almost felled her, and she knew then, a part of her would hunger for him always.

"But I see you...and you are *alive*," Kala said, with calm logic. "That is what is most important."

Their love affair had been brief, but she'd come to recognize what he was to her, and what another would never be. He was her warrior, her partner, her strength as well as her weakness and she had walked away. He would always cloak her with layers of protective violence if she allowed him to do it. When she would find forgiveness and administer justice, he would deliver pain and vengeance. And upon her death, which would be inevitable for her kind was not immortal, he would slaughter.

"Let's go. We need to find proper clothes and connect with those loyal to our house."

It took them hours, but they carefully made their way through the network of caves, pausing at intervals to seek the enemy, Shilah with her telepathy and Kala with her foresight. They made their way down the caves and ice tunnels for miles until they spilled out onto the lawns behind the building of the Senate. Shilah could have covered the journey in minutes while carrying Kala on her back, but she wasn't ready to reveal her new abilities just yet, not even to Kala given they would soon be around other telepaths. Shilah saw the sweat glistening on Kala's skin and heard her increased heart rate, but the journey had felt like a stroll to her. She felt like a predator roaming her jungle, aware of everything, she could even feel the subtle changes in the atmosphere as the sun dipped behind the mountain to herald the night.

The large white building loomed several meters away, climbing four stories tall, and it was the only place in Dxyriah not modernized by their advanced technology. It was not allowed within the walls of the Senate or on the grounds, and the round structure with its many round Corinthian columns and balconies had the same design that was displayed in their history books. Prince Quan had only been able to attack her coronation for it had been done in the temple of the high priestess, another place where no technology was allowed.

"There is no one ahead."

They sprinted across the open lawns to the side of the building. Shilah stayed low, sticking as close to the side of the building as she could. In the far distance, their once vibrant city was quiet, only a few hovercrafts zipped through the skies, and only one rover craft rolled over the steel-plated road. Unable to resist, she peered up at the mountaintop which loomed high behind the Senate to Castle Ashmir, her home. Seemingly built into the rock atop the highest mountain of Dxyriah, her castle was like a small city unto itself, with at least six hundred men and ladies of the court residing there. It boasted large glass structures with sweeping terraces and turrets, gleaming pyramids, statues, and columns.

Taking a steadying breath, Shilah lifted her chin. "The map leads to an underground bunker of olden times beneath the Senate."

"The bunker the rebellion used?"

"Yes."

Kala closed her eyes, and energy buzzed around her and then a smile burst on her lips. "My power can be handy," she said with a low chuckle. "Rah Blevinstoke is in that bunker now, with several loyal supporters. I see a clear path, follow me."

Tension seeped from Shilah's veins, and she allowed Kala to lead the way as she used her vision to guide them to a side entrance, then down the underground drains for a few minutes, and then to an iron door.

"They are in here."

"Can you see why they are here?"

Kala closed her eyes again. "No."

Shilah nodded, flared her powers, brushing against the mind of everyone inside the bunker. Thirty-nine people in total. She found Rah's thread and brushed against his mind, a stirring of warmth. She felt his alarm, his hope, and his fear. Carefully by-passing the thread, he had connected with the hive Psychic Net, sliding with deft skill through his various synapses, she spoke.

"Rah, it's Princess Shilah. I am here."

A loud groan sounded, of iron grinding against iron as the blot of the massive door slid back, and there he stood. Ignoring protocol, he drew her into a fierce hug, his thoughts of relief and joy spilling to her.

They stepped into the upper floors of the spacious bunker, which had been designed to hold eight hundred of their people. A large table was in the center with various maps, scrolls, and legal books strewed about. What she saw of the resistance force so far was made up of several army generals, a few of their scientists, and even a senior member of the Senate, Prince Novar— her former consort.

She faced them, so many feelings burning through her. "Thank you all for being here. I fled Serange because—"

"We know why you ran, princess," Rah said, his gaze jumping from one member to the other. "Your home was viciously attacked, and you lost people you love. You saved your life, and Princess Kala's, and now you've returned to us. That is all that matters. If you had stayed, you would have died, for none of us, expected or was prepared for the prince's action. Now we are prepared, and we will only look forward, not behind."

A lump formed in her throat. Her people stared at her with varying degrees of emotions—shock, relief, joy, and pain. Still, at the heart of it all, she was surrounded by trusted friends and supporters, and the air filled with camaraderie, with acceptance, with belonging.

Megladine stepped forward, scanning behind Shilah before relief wilted her shoulder. "I've been tormented with visions of darkness ravaging our city, Princess Shilah," she said huskily. "A decision was made that has changed something, and I am glad for it."

Shilah's knees went weak. "You no longer see this slaughter?"

"All I see is hovering darkness waiting, but I do not know for what it waits. But I prefer such an outcome than the pain and death I saw before."

The small crowd parted as she made her way over to the table. "What is all this?"

"We have been making plans while we awaited your return. We had every confidence both of you would come back," Rah said. "The Senate declared you both dead at Prince Quan's insistence. We will slowly spread the word that you've returned and put pressure on the Senate to convene immediately."

"They will demand proof," Baron Shaffer said, stepping forward.

"And the proof will be provided when you appear at the Senate meetings," Prince Novar said, his eyes warm and sensual. "Prince Quan has demanded the Federated Coalition of Senates to assemble, and a date has been set for six days from today. We suspect his greater agenda will become known at the meeting, so we must meet with our Senate before then."

Shilah frowned at the gentle flutters along her mind for a telepathic connection. She closed him out, refusing to connect with him outside of the Psychic Network. It oddly felt like a betrayal to the intimate bond she'd formed with Lachlan Ravenswood.

"Prince Quan broke the laws with his barbaric actions. The foundations of his plan before rested on ending the Symonrah bloodline. He failed. He will have no choice now but to meet you on the floor of the Senate," Rah said. "We've prepared all the legal arguments, and we have been thorough."

Kala jerked, and a small cry slipped from her. "I see hundreds of soldiers scouring the city, breaking into homes searching for us at his command. They will not rest until our death is secured. Unrest will rise for those who believe he has no right to the throne will be emboldened by our return and will fight. Lives will be lost. Dozens," she ended hoarsely.

Megladine's lips flattened. "The Prince will do everything to prevent you both from reaching the Senate."

"We must hide you until we've convened the Senate. And only after you're both hidden can we let it be known you're alive, princess. And we must assemble the Senate immediately. Too long a delay will be disastrous for our city," Prince Novar said, moving to stand beside Shilah.

Everyone's murmur of assent filled the bunker.

"Do we know why Prince Quan has acted with such rank disregard for our laws?"

Prince Novar stared at her for several moments before saying, "He has made a petition to the Senate to repeal aspects of the bloodline laws. He has proposed a motion that Impure be allowed to marry, even if they should remain sterilized."

Her gaze jumped to Megladine who was looking at Rah with such naked longing it was painful to witness.

Kala stepped forward. "The kingdom of Arcadia sent such a request to our brother. All three Senate branches of the three kingdoms must agree about overturning any part of the law that has been the bedrock to the society we lived in. My brother said no. To allow even an adjustment is to threaten the golden age we live in. It will start with marriage. Then perhaps sterilization will fail. A child will be born in secret. Then another. And another. And before we know it, we may have another Na'Vita. That risk we cannot allow."

Shilah's stomach rebelled, but she fought hard to stay in control, breathing deep. *"You've never told me this, Kala."*

Her sister froze. *"I am sorry, sister. I was afraid...afraid you would have agreed with Prince Quan."*

"Do you think so little of me that I would put my desires above

the safety of our future generations?" And the temptation was there, the hunger for another life for those who had been branded Impure. But why did Prince Quan seek such an alteration to the law? Was he impure?

Shilah took a bracing breath. "Where is our hovercraft? Has Prince Quan taken command of it?"

"No. All its systems had been shut down, and the prince has not been able to override it."

The operation and internal defense mechanism of their hovercraft, and home were controlled by Arrow, who was programmed to respond only to Kala and Shilah. Arrow had access to all the databases in Dyxriah. And they had armbands that they uploaded his intelligence on, and once they were within range of any technological construct, he could infect it with a virus and take control of it. Their father had been the creator of the Prime Sentient 2.1, and there had been no development in their realm that surpassed it.

Arrow had been programmed to respond to whoever ruled Castle Ashmir and was the most powerful sentient intelligence of their realm. Almost all other households operated on model 1.5. Knowing that the command of her household interface would be integral to Prince Quan, she had used her telekinetic powers to input the kill code that would deactivate it as she fled. There had been a possibility Arrow would not have responded to the prince's commands, but his attack had been so well coordinated and brutal she hadn't taken the chance.

"Your craft is at my hanger below my castle," Prince Novar said. "In the confusion, I anchored it to my craft and zipped it away. It would be my pleasure for you both to be guests in my home. We must move with the utmost secrecy of course," he said, removing robes from a bag, and handing them to her. His dark green eyes caressed her face. "With your new Imperial powers, I assume it would be no great feat to scan the minds of those we pass to see if they are suspicious and to plant a suggestion of seeing me with two high priestesses."

It would be possible but such an intrusion, slipping into citizen's minds and manipulating their memories, was against the law. And if she were not skilled enough her telepathic breach would alert the network and the PsyNet Protectorate. "Let us keep my return to only those in the room. I know many of our people are with us, but for now, awareness must be contained tightly. We are at war with Prince Quan, not our people. I have no wish to break the law and betray their trust. If it is one of Prince Quan's supporters who see us, and even with our disguise believes it is me, I will trap them in a temporary illusion. But we must not harm a single one of our denizens."

They nodded. She faced Prince Novar. "If you have a hovercraft nearby, it should take little effort to slip away to your castle and to the underground docking bay. We are not expected unless the prince has foreseers working with him."

No one could say, and in short order, they wrapped the meeting up and quietly dispersed. Only Kala and Shilah went with the prince, and as they boarded his hovercraft and whizzed through the sky, there was no alert along the PsyNet or any alarm sounding through the system.

In short order, they reached his castle, and a hole appeared in the mountain as the sleek craft dipped low and swooped down to its hanger. The doors opened, and relief swarmed through her to see her aircraft as he'd said. It looked unscathed, exactly how she'd left it with its smooth curves, alternating panels colored in silver and others in gunmetal blue, and the ruby red Symonrah sigil painted over the entire bow. It was their home away from the castle. It had all the amenities required to house a small family of royals on their journeys about the kingdom.

"Thank you, Novar," she said, glancing at him.

He nodded, clasping his hand behind his back. "I will have rooms prepared. I'll have your chamber placed next to mine."

Her eyes jumped to his, and in his gaze, she spied a feeling that was far too intimate. Lachlan's promise of death should another man touch her burned through her memory, and Shilah bit back her groan. Not that she was even tempted to entertain her former consort, but she had enough to deal with and now had to add rebuffing his advances to the mix. Their moment had been over fifty years past, and it still shocked her that after all that time, he wished to renew his advances.

"There is ample room in our hovercraft for Kala and me. Your castle is not as contained as it should be, and the secrecy of our presence will be compromised there. Below ground, we will be as safe as possible until we meet with the Senate."

He hesitated, then said, "That could be days, Shilah. I will work to have the assembly soon, but I cannot promise less than three days. An underground hanger is not fit for you."

"It will do," she said firmly. "Our ship has all the necessities to provide for us for a few days. And it will raise suspicion if you are seen coming down here."

With a soft sigh, he made his way to a door, scanned his eyes, and stepped through when it opened. It closed behind them, and Shilah turned to the craft, reaching out with her telekinesis to the dashboard enclosed within and entered the code that would power the craft and activate Arrow on the vessel.

The hover hummed to life, the sleek silver craft emitting the softest frequency as it powered up. They walked up to the ramp, and the door opened, sensing the signature of both. They went on board. Within the craft it was designed for relaxing comfort, the main room was softly furnished in shades of pale blues with a carpet of deep green and windows out into the night. Shilah barely glanced at the main cabin her mind concentrated on instructing Arrow where it was to take them and what it was to do.

"Welcome, Princess Shilah, Princess Kala," a melodious electronic voice said from the speakers of the vessel.

"Arrow, I need all views and angles of the city upon the monitors," she ordered her PSI. "And the laws enacted since the rebellion on bloodline inheritance and separation of powers."

"Permission to access the city's mainframe, and great archives princess," he replied, the walls of the hovercraft rippling as a holographic computer screen opened in the center of the ship, a blue light glowing at its center.

"Permission granted," Shilah said, flowing over, and swiping her fingers across the large screen which had displayed the laws of the kingdom as outlined by her ancestors and read for several minutes. The law was clear, and the rule of Dxyriah would soon return to her bloodline.

"Shilah," Kala said softly.

She closed her eyes and faced her sister. Kala's dark red hair was tangled around her face, and bruises were evident under her eyes. "You look tired, Kala. Get some food from the processor, and then rest. The next few days will be challenging."

Kala looked on the verge of tears, but she squared her shoulders. "We need to talk."

"We do not."

"Shilah please, I thought it insignificant and I—"

"You thought it insignificant to mention that Prince Quan, the only man to do so in over seven hundred years, petitioned for my brother to revise the treaties on bloodline inheritance and support such a motion to the Federated Coalition?" Shilah bit out furiously. "Or thought it insignificant even after our brother, his wife, our nephews, our uncle and aunt were murdered? You thought it insufficient to not tell me even *after* he attacked my coronation?"

The craft trembled at the wash of energy which leaked from her emotion.

Tears slipped down Kala's cheeks, but Shilah felt unmoved.

"We scoured the files for evidence on who could have murdered Torren. We found no petition from Prince Quan and the Kingdom of Arcadia, so that means someone hacked our mainframe and stole them. But you knew the petition had been made to Torren, and the revelation of that knowledge would have pointed us to a suspect, and perhaps prepared us for the attack."

"It wouldn't have prepared us!" Kala cried. "If I had known…If I had known Shilah that Prince Quan would have acted with such cruelty, I would have mentioned it. I never dreamt of such betrayal. I was afraid…."

Shilah advanced on her, hot anger riding her. "Afraid that because I am an Impure, and as I hunger for life beyond duty to the realm. I would have…what? What would I have done, Kala? Ignored our history and laws for my selfish desires? Supported the prince in his request? Revealed my status as an Impure and the shame that I'd been hiding it for so long?"

Her sister ran into her arms and hugged her tightly. "I am so sorry," she whispered hoarsely. "I was so stupid, and I did not think. I let fear and grief rule my actions when I should have been more sensible."

Shilah returned the hug, wanting to scream at Kala, but also understanding what had driven her actions. Battling the emotions pounding through her Shilah thought logically. "Prince Quan did not plot this in weeks, Kala. Or months. This was years of machinations, and even if our investigators had been led to his door, I am certain he had a plan for that eventuality."

She held her sister as she cried for several moments. "Come, let us wash, eat, and then get some rest. Dawn will be here within a few hours, and we can do nothing with our tired brains."

They parted, and Shilah made her way down the long steel-plated corridors of the ship, and to her room. Pressing her palm to the identification pad, the door slid opened, and she stepped inside. Nothing had changed since she last saw it, the design was still programmed to her last request, blacks, and deep purples to match her depressed state at the time, and various images of her lost loved ones fading in and out with different patterns across the surfaces of the room. With a weary sigh, she made her way over to the bed and lowered herself.

"Arrow display starry skies and sounds of flowing rivers."

"As you command Princess." The calming sound of rivers filled the room, and the walls went ice black with the sparkle of stars from various constellations covering the ceiling.

Grief rolled over her like the roaring waves of an ocean. They spun through her, swarming her senses, and drowning her in pain. For the first time in months, Shilah allowed herself to cry unchecked, without berating herself for the weakness. She cried until her throat felt raw, her eyes felt swollen, a desperate hole in her heart that would not ease. Shilah did not understand it, but her chest pained her.

Frantically she rubbed at the spot and almost against her will, the mating thread flared to life, and with a sense of shock, she felt the resonance vibrated and reach through the stars. Her heart leaped with joy despite her determination to keep her perspective. Their thread opened even wider, and she became a stealthy shadow in his mind, powerful enough where it was as if she saw through his eyes. She watched him as he administered justice in the court of his keep. Two men who'd fought over a female had been ordered to fight to the death. Curled onto her side, exhaustion pulling at her, Shilah watched the two Darkans as they battled for hours, bleeding and torn, tired but each determined to be the conqueror.

Lachlan observed it all with impassive coldness from atop steps. His people stared at him, but instead of showing apprehension at the ruthless changes evident in him, admiration and respect flavored their chakras. As if he tired of the display, he ordered them to be thrown into the dungeon for three days to cool their ardor and then they would be released.

The crowd in the hall of the court solarium dispersed, and a Darkan appeared before him.

"I've found the warlord."

The words came as if they had been said to her. A wave of primal vengeance and bloodthirsty triumph slashed through Lachlan and echoed through her bones. Their link vibrated harshly, reverberating with a discordant sound. Shilah gasped and closed the link, trembling. Something dark and powerful slammed against her shields, and her throat closed. Damn her curiosity and her need for him.

No more, she silently vowed, as exhaustion and the stress of the upcoming battle finally pulled her into the comforting arms of sleep.

21

Hours later, Shilah jerked awake, startled to find she had fallen asleep without eating or taking a shower. The mating bond was quiet, the silver and darkness gently sliding against each other. She pushed from the bed, and stripped off the filthy clothes, removing the plait from her hair and allowed the long tresses to ripple unchecked to her waist. *"Kala is all well?"* Not that anyone could have breached their defenses with Arrow crewing the vessel.

"Yes. I am glad you've finally woke. Would you like to break your fast with me?"

An olive branch her sister was desperate for her to take. Shilah could read the guilt and the fear Kala endured and softened. *"I will be there shortly. How long was I out for?"*

"Almost fifteen hours."

Shilah gasped. *"Any word from Rah?"*

"No. I've been watching the monitors over the city. All is silent. Too silent. It is as if our people are a shadow of themselves. The festival of lights is eight days away, and no preparations are being made. Prince Novar visited, and he's summoned the Senate for an

emergency meeting. He's promised to join us in a few hours with updates."

Shilah pulled from her sister's mind and stepped into the shower chamber, the chromatic tiles cool under her bare feet. The glass compartment slid open, and she stood under the hot spray of water, instead of using the more efficient air-dry method.

Had Lachlan found the warlord? From the intent in him, she knew he planned to kill the man. Temptation rode her to open the link and spy on him once more. She fought it, and after several minutes of the hot water beating on her tense shoulders, she admitted it was a losing battle. Every single part of her, heart and soul, her logical mind, seemed to have an overwhelming desire to be with him. Unable to banish the need she opened her mind, dipping into the well of her powers and connected with him.

He was a swirling force of violent rage, one so icy she shivered. He fought somewhere unrecognizable and under the wash of sunlight. Even without his beast, Lachlan was a merciless machine as he shattered bones and tore out chunks of flesh, slicing through arteries and vocal cords and flesh. She pulled her mind from his, leaning against the walls of the shower.

The violence she'd just touched within him reaffirmed that she had made the right decision in leaving without making any promise to return after the unrest. Something sharp tugged at her chest. Their bond. She quickly snapped open her psychic eyes, fearful that he'd been hurt.

She frowned. He was no longer on the battlefield but within the Darkage surrounded by his friends, and the king.

She sensed the intent in him to consume the healing elixir from Boreas with the hope it would restore the psychic wall she'd shattered. Shilah pressed trembling fingers to her lips.

He was ravaged with need of her. Memories of her scent and taste tormented him, and the only bloodlust soothed.

He tipped the gourde to his lips and consumed the powerful healing elixir. Bright blue energy washed from him, and then he stilled. Connected deep in his mind Shilah waited, her breath held.

"Does it work?" his friend Talon asked. "has your barrier returned?"

"No," he growled, the bitterness in the sound struck at her heart, and unable to help herself, she lifted her hands and touched his face. It was a simple brush of psychic energy, but he stiffened, tipped his head to the sky, and inhaled deeply.

Shock tore through her. He had felt her touch.

A swirl of shadows and he disappeared from his friends. He stood atop their mountain looking north toward the portal. *"Touch me again."*

The command burned along their link and she trembled.

"Did I imagine your touch? I am truly maddened by the loss of you?"

Every part of her ached for him, the giving lover, and the merciless monster.

He stood strong and powerful, but so lonely her throat ached. He stared unflinching toward the north, his familiar beside him, the beast's head under his palm. Shilah Could see the river shining through the trees as he saw it, even hear the flow of it as it traveled to his ears, feel the cold bite of the wind as it kissed over his skin. Her body became so sensitive, so in tune with him, she could feel the breeze caressing his arms.

She closed her eyes under the hot wash of water, and it was as if she was transported to his side and connected to his soul. Shocking emotions poured from him. Sorrow lived in him, breathed in him. And it was all for her.

She touched his lips, and a snarl tore from his throat, for

he had felt it. Snatching back her hand, she moved away. His turned his head, and it was as if he looked right at her. Their linked burned, flared with bright light and sinuous darkness.

"I feel your worry, my mate."

And then he was inside her mind.

She felt him in her, just as if they were sharing the same skin, merged together so deep she didn't know where he started, and she left off. She held her breath as his mouth drifted to her temple and then pressed his cool, firm lips to her ear. Then she reached for him, and the phantom disappeared.

"I miss you, Lachlan Ravenswood."

His anguish roared across their link….and with a harsh sob, she tried to close their connection. He did not allow it, his raw power pouring through the thread. Shilah ignored him refusing to look at him, closing her eyes tightly as she completed her shower. She cupped a handful of water and watched it run through her fingers.

The feel of a phantom caress against her tender nipples, the press of a kiss against her lips, the stroke of his finger down her throat and lower to slip inside her body, was all in her mind, but she felt as if he was right there touching her.

She gasped, trying to pull away from the connection but he did not allow it, his hold on their thread ruthless in its intensity. His scent wrapped around Shilah like a tight embrace, hot, arousing and comforting. Her pussy became wet and heated, longing for his touch. Even from such an impossible distance, their link burned with a dark-silver fire, and when her eyes snapped open, he was right there in the shower, peering down at her.

Phantom arms caught her chin in his hand and tipped her head up, forcing her to look into his eyes. *"I'm not going insane. You can feel and see me, just as I can see and feel you."*

"Yes," she whispered, reaching out and touching him.

His eyes closed, and he shivered his pleasure as if she had really touched him. *"I feel the heated pad of your finger on my cheek...I smell you, my mate."*

And she smiled, the ache in her heart easing. *"I hardly understand it, but I miss you, Lachlan Ravenswood, quite desperately."*

He made no reply, merely watching her in that calm way of his. And then she felt it, kisses all over her body, nips, and licks as he fed her mind and aroused her body. The arousal in her built and built with no end in sight. She heard her own strangled sob of pleasure as if from far away. A wave of weakening hunger swept through her, and it was more for than just sex with him. She wanted to be held, to share her fears with him.

Immediately the burning need disappeared, and phantom hands hugged her from behind and flushed her to his chest.

"What do you fear?"

She wanted to tell him, rest her fears and doubts on his shoulders, always. She wanted to trust in his strength and not fear his brutality or retaliation if something were to ever happen to her. The pain of that realization had her body tightening until she was on the verge of shaking.

"Let me come to you."

"Never."

She stopped the flow of the water and using her telekinesis turned on the crystal spray which cleaned her body within seconds. Another pulse of air dried her, and she stepped from the shower stall and went into the sleep quarters. She quickly dressed in a silver sari, conscious of her Darkan's psychic eyes watching every dip and hollow of her body. His phantom touch brushed against her nape and her bared stomach, and she saw him as if he were there, as he dropped to his knees and pressed a kiss above her navel.

A sharp knock on the door had her spinning around, and Kala entered. Her sister faltered. "Shilah, there is a strange light glowing around you! What is it?"

The fire of their connection had engulfed her body, the thread humming with a sweet resonance only she and her lover could feel.

"It is nothing," she said huskily, firmly closing their link, and marching from the room to prepare the arguments for the Senate.

THE SWEET SCENT of flowers wafted through her nostrils. Shilah knew she wasn't alone the moment she woke. A wall of heat pressed into her back, and she wiggled, scooting back against the man that held her with such tender possession. His body felt as hard as *valnetium*, unyielding, his arms strong, surrounding her. His scent wrapped around her, and she purred, feeling safe, content. She *felt* him inside of her, a part of her. Every breath she drew brought him deep into her lungs.

"Did you sleep well, my mate?"

Lachlan Ravenswood's low, husky growl shattered her sleepy contentment. Her heart lurched, her mouth dried, and a multitude of emotions jumbled through her—the most prominent longing for the man behind her. She inhaled deeply, and it took several moments to realize he wasn't there. A peculiar loss scythed through her heart. There was a deep part of her that hungered to see him beside her. It had been five days since she'd been in the ship, waiting for news on the Senate call to assemble. And each day, Lachlan visited her, or she'd slipped into his mind and visited him. There was always a sharp sense of disorientation, an awful tug of fear that he was really within Serange before she'd accepted what they saw was the Darkage, his touch, kisses, and loving words filled her soul for hours because of the strength of their mating bond and her tremendous psychic abilities.

Their link flamed with familiar dark silver heat, a bond forged between them that could never be broken, and one that she'd never want to see shattered. She twisted on the silken sheets, facing him. Several days' worth of beard shadowed his jaw. He looked even more ruthless, but his eyes were alive with swirling needs. She reached out and touched his lips. She felt the softness against the tip of her finger. He growled low, a purr of deep pleasure, and her heat tumbled sweetly inside her chest.

"You visit me every day," she whispered. *"And torment me with things I shouldn't crave, but how I want you."*

He brushed a hand across her cheek tenderly. *"I would crush an empire for you."*

And that was what she feared, but he was brutally unapologetically himself.

"But for you, I will also show mercy."

The shock of that promise, given in such a solemn tone tore through Shilah. Her hands trembled as she slipped them around his neck, drifting even closer to his body. *"What do you want from me, Lachlan Ravenswood?"*

"Your heart...your soul...your laughter...your happiness."

A hunger for him flamed in her chest like a living entity. She smiled, unable to halt the rush of tender feelings humming through her.

"And that my mate...that I wish to see." The pad of his thumb traced the curve of her lips. *"Your smile makes the bleak cold flee, and I imagine that is what it feels like to bask in the ray of your sunshine. I've brought you something."*

She glanced down and blinked. *"Flowers?"* The most beautiful she'd ever seen. An array of purple, and blue flowers with a dark red vein at the heart of each.

When she looked up, she found such longing and hunger in his eyes mirroring the desires of her soul.

She leaned closer to him, her mouth scant inches from his. *"They are lovely. Where did you find them?"*

His finger brushed against her lips, and suddenly she was there, where he stood. Dense, savagely beautiful jungles with wild creatures surrounding him. He lay on the ground, the grass rich and lush, a luminous waterfall rushing off the hill behind him. It was a hidden alcove, verdant and more beautiful than anything she'd ever seen. She lay atop him, peace seeping into her bones, the fine spray of the roaring waterfall misting the air. She could feel the individual droplets on her skin, breathe the scent of damp earth into her lungs.

She lifted the flowers to her nose and inhaled. They smelled dark and mysterious, very much like the man himself.

"I can feel your worry, my mate. Rest your fears on my shoulders."

It was an invitation to trust him with her deepest fears. She assessed him briefly, he could have followed her to her world but did not because she wished him to stay away. And she knew regardless of how perilous her situation was now, he would not go against her desires.

She opened her mind to his, showing him all that had transpired since her arrival. *"I cannot keep wondering why the Senate crowned Prince Quan. He is not of our kingdom. There are many princes here who are fit to lead if it is believed the Symonrah bloodline's reign has ended."*

His phantom arms dragged her atop his body. *"They fear him."*

"Our history has taught us it is unwise to allow a ruler to reign with fear. Dxyriah has an army, why has the Senate not mobilized them if they fear Prince Quan?"

She felt the warrior in him turning over her words.

"He has the support of those in your Senate."

"That is what I fear."

"You are wise and intelligent, mate, they will see the wisdom of your words."

Warmth burst inside her chest, and with a sigh, she snuggled even deeper into his arms, wishing she was in the Darkage with him.

"There is someone I'd like you to meet, Shilah."

With a blink, they were within his halls. A young girl walked over to him, a hesitant aura about her, but her eyes shining with absolute faith and acceptance.

"She is over four hundred years," he said with some amusement. *"She denies the beast inside her and does not let it out. This is my sister, Nayia Ravenswood. I have hopes that you will meet and speak with her one day."*

Unable to speak, Shilah nodded, enthralled by the way he greeted his sister, the careful way he spoke and touched her.

"Does she live at your castle?"

"I have avoided her since I returned from Mevia. The malice is too much for her. I feared how she would react to me in such a state given our history with the beast."

Shilah glanced up at him. *"And now?"*

"The more I'm connected with you, my mate, your light anchors the malevolence."

Three little boys barreled around the corner, and with fierce roars, they rushed toward him.

"These are Nayia's sons."

Shadows darted from his feet, and grabbed them, hanging them in the air, upside down. They shrieked, loving it, and at that moment Shilah irrevocably lost her heart to Lachlan.

For once in her life, she was desperate to allow her heart to overrule her mind and logic. Needs long denied rolled over her like an ocean of fire. She saw it—the promise of a future with him, the man within the beast, the darkness, and the light. At this moment, Shilah wanted to belong to him as she'd never wanted anything in her entire existence.

22

A couple of days later, a shrill sound alerted her that a hovercraft approached the underground docking area. Kala glanced at her, her eyes deepening, and she peered into the future. "It is Rah and Megladine. They have news."

At last. The inaction and lack of information had been driving her mad with frustration. She'd spent the previous six days locked away, not venturing out of the hovercraft despite Prince Novar's numerous invitations. She'd read over the bloodlines laws until they had been interred in her mind, watched the city through the monitors, and re-watched the memory feeds of her brother with his wife and children.

Those moments were the hardest, for it had been difficult to watch their happiness and recall how brutally their lives had been taken. The family hovercraft had malfunctioned in the sky, and before they had ejected from the ship, their vessel had crashed into the side of the mountains. It had been the investigator's belief their vessel had been hacked, their path redirected, but there had been no electronic footprint to follow. How quickly their hovercraft had crashed into the mountain, without their Prime Sentient

Intelligence canceling the potential hack led Shilah to believe the attack had been made by an assassin with telekinetic or teleportation powers. There had been no virus redirecting their system and taking control of the ship's mainframe, only raw, brutal power as they slammed the ship into the mountains.

Grey metallic cubes rippled in the air as Arrow used nanites to take a physical pixilated shape. He then spoke through the interactive construct of the vessel. "Baron Rah Blavenstoke and Megladine K'tair seek permission to dock."

"Arm the high beams," Kala said, moving over to the large windows of the ship, so she could keep the approaching craft in her line of sight.

Their hovercraft door slid open, and Rah and Megladine boarded. There was an air of satisfaction about them, and from the tender way Rah brushed against her, Shilah surmised they had been intimate. A profound ache filled her. Megladine had already been sterilized when her family had revealed an Alpha telekinesis genesis along with her foresight, but the law still prevented her from seeking a life partner. Despite her inability to produce children, Rah loved her with every breath in his body, and Megladine had the same love and respect for him. It was heart-breaking that they had to hide their relationship or face the full force of the bloodline law. When she'd just discovered them in bed together, quite by accident, Rah had expected her to report them. She hadn't, and Shilah knew he'd never understood why she did not.

It had been the first time she'd compromised her honor, but it had hurt something in her at the thoughts of Rah losing the woman he loved. It would have been a judgment of death for Megladine.

"The meeting has been convened, and we leave for the Senate now. It is not being broadcast for we do not wish to stir unrest within the kingdom until the best way forward to declare you both still live."

Kala made her way over. "I've seen what will happen if our people know we are alive. They will march to the Senate doors, and there will be a riot and lives will be lost. I cannot see what inflames the riot, so it is best we make an announcement after we've removed Prince Quan from our kingdom."

Megladine eyes swirled with power. "I do not glimpse the future you've seen, Princess Kala." Then she cast her lover a sideways glance, and a radiant smile creased her lips. "But I do see a future our kingdom will celebrate in."

Unease slid down Shilah's spine. "And what future is that?"

Megladine shifted her regard to her. "I see no death of our people, and that is every reason to feel relief. For months my dreams have been haunted with darkness and despair. Now it isn't so."

The tension seeped from Shilah. "I will be ready within a few minutes."

She made her way to her room and opened the glass partitions that housed her suits. It would not be the full regalia of a princess, but it would be enough to meet the Senate. There she dressed in a dark blue bodysuit, which fitted her body like a second skin. She grabbed her weapons belt and banded it about her waist and took up her high beam gun and slipped it in the holster belt. Then she tugged on the overdress, that was similarly molded to her upper body and down to her hips, then the skirts flowed to her ankles. Each side of the flowing material had thigh long slits, so she could easily access the blasters on her hips. Next golden armbands were secured to her upper and lower arms. Using her telekinesis, she brushed her hair until it rippled down her back in cackling energy, and then braided it in a single plait. Shilah then slipped on her boots, ensuring another high beam gun was secured in the holster on her boot.

And the entire time, she felt Lachlan Ravenswood in her mind, daring her to connect with him as she had done days ago. But Shilah had been strong and had denied the connection, but not strong enough where she hadn't lain awake hungering to simply feel his warmth and scent around her.

Shilah exited to see that Kala was similarly dressed. Rah glanced at the blaster on her hips. "You know the Senate will be opposed to you taking weapons into the chamber."

"They can oppose all they wish. Prince Quan should not have been crowned, even if they had believed the Symonrah bloodline had ended. Another Prince from our Kingdom should have been called to serve. Quan flouted the law, and they allowed him to."

He nodded, and they made their way from the vessel. Prince Novar and several supporters from the resistance waited. Prince Novar smiled at her, although there was no humor in his eyes. A pervasive tension entered the group, and they did not speak after greeting each other. Their party made twelve in total as they moved toward a large steel plated rover craft. A short, stocky man dressed in white waited by the rover. She glanced at Rah who flanked her left.

"Is that man with us?"

"Yes. He is from O'andor. I've hired him to teleport us to the halls of the Senate. The less time we spend in the open, journeying there, the better."

"And he is to be trusted?" she asked, even as she delved into his mind, reading his intention which resided in the wealth promised for the job, nothing more.

Rah's gaze was restless, moving over the street, up into the buildings and along the ground. They stopped at the teleporter, and he glanced around furtively. Tension rose in

Shilah and knotted her stomach. It was evident they anticipated Prince Quan uncovering the route they might travel to the Senate and execute a pre-emptive strike.

"Please, everyone hold hands."

They complied, and then he touched Rah. A flash of light blinded Shilah, and then with a blink, they were in the building of the Senate. Her stomach roiled, and several of their party bent over heaving. The halls were quiet, and Shilah did not linger in the corridors but made her way to the chamber. Rah went before her and opened the door. She entered, and a hush descended over the gathering council.

All two hundred and eighty-five members of the Senate were seated, clothed in white robes. Shock blared from some of their auras, and relief from others. Prince Quan was there, seated on the high seat where the ruler of the kingdom should sit. His arrogance set her teeth on edge, and anger pounded through her veins.

"We will sit below the Prince," Rah murmured.

"No," Shilah snapped. "I will not recognize that he has a right to my throne when he does not."

She made her way around the circular gallery, heading toward Prince Quan. His eyebrow arched in sharp inquiry, and a mocking smile curved his lips. All the princes, High Priestesses, and Barons of the Senate watched her. She could feel their eyes on her, feel their assessment of her actions.

She paused right before Prince Quan. His eyes too were like perfect diamonds— colorless, hard and sparkly, and ringed with black. He was an imperial in his genesis and very dangerous. He was also shockingly handsome with his jet-black hair, and chiseled cheekbones.

"You are in my chair, Prince Quan. Remove yourself."

His gaze narrowed thoughtfully on hers. He was the kind of man to demand complete loyalty from his followers, and he got it through intimidation. No doubt he believed because she had fled, she was weak. "I am the Prince of this Kingdom, Princess Shilah and—"

"I am not certain if the laws of *your* lands are different to ours," she said with a deliberately mocking smile, reminding him and the Senate he did not belong to their kingdom. Her chin went up. She refused to look away, holding her gaze steady on his. "I am Princess Shilah Symonrah, and you are on *my* seat. I will educate you today on the steps you can take to challenge my position, until that time you are *only* the ruling Prince of Arcadia and an interloper in Dxyriah. I am at a loss how the Senate did not correct your impudence when you planted your ass here."

A choked laugh from Rah ended quickly, and several murmurs swept around the chambers like a wave.

"We were not sure you were really alive, Princess Shilah, the Senate meant no disrespect. Of course, we would not dream to recognize any claim made by Prince Quan if this council had irrevocable proof that the Symonrah bloodline lives," High Priestess, Elizabeth G'undar said from the far left of the chamber.

Prince Quan's expression of mild amusement did not change, but he flowed gracefully to his feet, and stepped away from the seat, lowering himself into a highchair on the next level of the chamber.

Shilah sat, and Kala took the seat to her left. Rah did not take his place but positioned himself above her, as if he was a bodyguard.

The high priestess continued, "The Senate has been called to assembly to answer the charge that Princess Shilah is not fit to rule the kingdom of Dyxriah. Prince Quan has put forth that the Symonrah line has—"

Shilah laughed, low and softly, but it was enough to arrest everyone attention on her. "That is not the agenda for this meeting, high priestess."

There was a niggling sense of wrongness Shilah could not put her fingers on. Though the Prince and his supporters had willingly appeared before the Senate, something warned her that all was not as it seemed. But what? She couldn't anticipate it. The Senate comprised all the ruling Princes, Princesses, the High Priestess and her chief acolytes, and the Barons who made and administered the laws of their kingdom. As a unified body through voting, they would be the ones to determine the fate of Prince Quan. If it was up to her, Shilah might have ordered immediate banishment to one of the exiled planets. In their kingdom when a peer of the realm committed a crime, they could only be judged by fellow peers in the Senate who would give them a chance to defend themselves.

She fully expected the judgment of exile, for the crimes he had committed against her family was one of the most heinous. Since the division of the three kingdoms more than two thousand years ago, there had been no fight by a usurper to oust a ruler from their throne. The laws of inheritance had been created, and he had broken seven tenets with his cruel actions. If only a penalty of death could be levied against a prince. Shilah stood. "Prince Quan tried to take over Dxyriah by circumventing the law. *That* is all that should matter today," she said, holding the eyes of the Senate. "If Prince Quan wanted to challenge my rule, he should have shown his proof that I am an unfit ruler and a new head of the monarchy was needed, then demand a trial by combat if I refused. He did neither. He acted like a sniveling coward and took the lives of innocent people under my protection. I *demand* justice, and the Senate will render it today."

She glanced around the Senate, assessing their reception to her impassioned plea. Rah nodded approvingly from where he stood, and Kala offered a smile of support. Shilah moved down a few steps toward the wide-open floor of the

Senate. "Prince Quan orchestrated an attack on my coronation three months and eight days ago. He murdered fifty-eight of our people in his senseless quest. I am the witness to his atrocity, and my sister, Princess Kala is also witness. You will hear our testimony in full, of how he stormed the gates of our sacred temple with his bands of assassins, you will hear how he hunted my sister and me through the underground caves, and you will find him guilty."

Prince Quan clapped mockingly, stood, and descended a few steps while looking across the Senate.

"The princess has tried to remind you that you are from Dxyriah and I am from Arcadia. The princess forgets we are all Serangites. We are one people, one race, who have been cruelly divided through the archaic bloodline laws. The Symonrah family proved they were not open to a different way of thinking for the inclusion of all Serangites."

Several princes of the Senate nodded, glancing at each other, their expressions she did not understand. She inhaled, freezing as with her heightened senses she smelled a fragrance she could not identify. It tasted bitter.

Deceit.

The dark whisper deep inside felt as if it came from someone else. And she searched along the thread to find it quiet. It had been her newly enhanced senses at work alone. Her awareness seemed to sharpen with every breath she took, along with knowledge of each beating heart. Shilah studied the members of their Senate, trying to discern whose loyalty she might rely on. It was not logical to try and read their thoughts. That was an illegal act, and she was here defending the law which needed to be upheld.

The Prince's voice rang with power and conviction as he snapped, "We've become cowards. Once we traveled the stars, our borders were opened for trading, slavers docked in our ports, and we sold the best of technologies throughout the galaxies. We had a prime fleet of ships, we conquered and had colonies off-planet. What do we have now? *Nothing!* We deceive ourselves that we are in the Golden Age. We are a *weak* planet that fears the powers we were given. With my rule, we will become all that we should be. We will be Serange, and no longer a three-monarch triumvirate! A Na'Vita is rising, and, where is she? Exiled from our planet by your brother, living a life of poverty and degradation as the personal slave to the Titan King. Our people in exile are more powerful and revered than us, and this is palatable to you? To Dxyriah, to O'andor?"

"You are power hungry and delusional, Prince Quan," Shilah snapped coldly. "We have laws that you've broken. You may have hidden your psychic print, but I know you murdered a ruling Prince of Dxyriah, my brother, and preen as if those cowardly actions have no consequences. As ruler of Arcadia, you are not exempt from Dyxriah's justice. The last Na'Vita ruled with tyranny, and we have the unedited stream records of his senseless slaughter of over one hundred thousand of our people. Men, women, children who were *innocent* of any crimes. Our world had been lawless, working with slavers, and mercenaries from off planet as our Na'Vita king sought to consolidate more power. Is that the rule you would wish to return the three kingdoms of Serange to? Are you so misguided you cannot see the laws have given peace to our kingdoms and our lands have flourished? Instead of warring with other planets, the brightest minds turned to develop our world, and now we have medical units that can cure diseases, reverse the aging process of our people and regenerate body parts. We have buildings that rival the greatest architecture of the galaxies. Our people have thrived and evolved, and your self-serving ideology and ambitions will not take us back to the dark times!"

"Our people?" he murmured caustically, power humming

through the air around him. "I've been tracking the exiles, they number in the thousands, Princess. And they wander aimlessly without a home, a planet to call their own, a people, a culture to connect with. Some are enslaved for their powers by other worlds, and they have no one to defend and liberate them for they have no people! That is what these bigoted laws have done to *our* people."

"They were given a choice!" she snapped, glaring at Prince Quan. "They chose exile!"

"Not much of choice. A life without a family, without love. Is it different from an exile to another planet?"

Her heart trembled. "It is just as cold and harsh, but our views on the law does not give us impunity to challenge it with murder and disgrace which you have done, Prince Quan. I judge you guilty of the crime of murdering fifty-eight souls of the castle, and I request the Senate to approve the trial."

Prince Quan laughed and flowed closer. "Do you believe this is why the Senate has gathered, Princess Shilah? Do you believe that popinjay by your side had the power to command the princes of the land to gather at his request?" There was a wealth of knowledge behind those cold eyes. "No…it was done by *my* request."

To her left, Prince Novar stiffened.

"If you wish to challenge me, Prince Quan, I accept."

A cold smile curved his lips, as he too moved down several steps. "Do you now?"

"Yes. I am impure," she said softly.

The Senate chamber blanketed with a startled silence. She waved her hands, and the empty chair to the left levitated and swept across the room. Kala's face was white, her eyes wide with terror.

"An Alpha in the telekinesis genesis. I know the solitary life I face with my declaration. I must submit to the law or choose exile. I believe so strongly in the laws enforced to protect our kingdoms, I declare my status to the Senate. I do not sit on the sidelines, not imagining the fate or the hardship those who are impure experience. But I have watched the recordings of our history and the long, brutal fights of the Rebellion wars. I have seen children littering our streets, their throats crushed, their eyes filled with the horrors of their deaths. We have seen the evidence, and it is our duty as the rulers of Dxyriah to keep the bloodlines separate and never allow such consolidation of powers again into our land. It is our duty," she said fiercely, spinning around, meeting the eyes of the princes and princesses of her kingdom.

"Well, this should be easy then, for with such a revelation she is not your next ruler," Prince Quan said coldly.

A prince rose up, a silent wraith, blade in hand. Shilah frowned and before she could question his actions, he slashed, and blood spurted from her throat. The entire scene was surreal, an unimaginable nightmare of violence and gore and screams echoing from the gallery. "What are you—"

She stumbled, leaning against a high chair, gripping her throat. If not for the blood of her Darkan lover running through her veins, she would be bleeding to death. She could feel the flesh in her throat knitting from the inside, checking the flow of blood.

Pain slashed through her side as Megladine stabbed her.

Rah's roar of rage was from a distance, and Shilah stared at her uncomprehendingly. "Megladine, what—"

Another stab in her shoulder blade drove her to her knees. They were betraying her family. She did not even want to understand what the prince had promised them, but the entire Senate was betraying her family. Shilah's grief was overcoming her ability to function. Pain hazed through her mind.

Shilah lurched to her feet and stumbled back to the high chair when at least a dozen different members of the Senate stabbed her. Their attack was unrelenting, and she distantly heard Kala's screams of denial. The pain had gone from a dull ache to agony in a few short minutes. Everything she had ever believed in trembled, and deep inside she wept. She could feel their intent to murder her, despite her family had been the rulers of this kingdom for over six generations. They had no right to covet her realm, except for the greed in their hearts and minds.

"Do you believe I did not see your arrival?" Prince Quan said with a smile at Megladine who hurried over to his side. "Do you believe me so weak you entered this city, and I did not know? You met no resistance because I wanted you here, Princess. The Symonrah bloodline will end today."

Rah was held upright against the walls of the chamber by an unseen force. He struggled and screamed, but there was no give in the power that held him up. Pain and betrayal seeped from his aura as he stared at the woman he loved with his entire soul.

Megladine stared at him, a sob tearing from her throat. "I did this for *us*, Rah. I love you. And they…" she waved at Shilah and Kala. "Their barbaric laws make it impossible for us to be together. Prince Quan has a vision I believe in, my love, and you will believe in it too."

Another wave of pressure slammed into Shilah, throwing her to her knees. Dozens of members from the senate swarmed toward her, attacking relentlessly.

They would kill her and Kala today. A raw, savage wildness roared in response, urging her to retaliate, but she could not use her powers to murder these people. Her people. Everything around her blurred, and it took a moment to realize her eyes were swimming with tears.

A swell of voices holding heavy grief swamped her senses,

and with a sense of shock, she realized the very people who murdered her, also mourned her. They believed she and her family stood in the way of progress for their kingdom, that they held onto laws that made them weak.

The knowledge broke her apart and shattered something deep inside. A stirring came in her mind, she closed the link with all her Imperial strength. Lachlan Ravenswood could not know she leaned against a high chair, being relentlessly stabbed. Shilah stumbled and dropped to the ground, too weak to stand. Prince Quan's polished boot came in her periphery, and everyone held back.

"Your death will not be in vain, Princess Shilah," he said, something akin to regret gleaming in his eyes. "Your body and Princess Kala's body will be mounted above the Senate as an example for those who honor the old laws. This will spark a revolution, parts of the city will burn, we will lose people, but we will be reborn in a world that is stronger than before. Our people will be unified, and Serange will enter a new era."

In her periphery Kala trembled, and her eyes swirled with power. Her voice echoed in the Senate, as she said, "Mercy and love shall lead the kingdom to ruins. It will come, a creature of darkness and terrifying rage and it shall slaughter, and feast…you are its anchor to the light, and your death must not come to pass." Then Kala gasped, and trembling stumbled over to a chair and lowered herself in its comforting cushion as the vision released her.

Prince Quan grabbed Shilah's throat with the power of his mind and crushed. A wail of agony slipped from her, a sound that should have been impossible given the merciless hold he had on her neck. For a moment she felt as if every bone in her body would shatter. Her mind expanded, but instead of fighting him she reached out to Lachlan, wanting to see him, to feel him.

A monstrous, remorseless fury pounded through their link with such suddenness that it was shocking. His roar of agony slammed through their connection, and as impossible as it seemed, Shilah felt the force of the speed and unremitting rage hurtling through the Darkage and towards her through the distant stars.

"I love you!" His declaration was a garbled roar of rage and pain. *"Fight for me."*

Even at such a distance, her light and soul anchored Lachlan and gave him peace, pleasure, and love. Even if they were not together for years to come, should her thread of life snap, and their connection severed, the world would see the monster within. Her people would suffer for the darkness would blame them.

Nothing in her life had prepared her for the siege on her senses. Lachlan's emotions poured through their link. Rapid images of the first time he saw her, the awe he'd felt, the reluctant attraction, the fierce sense of his other half completing his soul. They morphed to his fear when she was attacked in the forest, his rage, his hope that she would walk by his side forever. The soft musical sound of her laughter as it had wrapped itself around his heart and sinking into his bones and lit inside his soul with happiness. The taste of her skin. His feelings were strong to the point of crushing.

And then it flamed through her. *Love*.

Hopes and dreams which had once fragmented around her reshaped and bloomed through her like molten lava. "I love you," she whispered achingly to him, even as the darkness of death called to her.

"Then do not leave me," the quite plea had no violence throbbing in it, just anguish and love. *"I am but a shadow without you, Shilah Symonrah."*

"For you Lachlan Ravenswood, I will become." Her promise tore at something she wasn't even sure she recognized. It ravaged her sense of justice, the gentle teaching of mercy and love her parents had instilled, and her sense of honor and duty to her people.

It was upon that promise of love and understanding what she meant to the man and monster, Shilah broke everything she'd ever believed in. The men and women standing before her would always try to kill her, to plot and overthrow her realm. Justice was not enough and would never be enough.

"Queen of darkness you shall become and at your feet the blood of our people will flow," the whisper of her sister floated on the air, mingling with the shocked murmurs of her people at the wave of power that washed across the chamber.

Her soul shattered. A cry slipped from her, and uncaring that she might appear weak, tears slid down her cheek. And then she released the unremitting swell of her power. She crashed into Prince Quan's mind, ripping through his memories with brutal precision finding his darkest fear and multiplying it in his thoughts. His brutal hold on her throat released, and she could feel the crushed muscles already healing. Without Lachlan's blood in her veins, she would have died.

Feeding a dark fear in the prince's mind, he screamed and slapped at his head. His eyes landed on her, and she felt the buzz of his powers as he gathered them to attack. She flashed, using shocking speed to rush behind him, grabbed him with her telekinesis and slammed him into the wall.

The princes and princesses of the Senate surged towards her, their mental waves slamming into her mind. She spun with grace, twisting to keep them in her site. "I am an Imperial," she taunted, ignoring the blood dripping to the stone floor from her stab wounds.

Her powers surged, and she felt the life pulse of every man and woman in the Senate. She dipped into the well of her power, connecting to the Psychic Network of her people. Shilah did not stop there. With a harsh scream, she allowed the well of her energy to spill through her veins. Then she unleashed the power that was now a throbbing beat inside her and crashed past thousands, millions of barriers into people's mind. The energy arced and spread until it consumed every cell in her body.

Her presence was a dark throb of energy within their minds as she connected with every citizen of the three kingdoms of Serange, a feat no Imperial telepathic had ever done. The sensory overload crushed her head in a vice and twisted hard knots in her stomach. She waded through it, uncaring that blood ran copiously from her nose.

"I am not my brother who was slaughtered with his family for greed. I am Shilah Malia Symonrah, and all who come for my bloodline will only know death. Citizens of Arcadia, I judge your crowned Prince Quan guilty of the crime of murder, and treason against Dxyriah and his fellow Serangites." She fed to their minds, her memories of his vicious attack, her fear, and the horror of fleeing to another realm. She shared everything. *"I judge him guilty for his crimes against this monarchy and the punishment is death."*

Shock echoed from several minds, denial roared from thousands, and thousands of others agreed. But what they wanted did not matter. Not in this instance. With ruthless precision, she found his thread of life, and sliced it. He dropped to the ground, his screams of terror no more.

In her sister's eyes, she saw the regret, the love, and the fear.

Darkness flowed through Shilah, violence blossoming through her mind as she waded through, slaughtering, and sending a message to the traitors of her realm. Those who had not fallen hurriedly bent their knees and bowed their heads to her power and sovereignty, but she showed no mercy. And with the neural connection formed with all citizens across the three kingdoms, they witnessed it all. Their impressions flowed through her.

The Dark Queen
The red queen
Queen of Darkness.

But she remained unmoved, flashing with speed, ripping through minds, and commanding death. She stood in the center of the carnage she'd just wreaked. From the Senate, she'd kill over one hundred people. Sorrow rose in her, but she battled it down. They could not know with this sacrifice, what she had saved her people from. And what she had to save Lachlan Ravenswood from.

Kala wept, staring at the bodies on the floor, then she pushed to her feet and stared at Shilah. There was gentle acceptance in her eyes. "I've always seen myself on the throne, in your stead, Shilah. I simply never knew how I got there. Now I know. I promise you, I see that I will be at the helm of a revolution years from now, and I will also be at the helm of the ashes our world will rise from. I see the peace and happiness of our citizens, and a man whose face I yet cannot see but know I will love him with every emotion in my soul. I've not seen you beside me, and for so long I feared it was because you died…. But I just saw a vision of you years from today, with your children and your mate beside you."

Shilah's legs trembled, and then she fell. Her body made no impact, instead powerful hands caught her and gathered her close. A finger touched her cheek with exquisite gentleness. Her heart sang when she recognized the familiar, comforting feel of Lachlan. She wanted to wrap her body around his and lose herself in his protective strength. She inhaled deeply. *"You came."*

"Always."

Then the shadows swallowed them, and he took her away.

∽

Lachlan flowed with the shadows, taking his mate away from the place which had filled her with such an abject sense of despair and betrayal. Picking images of the castle from her thoughts, and how much she had missed the palace, he roiled with the shadows, breaching the fortress and spilling into her palatial chambers. He felt edgy, the sense of terror that he'd lost her still coating his senses. A terrible craving to forge their bond in the most primal way pummeled him. He ruthlessly contained the need, for her, for himself, and because he wanted to show her, he loved her more than anything in his entire world. That she could trust him to place her happiness above anything else.

Her tears wetted the skin of his neck where she'd buried her face, softly sobbing. Lachlan did not disturb her, he merely used memories of her home to fill a large gold inlay bath with steaming water. Her incredibly long and very pale lashes fluttered against his jaw. Her eyes opened, her gaze flicked up to his face, lingered on his mouth for a heart-stopping moment before her eyes met his. He set her gently on her feet and stripped the bloodied garment from her body. Lachlan had the curious sensation of tumbling forward. He wanted to drag her into his arms and kiss her forever, but he only stooped and removed her boots. With a swirl of the shadows, he could have her undressed within a second, but he wanted to savor touching her. How he'd missed her.

After removing her boots and every strip of blood-soaked clothing, he stood and loosened the tightly braided plait her hair had been caught in. The entire time she watched him, with huge, somber eyes. Her small teeth bit nervously at her lip, drawing his attention to the fullness of her soft mouth.

The softest of hands touched his cheek. "Hello, Lachlan Ravenswood." Then with a sigh, she hugged him, tightly, breathing in his scent, and releasing the air of fear that had lingered within her. Trust flavored her senses, and he returned her fierce embrace.

With a swirl of the shadows, he immersed her in the spacious bath.

Large, heart-stoppingly vulnerable eyes peered up at him. *"Will you not join me?"*

Another pulse of shadows and he was in the bath, naked, with her sitting astride him. Her eyes were wide pools of pain and haunting emotions. Their link flowed with energy, with her raw power as she sank into his mind seeking comfort. He held her, offering her warmth and protection without asking anything in return.

"I killed them," she whispered. "Men and women I've known my whole life without offering them the benefit of a trial as our law demands."

"You defended your life." And saved them from a far worse death than what he would have subjected them to if he'd arrived and found her lifeless body.

"I cannot stay here in Serange."

"If you wish to remain and govern your kingdom, I will ensure it is done."

A watery laugh slipped from her. "I want to be at your side, loving you now and forever. The laws that I fought so hard to uphold will require Kala to be crowned Dyxriah's ruler. I…I will advise her and help her select the team needed to shepherd her into her rule, but when that is all over I want to live where ever you are, Lachlan Ravenswood, for *I love you*, quite desperately."

Everything in him—every thought, every one of his senses, arrowed on every nuance of her face.

"I entrust my heart to you," his mate vowed softly, her eyes soft with love.

His heart pounded, and his mouth went dry. His body burned for her, an unmerciful, relentless, savage need. "And I will keep it, always."

She smiled, and her happiness burned along their thread. The chain of their link curled around their body like the whip of dark silver fire.

"Life in the Darkage will not be easy. The seven kingdoms will march to war soon. But I promise you, I will protect you with every breath in my body, *always*. Your life and happiness will always be my priority."

She leaned in and brushed her lips against his, then lower over his jaw. Her tongue was like a stroke of silk across his skin. She barely touched him, featherlight, but it was the most sensual sensation he'd ever experienced.

"And I promise you the same, Lachlan Ravenswood. I am not as soft and fragile as I seem. I will guard your happiness and soul with every breath in my body, and you'll have my love forever."

Her voice caressed him like a physical touch, soft, smoky, soothing, sensual, and the darkness within was content.

"I must warn you, I do plan to stay in Dxyriah to aid my sister for several days, and to register for exile. I do plan to visit Serange often, and my sister, if it will be allowed."

"It will be," he promised, working very hard to keep his tone mild, and not to echo the brutal resolve flowing through his veins. Anything that would cause her unhappiness was a threat.

She rested her forehead against his. "How I ache for you." Then she reached between them and took his length in her soft palms. She couldn't encircle his width with the delicate fingers of one hand, so she held his cock with both hands, shimmered down and lowered her mouth toward his jutting length which had risen above the water. His entire body clenched, anticipation shivering through him. That first hot stroke of her tongue had a growl slipping from him.

He pulled her up, his hands no longer gentle, though he fought to keep from bruising her with his strength.

"You forget your blood has changed me, touch me without the fear that I might break," she teased, brushing against his mind with sweetness and passion.

He twisted with her, and she braced her hands on the bath. Gripping one edge of the tub, he braced his weight above her, using his other hand Lachlan arched her hips from the water and trailed his lips over the sparkling droplets of water down to her belly button so his tongue could take a leisurely dip. He went lower, tasting and breathing her aroused fragrance into his lungs. He lapped at her wet sex with a gentleness he hadn't thought himself capable of, especially given the hunger flaming through his body.

"Lachlan!" She moaned his name in a needy voice that threatened to shatter his rigid control.

Rising above her, he flowed with the shadows, so she was once again on top, her knees bracketing his hips in the bath. He curved her body to his, pressed his length against her wet, scalding entrance and thrust upward. He entered her slowly, inch by, deliberately slow, inch, holding her still until she was seated fully on his throbbing length. Everything was wet, tight heat and pleasure so intense his entire body trembled.

"I love you," she gasped, the stars in her eyes fracturing, powerful emotions pouring through their link, which had wrapped around them, burning them with fire.

He gripped her lush ass in his palms, urging her up, and then down, lifting her and dropping her again and again, gritting his teeth at the sublime ecstasy of her tight sheath. Her muscles clenched on his cock as he whispered his words of love against her lips. *"I could taste you forever and need nothing else to sustain me, my mate."* Not blood, or negative energy. Just this woman herself.

Their minds merged. Her soul invaded his, peeling him down to the barest essence—the man linked within the darkness. She rode him, slow, but deep, her eyes opened on his. Her body was damp with sweat, her cheeks were flushed pink, her lips glistened with his taste, and her eyes burned with love and passion. The ache of her slow ride was sweet and terrible. His mate trembled, her breath coming in shallow, ragged gasps. She took him, with slow, provocative rolls of her hips, their eyes connected, never closing, even when the pleasure threatened their sanity.

Passion rocked his body with jarring force. He curled his fingers around the nape of her neck and drew her closer. When he sank his fangs into the curve of her throat, he was gentle, showing restraint when he wanted to devour her. He drew her exquisite taste into him, and he fed her mind with his need of her, his love of her, and his promise that she would always be cherished.

He lifted his head. Her blood seeped from the two pinpricks and trickled down the creamy slope of her breast to her taut nipple. He cupped her breasts in his hands, his thumbs brushing her nipples before he dipped his head and licked the blood from their berry ripeness.

A deep hum reverberated through their link and her scream of release rippled through his mind, and wetness bathed his cock. He pulled her closer, caging her in his arms, gliding his hand down her back to the curve of her buttocks where he gripped her.

"Ride harder."

A small keening moan escaped her throat at his

command. She grew slicker, her heart pounded, the scent of her arousal got spicier. Her fingers gripped his hair, and she rode him, sliding her wet, yet impossibly tight pussy over his aching length.

The temptation of tasting him was a dark whisper in her soul.

"Drink of me."

She dipped her head and kissed along the corded muscles of his shoulder. Small, wickedly sharp fangs struck his neck. Lightning sizzled through his body. He jerked, water sloshed from the bath onto the floor. Another shockwave of pleasure washed through her and ecstasy crashed upon their senses. She shuddered, her pleasure ripping through her life fire as she climaxed on his cock, dragging his release from deep inside him.

He rolled over dipping into the shadows, taking her with him so that she sprawled across his chest as he appeared on her enormous bed. The smell of lavender and honeysuckle mixed with sex, hot and wild, lingered on the air and on her body. Satisfaction rumbled from him, and she smiled.

Lachlan wrapped his arms around her, holding her tightly. In the war to come, he would protect his love with all means possible.

"I know you will, but you won't have to. I won't be soft. I'll be the steel to your blade even when it is merciless, the light to your darkness, and I will be your queen in all ways when needed."

He'd never felt more content—or more complete.

The End

AUTHOR'S NOTE

Thank you for reading Lachlan and Shilah's journey to Happy Ever After. I am sending a huge thank you to everyone who messaged asking me about *The Amagarians*. Your encouraging kind words, love, and patience have meant the world to me. My health has been an albatross for the last several years, and I've been slower than I want to be. But I thank God every day that I have such fantastic support from my husband, family, friends, and fans.

This is the series of my heart, and while I'd wish to have more Amagarians out, my health will always come first even if that means stop writing for a while, but I will always resume once I am better. I am delighted to say my aim for the next few years is to grow this series to the full potential I have always imagined. And that potential ranges from exploring the seven kingdoms of Amagarie, the legends of Darkans (vampires, werewolves) on Earth, and Sci-Fi stories featuring heroes and heroines from the world of Serange and others in their galaxy.

The next book in the Amagarian series will continue with the witch Amirah's journey to love in **Eternal Promise or**

AUTHOR'S NOTE

Eternal Abomination (*I am still undecided which title is best***).** A novella featuring Xian and Gavyn, with lots of peeks on how Tehdra and Ajali have been doing in **Eternal Phoenyx,** will be released the same month as Eternal Promise/Abomination.

I've received dozens of messages asking me about King Gidon Al Shar's book. I promise you, he will be getting his story. I need to find the woman capable of loving a man such as Gidon, though I believe I've already found her in the Kingmaker's daughter. I will be releasing a novella, **Darkness Rising: Gidon**, showing a peek of his life before he was king, the history of how he lost his family and became bonded with his pack of beasts—the Cerberus. His full book, **Eternal Legacy** will be released a few books after that. 😊

I hope you will consider leaving an honest review of how you felt about **Eternal Damnation**, adding to my rainbow. Because I promise you, reviews are gold to an author, and they do help readers decide if they should give a series a chance.

If you have not read book one as yet, **Eternal Darkness**, or book two **Eternal Flames** you can grab a copy or read for free through Kindle Unlimited!

To keep updated with the latest release in this series, please sign up for my newsletter! P.S. I also write sensual historical romances, so my newsletter will also feature updates from those books.

Love,
Stacy

GLOSSARY

Ageni: The order of death placed on a person by the King of their nation if judged a traitor.

Aria: The Kingdom of Earth and Sands. The hardest know metal—Valnetium—of the several kingdoms are mined from the ground of Aria. Citizens with excellent chakra control can manipulate and control the earth.

Avindar: The Kingdom of lightning. They are famous for their crystal which is used as an energy source for most Amagarian households. Citizens with excellent chakra control can manipulate and control lightning.

Boreas: The Kingdom of Wind and Mountains. They are one of the two kingdoms to possess the mystical healing elixir. Citizens with excellent chakra control can manipulate and control the wind.

Caelum: The Kingdom of Water. Most of the realm is underwater, and they are the second kingdom to possesses the mystical healing elixir. Their city, Atlantis is fabled across the Omniverse. Citizens with excellent chakra control can manipulate and control water.

Chakra: Life-force used to form mystical techniques by

GLOSSARY

molding and releasing the physical and spiritual energy present in the body—gained from training and experience.

Cerja: A tattoo of Demon beasts with which each Darkan is born. It is located on the right shoulder blade on non-bonded Darkans but covers the entire back and spills to the front in bonded Darkans.

Consort: The lover of a royal. Held in high esteem by peers of the realm and it is considered a privilege to be chosen as a royal consort. A consort must be of equal rank before royal scion can wed him/her.

Darkage: Kingdom of darkness and Shadows. Citizens with excellent chakra control can manipulate and control the shadows. They are also the only citizens of Amagarie to have the presence of another chakra living inside their people.

Flash: the art of using one's chakra to move with such speed it appears as if one blurs.

Hari: Servant in the royal household, mainly for sexual favors.

Keni: A powerful mystical technique unique to the head families within a kingdom. This technique can be gained only through inheritance from a particular bloodline; hence, the term "bloodline keni."

Demons: Powerful, malevolent spiritual beings who reside in pure chakra.

Mevia: The Kingdom of Sound. Citizens with excellent chakra control can manipulate and control sound waves.

Nuria: The Kingdom of Eternal Fire. Citizens with excellent chakra control can manipulate and control fire.

Ricarkri: Formal name/title for the leader of each kingdom. Not every king is the Ricarkri. In such cases, the Ricarkri is the right hand of the king.

Serange: This planet is divided into three kingdoms—Dxyriah, Arcadia, and O'andor. The citizens of these three kingdoms possess abilities such as telepathy, telekinesis, teleportation, and in rare instances the gift of foresight.

Senjis: Darkans that are taken over by their demon essence.

Shenkiri: mystical elements that citizens of the seven kingdoms with powerful chakra control wields—elements such as shadow, water, wind, sound, fire, lightning, and the earth.

Sherras: Blades of the Nurian King: ten of his most trusted and skilled warriors.

Shiktre: A unique skill to the Darkan population. The ability to use the dark and shadows to move faster than the eyes can track.

Taijiu: The body art of dismembering and killing without the use of weapons—hand to hand combat.

The kingmaker—a man who was a shadow in Amagarie but lauded for his brilliance and cunning. His identity had been a mystery for centuries, and whenever he stirred, destruction ensued because he was brutal and incited anarchy.

Witches: Powerful beings that conjure, incant and cast spells. There are three covens of witches—The White Queens, The Black Queens, and The Red Queens. Male witches are rare, and they are referred to as **Warlords.**

OTHER BOOKS BY STACY

The Amagarians
Eternal Darkness
Eternal Flames
Eternal Damnation

Forever Yours series
The Marquess and I
The Duke and I
The Viscount and I
Misadventures with the Duke

The Kincaids
Taming Elijah
Tempting Bethany

Rebellious Desires series
Duchess by Day, Mistress by Night
The Earl in my Bed

Wedded by Scandal Series
Accidentally Compromising the Duke

Wicked in His Arms
Kidnapping the Marquess

Scandalous House of Calydon Series
The Duke's Shotgun Wedding
The Irresistible Miss Peppiwell
Sins of a Duke
The Royal Conquest

ACKNOWLEDGMENTS

I thank God every day for my family, friends, and my writing. A special thank you to my husband. I love you so hard! Without your encouragement and steadfast support, *Eternal Damnation* would not be published today. You encourage me to dream and are always faithful in your incredible support. You read all my drafts, offer such amazing insight and encouragement. Thank you for designing my fabulous cover! Thank you for reminding me I am a warrior when I wanted to give up on so many things.

Thank you, Gina Fiserova for being so wonderful and supportive always. You are a great critique partner and friend.

Readers, thank you for giving me a chance and reading my book! I hope you enjoyed it and would consider leaving an honest review.

Thank you!
Stacy

ABOUT STACY

Stacy Reid writes sensual Historical and Paranormal Romances and is the published author of over sixteen books. Her debut novella The Duke's Shotgun Wedding was a 2015 HOLT Award of Merit recipient in the Romance Novella category, and her bestselling Wedded by Scandal series is recommended as Top picks at Night Owl Reviews, Fresh Fiction Reviews, and The Romance Reviews.

Stacy lives a lot in the worlds she creates and actively speaks to her characters (aloud). She has a warrior way "Never give up on dreams!" When she's not writing, Stacy spends a copious amount of time binge-watching series like The Walking Dead, Homeland, Altered Carbon, watching Japanese Anime and playing video games with her love. She also has a weakness for ice cream and will have it as her main course.

I am always happy to hear from readers and would love to connect with you via my Website, Facebook, and Twitter. To be the first to hear about my new releases, get cover reveals, and excerpts you won't find anywhere else, sign up for my newsletter, or join me over at Historical Hellions, the fan group for historical romance authors Tamara Gill, and me!

Printed in Great Britain
by Amazon